Water dripped off them both, creating puddles on the stones beneath their feet.

Nora wiped some from her eyes and laughed. With her hand still captured in his, Colin reached out and brushed strands of dampened hair off her forehead. She gazed up at him, her large, blue-green eyes full of sincerity and . . . longing? Her slightly parted lips seized his attention, and he tugged her closer. Could she hear the rapid thudding of his heart over the sound of the rain?

Colin leaned toward her. When her eyes closed, he needed no further prodding—he narrowed the hairsbreadth distance between them. He skimmed his lower lip against hers, the feel of it so soft and smooth beneath his touch. The whispered kiss stoked fire within him and was all the proof he needed to know her lips were even more delectable than he'd imagined. He wound his fingers through the hair at the nape of her neck and kissed her fully on the mouth.

It was as if he was soaring in his plane again—the euphoria and vibrancy of kissing Nora was the same as flying. He wanted it to last forever, to give in to the passion stirring between them . . .

ACCLAIM FOR *HOPE AT DAWN*

"Readers seeking enlightening historical detail or a comforting story in which faith and rectitude overcome bigotry will be entertained."
—*Publishers Weekly*

"I very much enjoyed the book because of the subject matter and because of the way it was written."
—Romance.NightOwlReviews.com

"The author magnificently captures the Zeitgeist, the spirit of the time, how people really thought and behaved in that era, and how prejudice affects every life it touches . . . *Hope at Dawn* was a wonderful discovery . . . I highly recommend it."
—FreshFiction.com

A Hope
Remembered

A Hope Remembered

by

Stacy Henrie

FOREVER

NEW YORK   BOSTON

Forever
Hachette Book Group
1290 Avenue of the Americas
New York, NY 10104

www.HachetteBookGroup.com

Printed in the United States of America

First Edition: March 2015
10 9 8 7 6 5 4 3 2 1

OPM

Forever is an imprint of Grand Central Publishing.
The Forever name and logo are trademarks of Hachette Book Group, Inc.

The Hachette Speakers Bureau provides a wide range of authors for speaking events. To find out more, go to www.hachettespeakersbureau.com or call (866) 376-6591.

The publisher is not responsible for websites (or their content) that are not owned by the publisher.

To my kids.

*Whether in life, in motherhood,
or on our adventures in "Engly," I can't
think of three people I'd rather
journey with than you.*

Acknowledgments

This series, and this book, is far better than I could ever make it on my own due to the expertise and help of Jessica Alvarez, Lauren Plude, Julie Paulauski, Joan Matthews, and the entire team at Grand Central Forever. A heartfelt thank-you as well to Elizabeth Turner, who created the perfect cover for Nora's story.

I would be remiss if I didn't thank some of the wonderful people we had the privilege of meeting during our trip "across the Pond." Thanks to Bill and Diane for their gracious hospitality and kindness. I can't think of a more idyllic place to stay in the Lake District than their wonderful farm and cottages. Much thanks to Jean, too, who so kindly and willingly educated me on the ins and outs of sheep farming. A thank-you goes as well to the sweet hosts at Kiplin Hall, who not only gave us a tour at the tenth hour but taught me the true English way of offering tea. A final thanks to Megan for a wonderful day at the

Imperial War Museum in Manchester and the Youngs for a delicious, authentic British meal.

Thanks to my dad for sharing his love and knowledge of aviation and bettering my flying scenes because of it.

Thank you always and forever to my husband and kids. Having you along on this last trip to England made the experience even better.

Of course, no thank-you list would suffice without mention of the readers of my Of Love and War series. Thanks for your enthusiasm for these dear characters and the time period. I've loved sharing these glimpses of the First World War together.

Author's Note

Being the life-long Anglophile that I am, I knew I couldn't pass up the opportunity to set at least one book in this series in England. Thankfully Nora and Colin didn't complain! My first time through the Lake District as a college student, I fell in love with the unique beauty and wild strength inherent in this part of Britain. Visiting it again, some fourteen years later, reaffirmed all that I remembered and loved about Cumbria and also gave me the chance to experience the place as Nora and Colin might have.

Brougham Castle and Keswick are both actual places in the Lake District. The history behind the castle is also factual, and the ruins are as gorgeous in real life as I hope they sound in fiction. While Larksbeck and Elmthwaite Hall are both my fictional creation, I did my best to keep the architecture, weather, and topography in keeping with those found in the Lake District.

Sheep farming is an important way of life in Cumbria. As Jack points out in the book, the Herdwick sheep have been in this region for hundreds of years. It was my immense good fortune to be educated by Jean, a Lake District sheep farmer, who explained to this suburbia girl the many aspects of sheep farming. Any errors in that regard are mine alone.

I wanted Colin to have a responsibility in the war that was as unique as the Lake District, something that isn't always given large attention when WWI comes to mind. For those reasons, I decided to make him a member of the Royal Flying Corps (RFC). Before the war ended in 1918, the RFC combined with the Royal Naval Air Service and took the more familiar name of the Royal Air Force (RAF).

If being a soldier on the ground seemed like madness during the Great War, then being one inside the cockpit of airplane was even more so. While the world, then and now, glamorized these pilots, their job was not an easy one. Most pilots at the beginning of the war were lucky to survive two weeks—to survive the entire war was nothing short of a miracle.

The Germans, with their more sophisticated planes and ruthless killers like the Red Baron, weren't the only challenges to Allied pilots. Many of them had logged less than twenty hours of flying before joining the combat in the skies. Learning to actually fly one of these newfangled machines wasn't a simple task either. A number of deaths occurred, not in the famous dogfights over the battlefields, but in practice. Then there was the absence of parachutes, thought to encourage a pilot to bail instead of sticking out the fight, in the event a pilot's plane was hit.

While the work of WWI pilots, both in battle and reconnaissance, was significant, these men didn't escape the brutality of war simply because they were in the skies. Like all soldiers, they lost friends and relatives and the innocence of life from before the war. They likely experienced the same feelings of survivors' guilt as their comrades on the ground.

"Shell shock," or post-traumatic stress disorder (PTSD), gained more attention during the First World War; however strides in helping soldiers deal with the effects of war on the brain and body would still be a long time in coming.

After four years of war, Britain experienced a postwar economic boom, but it was extremely short-lived. A recession followed, with unemployment reaching an all-time high in 1921. While other countries enjoyed relative ease and success during the "Roaring Twenties," political, social, and economic upheaval remained prevalent in Britain.

For more information on Britain and the First World War, I recommend reading *First World War Britain*, by Peter Doyle (2012).

The Great War changed the world forever and not just in the number of deaths from combat or influenza. The world emerged from the First World War far less naïve as a whole, a bit more hardened, a little more resistant to the ways things had been done in the past. Social changes were occurring everywhere. And while many clung to the old way of life, there were countless others who were ready to embrace this new bold world—making it not only an intriguing time to live but an intriguing time to write about, too.

A Hope
Remembered

Prologue

France, August 1917

"Are you the Ashby brothers?"

Colin stopped wiping the already gleaming biplane and glanced over his shoulder at the tiny man standing just outside the shadow of the Sopwith Camel. "We might be. Who's asking?"

A look of excitement lit the man's angular features. "Charles Rushford from the *Daily Mail*."

A journalist? Colin tucked his damp rag into the pocket of his trousers and shot Christian a grin. "Our fame precedes us."

Christian shook his head as though he weren't amused and climbed to his feet, the book he'd been reading tucked beneath his arm. But Colin didn't miss the glint of laughter in his older brother's blue eyes.

"Nice to make your acquaintance, Mr. Rushford." Christian extended his hand to the journalist. "I'm Christian Ashby and this is my brother, Colin."

"The pleasure's mine," the man said, pumping Christian's hand. "I've been following the flying careers of you and your brother for some time now." His gaze lingered over the aeroplanes lined up outside the hangar as if they were Christmas gifts.

Colin could easily relate. The moment he'd first placed his hand against the hardened cloth body of an Avro 504 he'd been rocked with the sensation of coming home.

"Mind if I ask you a few questions?" Mr. Rushford asked, shaking Colin's hand next. He waved a small notebook and pencil at the hangar.

Christian threw a glance at Colin. No words were necessary to guess his brother's unspoken question. Would talking to this journalist be something their father approved of or not? Colin gave a decisive nod. No harm could come from simply talking to the man. Maybe an article about the two of them would convince Sir Edward Ashby that both his sons were worthy of his name.

"All right, Mr. Rushford." Christian motioned for the man to follow them into the hangar, away from the rays of the afternoon sun.

Colin located two chairs and brought them over for Christian and the journalist. When he didn't spy a third, he chose the edge of the nearby table for his own seat.

"Tell me first what you like about flying aeroplanes." Mr. Rushford balanced his notebook on his knee, his expression expectant.

"Freedom." The word burst from Colin's mouth before he'd even finished thinking it.

"Freedom?" Mr. Rushford dipped his head in a thoughtful nod. "How so?"

Colin hid his embarrassment with a shrug, though

he knew the reasons he'd spoken the word aloud. Ironically, it was only in this hellish world, where he'd defied death more times than he could count, that he'd found true freedom and purpose. Freedom from his father's disapproval or the constant pressures to be more like his reserved older brother. He'd found freedom in discovering he could do something better than Christian, too. While his brother was an excellent pilot, even Christian himself had conceded early on that Colin was the one with real talent when it came to handling an aeroplane.

"There's a sense of liberation that comes with being in the sky," Colin said quietly. He kept his eyes focused on Mr. Rushford's rapidly moving pencil instead of on his brother. Would Christian find his response foolish? "It's a place far removed from the earth and its human struggles." He crossed his arms over his chest and gave a rueful laugh. "At least until you spy a German Fokker diving straight for you."

Christian's approving smile eased the tension pinching at Colin's shoulders. He hadn't embarrassed his lifelong hero with his spontaneous answer. "I agree with Colin."

His older brother launched into a short but heartfelt speech about honor and doing one's duty as a pilot. Colin had to bite back a chuckle at how much Christian sounded like their father. No wonder he'd been born the oldest, the one to inherit Sir Edward's title of baronet and the family estate back home in England.

"I understand you two hail from the Lake District?" Mr. Rushford said.

"Elmthwaite Hall, near the tiny village of Larksbeck." Christian's tone was colored with pride.

"So that's where you'll return after the war?"

Colin answered "no" at the same moment Christian gave a resounding "yes."

The surprise on Christian's face brought the sting of regret to Colin. He hadn't yet voiced to his brother the idea he'd been contemplating of traveling, once the war was over, and seeing more of the world, hopefully from his own aeroplane.

"You're not?" Christian asked. Mr. Rushford looked at both brothers in turn. He clearly sniffed a story, but Colin didn't want something leaking to their father before he'd had time to explain.

"Right afterward, yes," Colin amended. "But I'd love to see more of the world, too. Maybe even purchase my own plane."

His answer seemed to satisfy the journalist, though Christian still appeared troubled as they finished up the interview with a few more questions about life in the Lake District and their experience in France.

Colin noticed none of the man's inquiries delved into the ugly parts of flying in the war. The constant possibility of injury, burns, or death; the loss of friends and those he'd only known a few days; the revolver in the plane intended for ending life instead of having it taken involuntarily. Apparently the people back home didn't want an accurate portrayal of a pilot's life. Only the perceived glamour and adventure.

At last Mr. Rushford stood and pocketed his notebook and pencil. "Would you mind posing for a photograph?"

Nodding his head, Christian rose to his feet as well. "That would be fine."

The man went in search of his photographer, who'd apparently been taking pictures of the aeroplanes and some of the other Royal Flying Corps pilots.

"Did you mean that?" Christian demanded, the moment Mr. Rushford was out of earshot. "About not coming back to Elmthwaite?" He stared hard at Colin. The look was so like their father's that Colin began to squirm. "Mother and Father would be crushed. Especially having us gone so long already."

"Please," Colin said, shoving his hands into his pockets. "Mother may be a bit heartbroken, but Father will be relieved to have me off somewhere else."

Christian's jaw tightened. "That isn't true, Colin. He cares about you, as much as Mother. We need you at home."

"What for?" The question came out harsher than Colin had intended and he hurried to temper his tone with a light laugh. "Without me, there'll be one more place setting for dinner parties and an extra room for house guests."

"Is that all Elmthwaite is to you?"

Colin couldn't meet his brother's intense gaze. "Come on, Christian. You know I'm only jesting. I love the house and the lake and the summers up in Scotland. But I wasn't born and bred to take over that sort of regimented life."

Christian raked a hand through his sandy brown hair, his agitation evident. But Colin couldn't place its source. Why should Christian care if he chose a different path? While they'd experienced a far better childhood than many of the men they flew with, Colin had also dreamt of the day he would be free to choose the course of his life, unlike Christian.

"You must promise me something." Christian gripped Colin's shoulder, his voice full of gravity, his hand heavy.

"What is it?"

"If something should happen to me..."

Colin brushed off Christian's hand and stalked away from the table. "Don't talk like that. We've made it this far; we'll make it till the end of the war. You'll see." His brusqueness hid the coil of panic unraveling inside him. He couldn't imagine a world without Christian in it. Their bond ran as deep as brothers' could—sometimes Colin felt as if they were different sides of the same coin. Who else had looked out for him, championed him, from his earliest moments on earth? "Besides, I'm not baronet material, Christian. We both know that."

"Promise me," his brother went on with equal resolve, "that you won't ever turn your back on Elmthwaite Hall."

"But I want to travel—"

"You can still do that. Only I want you to promise me you will always find your way back."

Colin gritted his teeth, even as his determination to permanently stay away began to crumble. "Why?"

"Because it's our life's blood, Colin." He stepped closer and placed his hand against Colin's heart. "Our heritage. Our home. Promise me you'll keep it as such?"

Blowing out his breath, Colin lifted his eyes to Christian's. He'd never been able to refuse a request from his brother. He would do anything for him. "I promise."

The relieved smile on Christian's face succeeded in cutting away the last of Colin's resolution to avoid home. "Thank you." He lowered his hand and cocked his head toward the hangar opening. "What do you say we pretend we're Charlie Chaplin for this photograph?"

Colin laughed at the rare showing of Christian's teasing and exited the hangar at his brother's side. The photographer insisted on their being in full flight gear—trousers, helmet, leather coat, boots, scarf—everything but their goggles. Since it was nearly time for patrol anyway, Colin and Christian complied.

Once the photographer was finished, Colin checked every inch of his plane and climbed aboard. He scanned the small cockpit: stick, rudder pedals, throttle. Using all three in concert to control the plane felt as familiar as breathing.

Please let this work out, Lord, according to Your will. It was the same earnest prayer he made each time he flew, the one brief moment he and God acknowledged each other.

With the engine started, Colin throttled up and guided his plane down the grassy runaway, knowing Christian was right behind him. In this one facet of their lives, Christian let him take the lead.

His plane rose into the sky, leaving the airfield and the warmer temperature far below. Adjusting his goggles, he scanned the air for German planes. Nothing marred the peace of the late afternoon, though, except the roar of the other planes in his and Christian's squadron.

The promise Christian had elicited from him repeated in Colin's mind. Could he fulfill it? Would stopping off at Elmthwaite several times a year meet his brother's request? He hoped so. Although the idea of being home never sounded so bleak at the thought of Christian being there, too.

The sudden cacophony of machine gun fire rang above the noise of the engine in Colin's ears. Coming out of the sun, six German aeroplanes dove steeply through the sky toward the Camels.

Instinct from days and months of flying took over, calming Colin's mind and guiding his hands through the turns, climbs, and descents of another dogfight. While it might appear from below to be an elaborate sort of dance, he knew it was anything but beautiful. This way of fighting was every bit as deadly, if not more so, than the battles on the ground.

Some of the chaps he'd talked with today about England and the girls they might want to marry would likely not be flying back with him tonight. He counted himself lucky every time he made it through another two weeks at the front lines. A few of the chaps he'd flown with early on in the RFC hadn't made it through even one set of fourteen days.

Bullets strafed the side of his plane, and Colin jerked the stick back to climb out of the line of fire. It was time to take down this German before the German took him down.

He maneuvered the plane upward, looping over to come behind the German plane, then opened fire on his machine gun. Riddled with bullet holes, the plane began smoking, its nose dropping lower and lower. Colin closed his mind to the guilt, to the flicker of thought about who this other man might be. If he didn't, he'd freeze up, and that meant certain death.

When the enemy aircraft plummeted toward the earth, he jerked his gaze away, unable to watch the crippled plane strike the ground, the pilot still inside.

At a hand signal from his squad leader, Colin banked his plane around and followed the lead Camel back toward the airfield. He looked for Christian on his left and right, but he wasn't concerned when he didn't see him. His brother was most likely behind him.

Colin landed his aeroplane and quickly did an assess-ment of the damage. More holes, but nothing to keep him from flying again. Goggles in hand, he strode toward the others, looking for Christian.

Another pilot and his good friend, Andrew Lyle, climbed off the wing of his Camel. When he removed his goggles, his face appeared unusually white.

"One get a little too close that time, Lyle?" Colin joked as he approached.

Lyle flinched and shook his head.

"Where's Christian? He's flying slow today, the old man."

"You didn't see…" Lyle rubbed a hand over his ashen face, his next words barely a whisper. "I'm so sorry, Colin."

"Sorry?" Shards of fear sliced through Colin, cold and ominous. "What are you talking about?"

"It's Christian. He…he was shot down."

Colin fell back a step. "No. He's only slow. I was right there, Lyle. I didn't see him fall."

"I barely saw him." Lyle's voice was too calm, too de-void of emotion now.

Fury ripped through Colin's denial. He fisted Lyle's coat and glared at his friend. "Are you joking with me? What happened to my brother?"

Lyle hardly blinked, his gaze full of pity. "Gunfire ate up his plane. He was dead before he hit the ground."

Christian dead?

Colin scanned the nearby planes, hoping, praying, Lyle was wrong. He'd see his older brother striding toward him, that disgruntled frown on his face before he repri-manded Colin for his risky flying. But no one appeared except the other members of their squadron. Colin read the truth of Lyle's words in the way none of them would meet his eye, the way their heads hung low with suppressed grief. Slowly he released his hold on Lyle.

"Can we get another picture, chaps?" Mr. Rushford said, hurrying toward them. "Group you up around one of the planes there?" He stopped his frenzied steps and frowned. "Where's your brother, Mr. Ashby? We need him in the picture, too."

"He's dead."

The voice sounded so unlike his that Colin wondered for a moment who'd spoken. But the searing pain in his throat and the horrified look on Mr. Rushford's face as the man stared openmouthed were proof enough that Colin had said the words himself. Words that sank deep like a knife wound through his chest, cutting and tearing his world into irreparable pieces.

"If it's all the same to you, Mr. Rushford, I'll sit this photograph out." He didn't wait for the journalist's reply. Instead Colin marched away from the group as fast as he could walk, his goggles strangled between his hands, his heart and mind wrapped in shock.

His brother was gone and nothing would ever be the same again.

Chapter 1

Iowa, May 1920

Nora led the strangers into the parlor, their footsteps sounding unusually loud against the polished wood floor. Her gaze swept the tidy room with theirs and settled on the upright piano. How forlorn it looked stripped of its usual sheet music and family photos. The latter she could take with her, but her courage fractured a bit at the thought of someone else playing the instrument that had soothed her loneliness more times than she could count. The piano would be too costly to cart to England, though, and so like many other things, it would have to be left behind.

"What a spacious room," the woman said, her hand resting on her protruding belly. Her husband draped an arm around her shoulders, the other hanging lifeless at his side. Wounded in France, he'd informed Nora in his letter of inquiry about the farm she was sellling.

"Perfect for all those children we're going to have." He pressed a kiss to his wife's forehead.

Nora folded her arms and looked away, the sting of resentment piercing her at their happiness. She didn't need further reminders, however unintentional, that her life had been—and was about to be again—irrevocably changed.

Nothing about the last two years matched her girlhood dreams, dreams that had included a husband and family. If Tom Campbell had survived the Great War, all those hopes would have been realized. He would be standing here now, instead of two strangers. It would be his arms holding her close, his lips kissing her, and she wouldn't be trying to sell the only home she'd ever known.

"The kitchen is through there." Nora forced a friendly tone to her words. The more they liked the place and her, the less likelihood of having to endure more people she didn't know traipsing all over the farm.

The couple moved past her and stepped into the large, sunny kitchen. Nora followed. She rested her hands on the back of one of the chairs. How many times had she sat here rolling dough for her mother or eating meals with her parents? They'd been gone more than a year, but the memories entrenched in every space of the farm kept them close, as well as increased the pain of missing them.

"The house comes with all the furnishings?" The young man's eyes were trained on the icebox.

"Yes." Nora recalled the day her father had brought the icebox home in the wagon—a birthday gift for her mother. Grace Lewis had been so happy she'd cried. It was one of many surprises, big and small, her father had delighted in giving "his girls."

"You don't want to take any of it with you?"

Wanted to, yes. The piano, her bed, her father's rocker, her mother's gramophone. "It might be rather difficult to get an icebox all the way to England."

The young man chuckled, bringing Nora instant relief that she hadn't offended him. "England, huh? Heard things aren't going so well there right now. I would've thought more of them would be coming here, than anyone going there."

Nora had read something similar in the newspaper, but she wasn't concerned. Caring for the farm alone since her parents' deaths, she'd learned how to stretch her nickels and dimes and how little she and her dog, Oscar, could subside on. "Actually, I inherited some property there."

"A big manor house, huh?" He laughed at his own joke. "I met some of those rich Brits overseas. Decent guys, though most of them never worked a day in their lives before the war."

There likely wouldn't be any rich Brits where she was going, Nora thought as she watched the man's wife fingering the red-checked curtains over the window. She fought the urge to ask her to stop. She'd helped her mother sew those curtains one blizzardy day years ago. The bright color had brought instant cheer to the room and made the winter weather more bearable.

"It isn't really a house," she replied, trying to focus on the conversation and not the way the woman continued to run her hands over the kitchen furniture. "It's a cottage— on a sheep farm."

"A sheep farm?" The woman didn't bother to hide her incredulous tone. "That's a rather unusual occupation for a woman on her own."

Nora swallowed hard, hating the way the woman's

words stirred up her deepest fears. Could she really give up the only life she'd ever known to do something she'd never done before? In a place so vastly different from hers here in Iowa? Like her parents, the farthest she'd ever traveled was Minnesota.

Clearly not expecting a reply to her candid remark, the woman asked eagerly, "Can we see the upstairs?"

"Of course." Nora bottled up her uncertainty and motioned them ahead of her, back into the parlor. "There are three bedrooms up there."

The couple exchanged a smile and started up the stairs, but Nora paused with her foot on the first step. Did she want to stand by while the two of them, nice as they were, looked at and touched more of her things? Things she'd be forced to leave behind because they wouldn't fit into her suitcase?

"Take all the time you need," she called up to them. "I'll be outside."

She slipped on a sweater to guard against the spring chill and let herself out the front door. The sound of the screen slamming shut behind her was both comforting and familiar. Nora moved down the porch steps and across the yard. Oscar trotted up to her side, his tail wagging. She stopped to rub the soft, brown fur between his ears, wishing again that she could take him with her. The old hound dog would detest being cooped up on a ship, though, and Tom's younger brothers had already consented to permanently caring for him.

Nora crossed the road running in front of the farm and slipped beneath the leafy limbs of the giant oak tree that stood like a sentinel before the fields. Oscar moved off to explore.

For the first time since the couple had arrived, Nora managed a full breath of air. She circled the trunk to peer at the carving Tom had cut into the bark years earlier. Lifting her finger, she traced the worn outlines of the heart and the letters whittled inside: TC + NL.

Tom had kissed her for the first time under these branches. She'd bade him good-bye in the same place, the night before he and his brother Joel had left to fight in the war. This tree had also been privy to Tom's promise to marry her when he came back and Nora's anguish when she'd received word he wasn't returning.

She shut her eyes and leaned back against the rough bark. Memories of Tom washed over her with such intensity she could almost believe when she opened her eyes she'd see him walking up the road, ready to pull her into his strong arms, as he'd done countless times before the war. His teasing manner and quick smile had been the perfect complement to her more serious nature.

A tangible ache throbbed in her chest and Nora pressed her hand against it. It had been two years since Tom had been killed. When would missing him hurt less? When would she stop feeling bound to a promise neither one of them could fulfill anymore? The life they'd hoped and planned for might be gone, but she still had to move forward. She had to stop dwelling on the past. Maybe then she'd find peace from the pain.

Opening her eyes, she pushed away from the tree and removed the wrinkled envelope from her skirt pocket. She'd memorized every word of the letter—about her being the next of kin to inherit Henry Lewis's sheep farm in England's Lake District. Letters had arrived sporadically through the years from her father's uncle, but Nora was still surprised to learn the man had died. And that like her father and grandfather, the man had so few living relatives.

She'd nearly written her great-uncle's solicitor back and declined the offer of the sheep farm. She had a home and a life here. Yet the prospect of a fresh start, in the land of her heritage, took hold in her mind and wouldn't leave her alone.

For the next week as she milked the cow, fed the animals, and tended the farm, the idea consumed her every waking thought until she finally relented and wrote a letter of acceptance. Even after posting it, though, she couldn't say why she'd agreed to go. Tom's sister Livy, and Nora's best friend, had certainly questioned her reasons for leaving. But the only thing Nora could say was "I have to."

She smoothed the envelope as she admitted in a whisper, "I don't know anything about sheep, Tom. But this is my chance to leave, like you did." She splayed her free hand against his carving. "I don't want to leave behind the life we dreamed of here…" Her voice hitched with a swallowed sob. "And yet I have to learn to live without you. Don't I?"

A movement across the street caught her eye. The couple was exiting the house. Nora pocketed the letter, eyed the carved heart once more, and stepped from the shade of the tree.

"Everything's just lovely," the young woman said as Nora came to a stop below the porch.

"We'll take it," her husband added. "How soon can we move in?"

Nora cleared the tug of sorrow from her throat and

managed a tight smile. "You can move in next Thursday. I'll leave the key under the mat."

They settled on a price, which was a few hundred dollars less than what Nora had asked for, but she'd expected that. After all, she could only do so much running the place alone. The young man promised to bring the money over tomorrow morning.

"Do you have family there?" The woman asked the question in a gentle voice. Had she sensed the heavy finality settling like a rock in the pit of Nora's stomach? "In England, I mean?"

Nora shook her head. "Not anymore."

"Then why go?" Genuine concern shone on the other woman's face as she allowed her husband to help her down the stairs. "If I had this place, I don't think I could leave it for the unknown."

Nora let her eyes wander over the house, the yard, the barn, the old oak tree. This had been her home for twenty-three years. So many dreams and hopes had been sown and shattered here. But now it was time to pick up the pieces. To leave what felt comfortable and familiar and hopefully find the peace that had eluded her the last few years.

When she turned her attention back to the couple, she didn't need to infuse her response with feigned confidence. "I believe I'm ready for an adventure." The words sank deeply into her soul, and a tingle of excitement eased the knot of regret in her stomach.

"Judging by the state of things here, Miss Lewis, I think you'll do well on your sheep farm." The young man extended his hand toward her. Nora shook it firmly and offered the two of them the first genuine smile she'd been able to muster all morning. "We wish you all the best across the Pond."

Lake District, England, June 1920

The wheels of the Avro 504 biplane caressed the grassy runway. Colin Ashby cut the engine, and the plane coasted toward the far end of the lawn, where his valet stood at attention, waiting. What did Gibson want with him now?

Before he could strike the line of trees bordering the grass, Colin turned the vehicle to face south, toward the lake. The plane rolled to a final stop, its left wing a mere two feet from the chest of the expressionless and unmoving Gibson. Colin bit back a laugh. Apparently even the possibility of being sideswiped by an aeroplane did nothing to crack the man's stoic demeanor.

Colin pulled the goggles from his face and climbed out of the rear cockpit onto the plane's wing. "What did you think of that landing, Gibson?" He leapt to the ground. "She kissed the runway with hardly a shudder."

Gibson inclined his balding head in a stiff nod. "Yes, sir."

Once he had the wheel chocks in place, Colin removed his flying helmet and let his gaze roam over the surrounding mountains. How different they looked from the air, like a child's creation rather than imposing peaks. From the sky, the sheep on the fell were ants and the lake beside Elmthwaite Hall was a puddle.

"You are late, sir."

"Am I?" Colin cut a glance at the still lit sky. Full dark wouldn't arrive for another few hours, but it must be after eight o'clock if he was already late for dinner. He'd flown longer than he'd intended.

"Your father and mother are in the dining room now." Gibson tucked his hands smartly behind his back. "Their guests arrived some time ago."

"Very well." Colin ambled toward the great house, in no hurry for the dinner party awaiting him. Gibson managed to stay beside him, even as the valet's steps remained clipped and precise. "Which distinguished guests are we to share our meal with tonight?"

"Lord Weatherly, sir, and his wife."

"No one else?" Maybe his father had finally tired of trying to marry him off.

Gibson pinned his gaze straight ahead. "No, sir. Although their daughter, Lady Sophia, is with them."

"Ah." The game wasn't over yet. "Have you seen Lady Sophia, Gibson?"

"Yes, sir."

"Is she as severe looking as that last girl? What was her name?"

"Lady Josephine," Gibson supplied.

Another earl's daughter, but not much to recommend her beyond her title. "Tell me, Gibson." Colin stopped and turned toward his valet. "Who is less plain? Lady Sophia or Lady Josephine?"

Gibson kept his eyes focused forward, but a muscle in his jaw ticked. Colin recognized the telltale sign the older man was slightly uneasy. He squelched a smile. So women, not aeroplanes, were a source of discomfort to the valet. The moments when Gibson broke character were rare enough that Colin deemed each one a victory.

"I would say . . ." Gibson coughed behind his fist before

lowering his arm. The perfect control returned to his lined face. "Lady Sophia is quite lovely, sir."

"Is that so?" Colin set off toward the gray stone house again. "Then I shouldn't be ashamed of making an entrance to attract this beautiful woman's attention, should I?"

Without so much as a quirk of the lips, Gibson tipped his head in acquiescence and opened one of the massive front doors for him. Colin stepped inside the entry and headed up the carpeted stairs, all the while silently counting off the seconds before his father would appear.

Six…seven…eight…

"Colin." Sir Edward barreled out of the dining room.

A little slower than normal. Colin pivoted on the landing to face his father.

"Yes?" He schooled his face into a droll expression, while fighting the raw irritation rising inside him. He'd seen far too many lives cut short not to want to live his own. A man of twenty-six ought to be in charge of his own life—be allowed to make his own choices. He didn't need society to tell him when to eat or change or fly his biplane. His older brother, Christian, hadn't minded the rote routine of their life as sons of a baronet, but Colin had long given up the notion of being like his childhood hero.

Nearly three years had passed since the day Christian had been shot down during a dogfight with the Germans, but Colin still couldn't think of his brother without sorrow and regret tightening his chest and constricting his breath. As if a part of him had ceased to function at that exact moment, and yet, he must somehow live and breathe despite the pain.

Things would have been much different, in all their lives, if Christian had lived.

"You are late." Sir Edward came to stand beside the polished banister. "The earl and his family are already here. We waited in the drawing room for you, but we could delay the meal no longer. How does it look to have you waltz in at your leisure?"

Colin gestured at his flying jacket and trousers. "I could come in now, Father, instead of keeping all of you waiting."

Sir Edward's face turned a shade of red Colin hadn't yet seen, but the twitch of one his blue eyes was an all-too-familiar sign of fury. "You will do no such thing." He spun toward Colin's silent valet. "Help him into his dinner clothes, Gibson, and be quick about it."

"Yes, Sir Edward," Gibson said with a half bow.

"And when you finally decide to grace us with your presence in the dining room, I expect you to behave, young man."

His father's tone allowed no argument, making Colin feel as if he were a child again. He despised that feeling. Without a word, he resumed climbing the stairs. The deep red carpet muffled the sound of his agitated steps. His cap and goggles were gripped so tightly in his palms his fingers began to ache.

He didn't spare a glance at the ancestral portraits in their gilded frames lining the long hallway to his room. The somber faces were likely to stare back at him with as much disapproval as his father had. He didn't want this life anymore, never had. Why couldn't his father accept that?

Once Elmthwaite Hall had meant happiness and security to him. Now the ornate furnishings, the incessant rules, and the inability to do anything on his own reminded him more and more of a prison—one built on tradition and money and expectations. If only he could leave...But he'd given his word to Christian that he wouldn't abandon the place, and he could not go back on that, especially in his brother's absence.

Colin tossed his flying gear onto his bed as he entered his room, newly redecorated in brown hues. In the adjoining washroom, he ran cold water in the sink and began vigorously scrubbing the dirt from his face. The shock to his skin helped cool some of his anger. Scrubbed clean, he allowed Gibson to help him change into dinner attire.

"You look well, sir," Gibson said as he removed imaginary lint with a brush from Colin's black tailcoat.

Colin fought the urge to peel off the jacket and bow tie. Both felt as restricting as a straitjacket. He wouldn't be able to relax until he'd shed the suit in another few hours.

He stared at himself in the full-length mirror. The dark hair and eyes were from his mother, his height from his father. He'd passed Christian up at the age of sixteen, despite his brother being two years older.

I suppose I can't call you my little brother anymore, Christian had said that summer. It was one of those rare moments when he'd set aside his usual seriousness to tease Colin. Just as he had the day he'd been killed.

Through the mirror, Colin's gaze sought out the now blank spot on the wall where someone had hung the grainy newspaper photograph of him and Christian, taken only an hour or so before Christian's plane, with him inside, had been shot down. Now it seemed as if the two events were separated by mere moments of time.

In the first he and Christian were answering questions from the *Daily Mail* reporter and grinning like Charlie Chaplin for their picture, and in the next his brother was gone.

Colin had removed the picture and stuffed it into one of the bureau drawers the instant he arrived home from France. He wanted to remember Christian, but the visual reminder of that fateful day cut too deep to see each time he opened his eyes on a new morning. Even now the memories gripped him like a vise.

A cough from Gibson, thankfully, managed to break the hold of the past. It was time to go down.

"Thank you, Gibson." It was the least he could say. While Colin despised not being able to do for himself as he'd grown accustomed to during the war, he instinctively understood Gibson took his role of valet seriously. In spite of Colin's reticence, the older man wanted to fulfill his duty.

Leaving his room, Colin descended the stairs, his hand moving along the banister. How many times had their butler, Martin, scolded him for sliding down the wood? A smile lifted the corners of his mouth at the thought, momentarily dispelling the grief that shrouded him, but the happy recollection faded as Colin paused outside the dining room.

The murmur of conversation and the smell of food drifted out to him. He hated having to play the part of dutiful heir and disappointing his father even more with his fumbled, halfhearted attempts. Christian had been born to do this, not him.

Colin arranged his face into a casual expression, his only defense, and entered the brightly lit room.

"There you are, Colin." His mother smiled, her manner warm.

He circled the table and placed a quick kiss on her cheek. "Good evening, Mother."

"Colin," his father intoned with less congeniality, "I would like to introduce my good friend Lord Weatherly; his wife, Lady Weatherly; and their daughter, Lady Sophia Fitzgerald."

"Lord Weatherly, Lady Weatherly, welcome." Colin tipped his head in acknowledgment of the earl and his wife, then turned his gaze on their daughter. Gibson hadn't been wrong—Lady Sophia was nice to look at, with her artfully arranged blond hair and glittering hazel eyes. "Lady Sophia."

She held out a gloved hand to him. "Mr. Ashby, a pleasure to meet you."

"The pleasure is mine." He bowed over her hand, noting the way she gripped his fingers, confidently, almost possessively, before she released him. Would she prove to be like every other young lady his father had paraded through the house of late? The war had brought a dearth of wealthy, eligible young men, which meant Colin truly had his pick of whom to marry. Only problem was he had yet to find a young woman with more than a pretty face and coy manners to recommend her.

He took a seat beside Lady Sophia. One of the new footmen, hired to replace those who'd been killed in the war, appeared at his elbow with a tray of food. Colin filled his plate and tried to ignore another reminder of how things and people had changed in the last six years. He took a bite, realizing he was famished. Flying typically heightened his appetite.

"Your mother was telling us about your aeroplane." Lady Sophia leaned toward him as if imparting a great secret.

Colin dabbed at his mouth with his napkin. "Yes, I enjoy flying." He schooled his tone to match hers; although he couldn't help wondering how truly interested she was in planes and flying. Several of the ladies he'd met recently had shown great enthusiasm for his aeroplane until they realized it wouldn't better their chances with him.

"You were a member of the Royal Flying Corps, correct?" she asked.

He nodded.

"How thrilling."

Images marched through Colin's mind—the explosion of artillery, the sinuous line of trenches, the tiny figures strewn like straw over the battlefield. He'd once thought the same thing about being a pilot, until he lost his first friend in a dogfight with the Germans. Colin had watched helpless as the man, shot dead, plummeted to the mud-churned earth in his smoking plane. No, *thrilling* wasn't the word for it anymore.

He settled for a simple "yes" before taking another bite of food. Sir Edward sent him a hard glare from his spot at the top of the table. Colin didn't miss the insinuation—he was expected to entertain the earl's daughter. Swallowing the annoyance clogging his throat, he turned to his dinner guest and inquired with a charming smile, "Tell me, Lady Sophia, how are you enjoying your time in the Lake District?"

"Very much." She offered him a brilliant smile, which almost made him forgive her naïve comment. Of course someone like her, pampered and sheltered her entire life, couldn't be expected to understand the atrocities of war. Hadn't he gone off to fight in part to preserve such innocence, to keep it from being destroyed? "In fact," she added with a light laugh, "I almost prefer it to London. I love the cooler summer weather and the green fields and mountains."

"You should see them from a plane." He regretted the words at once—he hadn't meant to imply the invitation Lady Sophia would likely read within them.

Sure enough, a glint of triumph lit her eyes. "What a lovely idea, Mr. Ashby. I think flying in your aeroplane would be marvelous."

Colin studied her flawless face for a hint of sarcasm, but found none. He'd received plenty of terrified exclamations from other girls about his flying. Perhaps there was more to Lady Sophia than he'd surmised.

"I may be able to provide you with an opportunity to fly before you return to London," he hedged, "if your father agrees, of course."

A mischievous smile tweaked her red lips. "Then I must make him agree." She laughed again. Colin smiled in return and felt himself relax slightly. The dinner was going better than he'd expected.

The conversation between their fathers centered around the country's rising number of unemployed workers and its floundering economy. Colin listened as he ate. He hated the feeling of guilt and helplessness that accompanied the news that so many returning soldiers still couldn't find jobs. These were the men he'd flown alongside. Yet here he sat with plenty to eat and no fear of the future. If only he could think of some way to help.

"What do you think of the unemployment of our brave

soldiers, Lady Sophia?" Colin glanced at her. Would she respond with the intelligence and compassion he hoped?

She frowned. "It's most unfortunate. All those men without jobs." Colin nodded in approval until she continued, "I am grateful they are home and the war is over, though. Now we can put the fighting behind us."

"Almost as if it never happened?" he murmured. There were times the war felt more like a long, horrible nightmare. Something one could simply shake off as unreal in the bright light of morning. But when Colin walked past Christian's empty room, the truth of what he'd seen and experienced in France would hit him with all the force of a German Fokker biplane. In those moments his life at home felt like the dream, and the war the reality.

"Why dwell on the unpleasantness," Lady Sophia intoned, breaking into Colin's troubled thoughts, "especially in such a pretty place like Elmthwaite Hall? Here one can almost believe such a horrid thing as war doesn't exist at all." She took a sip of her wine. "I'm quite ready to talk about much more rewarding topics of conversation."

He had to force his next question through clenching teeth. "Such as?"

Once again, his hopes of finding a woman not given over to frivolity had been dashed. How many more of these meaningless conversations, dinners, and weekend house guests would he have to endure before his father realized there wasn't a single young lady that piqued Colin's genuine interest?

"We could talk about fashion or jazz music or dancing. It's wonderful to have dance partners again. Though some of the men can't dance like they used to, what with their injuries and all." She placed her hand on Colin's sleeve, her gaze flirtatious. "Thank goodness you made it back in one piece, Mr. Ashby. We shall have no trouble dancing, you and I."

Sharp anger rose inside him, tightening his collar as effectively as his bow tie. The war and its effects, which Lady Sophia could so easily dismiss, had forever changed his life and the lives of thousands of other soldiers. Colin would never understand how people could so easily brush those sacrifices aside just because the fighting had ended.

"I'm glad to hear your mind is again at ease, Lady Sophia," he ground out despite his hardened jaw, "with all this war nonsense over. I shall be sure to thank the Good Lord tonight that I didn't lose life nor limb, so that I might continue dancing." The room felt suddenly too hot and confining. He threw down his napkin, unable to bear the thought of remaining a moment longer. "It is a shame, though, that my brother did not fare as well. He was the better dancer, you see."

He rose from his chair. "Please forgive me, Lord and Lady Weatherly. Lady Sophia." At least she had the decency to blush. "I'm afraid I have urgent business to attend to."

"What's this, Colin?" The anger in Sir Edward's blue eyes belied his casual tone. "The ladies haven't yet retired to the drawing room."

"I am sorry, Father. It cannot wait."

Colin noted his mother's deflated expression with a prick of guilt before he spun on his heel and marched out of the dining room. He paused long enough in his escape to undo his bow tie and loosen the chokehold of his collar.

At last able to breathe again, he moved toward the stairs but stopped when he spied Martin at the front door.

"I am sorry," the butler said in firm tones, "but I cannot disturb Sir Edward."

Though Colin didn't catch the person's reply, the voice was decidedly feminine.

"You may call again in the morning. Good night." Martin began to close the door.

His curiosity getting the better of him, Colin strode forward. "Hold on a moment, Martin. Who's come to call this late?"

The older man stepped back and gave Colin a slight bow. "Master Colin." Martin persisted in using the childish title. Colin had long ago given up correcting him—he'd likely be "Master Colin" until he died, even after he became baronet.

Colin peered out the door. A young woman stood in the pool of light from the entry. She looked to be a few years younger than himself, though she exuded an air of dignity that disguised her true age. Her coat and dress, while tidy, had clearly seen better days. Beneath her wide-brimmed hat, her red hair had been gathered into an attractive knot, which extenuated her slender neck.

A glance beyond her into the still brightly lit evening showed no waiting wagon or automobile. She'd clearly come here alone. But why? Strangers were rare in Larksbeck, and even more so at Elmthwaite Hall.

She didn't squirm beneath his scrutiny, but Colin noticed a flicker of exhaustion pass over her face as he studied her. How far had she come? He didn't like the thought of turning her away, as Martin intended, especially seeing that hint of fatigue. A tug of compassion and interest prompted him to step back and motion her inside. "Why don't you come in?"

The woman looked from him to Martin, then apparently sensing no further complaint from the butler, she crossed the threshold into the house. "Thank you. I promise I'll be brief."

Her voice revealed her American origins as the brighter light revealed details about her person that Colin hadn't yet noticed. Light freckles draped her nose. Her eyes, wreathed by long lashes, were the color of the lake in spring. She clutched a battered suitcase in one hand and a wrinkled envelope in the other. Her gaze flicked to the nearby marbled table topped with its ornate vase of flowers, but their opulence seemed to have little effect on her.

Turning those arresting blue-green eyes on him, she managed a faint smile. "As I told the gentleman here, my name is Nora Lewis. I'm the great-niece of Henry Lewis, and I've inherited his sheep farm. I was told Sir Edward Ashby could help me locate a Mr. Green, who would give me the key to my property."

Old Man Lewis had a great-niece, and an American one at that? Colin walked by the Lewis sheep farm and cottage nearly every day. He'd expected the property to go to the Tuttle family, though, who were related to Henry by marriage.

"As I already informed her, Master Colin, Sir Edward—"

"You are right, Martin. Father cannot be disturbed." He turned from the butler's annoyed expression to Nora Lewis. "Perhaps I might be of help, though. I'm Colin Ashby, Sir Edward's son." He had no idea why he felt

compelled to help, other than a vague notion that if anyone was to her assist her, it must be him.

"Mr. Ashby." She nodded in acknowledgment. He
liked the sound of his name spoken in her American accent. "Could you tell me where I might find Mr. Green?"

"Mr. Green is my father's land agent, but he doesn't
live here at the house. His home is down the lane a bit.
You passed it on your way."

The tired lines on her heart-shaped face deepened. "I
see. And which house is Mr. Green's?"

"It is late, Miss Lewis," Martin interrupted with dismissal. "I suggest you return in the morning and all will
be set right."

"Where is she to go, Martin?" The fierceness in
Colin's tone surprised himself.

The butler drew himself up to his full height, which
still meant his gray head only came to Colin's chin. "The
inn in the village, Master Colin."

"No," Colin said, shaking his head. Not only was Nora
clearly exhausted, but if she went to stay in the inn, his
curiosity about her wouldn't be satisfied. What had moti-
vated this beautiful young woman to come here, alone, to
claim a sheep farm? "You are welcome to stay the night
here, Miss Lewis."

Nora pocketed her envelope and fixed Colin with a determined look. "I appreciate the offer, Mr. Ashby, but I
would very much like to stay the night in my own house."

Colin bit back a laugh. He wasn't sure whether he
ought to remind her of the likely deplorable state of "her
house" or congratulate her on her fortitude. Her gumption
only added to her growing intrigue.

"Very well, Miss Lewis. I will show you to the Greens'

home." He shoved his bow tie into his pocket. "Martin, will you please tell Father I've stepped out?"

"Yes, Master Colin."

He ignored the disapproving tone of the butler and waved Nora out the door, ahead of him.

A small smile broke through her weariness. "Thank you, Mr. Ashby." She gave a polite nod to Martin, despite his abruptness. "Good night."

Colin followed her outside and onto the gravel drive. The crunch of their shoes filled the silence between them. They hadn't gone far before a low whine sounded, accompanied by the soft pad of paws. Colin stopped to allow Christian's yellow Labrador to catch up. The dog trotted over to them and began sniffing Nora's skirt and shoes. Colin fully expected her to shy away from the big but gentle brute, but instead, she knelt down and scratched the animal behind the ears.

"Who is this handsome fellow?" Her voice held more animation than Colin had yet heard.

"Miss Lewis, meet Perseus."

She glanced up at Colin over her shoulder and smiled. Not the reluctant smile of moments ago, but a genuine one that brightened her gaze. If he'd thought her eyes captivating before, now they were positively mesmerizing.

"Perseus? Do you like Greek mythology?"

It took him a moment to shift his focus from her blue-green eyes to her question. "My brother, actually."

Before the stab of grief could fill him at the mention of Christian, Nora spoke again. The wistfulness in her voice served as the perfect antidote to his own pain. "I have a dog back home. But his name is nothing so original." She gave Perseus another pat, then stood. "It's plain old Oscar."

"I have an uncle named Oscar."

"Oh." Apology etched her face. "I'm sorry. I didn't mean to imply—"

Colin broke his deadpan expression and chuckled. "I don't really have an Uncle Oscar, Miss Lewis. However, if I did, I think that's a perfectly dignified and sensible name."

He caught the quick showing of an amused smile before it vanished. Nora fell into step beside him, Perseus at their heels.

"How did you come from the station?" Larksbeck didn't have a train station. The closest one was a good hour's drive away, longer if the mud was bad. It would take several hours to traverse on foot.

"I walked."

Colin's eyebrows shot up with surprise. He couldn't imagine Lady Sophia, or any of the young women he'd recently met, making such a long walk. The more minutes he spent in Nora's presence, the more his admiration for her grew, along with an unfamiliar desire to know everything about her.

He tried to remember what he'd heard during the war about American women. They were bold, brash, independent—that's what his comrades had told him. Certainly Miss Lewis was the latter, to travel all the way here alone, to take over her great-uncle's sheep farm. He couldn't imagine her pining over the inefficiencies of dance partners as Lady Sophia had.

"Where in America are you from?" he questioned, hoping to draw out more information from her.

"Iowa."

"Is that where all the heiresses of sheep farms hail from?"

His playful question managed to coax another half smile from her. "I don't know. I've never met another sheep farm heiress."

"Nor have I. You're my first." He slipped his hands into his pockets. "What did you do in Iowa?"

"I ran my family's farm."

"Alone?"

Sorrow pinched the air between them as she paused. "Only recently."

He wanted very much to prompt her to elaborate, but he decided not to press the topic. "Did you have sheep there?" he asked, steering the conversation in a less discomfiting direction.

Nora shook her head, the trace of laughter in her voice when she answered, "No. We had a cow, horses, chickens, hay fields, corn. But no sheep."

"This is your first time caring for sheep, then?"

"Yes." There was no hint at hesitation or fear.

Colin's respect for her doubled at her answer. She would be tackling a brand-new skill, as he had when he'd first learned to fly. He missed learning new things. The war, though lengthy and awful, had given him a sense of accomplishment, a chance to work at tasks unfamiliar to him. Something akin to envy wound through him at the adventure that awaited Nora.

When she lapsed into silence again, he searched his mind for something else to say. *What's the matter?* he scolded himself. Conversing with women had never been a difficult task for him, especially not lately. The women

he'd met since returning home possessed a strong eagerness to talk to him.

Nora, however, didn't seem at all dazzled by what he'd
heard referred to as his "good looks and charm." He recalled the way she'd observed the ornate entryway at
Elmthwaite Hall with neither approval nor disapproval in
her gaze. In her unobtrusive presence, Colin felt suddenly
stripped away of all pretense and expectation. The realization left him feeling oddly vulnerable and yet liberated
at the same time.

He glanced at her, strolling silently beside him. Her
eyes took in the mountains, the languid lake, and him.
She offered him a quick smile, but he sensed it was
one of friendly appreciation, not one designed to im-
press like Lady Sophia's smiles. Nora's authenticity
demanded he act in kind, a thought that both intrigued
and unsettled him.

Walking here beside her, he was no longer Sir Edward's son or Christian's younger brother or the next heir
of Elmthwaite Hall. Tonight, in this moment, he was simply Colin—someone he hadn't been free to be in a very
long time.

Chapter 2

Nora waited outside the walled yard as Colin Ashby had instructed, while he knocked on the Greens' front door. Perseus sat beside her. She rubbed the soft fur behind the dog's ears, grateful for his calming company and the reminder of home in this unfamiliar place.

She glanced at the still-lit sky. What time did it actually grow dark here? she wondered. If she were back home, she'd be seeking refuge from the heat of the day. Perhaps taking a rest from running the farm by sitting on the porch, Oscar lying on the wood planks at her feet.

Instead she stood shivering, even in the summer air, in a country halfway around the world. Would she be able to learn sheep farming and make a life for herself here? Her great-uncle's solicitor, Mr. Shaw, certainly had his doubts, even if he'd tried to hide them behind a kind smile. Nora wouldn't soon forget his shocked expression when she entered his office and explained she was the great-niece of the late Henry Lewis.

But there's no going back, so please help me, Lord.

Nora set her suitcase down and crossed her arms to keep warmer. She had nothing back in Iowa, except for painful memories. This was where she would make a new beginning, one she desperately needed.

Footfalls disrupted her thoughts. She glanced up to see Colin striding toward her. His expensive suit looked out of place against the backdrop of the whitewashed stone cottage, and yet the man himself didn't seem so out of place here. He'd looked every bit the handsome prince from a fairy tale when he'd intercepted the butler, his black eyes warm with curiosity, his dark hair falling slightly over his forehead. But with his strong-looking shoulders and friendly manner, he could easily pass as a laborer in the right clothes.

He pushed through the gate in the wall, that easy smile lifting his mouth. "Your key, Miss Lewis."

Colin dropped the old-fashioned key into her open palm. The weight of it felt both ominous and promising. Would her new home be livable or a disaster after three months of being unoccupied? Whatever the state, she wouldn't go to the inn. The sale of the farm had provided her with enough funds to buy some new clothes and pay her travel expenses to England. She wouldn't part with what little she had left for a night at the inn.

"Thank you." She slid the key into her coat pocket beside the letter verifying her relation to Henry Lewis and her inheritance of his farm. "I appreciate the help."

She expected him to leave, to return to his grand house—with its lavish carpets, fresh flowers, electric lights, and marbled tables—though she rather liked his company. His had been the first show of friendliness in an otherwise long and tiring day of traveling.

Instead of bidding her good-bye, though, Colin glanced up and down the road, his hands returning to his pockets. "Do you know which farm is your uncle's?"

"No," she said, hoisting her suitcase again. It weighed so little. "But I have the directions."

"Old Man Lewis's place is back down this road, toward Larksbeck." He waved in that direction. "You passed it on your way up to the house. His lane veers off to the right. If you reach the bridge to the village again, you've gone too far."

Nora extended her hand to him. "I'll find it. Thank you again."

Rather than shaking her offered hand, he starting walking south. In the opposite direction of his home. Nora hurried after him, Perseus trotting alongside her.

"Look, Mr. Ashby. I'm sure I can find it."

"I have no doubt of that," he said without breaking stride. "But I can't very well allow you to bump around in the dark by yourself, can I?"

"But it isn't dark."

He chuckled, though he still wouldn't concede. "To allow you to go into a strange house, alone, would be ungentlemanly."

Her retort came swift, almost without thought. "And British men are nothing if not gentlemanly."

Nora pressed her lips together in shock. Had she really spoken the tongue-in-cheek comment out loud?

Colin stopped walking and burst out laughing. The deep masculine sound encircled Nora, filling her heart with something akin to pleasure, then floated off over the quiet lake on their left. "I take it you don't normally jest, Miss Lewis."

"No," she admitted with a soft smirk, her cheeks flushed.

What about this man put her in a teasing mood? It had been years since she'd made a man laugh. Tom had often praised her quick wit, but there were things she'd believed had died along with him.

Colin leaned close, his dark eyes full of amusement. "Then I shall endeavor to provoke some quipping from you again."

Nora's blush deepened as she peered up at him. She wasn't in danger of losing her heart—she'd promised it to Tom, and even in death, he had full claim to it still. But she couldn't help a sardonic smile at the thought of the sheep girl and the rich, handsome land owner ending up together. What would Livy have to say on that subject?

"Shall we?" Colin unpocketed one hand to motion her forward.

She moved in step with him, her feet throbbing inside her shoes after hours of walking. They trudged along in silence, but it wasn't uncomfortable. She felt no fear at walking alone with him. Perhaps it was the absence of darkness, despite being nearly ten o'clock, or perhaps it was more the sense of honor about him that told her she could trust him.

"Here's your lane," Colin announced at last. The path, no wider than a single wagon width, was lined on both sides with stone fences. Nora remembered seeing the ribbon of a road on the way up to Elmthwaite Hall, though she hadn't guessed it led to her new house.

Her heart beat faster at the possibilities of what lay ahead. She quickened her pace as the path ascended a grassy incline. Colin dropped behind as if he understood her unspoken need to view the place for the first time by herself.

At the top of the small hill, the land stretched flat for several acres before climbing toward the mountains. Nestled between two stands of trees was a two-story whitewashed stone cottage with slate shingles. The front doorway sagged and one of the windows appeared to be cracked, but Nora didn't care. It was standing—and it was hers.

She went to the door and fit the key into the lock. Colin came up behind her, while Perseus sniffed at the weeds growing beneath the windows. Nora twisted the key and pushed open the door. It moved inward with a loud creak. She stepped into a narrow hallway and set her suitcase on the floor, her nose filling with the dusty scent of uninhabited space.

To her left Nora found the dining room, to her right the parlor. Sheets shrouded most of the furniture, including the dining table and couch.

She walked past the staircase leading to the second floor and moved into the kitchen at the back of the house. A small table with three chairs stood on one side of the room. A sink, cooking range, and cupboard filled the rest of the space, while a washing machine guarded the corner.

Colin and Perseus appeared in the kitchen doorway. "What do you think, Miss Lewis?"

Nora glanced out the window above the sink—it had a lovely view of the mountains. "It's wonderful."

"The water comes directly to the house."

"Just like at home." She smiled in relief.

"Old Man Lewis did rather well for himself." Colin leaned against the wall at his back. "His family bought this land from my ancestors more than a hundred years ago."

"Did they want to sell it?"

"I believe they were in need of funds," he said with a touch of ruefulness in his voice.

"So where are my sheep?" Nora leaned over the sink to get a better view. A square field, enclosed by a stone fence and gate, lay directly behind the house, but it was empty. A stone barn sat beside the field, its doors shut.

Colin chuckled. "You won't find them out there. They're up on the fell."

She turned around. "The fell?" Apparently there were even words she would need to learn in this new life. *No matter, though*, Nora thought. She wasn't without a home or a way to take care of herself. There was reassurance in that.

"That's the name for the mountains. The farmers will bring the sheep down in the next two months for shearing."

"They wander around up there, on the mountains?"

He nodded. "All the sheep are marked—on the ear and with paint on their backs and sides. That way each farmer knows which sheep belongs to which farm. I heard that Jack Tuttle, one of your neighbors"—he straightened—"has been looking out for Lewis's sheep since his death."

Nora took note of the name; she'd have to learn where Jack Tuttle lived so she could thank him. "Anything else I need to know about the sheep?"

Colin laughed as he held up his hands in mock surrender. "Much more I'm sure, but that's all I can artic-
ulate on the subject." She couldn't help wondering the
real reason he'd insisted on accompanying her—not that
she minded. His company was proving to be as welcome as his dog's.

"That's good for now." She gave him a grateful smile
and glanced at the ceiling. "I think I'll check out the upstairs."

"I'll wait below," he said, waving her forward and giving her a slight bow, as if she were a queen.

Grateful to finish her final exploration alone, Nora
climbed the stairs, one or two creaking a bit beneath her
shoes. There were two bedrooms on the second level.
They were identical—each containing a bed, a small table, a bureau, and a fireplace. Which one had been her
great-uncle's? she wondered. Would he be pleased she'd
come all this way to take over his farm? She'd known so
very little about him, other than his name, where he lived,
and that he was related to her father.

She returned downstairs, her hand on the banister. Like
everything else, a layer of dust covered the wood. Nora
brushed her hand against her coat. A thorough cleaning,
a new pane of glass for the parlor window, a stocked cupboard, and the place would be comfortable.

Colin, a lit lamp in hand, waited with his dog by
the front door. The soft illumination helped chase away
some of the growing shadows. Lifting the lamp higher, he
peered into the parlor. "It all looks rather dusty."

"But nothing that can't be fixed with a rag." Nora's
scrutinizing gaze alighted on a horn-shaped object hidden
beneath a sheet. A thrill of excitement pulsed through her.

"That must be a gramophone." Her fingers mourned the loss of her piano, but a gramophone, like the one she'd left behind, would still provide music to sing along with.

She stepped into the parlor to get a better look, but instead of the click of her heels against the wood, her shoe connected with something that gave a frightened squeak. Startled, Nora jumped out of the way and crashed against Colin. He managed to keep hold of the lamp with one hand, while his other gripped her waist.

"Watch yourself," he said in a low voice, his breath warming her cheek. "There are likely more mice where that one came from."

Nora took a deep breath to still her pounding heart. But the heat of Colin's hand seeping through the thin material of her coat and dress, along with the solid feel of his chest against her back, caused her heartbeat to quicken instead of slow. It had been so long since she'd been held, especially by a man.

Their close proximity released a bevy of emotions inside her—anticipation, uncertainty, hope, fear—but she knew the danger of feeling too much. She would not risk returning to the depths of pain she'd endured at losing the three people she loved most. Pragmatism, not passion, had ruled her life the last nineteen months. And it would do so now. She forced herself to step away from Colin, stifling a shiver from the cold the absence of his hand created.

"Are you all right?" He reached out as if to touch her again, but his hand fell short before he lowered it to his side.

Afraid she'd sound breathless if she spoke, Nora settled for a nod.

Colin studied her face, his gaze penetrating. "May I ask you a question?"

Her dry throat felt drier still. What did he wish to ask? "Yes," she found herself answering, in spite of the concern throbbing beneath her skin.

"How does your family feel about you moving to England?"

Family. The word elicited a pang of sorrow in her chest. Nora fingered the sheet on top of the couch, allowing herself a single moment to feel the pain before she swallowed it back. "I lost my parents to the Spanish influenza over a year and a half ago. That's what I meant earlier about running things alone." She lifted her eyes to his and gave a halfhearted shrug. "So that leaves me. I have no siblings and no other living relatives."

"I'm sorry." The genuine tone of compassion made Nora feel that perhaps he, too, had experienced the death of someone dear. His next words confirmed her guess. "My brother was killed in a dogfight with the Germans nearly three years ago."

"He was a pilot?"

"We both were." The strangled tone told her more than his simple response. He'd been close to his brother. For a moment she wondered if, like Tom, this other Ashby had left behind a grieving sweetheart.

"That must be so very hard to have him gone." Nora studied the shadows at her feet, hesitating. Should she share more of her own story of loss? The feeling of trust she'd felt on the walk over with Colin returned, giving her the courage to push the truth from her lips into the air between them. "I lost my fiancé to the war."

"A double blow then," Colin said with equal gravity.

"Yes, but what family hasn't been affected? The war changed a great many lives."

She lifted her chin to find him staring at her, his expression a mixture of surprise and respect. A moment later, the emotion in his gaze faded and he passed her the lamp. "I must be getting back. It's a great pleasure to have met you, Miss Lewis."

"Thank you again for all your help, Mr. Ashby."

He paused at the door. "I wouldn't be much of a gentleman, or a British one, at least," he teased, making Nora flush, "if I didn't offer once more to let you stay at Elmthwaite Hall until this place can be properly cleaned."

"I'm perfectly fine staying the night here, as I said earlier."

"Even with the mice and dust?" His eyebrows rose with challenge.

Nora couldn't help a thin smile. It had been so long since she'd exchanged friendly banter with a man—she hadn't realized how much she'd missed it until tonight. "I'm not a stranger to such things, Mr. Ashby. I did grow up on a farm."

He smiled back. It was a rather nice smile, one that brought a twinge of warmth to her heart. "Very well." He let himself out the door. "Come on, Perseus."

The dog remained inside the house with Nora, his tail disrupting the dust on the floor as he wagged it back and forth.

"Go on, Perseus," Nora urged. She gave his rump a gentle shove with her shoe, but the dog refused to move.

Colin turned back and eyed the stubborn canine. "I have an idea, Miss Lewis. If you won't accept my offer of a clean room at Elmthwaite Hall, will you at least allow the dog to stay with you? After all, no true sheep heiress is without her dog."

The spark of warmth he'd incited within her grew, bringing the sting of grateful tears to Nora's eyes. She couldn't think of anything better in this strange, new place than the companionship of a loyal dog to see her through her first night. "You don't mind?"

"Quite the opposite." His hands slipped into his pockets again. "I would feel better knowing I hadn't abandoned you, alone, to the rodents."

Nora knelt beside the dog and rubbed his yellow fur. "Would you like to stay, Perseus?" The dog's tail swished faster as he attempted to lick Nora's face. He was as excited to stay as she was to have him. "All right then..." She rose to her feet. "I accept. Perseus may stay."

"I shall sleep better because of it." He gave her another mock bow, the kindness and interest she'd seen earlier still evident in his dark eyes. "Good night, Miss Lewis."

"Good night, Mr. Ashby."

She watched him amble down the lane before she shut the door. *What a puzzling man.* He held himself with all the bearing of one born to privilege, and yet his easygoing manner and genuine thoughtfulness didn't quite match the world she imagined he lived in. Had he always been that way? Or had the war deepened those contrasts? Nora found she very much hoped she had the chance to find out.

As she gazed about the cottage, she felt new energy seep back into her veins. Was it the relief of having completed her journey or the dog at her side or her time with Colin?

Whatever the reason, she didn't think she could sleep

just yet. Instead she walked to the gramophone and removed the sheet from it. A cloud of dust filled the air,
making herself and Perseus sneeze. Nora laughed as she
tossed the sheet aside. "Let's have ourselves a little music, shall we?"

* * *

Colin changed into his flight clothes, while Gibson stood
nearby, frowning. It was the one allowance Colin had
insisted on after coming home. Gibson could help him
dress for the day, for dinner, for parties. But when it
came to his flying uniform, Colin would dress himself.
He checked his appearance in the mirror, hoping with any
luck, he'd be halfway across the Lake District before his
father awoke.

He'd returned to a quiet house last night. His parents
and their guests had retired, while Colin had been helping
Nora. Still, he knew his father wouldn't let his behavior at
dinner go unchecked. For that reason, Colin had risen especially early and planned to spend the greater part of the
day in his aeroplane. Away from Sir Edward . . . and Lady
Sophia.

"Will you pass me my cap and gloves, Gibson?"

His valet handed him the needed articles and left the
room. Colin sat on the edge of his bed to pull on his cap
and gloves. Maybe he'd fly south today—over the Lewis
cottage.

How had Nora fared last night? He was grateful she'd
at least accepted his offer to let Perseus stay. She certainly
exhibited the same naïve bravery he'd witnessed in the
American soldiers he'd met during the war. Then again,

she wasn't a pampered heiress with servants to cater to her every whim like Lady Sophia.

Colin had taken one look at the cottage and declared the thing a disaster in his mind. The rickety stairs, cracked window, and dusty furnishings didn't discourage Nora, though. If anything, she seemed eager for the work.

He remembered feeling that way during his time in France, where he'd learned to fly, to work, to be disciplined. Now he felt mostly useless. Flying was the one thing that brought him satisfaction and purpose. When he soared over the world, he was free—free of his father's expectations and his brother's continued shadow. Up in the air, he could be himself.

His flying skills hadn't proven completely impractical at home either. He'd been instrumental in locating several groups of tourists who'd become lost on the fells, but those times were few and far between. Perhaps he ought to take up some other interest or work.

Like how to repair a cracked window, he thought with a smile. Wouldn't that infuriate his father?

When he returned from flying, he'd have to stop by the Lewis place, merely to collect Christian's dog, of course. His father would never condone a relationship with Nora Lewis. Not that she was interested in one. Colin had sensed as much when she spoke of her departed fiancé.

"Nothing wrong with looking out for one's neighbor, though," he murmured to himself as he stood and collected his goggles. He seemed to recall a sermon about that from his youth. Surely it would be ungentlemanly of him not to help.

He grinned as he remembered Nora's jest outside the Greens' home. Colin wasn't sure which had amused him more—her teasing or her stunned expression afterward. She might be quiet, but he suspected Nora of being quite witty. He looked forward to proving the theory correct.

A jaunty tune from the war filled his mind. He whistled it as he left his room and descended the stairs. Colin was looking forward to the day. Until he spied Martin standing at attention below. He'd hoped to rouse only the chauffeur to help him start the biplane, then slip away before encountering any of the other servants who might inform his father that Colin was about.

"Good morning, Master Colin," the butler said in a smug voice. "Your father wishes to see you in the library."

Colin forced back a groan. He hadn't outwitted his father after all. "Sorry, Martin. But as you can see, I'm off. I'll speak with Father when I return."

"You will do no such thing." Sir Edward appeared in the library doorway. "I need to speak with you. Now."

Though his teeth ground together, Colin nevertheless feigned an attitude of ease as he moved into the library. Martin shut the door behind them. Colin took a seat on one of several settees arranged around the large room and rested his arm along the back. "How may I help you, Father?"

"I see you're off to fly that contraption again." Sir Edward gave an indignant sniff as he crossed to one of the windows and stared outward.

"Shall I remind you that you purchased the aeroplane?"

Sir Edward frowned. "Only because your mother insisted. She thought it would pull you from your black temper. Instead, I fear, it's only heightened your insolence."

Colin forced himself to maintain his relaxed demeanor,

but his fingers betrayed him, gripping the goggles so tightly his knuckles must be white inside his gloves. "Forgive me, Father. Even my grief offends you. Perhaps Christian would have been less morose. Once again, it is a pity he died instead of me."

"How dare you?" Sir Edward blustered, turning from the window. "You mock his death."

Colin climbed to his feet—he wouldn't subject himself to his father's pointed barbs a minute longer. His voice came out calm, despite the anger churning in his gut. "It is precisely the opposite, sir. I wish he had not died because I will never be him, and it is obvious this family would have been better off if his life had been spared instead of mine." He started for the door, but his father's next words halted his retreat.

"There is more at stake here than your pride and freedom, Colin," his father bit out before his tone changed from bitterness to despair. "If you do not pull yourself together and do what you must, we will lose even more than we already have."

Colin turned back, surprise puncturing his frustration. "What are you talking about?"

Sir Edward ran a hand over his face, then sank onto the nearest couch. "I wanted to keep it from you. To allow you to live carefree, as your mother advised."

Nerves tightened Colin's stomach, reminding him of those first few minutes when he'd ascend the skies to square off with the Germans. "What do you mean?"

"The fact of the matter is we are living on the edge of a cliff." His father glanced around the library as if seeing it for the first time. "One that is crumbling under our feet as we speak." He leaned back against the cushions with a sigh. "My overseas investments did not weather the war. We are living on your mother's money at present, but that, too, will eventually run out."

Colin returned to his seat, his mind roiling with the news. He hadn't suspected financial troubles in the least. If anything, the way his parents had thrown parties and dinners recently, he'd imagined there was plenty of capital to be spent.

"What will happen to Elmthwaite Hall?" He had to know, though he feared the answer.

Sir Edward waved his hand in an arc that took in the bookcases and comfortable furnishings. "We may be forced to sell it, along with that aeroplane of yours, I might add."

"Sell Elmthwaite?" The air left Colin's lungs in a painful whoosh. His family had lived in this valley since the seventeenth century. He might feel confined here, but he knew no other home. He and Christian had been born and raised here, beside the mountains and the lake.

Still, the possibility of selling their ancestral home might not have pained him as much three years ago, before he'd made his promise to Christian. A promise exacted from Colin on the day Christian had been killed.

Promise me that you won't ever turn your back on Elmthwaite.

The strong resolve of Christian's voice filled Colin's mind as if his brother had once again spoken the words. Colin couldn't fail to keep the one thing Christian had prized more than anything else in the world, second only to their family.

"What about selling Brideshall in Scotland?" he pressed, anxious for some other answer to their troubles.

Nearly every summer that Colin could remember the family had traveled to their house in the Western Highlands of Scotland for holiday. The estate, Brideshall, sat on an island in the middle of the loch. While Colin hated to give up a place full of many other fond memories, it was far better than selling Elmthwaite Hall.

"I'm already preparing to sell Brideshall, which means we won't be going there this year. But I'm afraid the proceeds won't sustain us for long. Selling Elmthwaite would still have to follow." Sir Edward bent forward, his hands on his knees. "Unless…"

Colin lifted his head. There was a way out of this madness? "Unless?" he echoed.

"If you marry well, you can help save Elmthwaite for us and future generations."

Colin's jaw tightened at the thought of taking a wife for her money and not because of any real affection. "That's the answer? I marry someone like Lady Sophia and we're fine?"

Sir Edward snorted and sat back. "No, it's more than just marrying well. We need someone like the Earl of Weatherly to fund a project of mine that would give us a new source of revenue. Something the war hasn't touched. Fortunately for us, you have at least another week to redeem yourself with Lady Sophia and her father."

"What's this project of yours?"

A smile graced Sir Edward's face, softening his expression and revealing his enthusiasm. Colin had forgotten what his father looked like when he smiled. "I want to build a hotel by the lake, make Larksbeck more appealing to wealthy visitors."

Not a bad idea, Colin mused. "How would these visitors get here?"

"By automobile, of course. I plan to purchase three or four new autos and another chauffeur or two to maintain them. We'll bring the tourists straight from the railway to the hotel." His blue eyes flashed with eagerness. "The old stables can be converted to house the new automobiles."

Colin gave a thoughtful nod; his father had clearly given his plans much consideration. "What sort of hotel are you thinking of building? We can certainly afford some modest structure on our own, can't we?"

"Well yes," Sir Edward replied with obvious impatience. "But I want something large and extravagant. A hotel unlike any other in the Lake District. Which means we need serious investors, such as your future father-in-law, to help pay for the land and construction.

Ignoring the implications of such a reference, Colin felt the first stirrings of hope. He wouldn't have to break his word to Christian after all. "Where would you build this hotel?"

"On Henry Lewis's land. Next to Elmthwaite, his farm has the best view of the lake and is close enough to the village to be appealing."

His father's answer hit him like a fist to the stomach. An image of Nora rose inside his mind—the way her red hair had shone in the light of the lamp last night, the way his hand had fit snugly around her waist.

Sir Edward lifted his shoe to rest it on his knee. "I've been meaning to get that land back for years. And now that the old man has passed on . . ."

"That may not work, Father." Colin's hope began to shrivel beneath sudden doubt.

"Why not?"

"The place is already taken."

Sir Edward glared at him as if Colin were the one stopping his plans. "By young Jack Tuttle?"

"No." Colin didn't want to say more. But he couldn't remain silent, for Nora's sake. "A great-niece of Lewis's, from America, has inherited it."

"How do you know? Is she here?"

Colin worded his reply carefully. "She came to the house last night to collect the key. She'd already met with Henry's solicitor, who must have contacted her in the States and informed her of Lewis's death." He purposely left off mention of his part in helping Nora and going to the cottage.

"Martin said nothing of this." Sir Edward rubbed a hand over his chin, his brow knit with frustration.

"We didn't wish to disturb you."

"As if you hadn't already," his father muttered. He sat silent for a long moment, deep in thought, before he lowered his hand to the couch's armrest. "Is this woman alone?"

Wariness churned inside Colin at the calculating tone. "She is. Why?"

"Excellent." Sir Edward tapped his fingers against the fabric. "Then she may still wish to sell the place. Running a sheep farm, alone, could prove a difficult task, especially for a woman."

Colin recalled the determination in Nora's blue-green eyes. If anyone, man or woman, could manage the sad-looking cottage and farm, she could. Or at least she'd give it a real try. "I don't know that she'll want to leave, Father."

"Then you must persuade her." Sir Edward stood. Colin had always thought of his father as a large man, though he'd long ago surpassed his height by several inches. "There is money to be made with bringing tourists here. I know it. But we must have the Lewis property to do it."

He peered down at Colin, his blue eyes dark with intensity. "You've been blessed with certain gifts where the ladies are concerned, Colin. I'm certain you can ingratiate yourself with her. Then you will convince her this way of life is too demanding for a single woman to handle by herself."

Colin's gut soured at his father's request, making him feel ill. Thankfully he hadn't eaten breakfast. While he liked the thought of getting to know Nora better, he hated doing so under false pretenses. Much about him had changed during the war, but he wasn't so past feeling that he was in the business of swindling women out of their sheep farms.

"There must be some other way to save the estate." If he gave in now, when would the expectations ever cease? His life had stopped being his own the moment Christian's had ended. And yet a part of him, buried so deep he rarely stopped to consider it, believed he must have been spared for some reason, some purpose. But surely this couldn't be it. Helping save his home and family through deceit?

"I'm afraid we're all out of ideas." Sir Edward's hands drooped at his sides. He no longer looked imposing but old and weary. "Please, Colin. We need your help on this. I...need you."

The admission was the closest thing to approval Colin

had ever heard from his father, and it filled him with childlike optimism he couldn't completely squelch. Christian had been the favored son, while Colin had continually disappointed Sir Edward with his youthful charisma and a knack for finding trouble. But no matter how long he'd waited for his father's approval, it still wasn't worth the defeat of an innocent woman and a loveless marriage.

Even if they'd only met the day before, Colin knew without a doubt Nora was unlike the other women he'd encountered. She made him believe he was good enough simply by being himself. How could he destroy that trust by deceiving her?

He rubbed out a smudge on his goggles, his heart heavy and troubled. What would Christian do if he were here? Colin knew the answer at once. His older brother's life had been focused toward a single goal—the conservation of the estate and the title of baronet. Colin might have hardened himself against disappointing their father, but he couldn't bear the thought of disappointing Christian. He'd given his brother his word and he wouldn't go back on that.

For whatever reason, he hadn't died that day as Christian had. Now it was up to him to live for the both of them.

"Very well, Father." Colin rose to his feet, his shoulders bent in acquiescence of this newest burden. "I will do as you ask."

Chapter 3

Nora sat back on her heels to ease the aching in her knees. She felt as though she'd been scrubbing floors for an eternity. Her back was sore and exhaustion pulled at every one of her muscles. She'd been up late the night before cleaning one of the bedrooms so she and Perseus had someplace to sleep, then she'd risen with the sun to start on the rest of the house.

After tucking a few stray hairs underneath the kerchief she wore on her head, she rinsed her rag in the nearby bucket. Her stomach grumbled with hunger, loud enough to raise Perseus's head from where he lay by the kitchen table.

"Did you hear that, boy?" She laughed.

They'd already consumed the few cans of food Nora had found in the cupboards last night, which meant nothing to eat this morning. She needed to go into the village to buy groceries, but she didn't want to leave before Colin came to get Perseus. Surely he wouldn't allow the dog to stay indefinitely, though Nora would miss having Perseus with her. The strangeness of sleeping in someone else's house in a foreign country hadn't felt so overwhelming with a dog at her bedside.

"All this cleaning not only makes me hungry," she muttered to Perseus, "but warm, too." She shed her sweater and wiped the dampness of her forehead with the back of her hand.

In need of a breeze, she went to the back door and propped it open with a rock she found outside. Cool air filtered into the room, bringing a sigh of relief to her lips. Perseus climbed to his feet and trotted past her into the yard.

Nora lifted her gaze to the mountains. They were like imperial queens arrayed in emerald satin and opal jewels. Never had she seen peaks so tall. They left her feeling dwarfed, and yet comforted by their height. Would they one day feel familiar, like the fields and trees back home in Iowa?

She returned to her rag and bucket to start on the hallway floor. Once she finished there, she only had the parlor and dining room to clean before the entire cottage was livable. A noise at the back door brought her head up. Perseus had returned inside. Nora smiled at him, but the gesture turned to a frown when she caught sight of the muddy paw prints he'd left in his wake.

"Perseus, you brute," she scolded mildly as she tossed her rag down.

She shook her head and chuckled, but the sound quickly became a strangled sob at the thought of rewashing the kitchen floor. Nora leaned her head back against the nearby wall and shut her eyes. An image of life back home rose sharply into her mind, almost as if she were there. She could see herself seated at the piano, playing and singing, while Oscar listened, the smell of baking bread permeating the air.

Tears stung her tired eyelids. She'd expected things to be hard, at least in the beginning. She hadn't expected this feeling of complete fatigue and loneliness—one she hadn't experienced since the deaths of her parents when she'd been left to run the farm by herself.

Perseus licked her face, prompting Nora to open her eyes. "I know you're sorry," she said, scratching behind his ears. "I'm just so very tired." She released a heavy sigh. "Not a chance you could clean up your own mess and I could crawl back into bed for, say, three days?"

The dog cocked his head as if contemplating her request. Nora couldn't help laughing. How wonderful to have a companion again, even for a short time.

"All right, boy." She climbed to her feet and shooed him back out into the yard. "All is forgiven, *if* you stay outside."

Back in the kitchen, she surveyed the muddy tracks, her hands on her hips. "I guess this floor will be twice as clean." She dragged her bucket into the kitchen and commenced scrubbing away the paw prints.

The repetitious movement kept her hands busy but freed her mind to compose a letter to Livy, one she would write out later. She must tell her friend about finding the cottage intact, despite the obvious repairs and cleaning required to make it livable again. Then there was the beauty of the mountains and the lake to describe, and the fact that she currently had no sheep in her field.

What about Colin Ashby? How would she describe him to Livy? Nora stopped scrubbing and sat back, tallying up a list in her head. *Handsome, kind, charming, mysterious.*

"That won't do," she murmured to herself. Livy would take one look at those words and start urging Nora to get to know the man better.

She couldn't fault her dearest friend for wanting her to have a similar life to the one Livy enjoyed: a wonderful husband, a precocious little girl, and a baby on the way. But the death of a sibling was different than the death of a sweetheart. Livy couldn't understand why Nora had given up her dreams of marriage and a family at Tom's death. No amount of explaining could change that.

Perhaps she'd leave off mentioning Colin in her first letter from England.

A knock at the door interrupted her thoughts and pulled her to her feet. Could it be the man she'd been thinking about? Nora jerked the kerchief from her head and stuffed the worn cloth into her apron pocket. If only she'd been able to accomplish more cleaning before Colin's arrival. She'd hoped to show him a much-improved cottage and not the dusty, dirty one he'd viewed with mild disdain last night.

The person knocked again. Nora hurried down the hall and opened the door. Instead of Colin, a short, buxom woman greeted her, a bright smile on her round cheeks and a covered dish in her hands.

"Hello there." Her accent sounded more pronounced than Colin's. "You'd be Nora."

"Uh...yes, hello." Nora shook her head in surprise. How did the woman know her name? Had Colin sent her?

"I'm Bess Tuttle. Me and my children live down the lane. Next house you come to." She tipped her head in the general direction. "I've a cottage pie for you, just come from the oven. Didn't think there was much in the way of food here, not since Henry died. Quite sad we were. He married my mother's sister—God rest their souls." She placed a hand on her bosom and lifted her eyes upward for a brief moment. "Henry 'twas a good man and uncle, though a bit gruff at times. Can't exactly blame him, though, as I'm sure you know. What with losing all his kin, saving our family."

Bess didn't pause for breath until she'd finished her welcoming speech. Nora gaped at her. Which of the woman's many revelations should she respond to first? Her gaze dropped to the pie and she felt instant relief.

"Thank you, for the pie. That was very kind. Won't you come in?"

Bess handed Nora the dish and swept past her into the house. "Sorry state of things." She made a tsking noise in her throat as she glanced at the still dusty dining room and parlor.

"Actually, I've done quite a bit of—"

The woman went on as if Nora hadn't spoken. "My Mary and I came over a few days after Henry passed, you see, and did our best to clean up. Not that he was overly untidy, mind you." She walked into the parlor and ran her hand over the dark fabric of the settee. "I would've come several times more, but Mr. Green refused. Once I relinquished the key to him, he wouldn't give it back. He's a stodgy one."

Nora followed Bess down the hall, as if she were the guest rather than the other way around, and set the pie on the kitchen table. She wished she had some tea. Wasn't that what good British hostesses offered their guests? Embarrassment prickled her skin, making her feel even warmer than before. At home, she would have talked to Bess on the porch, maybe given her a glass of lemonade. But here, she felt out of place, a foreigner in a stranger's house.

If Bess noticed her discomfort, she didn't let on. Instead she marched around the room, clucking over the tidiness. "I haven't seen this room so clean in years. You've done good job of putting it to rights, you have." She glanced out the open back door. "Don't you worry about your sheep neither. My Jack's been looking out for them. He's a right, good young man, he is."

Nora recalled Colin mentioning something about a Jack Tuttle. "Please thank him for me."

The woman shooed away her gratitude. "I suspect you can thank him yourself, if you've a mind to. We'd like to have you down to our place for supper now and again."

"That's very kind—"

"Jack had hoped Henry would give the place to him. Henry has more sheep than we do, but that's before we'd heard he meant to give the farm to you." She fanned her face with her hand as if overheated, though she kept right on smiling. "Why look there? If it isn't Perseus? What's the Ashbys' dog doing here and without Mr. Ashby?"

Nora followed her gaze to see the dog lolling back toward the house, his tail wagging. How to explain? "Well, Colin...I mean Mr. Ashby offered to let the dog stay with me last night. I had a dog back at home, you see..."

"Yes, my Mary told me all about Mr. Ashby walking you down here last night. She works up at Elmthwaite

Hall as a maid, she does." Bess's curved face beamed with obvious pride. "Watch yourself with Mr. Ashby, though. A real charmer, he can be. Though he hasn't been the same since his brother died—none of them have. Christian Ashby was supposed to inherit the baronet's title and the estate, but now Colin will. Many a wealthy lady has her sights set on him, and none too subtly either, says Mary. He'll marry well, if Sir Edward Ashby has anything to do with it."

Nora's cheeks flooded with heat. She busied herself with brushing imaginary crumbs into the sink, so Bess wouldn't see her mortified expression. She'd been here less than a day and already her neighbors suspected her of setting her cap at the baronet's son?

Of course, she'd enjoyed her brief time with Colin and appreciated his help, but he was only being polite. A man such as he would never be romantically interested in an orphaned farm girl such as herself. As Bess had confirmed, he would marry a rich, refined young lady, and Nora, thankfully, didn't fit either one of those descriptions.

"Now let me have a look at you, love."

Nora reluctantly turned around, hoping the woman wouldn't notice the extra color on her face. Bess's brunette head barely reached Nora's shoulder, but she felt like a child beneath her neighbor's intense scrutiny.

After a long moment of silence—the first since Bess had shown up at her door—the woman smiled, her head bobbing with approval. "You are the mirror image of your mum, when she was this age."

Nora's own smile froze in place, then lowered into a puzzled frown. "How could you possibly know my mother? She never traveled outside of the United States."

"Henry's daughter Eleanor was my cousin," Bess prattled on, oblivious to Nora's mounting confusion. "She and I spent many happy hours together as young girls. I'd know her daughter anywhere."

"I'm sorry but my mother's name is Grace, not Eleanor. Henry was my great-uncle on my father's side."

Bess's cheery expression faded. "That's what they told you? Ah, poor Eleanor. Though it's probably for the best."

The hairs on the back of Nora's neck rose at Bess's strange explanation. Her earlier warmth dissipated as a chill swept up her spine. What was the woman talking about? "I don't understand." Nora shivered and folded her arms. "Who told me what?"

Bess paled. Her wide eyes darted about like a frightened animal's. "L-look at me going on about silly notions that don't mean ne'er a thing now. Just the ramblings of an old woman." She laughed but the sound resonated with hollowness. Nora hardly considered her to be old; Bess looked to be in her early forties. "Well, I suppose I ought to be heading home now."

Nora couldn't shake the peculiar feeling still churning in her stomach. What was Bess hiding? She wanted to press the woman with more questions, but she wasn't sure she would get any real answers. Perhaps later, when she knew Bess better, she could learn more. Although that didn't mean she couldn't do a little investigating of her own in the meantime. Colin might know what Bess's strange story was all about.

"It was nice to meet you, Mrs. Tuttle." She infused the words with genuine gratitude. Thanks to the kind woman, Nora could continue cleaning on a full stomach.

The blatant relief on Bess's face told Nora the older woman thought the odd turn in the conversation had been forgotten. "Oh no, love. Call me 'Bess' or 'Auntie Bess,' same as everyone else. Nobody's called me 'Mrs. Tuttle' since I lost my husband five years ago." She let herself out the back door. Nora trailed her outside. "When will we be seeing you for supper?"

"Um..."

"How's tomorrow night? Then you can meet my brood—all seven of them." She chortled as though she'd made a joke. "Don't know if I can hold Mary and the twins off much longer than that. They want to hear all about America."

A vine of panic wrapped itself tightly around Nora at the thought of sharing a meal with a room full of strangers. Though the idea of eating alone, without Perseus, held even less appeal. "I would love to join you," she heard herself say.

"Good. Now be sure to eat that pie." Bess wagged a finger at her. "I've got my work cut out to fatten you up, I have." With that, she disappeared around the corner of the cottage, still muttering under her breath.

Nora rested her shoulder against the doorjamb and released a tired chuckle. In Bess's absence, the cottage echoed with its earlier quiet. Perseus meandered to the door. He sat at Nora's feet, his head tipped to the side again as he watched her.

"I think I may have made a friend." Nora smiled down at the dog.

Another unusual friend, she thought wryly. *But a friend nonetheless.* The bleakness she'd felt earlier had disappeared in the wake of Bess's kindness and happy chatter.

The scent of warm food teased Nora from behind. She pushed away from the door, feeling famished. She'd tackle the rest of her work soon enough, but right now, Bess's pie smelled too heavenly to ignore a minute longer.

* * *

Colin halted beside the lane leading to Henry Lewis's cottage. He'd put off coming to see Nora, choosing instead to fly until well past lunch. The question he'd been debating all morning still plagued him. Could he continue to befriend her knowing what his father expected him to do where she and her sheep farm were concerned?

He jammed his hands into his trouser pockets and released a low growl. If only he'd managed to escape earlier, before Sir Edward had found him. Though Colin knew he wouldn't have been able to avoid his father forever. Eventually Sir Edward would have sat him down and repeated the same pleading request to save Elmthwaite. One that felt like an echo of Christian's from that fated day three summers before.

A lad with a fishing pole propped against one shoulder rambled up the road toward Colin. Headed to the north side of the lake, no doubt. The boy threw Colin a funny look as he passed, likely curious as to why the baronet's son was standing unmoving along the side of the road.

"You're being daft," he muttered to himself as he strode up the lane. He had to collect Christian's dog after all. Perseus would be awaiting their daily walk.

The cottage came into view a few moments later. The disrepair was every bit as visible as it had been the night before, and yet the house held an air of life about it today. Perhaps it was the way the glass panes shone in the sunshine, clear evidence someone had been at work inside.

Colin marched to the front door and knocked. As he waited for Nora to answer, he shifted his weight from one polished shoe to the other, staring at the hard-packed earth.

He caught sight of the door swinging open and lifted his head. Nora wore a faded blue dress beneath her apron, which accentuated the sapphire color in her eyes. Eyes that appeared to brighten with pleasure upon seeing him. Guilt rendered his mouth dry.

"Mr. Ashby." She smiled, the gesture enhancing the delicate features of her face. A very pretty face.

"I'm here for Perseus," he announced. Nora's eyes widened at his slightly curt tone and he stifled a groan of regret. He'd never persuade her to do anything this way.

Clearing his throat, he modified his request. "What I mean is, if you no longer require the use of my dog, I'd like to take him on his walk."

"Oh, yes, of course." She stepped back from the door. "Come in, and I'll find him. He's out back."

Colin ducked inside and his jaw slackened with surprise. If not for Nora's presence, he would have guessed he'd entered the wrong cottage. The sheets had been removed from the furniture and not a speck of dust could be seen anywhere. The two front rooms, though simply furnished, appeared tidy and respectable.

"Look at this." He waved his hand to encompass the dining room, hallway, and parlor.

"What do you think?" she asked, her question full of anticipation.

"What do I think?" he repeated. "It's a thousand times improved." He glanced down to find her earlier smile had deepened at his praise, revealing a tiny dimple beside her full mouth. He hadn't noticed it last night. A speck of what appeared to be gravy sat next to the bewitching dimple.

"You...have something there." He pointed at the speck.

Her cheeks turned pink as she swiped at the corner of her mouth with her fingers. Instead of removing the spot, though, she smeared it.

"Allow me." Colin wet the tip of his thumb and ran it from the corner of her mouth to her chin, wiping away the gravy. Her lips twitched at his touch, but she remained still. He allowed his finger to linger against her smooth, warm skin, his attention caught up in the blue-green recesses of her large eyes. What was it about them that captivated him?

"Must be some of Bess Tuttle's cottage pie." She broke free of Colin's touch to shut the door, disrupting whatever pull of attraction he'd felt.

Colin mentally shook himself. He was supposed to be charming her, not the other way around. "You met Auntie Bess?"

Nora nodded and moved down the hallway toward the kitchen. "She brought me a pie and invited me to supper tomorrow night."

"All the while conversing with herself without taking a breath," Colin joked as he followed her into the kitchen.

Nora's lips pressed together as if she were trying not to laugh. "She was very kind." Her voice choked with barely hidden amusement. Colin grinned in triumph.

She stepped to the back door and called for Perseus.

The dog tramped inside. On seeing Colin, Perseus wagged his tail and came to sit in front of him.

"Ready for your walk, ol' boy?" Colin scratched behind the dog's ears.

Nora began putting away the dishes stacked in several neat piles on the counter. "Where do you usually walk?"

"Around the lake or on the fell. Would you care to join us?"

"I would," she said, looking back over her shoulder, "but I need to buy groceries in the village and order a new windowpane."

"Right."

Now what? Colin thought with mounting frustration. His time with her was moving to a rapid end. Or was it? "Perhaps Perseus and I could walk somewhere else today. We could show you Larksbeck, if you don't mind us tagging along." He slipped his hands back into his pockets. Did he sound too eager?

"That would be nice." She put away the last of the plates into the cupboard and removed her apron. "Give me a minute to fix this hair of mine and I'll be ready." She faced the window as she began unpinning her hair.

Colin moved into the hallway, intent on waiting out front, but he stopped when he caught sight of Nora's unfettered hair. Free from its pins, it fell in red waves to the middle of her back. He stared, mesmerized, at the beauty of it. Would those tresses feel as soft and silky as they looked, slipping through his fingers?

As Nora began to rearrange her hair into a knot, Colin realized she could turn at any moment and discover him gawking. He beat a hasty and rather silent retreat to the front door, Perseus on his heels.

Outside, Colin took a cleansing breath of fresh air. He needed to clear his head, remain focused on his task, and not succumb to Nora's beautiful face or hair. It wasn't just her beauty he was struggling to ignore, though. Nora wasn't trying to capture his fancy, like Lady Josephine or Lady Sophia. She was simply being herself, and that was a quality he found as attractive as her person. If only the future of Elmthwaite weren't riding on his getting to know her and persuading her to leave.

Nora exited the cottage, her hair pinned back into place. A sweater covered her shoulders, despite the rare sunshine. She'd acclimate to the weather soon enough. Or perhaps she wouldn't, if Colin's father had his way. Regret flourished anew inside him, but Colin had grown rather good at ignoring unpleasant feelings.

"To Larksbeck, m'lady." He waved her forward with a slight bow.

Perseus bounded ahead of them as they fell into step and turned south toward Larksbeck.

"It's very beautiful here," Nora's appraising gaze roamed from one side of the valley to the other. "Everything is so green."

"Isn't Iowa green?"

"Yes, but in a different way."

For a moment he wondered about this place where she came from, what it must look like, how different it would be from the mountains and lake he'd always known. "Did you enjoy living there?"

Nora nodded. "Very much."

"Yet you chose to leave it, for the unknown."

He hadn't voiced it as a question, but she answered with a soft "yes."

She didn't elaborate further, and Colin decided he didn't want to press her for a confession of what she'd left behind in America or what she might wish to return to. He'd try a different tactic.

"I hope you'll find the village satisfactory." He tipped his head in the direction of the rooftops. "Larksbeck has only a few shops, and without the railway at our doorstep, we tend to be a bit isolated from the rest of the country."

"I don't mind. My hometown wasn't very large."

Colin threw her a tight smile. He'd been foolish to think he could easily dissuade a capable woman like Nora with a few well-placed reminders about her home in the States or the isolation of their tiny valley. Perhaps the villagers, with their typical reticence toward strangers, would succeed in convincing Nora that she didn't want to stay.

They crossed the bridge at the outskirts of the village a few minutes later. "We have the apothecary ahead on the left," he informed her. "Then Bagley's grocery shop. The doctor, blacksmith, and The Blea Crown are all on the opposite side of the street."

"The Blea Crown?"

Colin pointed to the combination pub and inn. "*Blea* means blue. Up the road, you'll find the church and the parish priest's home."

"It's very quaint," Nora said, her eyes showing her pleasure.

Colin tried to see the whitewashed buildings as she did. He and his family had spent little time in Larksbeck the last decade. As a child he'd roamed here often, but once he'd returned from university, his trips to the village became more and more infrequent.

"Where to first, Miss Lewis?"

She studied the shops. "I need food, of course, but I'm also out of soap. Would the grocers or the apothecary be the better choice for that?"

"If I remember right, the apothecary's wife, Mrs. Smith, used to concoct all sorts of scented fragrances and such."

"The apothecary it is then."

Colin and Perseus escorted her to the shop. She opened the door for herself, without waiting for him to do so, giving Colin a whiff of perfume and other chemicals from inside. Telling Perseus to stay, Colin joined Nora in the tiny shop. Mrs. Smith, herself, came bustling in from the back room, where her husband fashioned the needed prescriptions.

"What may I do—" She stopped short when she caught sight of Nora, one hand rising to her heart. "If I didn't know better, I'd say Eleanor Lewis had just stepped into our shop."

Nora's face drained of color and her mouth tightened. What about the woman's reaction bothered her? If anything, she was friendlier than Colin had ever seen. "I'm Nora Lewis. From—"

"America," Mrs. Smith finished for her. "I heard Henry meant to have someone contact you in the States after he died. I'm glad to see someone did." Her gaze flicked to Colin and she gave him a pert nod. "Mr. Ashby." When she turned to Nora again, she was all smiles. "What may I get you today, Miss Lewis? I hope you're not feeling poorly."

Colin remained near the door as Nora, once more composed, explained her need for some soap. He told himself it didn't matter if Mrs. Smith had instantly warmed to her. The grocer, Mr. Bagley, was a shrewd businessman and not inclined to friendliness where strangers were concerned. There was still time—and people—to persuade Nora that Larksbeck and her sheep farm, in particular, weren't right for her.

After today, Colin wouldn't need to do more than suggest the idea of leaving before Nora would be gone and Elmthwaite would be saved. Why then did he feel less than satisfied with keeping his promise to Christian?

"Ready?" he asked when Nora approached the door with a wrapped package and a loaf of bread.

"Yes." Over her shoulder, she called out, "Thank you, Mrs. Smith. It was nice to meet you."

"Lovely to meet you, too."

Before Colin could get the door for her, Nora let herself outside. He swallowed a frown as he followed, reminding himself of how independent American women could be. Or perhaps Nora had been doing things on her own for so long, she didn't realize there were others who might want to help.

"The grocers next?" he asked.

"Yes. Can you believe she gave me some of her freshly baked bread?" She sniffed the wrapped loaf as they headed toward the grocers. "Mmm. Smell this," she murmured, extending the loaf to him.

Colin didn't want to, not in the middle of the village street, but her enthusiastic expression wasn't easily ignored. What sort of woman didn't bat an eye at a rickety old cottage and hard work and yet became almost giddy at the scent of fresh bread? Colin had the sudden sense he wasn't the only one hiding behind a façade. He suspected a wellspring of feeling and passion lay beneath Nora's pragmatic personality.

To please her, he lowered his nose and inhaled the bread's scent. The smell immediately conjured up memories of slipping below stairs, to the kitchen, where Mrs. Quincy would let him sneak bits of raw dough for him and Christian. His brother, of course, would never do something so sly himself, but he didn't mind if Colin shared the spoils.

"It smells delicious," he admitted.

"I've tried to make bread as well as my mother did, but it never turns out like hers. But this." She inhaled the bread's aroma again. "I may have to ask Mrs. Smith her secret."

Colin edged ahead as they neared the grocers so he could hold the door open for her. Nora looked momentarily surprised by the chivalrous act, but then she smiled in gratitude and entered the shop. Her smile, and dimple, stirred a strange sensation in Colin's gut and filled him with a strong desire to help her again, and again.

With a frown, he dismissed the feeling. Being polite was the least he could do for Nora before she had to face the crotchety Mr. Bagley.

Colin trailed Nora to the long counter, where the grocer sat reading a newspaper. It all but hid the old man's face. Only his gray hair and wrinkled forehead poked above the top of the paper.

"If you will note the time on the clock above the door," Mr. Bagley stated in a harsh voice, "you will see I close the shop in ten minutes and not a minute later. And before you ask, I do not have any ladies' shoes and cannot say when the next shipment will come."

"I don't need shoes." Nora set her bread and soap on the counter. "I do need..." She withdrew a list from her dress pocket and began naming off the items. The paper sagged lower with each one. "Lastly, I'm wondering if you might be able to order me a new windowpane. One of mine is cracked."

Mr. Bagley threw down his paper, his mouth open. Colin waited for the man's biting retort to Nora's long list of requests at such a late hour, but it never came. The man's eyes widened in surprise. "Eleanor?"

Colin looked from the grocer to Nora and found her face growing white again. The references to Henry's daughter made her uncomfortable. Colin had been too little to know Eleanor himself, but those who did clearly thought Nora looked very much like her. He hadn't counted on the distant family connection to work against his father's plans.

"No. My name is Nora. I'm Henry Lewis's gr—"

"I'm Nathaniel Bagley, miss. At your service." He reached out to take her list. "Let's see if we can't find you those things you need."

"What about the time?" Nora threw a glance at the clock. Her tone sounded sincere enough, but Colin detected a glint of teasing in her eyes. He bit back a smile.

"Never mind that." Mr. Bagley came around the counter. "If you'll take that basket there, and follow me, Miss Lewis."

Mr. Bagley moved about the shop with the agility of a much younger man, all the while shooting wide-eyed looks at Nora. She caught Colin watching them and lifted her shoulders in a shrug. He responded with a puzzled shake of his head. He'd never seen the grocer act so affable. As a child, Colin had been rather intimidated by the gruff man who scowled each time Colin came in to buy a piece of candy.

When they returned to the counter, Nora's basket was nearly overflowing with items. Mr. Bagley rang up the purchases at the cash register, promising to order Nora a new windowpane tomorrow. "It should be here in a week," he said as she handed him her money.

"Thank you for your help."

"Do you sing, Miss Lewis?"

Nora appeared a bit taken back by the man's sudden question, but she answered in the affirmative. "I very much enjoy singing."

Mr. Bagley beamed. "I remember Eleanor's beautiful soprano voice. Just what we need. I direct the church's choir, you see, and we would love to have you join us. We practice Saturday mornings."

"I'd like that, Mr. Bagley."

Colin swallowed a groan. The more Nora became a part of life in the village, the less likely she was to want to leave.

"We could do with more male voices, as well." Mr. Bagley shot a pointed look at Colin, acknowledging him for the first time since he and Nora had entered the shop.

"Do you sing?" Nora spun to face him.

"Not as well as I can fly."

Mr. Bagley shook his head. "Don't let him fool you, Miss Lewis. The Ashby boys have sung together since the cradle. Nary a Christmas passed that we didn't hear them sing at the village celebration."

Colin fixed his attention on the canned goods lining the shelves behind the man. Memories of singing with Christian flitted through his mind and cut through his heart. Mr. Bagley had failed to mention there was only one Ashby boy now. Colin hadn't bothered attending the village's Christmas celebration last year—it hadn't seemed right without Christian.

He sensed Nora watching him. Did she perceive the pain he concealed behind his carefree demeanor?

"I'll see if I can persuade him," she told Mr. Bagley.

The grocer smiled with self-satisfaction at Colin. With great effort, he maintained a neutral expression, instead of the smug grin he wanted to shoot back at the man. Enchanting as Nora may be, she would never convince him to sing, let alone step foot inside a church.

Nora began gathering up her purchases. She clearly had more than she could carry, though she didn't ask for his assistance.

"Allow me." Colin removed an armful of items from her grip so she could pick up what was left on the counter. He stacked the loaf of bread on top of the pile and moved to the door. By shifting his load, he managed to free one hand to open the door for Nora.

Mr. Bagley's cheerful "good day" followed them outside—a far cry from his tone of twenty minutes before. Colin shook his head, amazed and frustrated at both shopkeepers' reactions to Nora. How was he supposed to convince her she needed to give up the sheep farm if everyone in Larksbeck continued welcoming her with open arms?

"Is there anything else you need?"

Nora glanced around the village. "Not this time."

Colin called for Perseus as he and Nora set off toward the bridge. The dog scampered past them, eager to explore the road ahead. Colin almost envied the canine's freedom.

Would he feel freer if he gave up trying to be something he wasn't, to please his father? If he refused to marry someone like Lady Sophia and stood back while Elmthwaite Hall sank deeper into debt? The possibility was tantalizing, but not when he calculated the cost. His freedom in exchange for Christian's eternal disappointment and the lost opportunity to make his father proud. No, he wouldn't trade those.

"Something wrong?"

Nora's question pulled Colin from his pensive thoughts. He rearranged his frown into a lazy smile. "What did you think of the village?" he asked, sidestepping her inquiry.

"I like it very much."

"I don't know that I've ever seen either shopkeeper so intent on making a customer happy."

"Only because they think I look like Eleanor Lewis." She frowned, her expression troubled. "What do you know about her?"

"She was Old Man Lewis's daughter, which would make her your father's cousin."

"Anything else?" she pressed.

Colin searched his memory for what he'd heard about Eleanor over the years. "I believe she married a chap from the next village over. He died shortly before their daughter was born. Eleanor followed him not long afterward."

"What happened to the baby?"

"I believe Henry gave her to some relatives to raise as their own."

"Interesting." She shivered as though cold, then

seemed to brush off whatever had caused her chill. "My father rarely mentioned his relatives in England. He never visited them, though we did get a letter now and then. His father, my grandfather, moved to America as a young man." Nora shifted her load. "How is Eleanor related to Auntie Bess?"

"Bess is Eleanor's cousin. Their mothers were sisters."

She gave a thoughtful nod. "I remember Bess saying something like that...among the other hundred and one things she told me this morning."

Colin laughed outright at her joke. Not wanting to pass up the opportunity to tease her back, he stopped walking.

Nora continued a few paces more before she turned around. "What?"

"Was that a jest I heard from your lips, Miss Lewis?"

Her cheeks went pink, but she didn't break eye contact. "Yes, Mr. Ashby, I believe it was."

"Colin."

"I'm sorry?"

"If I'm going to carry your groceries all the way home—a first for me, I might add." He could tell she was trying not to smile. "I think you ought to drop the 'Mr. Ashby' and call me 'Colin' instead. Makes me feel less foolish," he added in a feigned tone of annoyance. "If it weren't for my pride as a gentleman..."

"Colin," she said as if testing the word on her tongue. Colin instantly regretted his idea. Hearing her feminine and very American voice intone his name gave him more pleasure than he cared to admit. "Then call me Nora, please."

"I will...Nora."

Drat. He liked saying her given name as much as he

liked hearing her say his. A change of subject was definitely in order. "What were we discussing before we stopped?"

She shot him a mischievous look. "I believe it was how foolish you feel carrying my groceries."

Dash it all but she was beautiful, especially with that impish look in her greenish-blue eyes as she spouted off her witty remarks. Why did he want to convince her to leave?

Reminding himself of his duty, his promise, Colin reined in his feelings of attraction and forged up the road. "I remember now. You were maligning poor Bess Tuttle."

"I wasn't doing no such—"

"Speaking of dear Auntie Bess. Here comes her oldest son." The lanky frame of Jack Tuttle moved down the road in their direction. The young man's timely appearance was both a blessing and a curse. Colin needed some distance from Nora to clear his head, and yet he loathed someone else disrupting their privacy.

"Hello there," Jack said as the three of them met in the middle of the lane. "I reckon you must be Nora. Me mum told me all about you." He swept off his woolen cap, revealing his copper hair, and ogled Nora. "I'm Jack Tuttle."

"The one who's been watching my sheep?" Nora extended her hand to him. "I certainly appreciate you're stepping in like that, Mr. Tuttle."

"Call me Jack," he said, clasping her hand.

Colin's jaw tightened when the younger man didn't release Nora's grip right away.

"I'm guessing you know Mr. Ashby." Nora turned to Colin.

"Tuttle," Colin said with a tip of his head.

"Ashby," Jack ground out.

Colin suppressed a grin. The chap was still sore over the past, but the arrogant pup had gotten what he deserved. Jack had been entirely too cocky as a teenager. Probably still was, though Colin hadn't seen much of him since they'd both returned from France. If the dark look in Jack's blue eyes was any indication, the memories of a certain event were traipsing through his mind at the moment, just as they were through Colin's.

It had been his and Christian's last Christmas gathering in the village before leaving to fight. Sixteen-year-old Jack, four years Colin's junior, had cornered Lizzie Smith beneath the mistletoe. The girl's distressed look was evident from a distance. Christian would have typically been the one to intervene, but he'd been busy talking to the pastor. Colin couldn't leave the girl defenseless against Jack's awkward wooing, so he'd strode over and given Jack a dressing-down on how to win a lady's affections.

Blustering and red in the face, Jack had stormed off, but he hadn't retreated far. He still witnessed the rather passionate kiss of gratitude Lizzie bestowed on Colin. His and Jack's clash that night, and Jack's anger over not being old enough to fight right away, had sealed his contempt for Colin.

"Let me carry your things, Miss Lewis," Jack said. All traces of animosity evaporated as he addressed Nora.

"Call me Nora."

Jealousy tasted bitter on Colin's tongue. She hadn't asked him to call her by her first name until today, and yet she'd bestowed the honor on Jack after five minutes.

"Aren't you headed into the village, though?" Nora asked Jack.

"It can wait. I'd much prefer escorting you back to your cottage."

Clearly Jack had picked up a thing or two about how to treat a woman since Colin's long-ago scolding. That knowledge should have impressed Colin, but instead he felt annoyed.

Nora threw him a questioning look. He schooled his irritation to smile rakishly at her and mouth, "A gentleman." The corners of her lips rose at his teasing, revealing her dimple.

She relinquished her purchases to Jack and the two set off in the direction of her cottage. Colin stayed several paces behind them, though he remained close enough to listen and keep an eye on Jack. Nora plied the younger man with questions about her sheep, which he seemed more than willing to answer in great detail.

"Why don't I take you up on the fell tomorrow?" Jack offered. "You can see your sheep and get a feel for the land."

"I'd like that."

Colin frowned at her exuberant tone. He'd never considered Jack Tuttle competition in any way. Until today.

Nora laughed at something Jack said, making Colin grind his teeth together. He was supposed to be the enigmatic one. And yet... Was it his charm or his title and estate that attracted the ladies more? Nora wasn't impressed by his wealth or his position, so neither would help him in convincing her to give up her farm. Instead he'd have to get to know her as himself, as a friend. It was a terrifying and intriguing notion.

* * *

Nora half listened to Jack's explanation of the different tasks associated with sheep farming and what time of year they took place. The words wouldn't stick in her mind, though, because her thoughts were too fixed on Colin walking behind them. She kept remembering the way his dark eyes had watched her intently before Jack had shown up. Or how he'd removed the speck of gravy from her cheek earlier.

That look had the power to make her pulse trip a little faster, the power to make her feel things she'd buried deep. Nora crossed her arms, wishing she were holding her parcels instead of the two men. She wanted something to hold on to, something to keep at bay the vulnerability nibbling at her rational sensibilities.

Guilt accompanied her feelings of weakness. Colin had survived the Great War, thank goodness, but others, like Tom, weren't so lucky. He was the man she'd promised to wait for, to love, even if she could no longer make good on that promise. She wouldn't dishonor his memory or his death by harboring feelings for another man. Not yet, at least, and perhaps not ever.

Before she knew it, the three of them were standing in front of the Lewis cottage. Nora didn't remember turning onto the lane or climbing the low hill. Shaking herself, she collected her things from Jack. She wanted Colin to leave as well, but she couldn't very well carry everything alone.

"Thanks for your help, Jack. I'll see you tomorrow." She was looking forward to climbing the mountain and seeing her sheep for the first time.

Jack shot Colin a guarded look, then nodded at Nora. "I'll be by to collect you at five. Then we can go straight from the fell to my house for supper. You're still coming, aren't you?"

"Yes, of course."

With a tip of his cap to her and a frown for Colin, Jack tramped back down the lane.

"Let's bring the groceries through the kitchen door." Nora led Colin around the side of the cottage to the back. A glance over her shoulder showed his carefree manner had been replaced by a somber one. "Why doesn't Jack like you?"

Colin stared up at the mountains looming before them. "So you noticed his affability or lack thereof."

Nora gave him a pointed look, which elicited a chuckle from him. "What happened?"

"The simple story is this. Jack's girl of six years ago preferred bestowing a Christmas kiss on me than giving one to him." His shoulders rose and fell with another low laugh. "He's despised me ever since."

Nora couldn't say she blamed the girl. Given a choice between kissing Jack or Colin, she'd pick Colin, too. Her face grew hot at the thought and she busied herself with opening the cottage's back door to hide her reaction.

"It was entirely unsolicited, I assure you." He stepped inside after her. "He's also a bit touchy about not being able to enter the war until two years after Christian and I left, so I wouldn't mention that one tomorrow either."

"Just set everything there on the table," Nora directed.

Colin obliged, then stood back, eyeing the pile on the table. Awkwardness filled the air between them, a first since their meeting the night before.

"I'm grateful—again—for your timely help…Colin."

"My pleasure, Nora." His dark eyes lit with a slow smile.

Perseus appeared in the open doorway. Relieved at the distraction, Nora walked over to rub his fur. She would greatly miss his company. "It was nice to have a dog here last night."

"I hope it helped."

"Very much," she said without lifting her head. She wouldn't allow herself to be swayed by his handsome face and charming manners.

"I suppose we're off then." He and Perseus returned outdoors. Nora reached out to shut the door, but she stopped when she saw Colin turn around. Her heart beat faster as she met his gaze.

"If you should require anything else, please let me know." He tucked his hands into his pockets, a habitual gesture she already identified as his. "I'd like to be friends, Nora."

Gratitude for his honest admission lifted her mouth into a smile, though the tiniest sliver of disappointment cut through her at what might have been. Nora ignored it. She could offer him friendship, nothing more.

"I'd like that, too."

Chapter 4

A loud knock at the back door the next afternoon startled Nora awake. She studied the clock on the bureau through blurry eyes. It was already five minutes after five. After a busy day cleaning and weeding the overgrown garden, she'd stretched out on her bed, intent on a short nap. Instead she'd slept for two hours. It didn't help that sleep hadn't come easily the night before; she missed having a dog beside the bed.

She took a moment to rearrange her hair, then she hurried downstairs to answer the door. Jack stood on the stoop, his weight bouncing from one foot to the other.

"Ready for our walk?"

"Yes." Nora eyed the gray sky. "Let me grab my coat." She pulled it from the peg by the door and joined him outside. Pushing her arms through the sleeves, she drew the material around her as she shivered.

"We'll head up through the inbye to the fell."

"The inbye?" Another word she didn't know or recognize.

He motioned to the field ahead of them. "The fields by the farms are the inbye. And the fells are the mountains."

"Colin told me what fell meant."

Jack pulled his cap lower. "You sweet on him?"

"Hardly," she managed to get out past her startled laugh.

A smile appeared on Jack's face, though he made no comment. They entered the field through the gate and Jack shut it behind them. Nora studied the stone fence bordering the field. How many hours had it taken her ancestors to build the fence, stone by stone?

"The sheep," she asked, "what kind are they?"

"Herdwick. The Vikings are said to have introduced them to the Lake District." His pride was unmistakable.

Nora glanced at the mountain ahead of them. Its grassy skirt gave way to craggy rock and stubs of green higher up where the gray clouds hugged the mountain peak. Moving gray specks, which she suspected were the sheep, dotted its side.

She and Jack came to a set of small, wooden steps straddling the fence at the foot of the mountain. Before Nora could move or speak, Jack seized her hand and helped her up and over the fence. She quickly pulled her hand from his grip once her shoes were back on the ground. While she appreciated his attempt at being a gentleman, she preferred Colin's more subtle approach.

There I go, she thought with a frown. *Thinking of Colin again.*

She didn't want to think of the puzzling but kind baronet's son. Or the way he made her laugh with his jokes. Or the way his dark eyes glowed with interest when he looked at her. These were things she'd loved about Tom, too. She was simply missing him, in this place so far from their memories. Loving someone new wasn't an option. The potential for pain if she opened her heart all over again...Nora shuddered and drew her coat closer. Inhaling a deep breath of the damp air, she pushed aside the reminders of fear and heartache.

Her lungs and legs soon burned from the sharp ascent up the mountain, but Nora welcomed the exercise and the chance to stretch her limbs. Despite all the cleaning and weeding she'd done, she still felt a bit idle. She missed pushing herself through long, hard tasks as she'd done nearly every day on the farm back home.

After a time, Jack stopped. "Take a look. Prettiest sight in the world, if you ask me."

Nora turned from the mountain to face the valley below. Emotion stirred deep inside her at the sight. The deep blue lake, the imposing turrets of Elmthwaite Hall, the farms and partitioned fields—all of it spread out before them like a living, breathing canvas painted by the hand of God.

She could think of no proper descriptions save one. "It's stunning."

Jack grinned with triumph, as if he were part creator of the grandeur, and waved her forward again. Nora hiked after him toward a sprinkling of sheep. As they drew closer, she spied the lambs among the ewes. The animals began to stir and flee at their approach, but Jack moved swiftly and caught one of the lambs before it could escape. He brought the bleating creature to Nora. "This is one of yours."

Nora stroked the soft ears and ran her hand over the lamb's wooly black fleece. "I never thought I'd be like Mary in the nursery rhyme."

Jack didn't laugh as Colin would have. "You've got a good group of lambs this year. The few of your ewes with twins are in our field."

"You said the sheep will be sheared next month?" Thankfully she'd remembered something from their conversation yesterday.

Jack nodded. "End of July."

"Do the fleeces bring in a good profit?"

He set the lamb free, and the creature bounded away to its mother. "We sheep farmers do pretty well. It's not a rich life, but we make a decent living." His eyes narrowed as he stared in the direction of Elmthwaite Hall. Nora recalled the opulence of the entryway and grand staircase, to say nothing of the rest of the house she hadn't seen during her brief time inside. While lovely, she herself was living proof of how little one needed to uproot and make a new life.

Jack turned back to her, his tone boastful as he added, "I mean to get lots more sheep and have the biggest sheep farm in the Lake District."

Nora felt a twinge of regret at hearing his dream. Bess had mentioned Jack's hope of receiving the sheep farm from Henry. But it hadn't been Nora's decision, and she was grateful to her great-uncle for remembering her.

They started walking again, Jack in front. He led her along a narrow trail running across the mountain ridge, in the direction of Larksbeck. Sheep scattered ahead of them. He continued to share his plans for the future, which included a bigger farm with more cattle and pigs and a larger house.

Nora tried to focus on the one-sided conversation, but her attention kept straying to the beautiful landscape around her. Could she picture herself living here for the rest of her life? She glanced back over her shoulder for a moment at the Lewis cottage in the distance. She liked the new place, even if there was still work to be done with it, and the few people she'd met in the village yesterday had been more than kind.

Her greatest concern at present lay in the constant comparisons to her great-uncle's daughter, Eleanor. Being alone in the world, she wanted to be her own person, not live in someone else's shadow. *I've been living with shadows for a year and a half now*, Nora thought, folding her arms against the sudden ache in her chest. Had she traded one set for another? Only this time they were the shadows of strangers instead of those she loved dearly.

She also couldn't shake the eerie feeling there was more to this business about Eleanor, something she alone had yet to figure out. Perhaps she could get Bess to impart some answers today.

The practical mentality Nora had cultivated since her parents' deaths didn't fail her now, despite her troubled thoughts. While she might have to endure being compared to Eleanor, the result wasn't entirely bad. Because of it, she'd been accepted into the village, at least by the two shopkeepers she'd met. She'd also received an invitation to join the church choir, which meant she wouldn't have to give up music altogether, even in the absence of her piano. Then there were the friends she'd made so far—Colin, Bess, Jack.

God was watching out for her. The realization brought a semblance of peace. It hadn't been easy selling her childhood home to strangers or leaving her tangible connections to Tom and her parents. But she'd done it. Surely that meant she could carve out a life for herself in this valley.

A full and vibrant life? Like the one you had before losing Tom, and Mother and Father? The question pricked her heart.

"A contented one, at least," she firmly told herself. It wasn't safe or realistic to expect more than that.

Jack stopped to point at a cottage similar in structure to Nora's. "We live there." She spied sheep and cattle grazing in separate fields and flowers at the cottage windows.

Leaving the trail behind, Jack began climbing down the mountain. Nora struck out after him. They reached the field and climbed the ladder over the wall. Nora paused to catch her breath, while Jack removed his cap and wiped at his forehead with his sleeve.

"Can you teach me how to shear the sheep?" she asked, studying the thick gray coat of one of the nearby ewes.

"No need to worry about that. I'll see to your sheep, same as ours."

A flash of irritation tightened her lips. "I wouldn't feel right about that. I need to learn. It's my livelihood now."

Jack's frown mirrored her own. "Don't know what the other chaps will think of you being in the way, but we'll see." With that, he stalked toward the field gate.

Nora forced a steadying breath through her nose. She wouldn't push the point with him anymore this evening, but she was an independent woman who had to rely on her own two hands for her support. And she wouldn't let anyone, including Jack, bully her out of her rightful place here.

She picked up her pace and trailed him out the gate and into the cottage. They entered through the back door onto a scene of complete chaos. Bess stood at the stove, stirring something, and calling out commands in a loud voice. Twin girls worked to set the long farm table as they talked. Their older sister brushed the coppery hair of the smallest girl, who sobbed in protest. A teenage boy, also with reddish hair, added wood to the fire, and another boy rode a wooden horse around the room, whooping.

Nora shrank back against the door. Her recollections of visiting the Campbell home, even with Tom and his six siblings, hadn't felt quite so frenzied.

Bess glanced up as Jack approached her at the stove. "Oh, you're both here," she exclaimed.

The noise and movement stopped as if on signal. Eight pairs of eyes stared at Nora. She swallowed the sudden dryness in her throat, almost wishing for the loud madness instead. She didn't like feeling like a specimen to be examined.

Bess came over and looped her arm through Nora's. "Welcome, love." The older woman gently tugged her toward the center of the room, oblivious to her reticence. "You've already met our Jack here. So we just need to be introducing you to the rest of the Tuttles." She motioned with her free hand to the oldest daughter. "That there's Mary. She's the one what works up at Elmthwaite. Jon is next. Then there's the twins, Margaret and Martha. Joseph comes after them, and finally our little Ellie."

What if she couldn't remember all their names? "It's nice to meet you," Nora said with a tentative smile.

"Come sit down." Bess shooed her toward one of the benches drawn up next to the table.

Nora took a seat. The children crowded across from and beside her. Bess sat long enough to offer a blessing on the food, then lumbered to her feet again to ladle stew into bowls the twins passed around.

Before Nora could spoon some of the savory-smelling broth into her mouth, Mary asked, "What it's like living in America, with all them automobiles and big houses?"

Nora gave a self-conscious shrug. "A lot like living here, I suppose. My family had a good-sized farm, but we didn't own a car."

Mary's eyes clouded with momentary disappointment. "What about American fashion?" She leaned forward as she added, "I want to cut my hair and wear shorter skirts, but Mum won't let me."

"I heard that," Bess scolded. She brought a bowl of stew for herself to the table and sat down again.

"What about film stars?" Margaret or Martha asked. "Have you met any?"

Nora chuckled and shook her head before tasting her stew. It was every bit as delicious as Bess's cottage pie had been.

Everyone but Jack and Bess plied her with questions through the meal. A good portion of them she didn't have answers for, much to the obvious displeasure of her young crowd.

"Maybe she's not really American," Nora heard one of the twins whisper to her identical sister.

"I did go to New York on my way here." Maybe that would appease their curiosity.

"What's that like?" Mary's green gaze reflected her excitement.

Nora described the tall buildings and the crowds of

people. Ellie wanted to know what it was like traveling on a boat across the ocean. By the time their inquiries ceased, the remaining stew in Nora's bowl had grown cold. She didn't mind, though. Her uneasiness had faded and she rather liked the lively conversation—so different from her normal silent meals, with only her thoughts and memories for company.

"I have a question for *you*," she said, smiling down at Ellie seated next to her on the bench. "All your brothers' names start with *J* and your sisters' names start with *M*. Where does your name came from?"

"She's named after Mum's favorite cousin, Eleanor," one of the twins answered. "I thought you would have known that, her being your—" Her words ended in a sudden *squeal* of pain. Rubbing her arm, she glared at Mary, who scowled right back. "Why'd you have to go and pinch me?"

Bess, looking very red in the face, jumped to her feet and began gathering dishes. "Time to clean up, girls," she ordered over the clatter she was making. "Boys, see to the chores. Jack, you can walk Nora home."

No one would meet Nora's eyes now and the twin who'd spoken sat pouting as though in trouble. Nora scooted off the bench, uncertain what to do or say to restore the congeniality of moments ago. She wanted answers about Eleanor, but she didn't want to upset or cause trouble for anyone. "Can I help with cleaning up?"

Bess shook her head. "No, no. You're the guest. Jack will walk you back."

"If you're sure." The chilled feeling had returned. "I am perfectly fine to walk back, though—"

"Jack doesn't mind, do you, Jack?" Bess added dishes

to the sink. Mary, Ellie, and the other twin started in on washing them.

Jack put his cap back on and grinned at Nora. "Not at all."

Though she longed for solitude after the noisy dinner, Nora decided not to insist on walking home alone. "Thank you for the supper, Bess. It was delicious. The best I've had in a long time."

Bess's round cheeks turned pink as she waved away Nora's compliment. "Never mind that. Glad you could come. We expect to see you regularly now, you hear? I still plan to fatten you up, you know. You're as skinny as..." Her blush deepened and her mouth quickly closed over whatever she meant to add. "Well, go on now, love. And don't be a stranger."

Nora bade the rest of them good-bye. The coolness of the evening washed over her as she and Jack exited the cottage. What secrets were Bess and her family keeping from her? And why? She cut a glance at Jack, but he didn't look the least bit uncomfortable. If anything, the smiles he kept throwing in her direction unnerved her.

They walked in silence up the road toward the cottage. At her lane, Nora stopped and faced him. "I can make it from here." She stuck out her hand for him to shake. "I enjoyed the walk and the chance to see my sheep."

Jack grasped her hand and held fast. "Me, too."

"Can I come collect my sheep from your inbye field tomorrow?"

"I can take care of them for you, Nora." He twisted her hand in his grip and ran a thumb over her skin. "You don't have to worry your pretty head over the sheep."

Nora inwardly cringed—both at his words and his

touch. She needed to convince him to relinquish her sheep to her care, but how? The direct approach hadn't worked. Perhaps she ought to try feminine wiles, though she wasn't entirely sure what to do in that department. She'd never been very good at playing coy or being flirtatious.

"Please, Jack," she tried, squeezing his hand and giving him an earnest look. "I want to fit in here, but I need my sheep to do that."

He studied their hands, then finally lifted his gaze to her face. "Oh, all right. I'll bring 'em by tomorrow."

"Thank you," she said with a genuine smile.

He eyed her lips, making Nora gulp. Did he expect a kiss in return for bringing her sheep back? Rather than step closer, though, Jack released her and tipped the edge of his cap in a farewell gesture.

Nora waved good night and climbed the hill toward the cottage. The sky overhead remained gray and cloudy. She hugged her arms to her chest against the cold, though inside she felt a measure of contentment. Despite the disturbing incident at supper, the evening had gone well and tomorrow she would have a few of her sheep to tend to. She could think of only one thing that would've made the day even better—seeing Perseus again.

And perhaps his owner, too.

* * *

Colin plodded up the hill to the Lewis cottage, while Perseus scouted through the tufts of grass along the stone fences ahead of him. It had been a whole week since he'd been here last, not that he hadn't made attempts to see

Nora sooner. Each time he had set out to walk this way, though, guilt ate at him until he turned around. How could he face Nora knowing he had to persuade her to leave? Of course, he'd also been patching things up with Lady Sophia, which meant enduring hours of inane conversation. His head still ached.

The earl's daughter had dropped copious hints about riding in his aeroplane, but her father had insisted she wait for a drier day to fly. Thankfully for Colin, that day hadn't come until after their guests had at last departed Elmthwaite Hall. Flying was his sanctuary, and he no longer liked the idea of sharing such peace and freedom with just anyone.

Had Nora wondered about his absence? When he'd found himself thinking about her too often during his time with Lady Sophia, Colin had told himself keeping his distance was a tactical move. In war, one needed to keep the enemy on its toes.

He frowned at the thought of him and Nora at war, but perhaps the line of thinking would serve him better. Then he wouldn't be so enchanted by her red hair or soulful eyes or clever wit.

If he expected to find things the same after his week-long sabbatical, Colin was sorely disappointed. The cracked window had been repaired and the whitewashed walls of the cottage gleamed brighter. Nora must have painted them with a fresh coat. Gone were the wild plants and grass beside the door, too. The structure looked neat, tidy, and permanent. He hated the idea of seeing it torn to the ground to make way for his father's hotel.

Please, Colin...I need you.

The words echoed in his mind, bolstering his deter-

mination to fulfill his father's wishes and his promise to
Christian. Colin knocked on the front door. When Nora
failed to appear, he and Perseus headed to the back of the
cottage. Several ewes and their lambs now grazed in the
previously empty field beside the barn.

A loud noise, like the scraping of metal against wood,
came from inside the house. What was Nora up to? Colin
rapped his knuckle against the partially opened back
door.

"Come in, Jack."

Jack? Something akin to jealousy cut through Colin at
Nora's assumption. Jack had obviously been here enough,
during Colin's absence, that Nora expected him to be the
only one to arrive at the back door.

Time to change that.

Colin eased the door open and stepped inside. There was
no sign of Nora at the sink or the table, though the smell
of something cooking in the oven attested to her presence.
A movement in the corner of the room caught his attention.
Nora was kneeling beside the washing machine.

"Are you hiding?" he teased.

At his voice, she scurried to her feet. A kerchief covered her head, though tufts of red hair had escaped its
confinement. Flecks of dust rested on her cheeks and
shoulders.

"Colin." She jerked the cloth from her hair and used it
to wipe her face. "I ... um ... wasn't expecting you."

But you were expecting Jack? He swallowed the retort.
"I tried the front door."

Her gaze flicked to his, then away. "Sorry. I didn't hear
you."

Was she pleased or disappointed to see him again? He

couldn't tell and that annoyed him all the more. "What are you doing there?" He motioned to the washing machine, which now stood two feet from the wall.

"I can't get the crank to turn more than a few inches. Not very convenient when you have a week's worth of laundry to do."

A slight burnt odor filled Colin's nose. "What are you cooking?"

Nora gave a soft gasp. "The cottage pie. I completely forgot about it." She hurried past him to the stove and opened the door with a dish towel. "I think this beast of an oven has something against me," she muttered as she removed the pie, with its blackened edges, and set it on the counter. "I suppose the washing machine does, too."

"Why don't I take a look at the washing machine?" he volunteered. It was the perfect excuse to stay as well as a way to help ease her distress.

Her eyebrows rose and her eyes flashed with blatant skepticism. "This from the man who'd never carried groceries before last week?"

"I didn't just fly an aeroplane in the war, Nora." He removed his tie, jacket, and vest. After setting them on one of the chairs, he unbuttoned his shirt cuffs and rolled up his sleeves. "I learned a thing or two about how machines work as well."

"Be my guest." She waved in the direction of the washing machine.

Colin tried the hand crank. Sure enough, it would hardly turn. He bent over the machine and examined each of the gears. "I think rust is your problem. See?" Nora came to stand beside him. "If we clean some of it away and oil the gears, it should turn without difficulty."

She tipped her chin up, a mischievous glint in her eyes. "By *we*, I'm guessing you mean me."

He threw her a mocking glare to hide the grin that wanted to break through. "Would you mind getting *me* a rag and soap?"

"Of course," she chirped a little too brightly. She returned with the needed items and Colin set about removing the rust from the gears. "I'll see if there's a can of oil in the barn."

Nora disappeared out the back door. A moment later Colin overheard her exclaim at finding Perseus in the yard. A shadow of Colin's earlier jealousy returned. He shook his head in annoyance at himself. Now he was envious of his dog. How could he get Nora to be as thrilled at seeing him as she was Jack Tuttle or Perseus?

He was still trying to figure out a solution when she returned with a can of oil and began washing dishes. Quiet filled the room, except for the gurgle of water and the rattle of plates, but the atmosphere wasn't uncomfortable or strained. Colin actually found it peaceful.

Once he'd removed most of the rust, he generously oiled the gears. He didn't want the machine giving Nora any more trouble. When the gears shone like new, Colin reached for the hand crank a second time and gave it a twist. This time it turned easily.

"Your washing awaits, fair lady." He grinned in victory as Nora came over and watched him turn the crank once, twice.

"You did it," she said with a laugh. The sweet sound wove its way straight to his heart, as did the genuine smile and dimple she offered him.

A feeling of satisfaction pumped through Colin's veins,

making him feel almost light-headed and yet powerful at the same time. It felt good to be working with his hands, doing something useful. He pushed the washing machine back into place and started to roll down his sleeves.

"Oh no. Your shirt."

He looked down. Several oil spots marred the perfectly pressed garment. Gibson would not be happy.

"I know how to get those out." Nora extended her hand to him.

Colin looked from her hand to her face. "You want me to take the shirt off...now?"

An attractive blush rose into her cheeks but she nodded anyway. "We don't want the stain setting in."

With a shrug, Colin undid the buttons and pulled off the shirt. He'd never stood bare-chested in front of a woman before, but any twinge of discomfort was fleeting. Especially after being a soldier and having a valet help him dress most of his life.

Nora took the shirt from him, without meeting his eye, and retreated to the cupboard, where she pulled a tin from one of the shelves. She placed his shirt on the counter next to her pie and sprinkled something over the material, all the while acting as if he weren't there.

Clearly she was embarrassed to have him standing shirtless in her kitchen. Colin didn't wish to make her uncomfortable. Perhaps he ought to put his vest or jacket on while he waited.

He froze in indecision until another thought entered his head. Could it be that Nora wasn't so much nervous as she was attracted to him and fighting it? A smile lifted Colin's mouth as he crossed the room to stand next to her, intent on finding out.

* * *

"What are you putting on the stain?"

Nora jumped at the sound of Colin's voice near her ear. She'd been so focused on not looking at him that she hadn't heard him come up beside her.

"It's corn starch. I believe you call it corn flour here. It should help lift out the oil." She scrutinized the shirt in an effort to avoid looking at Colin. Even then, she couldn't help noticing out of the corner of her eye the firm muscles of his shoulders and chest. She mentally berated herself for offering to help with his shirt. Especially since he hadn't bothered to come by once in the past week.

The reminder of his absence, especially after his promise to be friends, imbued Nora with renewed practicality. She would not be charmed, even by his nice-looking physique.

"Tell whoever does your wash," she said, jabbing the shirt at his bare chest, "to rub soap into the spot as well."

Colin curled his fingers around his shirt, capturing her hand. Something thrilling, and a little frightening, raced through Nora at his touch and the way his dark eyes deepened in color as he peered down at her. She made a poor attempt at reclaiming her hand, but he held on.

"Thank you for fixing it."

She licked her suddenly dry lips. "It's the least I could do..."

"Nora." Her name sounded like both a caress and a cry. Colin glanced away and swallowed, all traces of arrogance or teasing gone. "There's something I—"

A knock at the back door interrupted his words. Before Nora could step away from Colin, Jack entered the cot-

tage and removed his cap. "I came to see…" His words
faded into silence as he took in the sight of the two of
them standing close.

Certain her face matched the color of her hair, Nora
yanked her hand from Colin's grip and stepped backward.
"Jack. How are you?"

Jack looked from her to Colin and back, his brow
furrowed. "I came by to see if there was anything you
needed before I headed to the fell." He frowned at Colin.
"Didn't mean to interrupt anything."

"Everything's right as rain here." Colin smiled at Jack,
though the merriment didn't reach his eyes. "I fixed
Nora's washing machine, and she, in turn, fixed my shirt."
He pushed his arms through the sleeves and began doing
up the buttons. Jack stood rooted to his spot.

The air in the kitchen crackled with unspoken tension.
Nora moved between the two men. "I appreciate you
checking on me, Jack. I'll see you for supper at your place
tomorrow night?"

Jack dipped his head, his cap strangled between his
hands. "Suppose I'm off then." He cut Colin another
scowl.

"Farewell, Tuttle." Colin unrolled his sleeves. "Nora's
in good hands."

With a glare at both of them, Jack smashed his cap
on his head and stalked from the room. He proceeded to
slam the door behind him, but it hit the door frame and
bounced open instead.

Nora pushed out a sigh. "You didn't have to be rude.
Jack's been very helpful to me this past week." *Maybe
a bit too much.* But she didn't voice that thought. Colin
needed no further ammunition against Jack.

"I'm sure he has," Colin muttered, his expression as dark as his eyes.

Nora pinned him with a piercing look.

"You're right." He finished buttoning his cuffs and slipped on his vest. "That was ungentlemanly of me."

She ignored his reference to her joke at their first meeting as she put away the corn starch and closed the cupboard. It was easier to keep her heart firmly locked if she held on to her disapproval of Colin's behavior. Plus it would also stop her from wondering what he'd been about to say before Jack's arrival.

"How may I redeem myself?" he asked as he pulled on his jacket. The amusement tugging at his mouth contradicted his contrite tone.

Nora folded her arms, contemplating a suitable penance. "I think your punishment needs to be twofold."

"Very well." He nodded. "What is your sentence?"

"First, you must join me for choir rehearsal at the church tomorrow morning."

The mirth drained from his face. "Nora." His voice held a note of warning. "That is entirely—"

"Second, you and Perseus can give me a tour around the lake. I've already been here a week and haven't even seen all of it."

Colin scowled. "A walk around the lake would be acceptable. But the choir rehearsal..."

"Please, Colin." She hazarded a step toward him, hoping he'd relent. "I sang with them last Sunday and they need more male voices."

She had another reason for wanting him there. Everyone had been kind at rehearsal and at church the following day, but Nora still felt uncomfortable with the continued references to her likeness to Eleanor. Apparently their similarities also included their singing voices. With Colin at the rehearsals, she wouldn't feel as awkward. She was beginning to think he was the only person in Larksbeck who hadn't known Eleanor.

Colin's brow knit in obvious annoyance, while Nora held her breath. Would he accept her proposal? Finally resignation settled over his countenance. "I'll go, but only once." He held up a single finger. "Once," he repeated. "I make no promises after that."

Grateful, she breached the remaining space between them and put her hand on his sleeve. "I agree to those terms." She couldn't hide her smile as she added, "Be careful, though, we might make a regular choir member out of you yet."

Instead of the light laugh she expected, Colin solemnly watched her. Though he didn't touch her, she felt as powerless to release his sleeve as if he'd detained her hand. She couldn't step away—his nearness drew her in like the promising warmth of a fire after being out in a storm.

"You know," he murmured, his voice low, "you are rather charming when you jest like that."

Nora's pulse stuttered to a stop, then sped up again like a train gaining speed. She tried to remember why she'd been angry with him, tried to remember why she couldn't allow anything more than friendship to blossom between them. But she couldn't concentrate on any one thought, except for the growing desire to touch the hint of dark bristles covering his jaw.

Colin studied her lips as Jack had done last week, but this moment couldn't be more different. A part of her, one growing more insistent by the second, actually wanted

Colin to kiss her. How long had it been since she'd last felt the press of masculine lips against hers?

Not since before Tom left.

The memory crashed over her with all the effect of an ocean wave. She felt suddenly ill and cold. Releasing Colin's sleeve, she stepped back, crossing her arms over her chest for warmth.

Forgive me, Tom.

She'd done nothing wrong, but even entertaining the idea of Colin kissing her felt like a betrayal. Her heart could never belong to anyone else. And yet, in this moment, the past felt more like a burden than a boon.

"I'll...uh...just get my sweater, then we can go on that walk." Nora went to pull the garment off its usual peg. Her hands shook slightly as she slipped the sweater on over her blouse. "Ready?"

A flicker of emotion gleamed in Colin's dark eyes. Was it disappointment? Frustration? Would he forgive her abruptness or understand the source of her pain? As quickly as it had come, though, the sentiment faded and Colin shot her a carefree grin. "After you, fair lady."

Chapter 5

Kicking at a pebble, Colin maintained his unhurried pace as he scowled at the road ahead. Why had he felt compelled to redeem himself yesterday? His comments to Jack Tuttle, while not exactly friendly, hadn't been hostile either and certainly didn't warrant having to attend choir rehearsal as penance. He'd only sought to put the younger chap into his place after learning how comfortable Jack was becoming in Nora's company.

Guilt simmered within him at the thought. Jack wasn't the only one getting too comfortable. The young farmer hadn't been the one who'd nearly kissed Nora in the kitchen yesterday. At least Colin hoped Jack hadn't. His glare deepened at the possibility, though he knew he had no right to be jealous. Unlike himself, Nora had the freedom to choose whom to love and marry.

He'd almost ruined his father's plan to save the estate by confessing the whole thing to Nora yesterday. Then there'd been his other moment of weakness when he'd been caught up in contemplating her full lips and what they might feel like to the touch. She'd seemed willing to let him kiss her, at least at first.

Before either one of them could make that mistake, though, Nora had leapt away from him, her blue-green eyes full of unexplained panic. Not that it mattered. However attractive Colin found her, however much he was quickly coming to crave her company, she wouldn't be staying. She would eventually leave and take his heart with her if he wasn't careful.

Their walk around the lake after the near-incident in the kitchen had given him a chance to clear his head and get to know her better. They'd talked some more about her farm back in Iowa and her parents. Her account of life there was liberally peppered with references to her deceased fiancé.

If Colin had thought her constant talk of Tom Campbell would serve as a greater reminder that Nora wasn't and never would be his, he'd been wrong. Each mention of her former beau stirred a flicker of disappointment and envy in his gut. It was almost a relief when their walk ended.

But now he had to see her again, and the problem was, he wanted to—very much.

Colin stabbed a hand through his hair. Life had been less complicated before the redheaded American had moved in down the lane. Flying his biplane and dodging his father's expectations had been his main pursuits. Now, because of Nora, he'd be stepping into a church for the first time since Christian's death.

Nerves drained his mouth of moisture. Why did he feel

as if he were about to face an entire squadron of German planes single-handedly?

Well, not single-handedly. He lifted his head to see Nora waiting for him at the end of her lane. She raised a hand in greeting as he approached.

"I wasn't sure you'd come." Her tone was teasing.

"A gentleman never breaks his word, Nora." His comment inspired the laugh he'd hoped for, though the words tasted bitter on his tongue. He wasn't being gentlemanly by almost kissing her—not when he planned to persuade her to leave.

They started in the direction of Larksbeck. "If you hadn't come soon, I was thinking of going up to the house and collecting you myself..." She threw him a small smile. "Though I suspected I might run into trouble with your butler again."

Despite his anxious thoughts, Colin couldn't help chuckling. "Martin can be a bit of a watch dog, but he's also loyal."

"What's it like having all those servants around to do your bidding?" He sensed no judgment behind her question, only curiosity.

"Until I went to Oxford and later to France, I didn't know any different." He tucked his hands into his pockets and propelled another pebble forward with the toe of his shoe. "I'll admit it was a bit odd at first, not to have Gibson or Martin around—Christian and I took a lot of ribbing for being the sons of a baronet. But we learned to manage. After a while, I found I rather liked being on my own."

"Was it hard returning to that sort of life? After the war?" Her perceptive question pleased him, but still he hesitated answering. Christian had always been the one who understood him growing up, the one he could truthfully confide in. Flying together in the war had meant having someone else to share every horrible experience, every guilt-filled moment. Colin had been able to cope because Christian was living through the same hell he was.

After Christian's death, there was no longer someone who knew him so well to talk over things. Colin had yet to verbalize to another living soul how the war and the death of his brother had changed things for him. Could Nora possibly understand? He recalled what she'd told him regarding her parents and her fiancé. Unlike most, she might be able to comprehend how his life had been altered. Her own had been greatly transformed, too.

Nora frowned at his silence, her eyes downcast. "You don't have to answer."

Colin shook his head. "I don't mind." Still, he had to pause further to formulate his thoughts, thoughts left too long unspoken. "If Christian had lived, I believe I would have looked forward to returning here. I'd always been allowed a bit more freedom than him."

"But his death changed that?"

"Yes . . . it did." The grief squeezed at his throat, like a hand clamped around his neck, intent on strangling the life from him. He coughed to dislodge the emotion and drive it back to the recesses of his heart.

"I'm sorry, Colin." Nora stopped him with a hand to his arm. "I'm sorry for your loss." He instinctively knew she meant more than Christian's death.

Fresh regret riddled his thoughts. He might not like the direction his life had taken since the war, but at least he had parents and a bevy of servants. Nora had no one.

As he peered into her blue-green eyes, full of sincere compassion, he vowed to keep his word to be her friend. He must still go along with his father's plans for the hotel, but that didn't mean he couldn't do all in his power to somehow help Nora.

Colin reached for her hand and studied the long, glove-less fingers. Tiny freckles dotted her skin. He ran his thumb over them. "Shall we get to it then?" he asked, lift-ing his head.

Nora's gaze widened. "W-what do you mean?"

He bit back a smile. She might deny it all she wanted, but she wasn't completely immune to his attentions. "To choir rehearsal."

"Oh…right." She slipped her hand from his and started walking—quickly.

With a low chuckle, Colin easily matched his stride with hers. They covered the remaining distance to the vil-lage in silence.

When the stone walls and bell tower of the church came into full view, Colin slowed his pace. Would he be mocked for stepping inside? Would the ancient rocks crumble around him in protest? He hadn't entered the building since the Sunday before he and Christian had left for the war. Pastor Randolph had given a sermon that day on trusting in God. A subject Colin couldn't claim exper-tise in, especially given that communication between him and the Lord had been relatively nonexistent for years.

Nora opened the door and waited. "You're coming in, right?"

He swallowed to bring moisture to his dry mouth. His hands, inside his pockets, felt clammy, his stomach sick. He felt worse than he had his first day flying. If it were anyone else asking… But he couldn't refuse the beautiful woman watching him with concern.

Forcing his feet to move once more, he gave her a deceivingly casual smile. "What have I said, Nora? Always a…"

"Gentleman," she supplied with an amused shake of her head. "Then come along, *Mr.* Ashby. We don't want to be late."

He held the door for her and followed her inside. Warm air and the cheery glow of lamplight greeted him as he made his way down the aisle behind Nora.

Mr. Bagley, the grocer and choir director, stepped away from the knot of people gathered near the small pipe organ and greeted Nora with a smile. When the old man's gaze alighted on Colin, his jaw sagged. "Mr. Ashby?"

"I've enlisted some help, Mr. Bagley." Nora shot Colin a look that bordered on pride. Had she sensed how much he dreaded this?

The old man recovered his shock. "Welcome, young man. We're pleased to have you."

Colin wordlessly tipped his head in acknowledgment. The other singers from the village eyed him with blatant curiosity. Just as he was beginning to squirm under their scrutiny, Mr. Bagley passed out hymnals and announced it was time to start. He directed the singers to their different spots near the organ. Colin took his place on the bottom row, while Nora went to stand at his far right on the top row.

As Mrs. Smith, the apothecary's wife and church organist, began playing the instrument with gusto, Colin shifted backward and peered over his shoulder at Nora. He caught her eye and raised his eyebrows, indicating the door at the opposite end of the church. Perhaps he could still make a run for it.

She lifted her hymnal and mouthed the words *a gentleman*. Colin threw her a feigned scowl. He'd rather be anywhere else at the moment. Nora returned her attention to the book in her hands, but Colin caught the trace of her dimple. She was trying not to laugh. Her amusement invoked his. He coughed to cover his own chuckle.

The notes of the song penetrated his thoughts. He recognized the tune, even before reading the title printed on the open page in front of him. "Nearer, My God, to Thee." His mother's—and Christian's—favorite hymn. He gave another cough, not to disguise his humor this time but to ease the assault of memories. In his distraction, he missed the opening cue from Mr. Bagley.

Colin easily found his place in the song and joined his voice with the other four men standing beside him. Two of them looked to be middle-aged or older, while the other two had to be in their late teens. Colin couldn't recall any of their names, though their faces all seemed familiar.

With his mind elsewhere, he struck a wrong note. He cringed inwardly with embarrassment. It had been such a long time since he'd sung, especially with others. He needed to concentrate. Doing his best to block out everything but the music, Colin kept his eyes focused on the words and notes of the second verse.

Though like the wanderer, the sun gone down,
darkness be over me, my rest a stone;

He could relate to this stanza. Since Christian's death, he had often felt darkness clouding his days and his future. Like a wanderer, he struggled to find some purpose, some usefulness to his life, that wasn't orchestrated or mandated by his father.

> *Yet in my dreams I'd be*
> *nearer, my God, to Thee.*

Only when he flew his plane did he feel any amount of freedom or hope. Might that be God manifesting Himself in his life?

Colin stopped singing to listen to the harmony around him. Though the mixture of singing voices blended well, he could still pick out a lovely soprano voice among the other parts. He twisted to glance up at Nora again. Her gaze was fastened on something across the church, her lips parted as she sang.

As he watched, she looked down at him. Her eyebrows rose in silent question. Colin shook his head in answer. He'd given his word; he wouldn't bolt, even if he felt horribly out of place. She paused, in singing, to bestow a full smile on him. Flying wasn't the only time he felt freedom. That was how he felt around Nora.

A look from Mr. Bagley drew his attention back to the song. Colin resumed his part, singing it with no trouble this time. The group worked their way through several more hymns before Mr. Bagley declared the rehearsal over.

After receiving a handshake and an expression of thanks from the old man, Colin exited the church with Nora. He blinked in the unexpected sunshine outside.

"What did you think?" she asked as they strolled through the village.

Colin pretended to frown. "It was every bit as horrible as I'd imagined." He couldn't show his enjoyment of the singing too easily.

"I see." Nora gave a thoughtful nod. "So that was a look of horror I saw on your face earlier."

Colin chuckled—she'd called his bluff. "Only a week here, and you're already as mocking as a court jester. What will several months do to you?"

She blushed. "I'm sorry. I don't—"

He stopped her with a hand to her elbow and a finger to her mouth. "I'm only teasing, Nora. I enjoy your ribbing…" Her lips felt warm and subtle beneath his touch, just as he'd imagined yesterday. "Quite a lot actually…" Would her mouth taste every bit as sweet as he hoped?

Her eyes widened as he continued to stare down at her. What had they been talking about?

"Morning, Mr. Ashby, Miss Lewis," a feminine voice called out.

Colin released Nora straightaway and turned to see Mrs. Bagley hanging wash on her clothesline. "Morning, ma'am." He tipped his head in politeness.

Had she observed the intimate moment between him and Nora? What had possessed him to touch her lips, and in the middle of Larksbeck?

He began walking again, Nora silently striding along beside him. If he meant to follow through with his father's demands—and he did mean to—he must avoid physical contact with Nora. It was much too distracting… and enjoyable.

"What time is church tomorrow?" he asked, as much for the information as to end the strained quiet between them.

"Nine o'clock. Why?"

Colin kept his gaze focused straight ahead. "I suppose I ought to show up for the actual performance. Bagley will be furious if I don't."

Nora reached out as if to touch his sleeve, but she lowered her hand to her side again. *Good*, Colin thought. *She needs to keep her distance, too.* But he couldn't completely ignore the slash of disappointment that cut through him at the absence of her feminine touch.

"That would be wonderful, Colin."

"I'm not promising to make this a habit."

"I understand." She shot him a look from the corner of her eye. "Thank you for coming, and not just for the singing. I think everyone was so surprised to see you, they forgot all about comparing me to Eleanor Lewis."

At last a topic he could discuss with ease. "Does that bother you?"

Nora lifted her shoulders in a shrug, but tension clouded her expression. "Sometimes it feels as though I ought to know her, since we're clearly alike. But I knew so little about my relatives here in England."

"Have you asked Bess?"

"Not outright." Nora folded her arms against her sweater, though the sun still shone. "She'll start to talk about Eleanor, then suddenly go silent. I know she's hiding something, but I can't figure out what or why."

Her distress brought an anxious feeling to Colin's gut. He didn't like seeing her so troubled. While the comparisons to Eleanor might be a way to divide Nora from the villagers, he wouldn't use them against her. Not when he'd vowed to be her friend. He would find some other way to persuade her to move from the sheep farm.

"Have you searched the cottage for some kind of journal or diary?" he offered. "Perhaps Eleanor kept one."

"That's an excellent idea." A smile graced her face once more. "The bookcase in the parlor is full of books. I might find something there."

They crossed the bridge and headed up the road toward Nora's lane. Colin placed his hands inside his pockets. If he could pretend for a moment his father's plans for the hotel didn't exist, he could admit to being closer to happiness than he'd been in a very long time. The sun cheerfully lit up the green fields, the trees, and the lake, evidence that the world refused to let melancholy have its way today. He began to whistle Christian's favorite hymn, the one they'd practiced first in rehearsal.

"Shall I pretend I don't hear you?" Nora asked, her tone playful.

"Hear what?" he countered with feigned innocence.

She laughed and turned to look at the lake. Colin whistled a few more bars as he studied her profile openly. What would Christian think of Nora Lewis? He certainly would have agreed with Colin about her being pretty. He would have also liked her kindness, her strength, her humor, but most of all, her faith. That was a quality she and Christian shared.

The time in the church had clearly affected more than his mood because he felt compelled to suddenly ask, "Do you believe the words of that song?"

"What?" Nora pulled her gaze from the lake to look at him.

"The song we sang first. All those ideals about God being near, even in darkness and sorrow?"

Her nod held conviction. "Don't you?"

Colin kicked at a rock. "My brother certainly did. Up to the day he and his plane were shot up by some German pilot."

Silence met his embittered words. He'd shocked her. Colin cleared his throat to apologize, but Nora spoke first.

"You think his faith did him little good?"

Once again her uncanny ability to strike at the heart of his thoughts caught him off guard. He trained his eyes on the road ahead, instead of on her earnest face. "Perhaps."

"Was he happy, up until his death?"

He considered the question. Christian had always been more serious and reserved than Colin, but he'd seemed happy. "I believe so."

"Do you think any of that came from his faith?" she gently prodded.

Colin frowned. Was she trapping him into an answer? He thought back to the war. Christian had often read his Bible when they weren't flying, and before they'd left for France, he'd enjoyed discussing spiritual things with the Larksbeck pastor. But had it made him happier? Colin wasn't sure. There had always been a quiet confidence about Christian, despite the expectations and pressure of being baronet someday—something Colin envied, then and now. Was his brother's confidence born of his faith?

"I'll concede his faith *may* have had something to do with his happiness." She wouldn't get more of an agreement than that.

Her silence implied acceptance of his answer.

"Do you think it was God's will he died?" The question, one Colin had wrestled with since Christian's death, was out before he could jerk it back.

Would Nora give him a trite response, as others had?

Colin tensed, his hands curling into fists within his pockets, as he waited for her answer. Quiet stretched between them. Perhaps no answer would be better than a hackneyed one.

Nora motioned to the blue sky filled with wispy white clouds. "When you are up there, in your aeroplane, how different is your perspective from being on the ground?"

"There's no comparison." He eyed the sky, thinking of his last flight over the Lake District the day before. Elmthwaite Hall, which seemed so large and monumental from the ground, faded to the size of a doll's house when he was high above the valleys and mountains.

"I don't believe it was God's will for any of those soldiers to die in the war." Nora stopped walking and turned to face him. Colin stilled to a stop as well. Unshed tears glittered in her blue-green eyes. Was she thinking of Tom Campbell again? "War is not something God condones, Colin, but men must be allowed to choose what they will make of their lives—good or evil. He cannot rob them of that."

She brushed at the corners of her eyes, then lifted her chin. "While I don't believe God wanted Tom or Christian to die, I do believe He has greater perspective than I do. Just like a pilot in his plane, who sees a much different picture than what we can from the ground."

Her gaze fixed intently on his, penetrating past his usual defenses of apathy and bitterness, straight to his heart. "When we go through heartache and loss, it's our right and challenge to discover what God wants us to do and become from those experiences." The resolve shining on her face only enhanced her beauty. "*That* is His will. To help us catch a glimpse of the wider, bigger perspective. To recognize and rejoice in those moments when He reaches down and compensates our losses."

The heartfelt words struck Colin with the force of a bullet, cutting through his doubt and anger and stunning him to silence. Was this what Christian had understood and lived? Had his faith given him greater courage?

"I didn't mean to offend." Nora glanced away. "I suppose I feel strongly about understanding God's will because I've dealt with losing three people I love very dearly."

Colin waited until she looked his way again before he spoke. "You didn't offend, Nora." On the contrary, she'd voiced her thoughts with compassion and sincerity. A desire to reach out and cup her face nearly overpowered him. To stop himself, he faced forward, away from her. "So is that how you see your sheep farm? As a compensation from God?"

He caught sight of the smile that creased her lips. "He's given me a chance for a new start here, and I'm grateful for it."

Renewed guilt rendered him unable to respond. How could he rob her of that new start? Was his father's plan worth such a price?

Colin fell into step beside her as they continued up the road. A memory from his childhood, one he hadn't recalled in years, pushed its way to the front of his mind.

He and Christian had been out hunting. Christian had bagged a nice-sized bird, but Colin hadn't shot a thing. Before returning to the house, he stopped to pick his mother a bouquet of wildflowers, so he would have something to show for all the time spent sloshing through the mud and trees.

Near the stables, he found Sir Edward exclaiming over

Christian and the "fine bird." Colin hurried up to show them his own gift, but his father's words stopped him in his tracks.

"When are you going to get your head out of the clouds, boy? Picking flowers instead of shooting?" Sir Edward shook his head in disgust. "It's a good thing your brother here is going to inherit or you'd surely bring Elmthwaite to its knees with all your foolish ideas."

Colin stalked away, throwing the silly flowers in the rubbish bin as he passed it. Later his father had muttered a quick apology, likely the result of Christian's explanation. But the hurt had already embedded itself inside Colin. He would never live up to his father's expectations because he would never be Christian.

"Are you all right?"

Nora's voice broke through the painful recollection. Colin blew out a breath, attempting to ease the tension radiating through him.

"Splendid," he said with an air of nonchalance. Years of practice had made it easy to disguise his true feelings. "Just thinking how I shall stay awake during the services tomorrow. Maybe a jab to the ribs?"

Nora studied his face for a moment, as though trying to perceive his real thoughts. Colin kept his expression neutral. "If you come," she said at last, "I promise to wake you, but only when it's our turn to sing."

He cracked a smile. The weight of the past didn't feel quite as heavy when he was with Nora. Too bad he would have to sacrifice her friendship to save his home and keep his promise to Christian. That didn't mean, however, he couldn't enjoy every minute he spent getting to know her. And he planned to do just that.

Chapter 6

Nora brushed a loose strand of hair out of her eyes with the back of her gloved hand, then hoisted the next rock onto the stone wall. Patching the barbed wire fences back home in Iowa now seemed a simple task by comparison.

After much persuasion on Nora's part, Jack had finally given up insisting he mend the walls himself and showed her how to fix the few crumbling spots. Nora appreciated his help and advice these last six weeks since she'd come to Larksbeck, but she still chaffed at his desire to do everything for her.

She positioned the outer-facing rock into place and stepped back to eye her work. This spot was beginning to look as straight and even as the rest of the dry-stone wall. Shading her eyes, she glanced up at the sun. The July morning was proving to be pleasant and only a few white clouds dotted the sky. Still, she was grateful she'd put on her rubber boots—or "wellies" as Bess had said they were called. Hopefully the sunshine would dry out the mud from the last heavy rainstorm.

Her gaze wandered to the few ewes and their twin lambs grazing on the other side of the green field. In less than two weeks, the farmers would gather their sheep from the fell for shearing. Nora was counting down the days until the event. Though the villagers continued to be friendly to her, she still didn't feel as though she belonged yet. Surely after the shearing, though, she'd be accepted as one of them and not feel so much like a guest, play-acting at being a sheep farmer.

A movement near the gate drew her attention. She looked over to see Jack striding across the field toward her. He, too, had on work gloves and wellies.

"Morning," she called as he came closer.

He nodded in greeting and studied the stone fence. Nora had a sudden urge to block her work from his scrutinizing gaze. He may be an expert at walling, as he'd informed her, but she didn't think her efforts paltry either.

"What brings you out here today?" she asked in a friendlier tone than she felt. "Does Bess need something?"

"No. I'm here to help you."

"Help me?" Nora raised her eyebrows in doubt. Didn't he really mean do it *for* her?

Jack rolled his eyes as though he could read her thoughts. "I've learned my lesson not to do it for you, though you might want to reconsider. Take these stones here..." To Nora's disbelief, he stepped around her and removed two of the rocks she'd carefully set into place. "They aren't going to work this way."

Nora forced a long breath through her nose as he repositioned the stones and reached down for a third.

"Well, come on," Jack said, an uncharacteristic note of teasing in his voice. "I told you I'm not going to do it for you. Pick up a rock, lass."

Nora shook her head with equal amusement and annoyance, but she bent down and hoisted another stone. Jack indicated where to place it. Though she wished she was doing the task alone, she wouldn't begrudge the extra set of hands—or expertise. Things would go much faster with both of them walling.

After a few minutes of getting in each other's way, Nora had the idea to form a brigade of sorts. She would pass the stones to Jack and he would situate them properly on the wall. At first he balked at the plan, insisting on doing the lifting. But Nora reminded him that, unlike her, he knew better how and where to place the rocks. Besides, she pointed out, the stones weren't too heavy. At last, he relented.

They spoke little as they worked, which suited Nora fine. Conversation didn't come as easily with Jack as it did with Colin. She concentrated on lifting the rocks, placing them into Jack's hands, then stooping for the next. After a time, her arms and neck grew warm from the exercise. She paused long enough to remove her sweater and place it on another section of the wall. When she turned, she caught Jack staring at her. A blush filled her cheeks and she hurried to hide it by picking up another rock. She wasn't blind to his lingering gazes, but she felt nothing more than friendship for him. She could only pray he wouldn't be hurt by her lack of romantic interest in him.

By the time the sun had climbed higher, they were well over halfway done. Nora offered to get them something to eat. While Jack continued to work, she went inside and gathered food for a lunch outdoors. When she returned to the field, they took their seats on the grass, their backs against the stone wall.

"It's a lovely day," Nora said, shutting her eyes and turning her face toward the sun's rays. She actually felt warmed through today, something she hadn't experienced in weeks. The cool, wet weather always seemed to penetrate straight through her clothes, chilling her even during the day.

Jack grunted in agreement. So much for starting a conversation.

"Tell me more about the shearing." Nora opened her eyes and took another bite of her sandwich.

"All of the farmers around Larksbeck spend the week going to each other's farms to shear the sheep. There'll be a competition for the fastest shearer. I won last year and two years in a row before I left for France." His blue eyes lit up as he spoke. "All the mums and daughters cook up a real nice spread of food at each farm. Then when all the sheep have been sheared, there's a dance in the village. If the weather holds, it'll be outside. If it rains, we'll squeeze into the Blea Crown."

"It sounds exciting. I'm very much looking forward to it."

Jack studied his sandwich. "Will you save me a dance that night?"

The morsel of food in Nora's mouth felt suddenly too large. She swallowed hard. Though she didn't wish to give him false hope, she could at least accept his offer of a dance. "I'd be honored to dance with the reigning shearing champion."

"I'm a wrestling champion, too, mind you," he added before digging into his sandwich again.

Nora nearly choked with laughter. Jack was a hard worker but not very modest about his skills. Once they'd finished their meal, she took the leftover lunch things into the kitchen, then returned to the field to help Jack. The sun began slipping behind gray clouds by the late afternoon and soon disappeared altogether. Nora put on her sweater once more.

She guessed the time to be three or four o'clock when Jack secured the last rock into place. Together they stood back to view their handiwork. A deep feeling of pride filled Nora at seeing the tidy, perfectly flush stone wall.

"Now that's walling done right." Jack removed his cap and ran a hand through his wavy red hair.

"It looks perfect." She smiled up at him.

"Glad I came to help you then?"

"Very much." And she meant it. "Why don't you come in and I'll make you a nice cup of tea."

"You're sounding more British every day."

Nora laughed at the compliment and did her best to ignore the appraising look on Jack's face. They headed across the field at the same time a familiar figure walked around the corner of the cottage.

"Colin." Nora lifted her hand to catch his attention. She sensed more than saw Jack stiffen beside her. The two men had barely acknowledged each other in public since the awkward moment weeks ago when Jack had entered her kitchen to find Colin standing there without his shirt on.

Colin waved back, though he remained by the cottage instead of entering the field. Nora noticed he carried something brown and moving in his arms. He'd been coming over several times a week with Perseus so the three of them could go for walks, but to her disappointment, she didn't see the dog around today. Even if Perseus wasn't hers exactly, she felt as if she still owned a dog with how much she saw of him.

Opening the gate, she let herself and Jack out of the field. "Where's Perseus?" she asked as she secured the gate.

"I left him home," Colin answered, "but I brought another friend along." He hoisted the wriggling bundle in his arms. It was a puppy.

"What a darling." Nora removed her gloves and hurried over to rub the puppy's head and ears. It playfully licked her hand. "Where did you get it?"

"Mr. Green's dog had pups a couple of months ago." Colin leaned over the puppy to add in a low voice, "I believe our Perseus is the sire."

Nora chuckled. "Is that so?" She ruffled the puppy's ears. "That's a lot to live up to, little one, when you have a father like that."

"I'm sure you'll teach her all she needs to know." Colin transferred the puppy into Nora's arms. The little dog began covering her chin with slobbery kisses.

"What do you mean?"

A mischievous smile lifted the corners of Colin's mouth, making Nora's stomach flutter despite the many times she'd told herself they were only friends. "She's yours, Nora." He tucked his hands into their customary spot inside his pockets. "I know you miss Oscar, so when I heard Green was ready to find homes for the puppies, I picked one out for you."

Nora stared into the big brown eyes of the dog. The puppy was hers to keep? So many nights she'd woken up and reached out to rub Oscar's fur, only to remember he was back in Iowa with Tom's family.

Colin shifted his weight. "If you'd rather pick one out yourself..."

On impulse, she went up on tiptoe to press a quick kiss to his cheek. His bristled jaw smelled nicely of soap and spice. "She's perfect, Colin. Thank you...thank you so much."

Embarrassed to meet his eye, she hid her face by nuzzling the puppy's soft fur with her nose. "Let's take her inside. You can come, too, Jack," she called over her shoulder. "I did promise tea."

Colin moved beside her as she carried the puppy through the back door of the cottage. "We'll get you some water and us some tea," she informed the dog as she set down her gloves and pulled a bowl from the cupboard. She filled the dish with water from the sink and placed it on the floor.

Upon release, the puppy lapped up the water with its tiny pink tongue. Memories of Oscar as a puppy filled Nora's mind and brought the sting of happy tears to her eyes.

"Green said his wife has already house-trained the dogs, so the pup shouldn't be any trouble in that regard." Colin took a seat at the table. "You might want to keep her on a leash, though, or tied up when you go outside, to keep her from wandering off. At least for a few more weeks." He leaned back in his chair. "Now what will you call her?"

Nora considered the possibilities as she filled a kettle

and placed it on the stove. The puppy had finished drinking and was now sniffing at Colin's shoes beneath the table. "I doubt I'm as knowledgeable about Greek mythology as your brother, but I recall hearing a story once about a female warrior named *Phoebe*."

As though she understood her namesake, Phoebe dropped her head to the floor, stuck her bottom in the air, and began growling at the broom. Colin chuckled. "I think for a daughter of Perseus, Phoebe will do nicely."

"Phoebe it is then." Nora went to the cupboard and pulled out three teacups. "Do you still want tea, Ja—" She twisted around, realizing Jack hadn't followed her and Colin inside. She peered out the window, but the yard stood empty. "I wonder where Jack went."

"Probably home. What were the two of you working on?"

"Walling." She put the extra cup away and removed two saucers. "Without his help, I wouldn't have finished it today. I need to thank him when I see him again."

"Did he happen to mention he's our current shearing champion?" The innocent question held a note of concealed laughter.

Nora was grateful she had her back to Colin so he couldn't see the smile he provoked. Schooling her expression, she carried the dishes to the table and sat down. "Be nice."

Colin lifted his hands in mock surrender. "It's the honest truth. Everyone around here knows it, most of all Jack. He's a shearing and wrestling champion." He grinned at her, as though he'd somehow overheard Jack's boasting.

"And what are you the champion of, Colin?" she shot back in Jack's defense.

The merriment on his face faded at once, making Nora wish she'd hadn't asked the question. "Ah." He picked at a knot in the table, his brow furrowed. "That is the real tragedy. Unlike Jack or Christian, I am not a champion of anything."

Compassion for him tugged at Nora's heart. Unable to resist its pull, she reached out and covered his hand with hers. "You're wrong, Colin. You're a champion of thoughtfulness." She motioned to Phoebe, who'd curled up by the back door. "Also in laughter, in manners, and in making me feel more at home here than almost anyone else—even on that first day."

The black of Colin's eyes had deepened as he listened. Nora's cheeks warmed under his silent examination of her face, and unseen energy filled the room. She'd felt this same electrifying feeling, seen that same look of desire on Tom's face, when he'd kissed her on her sixteenth birthday under the oak tree.

Was it wrong of her to feel this pull of attraction toward Colin, even when Tom had been dead for more than two years? She still felt as though she were dishonoring his memory and the love they'd shared from their youth by her friendship with Colin.

Besides, how well did she even know this man seated across from her? During their time together—on walks, at choir rehearsal, or after church services—she most often encountered the good-humored, carefree Colin. The one who hid his true self behind a ready grin or cynical rhetoric. There were times, though, when he allowed her glimpses into his heart. She cherished those moments, and yet she feared peering too closely, afraid of what she might find about herself there.

Colin could never pursue a romantic attachment with her, not as an heir to Elmthwaite Hall and his father's title. Opening her heart to him would only land her right back where she'd been when she lost Tom—heartbroken and alone.

The hiss of the kettle rescued her from her convoluted thoughts and kept her from dwelling on what Colin's intense gaze might mean or why the touch of his hand under hers felt so right and comforting. Nora jumped up, nearly upsetting her chair in her hurry. Ignoring a chuckle from Colin, she busied herself with pouring the steaming liquid and placing a single tea bag into each cup.

By the time the tea was ready, Colin was well into describing his most recent flight in his aeroplane, and the atmosphere in the warm kitchen had returned to normal. Nora sipped her tea as she listened, her glance continually wandering to Phoebe where she slept by the back door. How wonderful to have a dog nearby again. A feeling of contentment washed over her, and for the first time since coming to Larksbeck, she felt a sense of home.

* * *

An insistent yelp jerked Nora from sleep. She shot up in bed, her heart beating fast. What was wrong? Another yap followed by a scratch oriented her in the semidarkness.

"What is it, Phoebe?" Nora swung her legs over the side of the bed and patted on bare feet to the door, where Phoebe sat. "Do you need to go out?"

The dog barked. With a sigh, Nora opened the door and followed Phoebe down the stairs to the kitchen. She'd forgotten how much work a puppy—even a house-trained one—could be. Still she was more than grateful for the companionship.

She pulled her sweater from its peg and opened the door a few inches before turning to collect Phoebe's leash. In those few seconds, the dog wriggled through the opening and out into the night before Nora could stop her.

"Phoebe!" Nora raced into the shadowed yard. The cold, damp air swirled around her bare ankles and calves and made her shiver. Her pulse pounded fast and hard in her ears at the thought of losing the puppy after only half a day with her. "Phoebe? Where are you?"

Nora searched the flowers near the cottage, repeating her call for the dog, but it was as if Phoebe had vanished. The only noises were the milling about of the ewes and their lambs in the field. Worry and regret twisted Nora's stomach as she moved farther away from the house to hunt for the lost dog.

Several long, agonizing minutes passed before Nora heard the faint noise of Phoebe's whining. Relief coursed through her at the sound. The dog had to be close. Nora walked to the stone fence bordering the field and paused to listen. Phoebe's whines sounded louder.

Nora peered over the fence, but she couldn't see anything among the dark shadows. Dropping to her knees in the wet grass, she ran her hand along the rough stones near the bottom of the fence. She advanced slowly down the fence line until her fingers brushed soft fur.

"Phoebe, you naughty dog," she scolded.

Using her hands more than her sight, Nora determined the puppy had tried to climb through a hole in the fence, but the opening on the opposite end wasn't large enough to accommodate even her small body. The hole would need to be patched in the morning, to keep mischievous puppies out and little lambs in.

Nora felt around the hole a second time, trying to determine the best way to extract her puppy from the fence. Beneath Phoebe's feet her fingers brushed something smooth and metallic, rather than rough stone. What was the dog standing on?

"All right, girl, I'm going to help you out of there," Nora crooned as she gently pushed Phoebe into a lying position. With one hand on the dog's back and the other near Phoebe's rump, she carefully removed the puppy from the fence. Free at last, Phoebe scrambled up from Nora's lap to lick her chin. Nora chuckled and embraced the squirming pup.

"Let's not do that again, please." She wrapped a firm hand around the dog to keep her in place, then she reached into the hole for the metal object. After several twists, Nora pulled out a box. "I wonder what's inside," she murmured as she carried both the puppy and the box into the house.

Nora set the box on the table and secured the door before releasing Phoebe to the floor. "I hope you did your business before you got stuck because you aren't going back outside tonight."

The dog circled once, then flopped down beneath the table and shut her eyes, clearly exhausted by her little adventure.

A yawn escaped Nora's mouth as she hung up her sweater, but she wasn't sure she'd be able to fall asleep yet. Adrenaline over possibly losing the dog had fully awakened her.

After lighting a lamp, Nora sat down in one of the

kitchen chairs and examined the metal box. "Should we see what we've got here, Phoebe?"

Nora wiped the dirt from the lid with the side of her hand, revealing gold lettering and a picture of some sort. The box had likely been a cracker or biscuit tin at some point. So why would someone stow it away in the fence?

A mixture of curiosity and nerves had her holding her breath as she pushed the lid open an inch or two. Nothing jumped out and no foul smell tainted the air. Nora released her breath and opened the tin all the way. Dried flowers and pieces of lace and material sat atop a green leather-bound book.

She brushed aside the bits of material and crumbling petals to lift out the book. As she ran her fingers over the soft leather, her heart raced with sudden hope. Had she finally found something that belonged to Eleanor? The hairs on the back of her neck rose and Nora shivered. She'd searched the whole cottage for a diary of some sort, but she hadn't found anything of real interest beyond some old clothes and toys in the attic. Would she be disappointed once more?

"Only one way to find out."

She opened the cover and her breath snagged in her throat. Written on the cover page in faded but neat penmanship were the words: *This diary is the sole property of Eleanor Lewis.* The name *Galbert* was written on the line below.

"Oh, Phoebe. You, wonderful, wonderful dog." She knelt beside the puppy and stroked her silky fur. "All is forgiven."

Nora stood and collected the lamp and book. "Come on, Phoebe. Let's go back up to bed."

The dog followed her out of the kitchen and up the stairs. Nora set the lamp on the bedside table in her room and helped Phoebe onto the foot of the bed. The puppy nestled into the quilt and closed her eyes again. Nora climbed into bed, but she knew sleep was even further off than before. She had to read a little of the diary first.

Settling back against her pillow, she opened the book. A thrill of anticipation shot through her as she read the first two sentences of the first entry: *My name is Eleanor Lewis. I'm sixteen years old today and I'm in love.*

Chapter 7

Whistling to himself, Colin entered the dining room. Sunlight shone through the lace curtains at the full-length windows, adding to his already good mood. He served himself breakfast from the buffet, then took a seat beside his father at the table.

"Morning, Father." He arranged his napkin on his lap. "How's the state of the world today?"

Sir Edward glanced up from his newspaper and grunted in greeting. Clearly not everyone shared Colin's enthusiasm for the day—at least not at this hour.

Colin started in on his breakfast. He managed a few bites before Martin walked into the room and announced, "Letter for you, Master Colin."

The butler held out a silver platter with a single envelope lying on it. Colin took the letter and eyed the name written there. It was from his closest friend and fellow pilot during the war, Andrew Lyle.

When was the last time he'd heard from Lyle? At least three or four months ago. Colin read over the letter as he ate. Lyle spoke of London and the heat, and of the many ex-soldiers without jobs. Familiar guilt wrestled with the breakfast in Colin's stomach, marring some of his earlier good humor. He wished there was something he could do to help these men whom he'd shared the horrors of war alongside. Jobs were few at the moment, but he'd also heard a good number of the returning soldiers were too damaged in mind or body to secure employment.

Near the end of the letter, Lyle asked if he might come up for a visit. *I find myself in need of a change of scenery*, he'd written. *I can come at your earliest convenience.*

Colin folded the letter and slipped it back into its envelope. He rather liked the idea of having his war chum come to stay for a time. Only one thing about the letter struck him as odd—Lyle hadn't mentioned bringing his wife along.

"A pilot friend of mine, Andrew Lyle, would like to come for a visit. When shall I tell him to come?"

Sir Edward dropped a corner of the paper. "Where does he live?"

"London."

"Who is his father?"

Colin's jaw tightened at the question. In light of all England had suffered over the last six years, allowing only house guests of proper birth or origin at Elmthwaite felt not only antiquated but offensive. "No one you know, Father. He's the son of a humble solicitor. And one himself, I might add."

His father lowered the paper and frowned. "Then how can he afford to leave his clients by traipsing all over the country?"

Breakfast no longer seemed appetizing in the wake of his anger. Colin pushed his plate aside. When would his father ever choose to see beyond his own life? "He was injured in the war. The same war that took your son." The words hit home as Colin knew they would, causing his father's face to harden. "He's in need of a change of pace, which is what we can give him."

"And how long will he be gracing us with his presence?" Sir Edward shot back in an icy tone.

"I don't know." Colin wadded up his napkin and tossed it on the table. "But I'd think you'd show some compassion for those who sacrificed more than their time to preserve your way of life here."

His father's blue eyes narrowed. "My way of life? Is that all this is to you?"

"What if it is?" Colin countered. "There are soldiers begging on London street corners for money because they don't have hands or legs or arms to do anything else. There are those whose minds have been so shattered they struggle to simply exist. And yet here we sit…" A lump of emotion lodged in his throat, forcing Colin to pause. "Here *I* sit with all my faculties intact and money to spare, at least for now."

It was the closest he'd ever come to admitting the guilt he harbored over having survived, when Christian hadn't. The guilt he often felt that he could still walk and see and fly, when others couldn't.

His admission hung in the air like glass over the dining room, fragile and liable to shatter at the first dismissive comment from his father. Sir Edward wouldn't meet his eye. Instead he stared vacantly at something across the room, Colin and the newspaper all but forgotten.

Colin recalled the moment he'd first seen his father after coming home. The man who'd greeted him that day was a much older, more haggard version of the one who'd wished him well when he and Christian had left for France. Was it their money troubles that had caused the change, or Christian's death?

Colin pushed out a sigh, anxious to leave the room. He was more likely to succeed at teaching Perseus how to speak than to come to any understanding with his father over the war and the ways it had changed the world.

"I have to go to London next week to select our new automobiles," Sir Edward said, breaking the taunt silence. "Your friend may ride the train back with me on Thursday next." Colin recognized the attempt at a truce, albeit a tenuous one.

"Thank you . . . sir. I'll let him know."

He stood, eager to get a reply off to Lyle, before he went to see Nora and her puppy. The memory of Nora's delighted expression when he'd presented her with the little dog yesterday restored some of his good mood. As well as the recollection of her calling him a champion.

Good thing that table was between us, Colin thought as he pushed in his chair. Otherwise he might have given in to the overwhelming desire to kiss her soundly after her heartfelt speech regarding his good qualities.

"One thing more, Colin." Sir Edward folded the paper and placed it on the table. "I have men contracted to start reconstruction on the old stables when I return from London. I've also narrowed down the hotel design to two possibilities. Either one should be lavish enough to attract interest, even here in Larksbeck."

Colin wrapped his fingers around the back of his chair, bracing himself for what he knew was coming.

"How are you handling your part of the plan?" Sir Edward pinned him with a probing gaze.

"I'm getting to know her," he answered simply.

He wouldn't share how much he'd come to appreciate Nora's friendship over the last six weeks. Or how much he thought about her during the day, or how he preferred her company to anyone else's. If he admitted those things out loud, he feared he wouldn't be able to go through with what was required of him.

"And?" Sir Edward prompted.

"What, Father?" Colin pasted an innocent expression on his face.

Sir Edward pounded the table with his fist, making the dishes rattle. So much for their truce. "I'm not ignorant of the amount of time you've been spending with that no-name orphan. And now all you can say for yourself is that you've gotten to know her?" He pointed a finger at Colin. "Everything is riding on your persuasion tactics. You know this."

"Don't forget the part about my marrying Lady Sophia," Colin couldn't help adding, his voice coated with sarcasm.

Sir Edward scowled. "This isn't a game, Colin."

No, it wasn't. Colin knew that better than his father. He was the one playing with fire by befriending Nora with the intent to pull the rug out from under her when he convinced her to leave her farm...to leave him.

"I cannot build this hotel and bring tourists here without that property," Sir Edward continued, but he no longer sounded angry. His voice denoted only weariness. "Even a well-placed marriage will only add a few more years to Elmthwaite's survival if we don't build the hotel." His gaze found Colin's. "Are you with me or not? I need to know, before I go to London."

Releasing his viselike hold on the chair, Colin straightened. He wouldn't go against his brother's request or his father's plans, even if he wished he could. "Go ahead with your trip and converting the stables. I will get the property. You have my word."

It was the second time he'd given his promise to a member of his family. The words felt no less weighty today as they had when he'd said them to Christian before his death.

A rare half smile lifted the corner of Sir Edward's mouth. "Very good. When can I expect to begin building the hotel?"

"I don't think she'll accept your offer to buy the farm until after the shearing and the selling of the male lambs next month. Once she sees the work involved and the moderate income, she might be more easily persuaded to give it up." Remorse, scalding and thick, roiled through Colin at talking about Nora and her future with such detachment, but if he didn't, he would fail.

Sir Edward steepled his hands and tapped them against his chin. "You have a point. We should still move forward, as you suggested, on the rest of the plan. Come the end of August, though, I expect your part to be tidily wrapped up." His eyebrows rose in challenge.

"End of August," Colin echoed with more conviction than he felt.

At least he had the promise of another six weeks with Nora, before she left. And leave she would. Once she learned about his treachery, she wasn't likely to stay anywhere near Larksbeck.

He tried to picture his life the way it had been before Nora, but it was like trying to recall his life before the war. Both events had made deep impressions on him. The thought of continuing on here, without her, filled him with tangible pain. So he shied from it, telling himself he had time enough to settle into the idea once she was gone.

Sir Edward rose to his feet. "I'm counting on you, Colin." With that he left the dining room.

His last words repeated through Colin's head as he went to stand at one of the windows. The earlier sunlight was fast being blotted out by gray clouds. A noise at the servants' door drew his attention and he turned. One of the maids—Bess's daughter, if he remembered right—stuck her head around the door. Her cheeks flamed red when their eyes met.

"You can come in." Colin waved her inside. With downcast gaze, she entered the dining room, a tray brandished in front of her like a sword.

"Sorry, sir," she said in clipped tones. "I thought everyone had gone."

"It's fine. You can collect the dishes."

"I tried to come get 'em earlier"—she punctuated her words with a great deal of clatter as she placed plates and platters onto her tray—"but you and Sir Edward were talking, see…" She shot him a penetrating look over her shoulder.

Had she overheard them talking about Nora? Colin

frowned as he quickly reviewed the conversation in his head. He hadn't mentioned Nora by name, so the maid wasn't likely to know whom they'd been discussing.

"I apologize for delaying you," he said with a smile and as much charm as he could muster at the moment.

She blushed again, but she didn't say anything else. Instead she shook her head and continued with her task.

Colin exited the room and went to find Perseus outside. Despite the cloud cover, he and Nora might be able to squeeze in a walk before it rained. The thought cheered him, though he couldn't quite shake the uneasiness in his gut that the maid understood far more than he suspected.

* * *

Nora sat back on her heels and surveyed the garden. How could so many weeds have sprung up, seemingly overnight? She'd been out here every day the last few weeks, plucking up the bothersome plants, and yet new ones seemed to shoot up hourly among the herbs and vegetables.

"It's all this rain," she murmured. "Makes the weeds and everything else grow faster than a wildfire back home."

Phoebe barked in response and strained at the rope Nora had attached from the dog's collar to the gate post.

"I know you want to explore…" Nora bent and plucked another weed from the soil. "But after last night, I need to keep you tied up, like Colin said."

"What did I say?"

At the sound of Colin's voice, a tremor of anticipation shot through Nora's stomach. He'd come earlier than usual for their walk. Did that mean he wished to spend more time with her? She jerked at the weed between her fingers, ripping it out from its roots before tossing it away. If only she could eradicate her attraction to this man as easily.

"Morning." Nora climbed to her feet, brushing dirt from her hands. Perseus ambled over to sniff Phoebe, then trotted off. The puppy ran after the bigger dog as far as her rope would allow before she began barking in protest at being left behind.

With a chuckle, Nora walked over to console her dog. Colin joined her and bent down to pet the struggling puppy. "You were right about her needing to be tied up."

"Me? Right?" He shot her a mischievous smile.

It was a dangerous smile, one that always made her pulse sputter, as it did now. She focused her attention on the dog pawing at her knee. "She needed to go out in the middle of the night. But before I could get the rope on her, she charged outside." Nora let Phoebe lick her hand. "Isn't that right, girl?"

"Do you still wish to keep her? She isn't too much trouble?"

"No." She ruffled Phoebe's soft ears. "She might be an imp, but I think she's a perfectly wonderful imp."

"You and me both, Phoebe," Colin said, leaning back against the stone fence.

Nora chose to ignore his joke. Especially since he had that roguish look in his eyes. "You'll never guess what happened, though. She got herself stuck in the stone fence, and when I got her out, I found a box. With Eleanor's diary inside it."

"It's been out here this whole time? Bravo, Nora." Phoebe barked, making Colin laugh. "My congratulations to you, too, Phoebe."

Nora returned to the garden. "It's been quite a fascinating read." She set about tearing up weeds again. After a minute, Colin walked over.

"Are you going to tell me what it says?"

She squinted up at him. As usual he'd dressed in an immaculate suit and polished shoes. A rascally idea formed in her mind. "Are you as handy with weeding as you are with fixing my washing machine?"

"Much worse, I'm afraid."

"Too bad." She shrugged. "I'd be willing to tell you what I read, in exchange for some help weeding."

"You're serious?"

His incredulous tone nearly undid her feigned composure. "Yes."

Nora continued to work, until the silence proved too much. She peeked over her shoulder to see Colin had removed his jacket and was now rolling up his sleeves.

He scowled when he caught her watching him. "All right, you win. Which ones are the weeds?"

She pointed to some of the offensive plants. "All the ones that look like those."

He tore two up at once and flung them into her small pile at the edge of the garden, while grumbling something under his breath. Nora coughed to disguise the laugh rising in her throat.

"I'm almost halfway through the diary."

"After one night?" Colin sounded impressed.

"I've wanted to know more about her for weeks, so I had to keep reading." She scooted down the row of vegetables they were working on. "Apparently when she was sixteen, Eleanor fell in love with a young man who was seven years older than her. She doesn't refer to him by name, though. She simply calls him E in her diary."

"E? Why wouldn't she write his name?"

"I'm not sure." Nora tugged at a particularly stubborn weed. "They met at a dance in the village, and after that, they saw each other regularly, usually at a certain spot on the fell."

"I can think of only a few men in Larksbeck whose names start with E." Colin tossed more weeds on the pile. Was he working faster than her? Nora jerked at the obstinate weed and finally freed it. "There's Ebenezer Snow, but he's got to be sixty-five now—much older than Eleanor would've been. Then there's Egbert Croxley."

"What's he like?"

"Large nose, dull as a post. But maybe he was livelier as a young man."

Nora rolled her eyes. "Eleanor said E was very handsome and amiable. Anyway, this morning I read about E going to London and how much Eleanor missed him."

"London?" Colin rested one arm on his knee. "So he moved away?"

Nora had quickened her pace. She was nearly to the end of the row. "I don't think so. Eleanor made it sound as though he'd be away only a few months. While he was gone, she became acquainted with a young man named Matthew. She wrote how he played the fiddle beautifully and was very kind."

"She wrote out the other chap's name, but not E's?"

Nora nodded.

"An interesting mystery."

"Ready to start on the next row?" She threw the remaining weeds into the grass bordering the garden.

"How many more weeds are there?"

"Too many. I need to ask Bess what she does to keep them out. What do you use over at Elmthwaite to get rid of the weeds?"

"The gardener." Colin chuckled.

A strong desire to knock his arrogance down a rung or two filled Nora. She scooped up a handful of dirt and threw it at him, hitting him square in the chest. Colin's jaw went slack as he stopped weeding and looked from her to his vest and the brown mess there.

"I think you missed the weed pile, *Miss Lewis*."

A ripple of emotion ran through her at the low, husky quality of his voice. But she wouldn't back down. She wanted to strip away the pretense and cynicism Colin constantly hid behind to the man he truly was, the man she glimpsed for a few moments now and then.

"Did I?" she countered.

The roguish look returned to his eyes, deepening their color to ebony, as he threw a handful of dirt back at her. The soil alighted in Nora's hair and collar. She paused long enough to brush away the granules near her mouth before tossing more dirt at Colin. This time she hit him square in the side of the head. She tried to stop the laugh threatening to escape her lips at how ungentlemanly he looked, but the laughter won out.

With a growl, Colin pummeled her with more soil. Nora ducked as best she could, then scrambled to her knees to get a better throwing position. Dirt flew back and forth through the air between them. Beyond the garden, Phoebe barked incessantly at their game.

Nora didn't realize Colin had been slowly inching his way closer with each throw until his hand seized one of her wrists. She couldn't stop laughing, even though her sides hurt. When was the last time she'd felt this alive or carefree?

"Do you surrender?" He kept his gaze locked on hers.

"Never." She managed to sprinkle a bit more dirt into his hair. His face was mere inches from hers, close enough she could spot the individual particles of soil on his jaw. A boyish grin lit up his entire countenance.

"A truce, then?" Colin brushed some of the dirt from her cheek, his touch sending a shiver up her spine. Especially when his finger trailed her face to her upper lip and stayed there for several heartbeats.

"What are the terms?" Nora asked, hating the breathlessness in her voice. Could he hear the pounding of her heart? Would he request a kiss from her?

"I propose a rest."

"A rest?" She blinked in confusion.

"A rest from this war with the weeds." He pressed his forehead to hers. "Which you are losing, I'm afraid."

Without waiting for her answer, he pulled her down beside him as he sprawled on his back in the garden. Nora took a minute to catch her breath. Colin hadn't yet released her hand.

"You're ruining my plants." It was a halfhearted complaint, which he must have sensed.

"Yes, but I'm crushing the weeds, too."

She giggled as she stared up at the clouds trailing across the sky. A comfortable, friendly silence settled over them. Even Phoebe had stopped making noise. Colin let go of her hand, but he kept his fingers resting against hers so she felt the warmth of them against her skin.

A swell of gratitude filled her for his friendship. Working with him, teasing him—it was a nice way to spend a morning. Then why the lingering feeling of disappointment?

Because he didn't kiss you.

She'd expected him to and he hadn't—and this time, she realized with a start, she would have let him. That thought made her tremble with cold, despite the pleasant temperature. She couldn't fall in love with him—she wouldn't. For Tom's sake, but more important, for her own.

To prove her resolve, Nora scooted to the side, putting a few inches of distance between them. Immediately her right side felt bereft without his warmth. She stayed where she was, though, until she could sit up and smile at Colin with nothing but affability in the gesture.

Whatever happened, Colin Ashby would not overtake her heart.

Chapter 8

The automobile rumbled up the drive and Colin strode quickly toward it. He'd spotted his father's car from the air when the vehicle was still a ways off from Larksbeck. A few of the servants waited to greet his father and Andrew Lyle, but most would be preparing dinner. Sir Edward disliked eating late.

Excitement brought a grin to Colin's face as he went to stand next to his mother. He'd been anticipating Lyle's visit all week. The last time he'd seen his friend, the man was being loaded into an ambulance after enemy fire had cut up Lyle's aeroplane, the right side of his face, and his leg below the knee. The last few months of flying in the war hadn't been the same without Lyle around, especially with Christian gone, too.

When the car stopped, their chauffeur exited and opened the door for Colin's father. Sir Edward stepped from the vehicle, an uncharacteristic expression of cheerfulness on his face. He gave Colin's mother a kiss on the cheek and turned to Colin.

"I found the perfect autos in London, my boy." He squeezed Colin's shoulder in a rare show of fatherly affection. "Wait till you see them. Once the stables are converted, we'll have them sent up on the train."

"Sounds splendid, Father. What do you think of Lyle?"

"Oh, pleasant fellow," Sir Edward said with an air of dismissal. "Shame about his disfigured face and the false leg." He walked away to speak with Martin, leaving Colin annoyed.

His mother offered him a genuine smile. "I'm looking forward to meeting him."

Lyle climbed from the car and approached them, leaning on his cane. He had on his worn RFC uniform. The trousers hid the prosthetic that served as his left leg now. "Colin Ashby." He extended his free hand to shake Colin's in a firm grasp. One side of his face appeared normal and healthy, while the other drooped downward where the skin had been grafted around his right eye and cheek.

Colin hurried to swallow his guilt at having made it through the war physically unscathed. "Lyle. Good to see you again, old chap." He shook Lyle's hand, then turned to his mother. "Mother, this is Andrew Lyle. Lyle, this is Lady Ashby."

"I'm honored to make your acquaintance, Lady Ashby." Lyle made a little bow over his cane.

"The pleasure is mine," Lady Ashby said warmly. Colin felt a measure of pride at his mother's kindness. She never acted as anyone's superior in status or breeding. She treated Lyle as if he were a duke. "I feel as if we know you already with how much Colin spoke of you in his letters during the war."

"Only good, I hope?" Lyle asked.

"Yes, of course," she said with a soft laugh. "Your mother must be very proud of you."

A shadow passed over Lyle's face before he answered, "I hope so."

"Colin, I'll let you show Andrew to his room. Once you're both dressed for dinner, we'll eat."

"Dressed for dinner?" Lyle half whispered as Colin's mother went into the house.

"Welcome to Elmthwaite," Colin quipped. "Do you have dinner clothes?"

Lyle motioned to his jacket. "If this isn't dinner clothes, I'm sunk. I only brought a few suits, nothing fancy."

Colin clapped him on the back. "You can borrow some of mine during your stay."

"It's beautiful here." Lyle stared in the direction of the lake. "Even more so than you described."

Colin followed his friend's gaze. The lake sat still, reflecting the mountains and the patches of blue sky as perfectly as a mirror. How many hours had he spent on its shores, fishing and skipping rocks with Christian? He may not have loved Elmthwaite as much as his brother, but the thought of losing it had endeared the place to him, more so than he'd once thought possible.

"How is Mae?" He shifted his stance to look at Lyle. "You could have brought her along."

Lyle glanced from the lake to the gravel. "We are ... well ..." When Lyle finally lifted his head, Colin was surprised to see real anguish in his friend's eyes.

"We got a divorce, a little over two months ago. Although she'd been living with her parents for several months before that."

Remorse for his friend, coupled with the shocking news, tethered Colin's tongue for a moment. What could he possibly say by way of comfort? "I'm so sorry." Colin tucked his hands into his pockets and gave a regretful shake of his head. "I didn't know."

"Not your fault, chap. I wasn't ready to say anything in my last letter." A tight smile replaced the raw emotion on Lyle's face. "What about you, Ashby? Any pretty, single girls in this tiny village?"

Colin nearly said "one," but thought better of it. "You can see for yourself when we go to church on Sunday."

"You? At church?" Lyle barked out a laugh. "During the war, you wouldn't even get near a chaplain with a ten-foot pole."

He shrugged off the teasing. "It's not as bad as I used to think."

"Not bad? Who put you up to it? Your father? Your mother?"

"No." Colin spun around. It was definitely time to end this conversation. "Would you like to see your room? We'll need to hurry and change for dinner."

"If not them, then..." Lyle refused to move. "It's some dame, isn't it?"

Grateful Lyle couldn't see his face, Colin said evenly, "She's a friend, Lyle. And only a friend."

"Is she pretty?"

Colin swallowed, wishing he could deny it. "Yes."

"Kind, intelligent, interesting?"

"Yes," he repeated.

"Laughs at your jokes?"

The memory of the dirt fight with Nora in the garden the other week filled Colin's mind and he nodded.

"All the things you require in a wife," Lyle said with a note of triumph. "Believe me, I know. Christian and I heard that list of yours over and over again while we lay awake in that old château in France."

The mention of his brother, by someone who'd also known and admired him, didn't provoke the usual sadness. Colin was glad Lyle had come. Now if he would just leave off pestering him about Nora.

But Lyle wouldn't let it go. He came to stand next to Colin. "Why only a friend?"

Colin studied the intricately carved wood of Elmthwaite's front doors. "Now that I am the future baronet, my father has rewritten my list. Money and connections are at the top. And unfortunately, Miss Nora Lewis has neither."

"I'm the one who is sorry now." Lyle placed his free hand on Colin's shoulder. "Marriage without enduring love from both parties makes for a mighty burden indeed."

Colin thought of his parents. While he sensed a genuine, solid affection between them, he didn't know if either of them had been deeply in love with the other when they married. Is that what awaited him in the future? A marriage to a wife he felt fondness for but never true adoration? The idea appalled and depressed him.

Shaking off the despair that clung to him like mist on the lake, Colin forced a laugh. "You've only been here less than half an hour, Lyle, and already you have me as somber as a priest. Reminds me too much of the war.

Your job from now until you leave is simply to relax and enjoy your visit."

Lyle smiled, though his gaze remained serious. "I can't tell you how wonderful that sounds, Ashby." Colin suspected there was more his friend wanted to say, but he couldn't just yet. A moment later the soberness eased from his face and Lyle asked in an amused tone, "Will I have a chance to meet this *friend* of yours while I'm here?"

"As a matter of fact, you will. She'll be at choir rehearsal tomorrow." Colin leveled a hard glare at Lyle. "And not a word about my joining the choir. I was coerced, I assure you."

"I wouldn't dream of it." Lyle held up his hand in surrender. "I'm very much looking forward to meeting this Miss Lewis, though. Who knows, maybe a one-legged solicitor is more in keeping with her tastes than a future baronet."

Colin chuckled as he knew Lyle expected him to, but his mind revolted against the idea of Nora liking his friend more than she did him. If truth be told, he didn't fancy the idea of her liking any other man. And such a belief was liable to get him into real trouble if he wasn't careful.

* * *

The nervous bleating of sheep filled the air behind the cottage as Nora handed off another ewe to one of the three shearers seated on wooden benches. She'd grown used to the sheep's protests, though at first their plaintive cries had made her reluctant to wrestle them into the hands of the shearers. Once she saw the creatures were no worse for the wear afterward, even without their wooly coats, she threw herself into helping.

The occasional cheer from the gathered crowd for their favorite shearer added to the excitement pulsing through the late afternoon. The sun itself had even decided to join the festivities.

After five days of participating in the shearing at the other farms around Larksbeck, Nora felt particular pride that today, the last day of shearing, was her turn. She'd helped Bess and her daughters earlier in the week to prepare and cook enough food for the villagers who came to their farm. In turn, Bess had spent nearly all of the previous evening helping Nora ready the delicious fare now spread across the two tables Jack had set up outside.

The piles of wool—her wool—beside each shearer continued to grow larger. Jack was still in the lead as fastest shearer for the week. He lifted his head long enough to exchange a smile with her before bending to his task again. Nora wiped sweat from her forehead with the back of her glove, then tussled the next ewe out of the holding pen. Thankfully she'd brought her work trousers to England.

If Livy could see her now, working as a real sheep farmer...

Nora's thoughts returned to the letter that had arrived from her friend the day before. It was the second one she'd received since leaving Iowa. Livy had written about her daughter, Kate, and how very pregnant she felt. Her baby had likely been born by now. Had Livy given birth to another girl or a boy this time?

Nora recalled holding Kate the day after she'd been

born. Any nervousness she'd felt at holding a newborn disappeared as she drank in Kate's sweet smell and tiny features. A deep longing to be a mother herself filled her, bringing the mist of tears to her eyes, along with sadness at what might have been had Tom lived.

When would she get to see this newest addition to Livy's young family? Probably not before the child was walking or talking. The realization brought a wave of homesickness that tightened Nora's throat. Did life back in Iowa really have to go on without her?

Of course she was happy for Livy, very happy, especially since her friend hadn't escaped the last few years without difficulty either. But there were times when Nora felt as if her own life, whether there or here, hadn't followed the normal progression of everyone else's. Her life had stopped with the death of Tom and her parents, and every day she struggled to figure out how to start it moving again.

Livy's letter had also included the latest news of the Campbell family. All of them had enjoyed a visit from her oldest brother, Joel, his wife and son, and several of the orphan boys who lived in their home in Michigan. Nora wished she might have seen them. The last time she'd spoken with Joel had been right before he and Tom had left to fight.

It might have been awkward, though, she reminded herself as she handed off another ewe to the shearer.

While she still considered the Campbells to be the closest thing she had to family, she would have felt out of place with all of them there together. Being in their midst, without Tom, would have likely served as another painful reminder of her loss.

Of course Livy hadn't passed up the opportunity to ask Nora a few questions about Colin. Nora had finally mentioned him briefly in her last two letters, but her friend had perceptively latched on to the scanty references.

What is he like? Livy had penned. *Is he really the son of a baronet? Is he handsome?*

Nora cut a glance to where Colin and his friend Andrew Lyle were watching the shearing with obvious fascination. While she longed to sort out her mixed feelings when it came to Colin by confiding them to Livy, she found the idea too uncomfortable. Livy would be the last to judge, but Nora couldn't let go of the feeling she was betraying Tom. Especially by sharing her thoughts about another man with his sister.

"You're doing well, Miss Lewis," the farmer working beside her said. "We'll be done in no time at this rate."

A smile pulled at Nora's mouth. Her clothes were soaked with perspiration and she smelled of sheep, but she didn't care. This week she'd taken her rightful place alongside the other sheep farmers of Larksbeck.

"Shearers take a break," Ebenezer Snow, the official leader of the shearing, called out. Jack and the other two shearers stood and stretched their backs.

Nora seized the opportunity to get a bite to eat. She arrived at the food tables at the same time as a towheaded boy, who grabbed one of Bess's famous butter tarts and dashed off.

"That's enough tarts for you, William Shaffey." Bess shook a menacing finger at him. She was keeping the food tables well stocked. "His fourth one," she grumbled. "Now what can I get you, Nora?"

"A tart as well, please." She took the pastry Bess presented her and bit into the flaky, sweet goodness. "You can't really blame him. Your butter tarts are heavenly, Bess."

Bess shook her head at the compliment. "Go on with you, love. You just haven't had good English cooking before."

Nora gobbled up her pastry, then placed a hand to her middle. "I have this week. I don't know that I'll need to eat again until next year." They exchanged a laugh.

"How do you like your first shearing?"

"I've enjoyed it very much, especially getting to know the other farmers." Nora let her gaze wander over the other villagers, the shearers, the sheared ewes grazing in the field. "I didn't really feel as though I belonged here until this week."

"You belong more than you know, love." The reply was spoken in such a low voice, Nora wasn't completely sure she'd heard Bess right.

"Looks like Jack will win champion shearer again this year."

Bess nodded with pride. "He's faster than any shearer I know. 'Course he has got a bit more reason to show off today." She gave Nora a knowing smile.

The tart in her stomach tasted less sweet. How could she explain to Bess that she felt nothing but friendship for her son?

"I'd better get back. Thank you for watching the food, Bess." Nora brushed her hands free of crumbs.

"My pleasure."

Nora wandered through the assembled group back toward the shearers, saying hello and accepting compliments on behalf of Bess for the good food. She stopped next to Colin and Lyle. "What you do think?"

Lyle shook his head, his expression one of awe. "I've never seen anything like it."

"I haven't been to a shearing since I was a boy. I forgot how interesting it is to watch." Colin looked from the sheep to her blouse and trousers, an appraising gleam in his dark eyes.

Nora's face warmed and she quickly turned her attention to the spot where Jack and another of the shearers were conversing. "It can't be as easy as they make it look, especially to cut off the entire fleece in one solid piece like that."

"You're probably right." A determined glint entered Colin's gaze. "But I've made up my mind I'd like to try."

"In that suit?" She raised her eyebrows in challenge.

"This is my weeding suit, remember?"

Memories of that day in the garden flitted through Nora's mind, adding to her feelings of contentment. "What did you tell your valet about where the dirt stains came from?"

"I told him I was ambushed," Colin said with a sly smile, "by a whole regiment of weeds."

Nora laughed. "I guess if you have a mind to try, go ask Mr. Snow if you can switch with one of the other shearers."

"I believe I shall." He marched over to where Mr. Snow stood talking with one of the other farmers.

"Is he really going to do it?" she asked Lyle. She'd liked Colin's friend the instant she'd met him. Despite his injuries, he didn't seem overly bitter, only a bit lost at times. Nora could relate.

The young man chuckled. "Colin Ashby never backs down from a challenge. He'll do it or die trying."

Mr. Snow announced the shearing would begin again and that Nathan Duncan and Colin Ashby would be replacing two of the earlier shearers. Jack Tuttle would stay.

An exclamation of surprise rose up from the crowd at the older man's announcement. Nora noticed a number of the single young ladies from the village moving closer toward the benches, suddenly interested in the shearing when they hadn't been before. She returned to her post near the holding pen. Colin had removed his jacket and rolled up his sleeves, giving her another glimpse at his muscled forearms. He took a seat on the bench closest to her.

At Mr. Snow's call, she handed off the first ewe to Colin. The shearer whose place Colin had taken stood behind the bench, instructing him on how to shear the sheep. Shouts of encouragement rose from the nearby group— nearly all of them directed at Colin.

He worked slowly but meticulously. After a few minutes, he was well behind the other two shearers, but he didn't stop. The cheers for him increased. *Come on, Mr. Ashby. That's right, young man; put your back into it. You can do it, Ashby.* Nora found her attention riveted on him as well. His brow was furrowed in deep concentration, and beads of sweat soon formed there.

When the last of the wool dropped off the ewe, Colin straightened on the bench and shot the crowd a triumphant grin. The villagers cheered. He'd averaged only one ewe to two of Nathan's and three of Jack's. But the unadulterated joy on his face made him appear more the victor than either of the other two.

Nora couldn't take her eyes off him. Not only did he look impressively handsome with his rumpled hair, light bearded jaw, and muscular arms, but she suddenly realized she was seeing the real Colin. Here was the man he so often hid behind his jokes and nonchalant attitude. He twisted on the seat to smile directly at her. Nora swallowed in panic. Her defenses were useless against the power of this Colin and his dashing smile.

The farmer next to her prodded her with his elbow. "He said he's ready for another."

"Oh…right." Nora scrambled to give Colin a second ewe to shear.

His movements were quicker and more confident this time. He finished shearing this ewe in almost half the time the other had taken him. After that, he asked for one more. When he finished shearing that sheep, he announced he was finished and stood. The crowd swarmed him, clapping him on the back and offering their congratulations. The fuss interrupted Nathan's and Jack's progress. Nathan finished with the ewe in his hands, then wandered over to talk with Colin, but Jack hung back, a scowl on his face.

Nora's conscience pricked at the sight of Jack sitting alone. She strode over to him. "I had no idea you could shear that fast."

Jack didn't spare her a glance; instead he kept his focus locked on the villagers surrounding Colin. "Looks as though it doesn't matter, does it?"

"It's only because they've never seen a baronet's son shear a sheep before."

"Why aren't you over there?" he countered, finally looking at her. "I'd think you'd want to be the first to kiss your chap."

Nora frowned. "He's not my chap."

"Isn't he? I've seen the way you look at him."

She refused to argue with him or let his bad mood spoil the lovely day. "Congratulations again, Jack. Thank you for helping with my sheep." She turned and started to walk away.

"You don't know him, not really," Jack hurled at her back. "If you did, you wouldn't be sticking up for him. Not if you knew what I do."

Nora spun around, her hands balling into fists at her sides. At least Colin's remarks about Jack weren't malicious. "I shouldn't have to remind you, you're on my property, Jack. So I suggest you keep your opinions of Colin Ashby to yourself until you leave my farm."

He had the courtesy to look apologetic. "I didn't mean to make you angry, Nora. Honest. It's just, that man is always…" He broke off when she held her hand up for him to stop. "Sorry," he mumbled.

She forced a steadying breath to calm herself. "Apology accepted. You are still planning on saving me a dance tonight, right?" If she could get through it.

The anger left Jack's expression and he nodded.

"Then I'll see you tonight, Jack."

She returned to the holding pen. There were at least twenty-five sheep left to shear before everyone would head home to get ready for the dance at the pub. Would Colin and Lyle attend? Nora hoped so, though she couldn't free herself of the feeling that perhaps they ought to stay away. She hadn't liked the animosity burning in Jack's eyes just now.

Chapter 9

Music from the fiddles spilled from the open pub door, inviting Nora to enter. Despite the slight drizzle, some of the farmers were drinking their pints outdoors. A few of them called out a greeting to her. While their acceptance warmed her through and through, it did little to calm the nerves in her stomach as she stared into the crowded pub.

It had been too many years since she'd last been to a dance, and never alone. Tom had always gone with her. The remembrance only added to the feeling inside her of being unable to move. She couldn't enter or flee. If she did choose the former, would she be able to dance tonight without being plagued by memories?

Nora smoothed a hand over her waist, grateful she'd brought along more than one nice dress to England. She'd arranged her hair differently, too—half of it pulled back, while the other half fell long over her shoulders.

Another farmer exited the building, a mug in hand. "Evening, Miss Lewis."

She nodded in response.

"Better get on in there if you plan to dance. All the good partners will be gone." He chuckled.

Right. She could do this. She could enjoy the evening, with the friends and villagers she now felt a part of.

Taking a deep breath, she walked through the door and into the pub. Half a dozen couples were dancing in the middle of the room. A small crowd watched and conversed along the perimeter. Nora squeezed through the throng, the music drawing her forward like a bee to honey. Her feet itched to tap out a beat to the vibrant melody pouring from the instruments of the two fiddlers. She caught sight of Lyle seated in the corner, talking with Mary Tuttle. If Lyle was here, then Colin must be, too.

She searched the faces around her, but to her surprise, Colin wasn't standing along the walls. He was dancing and doing a fair job of it.

As if sensing her stare, he turned in her direction, and seeing her, he smiled. He looked very much as if he belonged here, just as he had earlier when he was shearing the sheep. Tom had possessed similar qualities, of being able to fit into any situation and putting people at ease with his ready smile.

For one brief second, she saw Tom instead of Colin. Any minute now she'd hear his voice call her name; she'd feel his hand clasp hers and pull her toward the dance floor. The memory felt so real she took a step toward him.

Someone jostled her from behind, jerking her from the past. Nora pushed out her breath. Tonight was about her life here, not the one she'd left behind.

The music ended and the dancers dispersed to find new partners. Where was Jack? She'd promised him a dance. Before she could locate him, though, Colin reached her side.

"Care to dance?"

"Yes, but I'm not sure how." The steps she'd seen him doing weren't like those she'd danced back home.

"Well, it's about time I taught you something." He held out his hand to her.

Nora hesitated, afraid to stir up the old memories again, then the notes of the next song filled the pub. She'd never been able to resist energetic music. "All right." She placed her hand in his.

Colin led her to the middle of the room. There were more couples this time than Nora had seen dancing to the last song, but the crowd had thinned along the walls to accommodate them. With her hand firmly grasped in Colin's, Nora followed his lead. The steps went perfectly with the tempo, and soon her anxiousness disappeared in the wake of newfound confidence. She'd never danced in such an animated way, but the music demanded it.

A rush of happiness engulfed her and she grinned at Colin. "This is nothing like dancing back in the States."

"Forget those sedate waltzes or tangos," he said near her ear so she could hear him. "Give me a good country dance any day."

"You're quite good at it."

"And that surprises you?"

"I suppose I didn't think to add dancing and sheep shearing to your list of talents."

Colin laughed, full and genuine, the warm sound embracing Nora. It reminded her of the look on his face after he'd shorn his first sheep. The more she came to know him, the more he surprised her.

The moment the music ended, Jack appeared at her side to claim his dance. While he smiled at her, his demeanor radiated bitterness when he glanced at Colin. Without a word, Colin released her hand, bowed, and walked away. Nora watched, with a twinge of jealousy, as another young lady latched on to his arm and pulled him back toward the dance floor.

"I won fastest shearer again," Jack boasted as the music started. "Fourth year. They announced it right before the dancing."

"Congratulations, Jack. We're all indebted to your quick shearing."

His gaze latched on to someone over her head, probably Colin. "Nice to hear there are some who fancy my skills."

Nora held her tongue—she didn't want to incite another argument.

A minute or two into the song was long enough to prove dancing with Jack was nothing like dancing with Colin. Where Colin's hand fit snuggly and warm against her waist, Jack's gripped her a little too tightly. No easy conversation or friendly banter flowed between them either. Instead Jack remained morose unless he was looking at her. Only then did he act pleasant.

The song ended at last, to Nora's relief, and she thanked Jack for the dance. To her chagrin, though, he kept her hand locked in his. Did he intend to dance with her again?

"Miss Lewis." Lyle moved quickly toward her, despite having to use his cane. "May I have the next dance?"

Nora nearly kissed him. "I would be honored."

Jack scowled at Colin's friend, but he finally let go of her hand and stalked away.

Lyle leaned close to say, "I'm afraid I can't dance these country jigs with this bum leg and cane, but you looked as though you needed a change in partners."

"Yes, thank you."

Lyle led her to a corner of the room, and while they didn't dance, Nora enjoyed talking with him. He was a congenial young man, who loved music as much as she did. More than once he expressed his delight at hearing her and the choir sing in church the previous Sunday.

Long after the one dance had ended, she lingered by him, happy to continue discussing their favorite pieces of music. Occasionally Nora glanced toward the dancers as she and Lyle spoke. Colin was always there, a different girl on his arm each time. The spark in his dark eyes showed how much he enjoyed the dancing, while the young ladies' starry gazes suggested they were more enamored with him than the festivities. Nora couldn't blame them. When was the last time they'd danced with a handsome baronet-to-be?

Once she spotted Jack standing alone in the opposite corner. He was watching the dancing, too, his expression hard.

"You'll have to come by and listen to my great-uncle's gramophone," she told Lyle at the end of their conversation. "It might be old, but the sound is still beautiful." A warm hand clasped her elbow.

"What's this? Lyle's invited to listen to your musical contraption and I'm not?" Colin glowered at her. "I'm hurt, Nora."

She pretended to ignore him as she smiled sweetly at Lyle. "What do you think? Should we allow a future baronet to our humble musical gathering? He probably has a whole room dedicated to music in that big house of his."

"He sheared three sheep today," Lyle pointed out, his face a mask of serious reflection.

"True." Nora gave a thoughtful nod.

"And he does appear to be quite popular tonight because of it."

"Good point."

Colin growled deep in his throat. "Are you two finished?"

"Almost." Nora turned toward him. "You're welcome to come with Lyle, if…" His eyebrows shot up. "You agree to dance with me one more time." It was her turn to dance again with her friend.

"I accept your terms." He tucked her hand beneath his arm and pulled her close to his side. In a low voice, meant for her ears alone, he added, "It would be my great pleasure to dance with you, and only you, the rest of the evening, Nora."

She couldn't stop the blush that flooded her cheeks, but she couldn't let him think he'd rattled her completely. "I doubt your many admirers would allow that," she whispered back. "But I'll accept two dances."

"Very well." He grinned and spun her onto the dance floor.

Nora laughed at his enthusiasm. If she didn't know better, she might have suspected Colin of being a farmer, instead of the heir to a title and a wealthy estate.

The dance steps came easily to her this time. But

whether that was because her country dancing had improved or because she had Colin as her partner, Nora couldn't say. She had to admit she very much enjoyed dancing with him. Their movements were perfectly matched and she felt content, even proud, to be at his side. Almost as if they'd been dancing together for years.

Like me and Tom.

In an instant, the pub, the crowd, and the lively music receded. Memories replaced the present in her mind. Instead of being in England, she was back on the farm in Iowa, waltzing with Tom. The gentle strains of the piano spilled through the screen door.

"Are you scared?" Nora whispered. "To go fight?"

Tom lifted his shoulders in a shrug. "Naw." A sheepish grin lit up his face a moment later. "All right. Maybe a little."

Nora stopped dancing and squeezed his hand where it still held hers. "I'm scared, too."

He cast a glance into the house where her mother sat playing the piano and her father read the newspaper. "Come here. There's something I want to ask you." He led her off the porch and to the oak tree across the road from the farmhouse. Nora rested her back against the rough wood, beside the heart Tom had carved there with their initials.

"You know I love you, Nora." He peered down at her, his expression unusually serious. "Always have, always will. Which is why I think we ought to get married."

Nora gave a startled laugh. Was he serious? It was hard to tell sometimes with Tom. "But you leave tomorrow."

"Not before I go, but the moment I get back." He cupped her cheek with his free hand. "I'd wake the preacher and do it now, but I don't like the thought of possibly leaving you a widow." He placed a finger over her lips when she started to protest such talk. "Not that I plan on doing anything else but returning to you. So what do you think?"

The answer came easily to her lips. After all, she'd wanted to marry Tom Campbell for years now—their families expected it as much as the two of them did. "Yes," she said, wrapping her arms around his waist and resting her cheek against his shirt. His steady heartbeat beneath her ear was a comforting sound. "The moment you get back, I'll marry you."

"I don't have a ring to make the engagement official." He eased back to see her face. "But if you'll promise to be mine forever, that's good enough for me."

Be mine forever.

The noise of the dance and the pub rushed back into her conscious mind, and Nora stumbled. Colin, not Tom, held her hand now. His firm grip kept her from losing her balance, but they'd gotten off tempo.

"Are you all right?" he asked. "You look like you've seen a ghost."

Almost. "I think I could use some air. Do you mind?"

Colin shook his head. "Follow me." He led her off the dance floor, through the crowd, and out the pub door.

Once outside, Nora gulped in a deep breath of the cool evening air. The light rain had stopped, though the sky was still littered with clouds.

"Where to, fair lady?" Colin hadn't released her hand yet, for which she was grateful. She relished the human contact to chase away her recollections of the past.

She pointed to the low wall behind the pub. They

walked over to it, and only then did he let her go. Tiny purple flowers dotted the stones. Nora plucked one, rubbing the soft petals between her fingers.

The girl Tom had left behind wasn't the same as the one who stood here beside a stone fence in the middle of the Lake District. She'd loved and lost and grown up in the process. So why did she feel compelled to keep her promise to a man who could no longer honor his end of their agreement?

She didn't have to search very deep to find the answer—it was fear. Fear of the pain and loss, if she were to fall in love a second time with someone who wouldn't stay.

Companionable silence settled around her and Colin as they stared at the row of mountains on the opposite side of the lake. She appreciated that he was willing to let her think and that he didn't feel an immediate need to disrupt the quiet.

She shifted her gaze to Colin's profile. Ever since arriving in Larksbeck, she'd found him intriguing. That interest had soon given way to trust and friendship the more time she'd spent with him. His company made her quiet life more exciting and less isolated. She enjoyed their walks around the lake, when he regaled her with stories of his youth or his time in France. She appreciated the funny faces he shot her during choir rehearsal when Mr. Bagley was preoccupied. She liked the challenge of matching his banter and teasing with her own. He'd become her dearest friend in Larksbeck.

And something more? her heart prompted.

Before today, she would have brushed the question aside, fearful of dishonoring the love she'd shared with

Tom. Tonight, though, Nora allowed it to seep into her thoughts. The very act of looking toward the future instead of the past felt as freeing as the Iowa sky and as soothing as rain on a parched field.

As she continued to study the handsome contours of Colin's face, a new question emerged. *What does he think of me?* Colin appreciated her friendship; that much she knew. Otherwise why would he choose to spend so much time with her? But did he see her as more than a friend? Seeds of hope, and fear, sprouted within her at the possibility.

At that moment, he turned to face her, causing Nora to glance away. Had he caught her staring? "You look rather serious."

"I'm fine."

A low chuckle emanated from him. Nora's stomach fluttered at the sound. "Don't worry. I won't pry your secrets from you." He reached out and fingered a lock of her hair. Even the whispered touch sent her heart racing. "I like your hair this way."

Nora looked at him to gauge if he was joking or not, but he watched her solemnly. "Thank you." His compliment pleased her, more than she probably ought to let it.

"You've never worn that dress to church before either. It matches the green in your eyes."

He noticed what she wore? "What of my work trousers?" she countered, to school her feelings. "You hadn't seen those before today either."

His voice held no trace of mirth or sarcasm as he said, "A beautiful woman like you would make rags look stunning, Nora."

The heartfelt words and the way he delivered them rendered her speechless. It had been so very long since a man had called her beautiful.

Lyle walked out of the pub then and approached them, saving her from having to form a suitable reply. "I believe I shall retire for the evening, Ashby."

"Already?"

"I can walk back myself," Lyle said, his gaze jumping between the two of them. Nora's cheeks flushed with embarrassment as she realized how it must have looked when she and Colin exited the pub together.

"Nonsense." Colin tucked his hands into his pockets. "Father is likely wondering where we ran off to after dinner. It's time I went back as well. Shall I send for the automobile?"

Lyle shook his head. "Even with a bum leg, it's too nice a night for riding in a car."

"Very well. Would you like to walk with us?" Colin asked her.

Nora wanted to, very much, but she hadn't spoken with Bess or Mary yet. "You two go ahead. I have some visiting to do."

Colin's face clouded with obvious disappointment. Nora pressed her lips together to hide a pleased smile. "We'll see you in church tomorrow then?"

She nodded. "The choir's singing, remember?"

"And you have a solo part."

The reminder brought a tremble of nerves to her middle—she'd never sung a solo in public before. Nora suppressed her anxiety, though, with the reminder that Colin would be there. He was her friend, after all, and his presence would help her stay calm.

After she'd bade the two men good night, she went in

search of Bess and her family. Mary and Jack weren't around anymore, but she found Bess and several of the farmers' wives inside the pub's kitchen. One of the older women spotted Nora and invited her to join the group. She happily complied.

Before long, one of the fiddlers announced the last song. The pub wasn't nearly as full as it had been earlier. Nora was asked to dance by a tall, skinny lad, probably five years her junior. Still, she enjoyed the opportunity to dance one last time. When the song ended, she slipped out of the pub. Dusk had now settled over the valley.

Nora breathed in the scent of wet earth as she walked toward her cottage. She'd enjoyed the evening and the whole week. The air might be chilly away from the crowded pub, but inside she felt nothing but warmth.

"Thank you," she whispered heavenward. "I don't know all Thy reasons for wanting me in Larksbeck, but I'm grateful to be here."

She smiled to herself as she climbed the hill to the cottage. A life here in England was beginning to feel not only possible, but gratifying.

The sound of Phoebe barking met her ears before the house came into view. *How odd*, Nora thought. Phoebe didn't usually mind being left alone.

Something about the dog's incessant yelping erased Nora's smile. She quickened her pace, but she stopped short at the sight of the jagged hole in her newly replaced window.

"Phoebe? Are you all right?" Nora rushed into the house, dread pulsing through her.

The puppy clawed at her legs as she entered through the front door. Nora knelt and pulled the whimpering dog into her lap. "What's wrong, girl?"

Phoebe jumped from Nora's grip and scrambled into the adjacent room. A large, dark object sat on the wood floor near the dining table. Phoebe growled at it.

Goose bumps riddled Nora's arms as she entered the room and squatted down to examine the object. It was a stone, like the ones used for walling. Nora glanced from the stone to the window. No wonder there was an ugly hole there—someone had thrown the rock through her window. But had it been an accident or a prank?

Below the window, she spotted a piece of paper. She picked it up to read the words scrawled in a heavy hand in the middle of the page: *Go back to where you came from.*

Icy prickles of fear chilled her entire body and stole her breath. Someone wanted her gone. As if in agreement, the cottage door flew open and crashed against the opposite wall. Nora's heart leapt into her throat as she scrambled to hide in the room's shadows. Phoebe launched into another round of frenzied barking at her feet.

When nothing but a blast of cold air entered the cottage, Nora climbed shakily to her feet and shut the door. "There, there, girl," she soothed, though her voice trembled as much as her body. "It was only the wind."

She leaned against the door for support, her gaze dropping to the paper still clutched between her fingers. All traces of happiness or acceptance had vanished like the sun on a stormy day. What to do now? But her mind felt too on edge to form any proper solutions.

"Come on, Phoebe. Let's get some tea."

Nora started down the hall, but stopped halfway to the kitchen. There was one thing she could do tonight. She returned to the front door and dropped the latch into place.

For the first time since coming to Larksbeck, she would sleep with the doors locked.

* * *

Colin jerked awake. His room was bathed in semidarkness, and except for the ticking of the mantle clock, silence permeated the night. Something had disrupted his sleep, though. He lay still, listening, his eyes staring at the canopy of the four-poster bed.

Just when he'd convinced himself he must have imagined the noise, a shout of pain and agony split the quiet of the house. Colin tore off his covers and shot to his feet. Was something wrong with his mother or father? He pulled on his robe, threw open the door, and paused to listen again. When the loud, anguished cry repeated, he realized it wasn't coming from his parents' rooms. It was coming from Lyle's.

Sir Edward lumbered into the hall, carrying a lamp. "What is the meaning of this, Colin?" Lady Ashby appeared as well, her dark hair arranged in a long braid down her back.

"It's Lyle," Colin said over his shoulder. He went to Lyle's door and knocked. The only response was another shout. Anxious for his friend, Colin opened the door and stepped into the room. "Lyle? Are you all right?"

He heard his parents come up behind him. His father's lamp cut through the room's darkness, illuminating Lyle's look of horror.

"Ashby, I can't shake them," Lyle screamed. He sat straight up in bed. "They're all over me." He flailed his arms as if trying to bat away a fly. "I'm hit; I'm hit."

Colin swallowed hard, memories slamming into him at hearing Lyle's words. The room seemed to fall away and he, too, was back in his biplane, the sky thick with German fighters. He'd motioned for Lyle to get back to base. Miraculously, his friend had, though it was the last time Lyle flew in the war.

A hand on his arm brought Colin back to the present. He glanced down into his mother's worried eyes. "Is he dreaming?"

Colin nodded. "Go back to bed. I'll make sure he's all right."

She took the lamp from his father and handed it to Colin. "Would you like me to ring for some tea?"

"No."

Lady Ashby kissed him on the cheek, then followed a grumbling Sir Edward out of the room. Not wasting any more time, Colin strode to the bed and set the lamp on the side table. Lyle was weeping now. Colin gripped his friend's shoulder and shook him. "Lyle. Wake up. You're dreaming. It's not real—not anymore."

Lyle fought his grasp, but Colin held on. He gave his friend another firm shake. "Wake up, chap. Everything's okay."

After another minute, Lyle's face relaxed and his eyes widened. "Ashby?" he said, his voice heavy with confusion.

Colin sank onto the end of the bed. "You were having a nightmare."

Lyle ran a hand over his jaw. "Did I disturb the house?"

"No." He needn't tell Lyle about waking his parents, and for all Colin knew, the servants hadn't heard a thing. "Would you like some water?"

Lyle shook his head. "I'm sorry to wake you."

Colin shrugged off the apology. "Does this happen often?"

The lamplight accentuated the red of Lyle's face and neck. "I can't help it, Ashby. I've tried everything—medicine, staying awake all night. Nothing makes them go away altogether. I'm surprised I haven't had more this last week." Lyle collapsed back against his pillows. "The nightmares are one of the reasons Mae left."

Colin studied his hands, wishing there was some way he could help. While his peace of mind might be bothered now and then with grief over his brother's death and the way his life had been altered, his occasional dreams about the war only meant a less than restful night—nothing compared to what Lyle was dealing with.

"At first, she didn't seem to mind my leg being gone or my half-ghastly face," Lyle continued, his voice low and full of pain. "She was real sweet with the bad dreams in the beginning, too. Making sure to wake me and offer comfort. But after I'd been home a month or so, things started to change. She didn't understand why I couldn't get out of bed to go to the office some days. My father and his partners were giving all the easy cases to me, ones that even the most inexperienced of solicitors could handle."

Lyle scrubbed at his eyes. "I hated feeling useless and pitied. By my parents, by our clients, by Mae. Eventually she found herself a job—said I didn't have to be the only one making money for us. She didn't understand that I wanted to do just that." He gave a sad shake of his head. "She started working later and staying over at her parents', so my nightmares wouldn't disturb her sleep.

It wasn't long afterward we decided things were over. I heard a few weeks ago she's engaged to some lieutenant."

"Bet he has nightmares like the rest of us," Colin quipped.

As he'd hoped, Lyle chuckled. "Probably worse, being army and all. Poor Mae."

"She's really better off with some fifty-year-old farmer than any of us ex-soldiers."

Lyle gave another light laugh. "Should have told her as much when I had the chance."

Colin stood and dragged one of the armchairs by the fireplace to the side of the bed. The more Lyle talked, the more he seemed to relax.

"Remember Hugh Shepherd?" Colin asked as he sat down in the chair. "After his first flight against the Germans?"

A real smile shone on Lyle's face. "When he threw up all over your boots?"

Colin laughed at the memory. "It was only funny because we all knew we'd come close to doing the same thing. Even Christian." He propped his feet on the bed and rested his elbows on the chair arms. "Wonder what Shep's doing these days."

"Heard he's back in Cornwall with his wife and two girls."

Lyle told him about running into a few other pilots they'd flown with. Soon the conversation turned to their time in France. Some of their shared stories made Colin laugh until his sides hurt; others brought a hard lump to his throat, especially those involving Christian or their other friends who hadn't made it home.

By the time the clock on the mantel chimed three,

Colin could barely keep his eyes open, and yet he felt strangely buoyed up as well. Releasing a yawn, he stood and bade Lyle good night. He shuffled back to his room and collapsed onto his bed, without bothering to remove his robe. A niggling thought in the back of his mind told him there was something he needed to do in a few hours, but he pushed it back as sleep reclaimed him.

Chapter 10

Sunday morning dawned gray and rainy, but Nora refused to let her mood match the weather. She firmly set aside her anxieties over the rock through her window as she ate breakfast and dressed for church. She spent longer than normal arranging her hair and choosing which dress to wear.

Only because I'd like to look nice for my solo.

But she knew the real reason. Colin would be at church again, and she wanted to feel as beautiful as she had last night at the dance when he'd complimented her.

Because of the rain, she left Phoebe in the house, instead of tied up outside as the puppy typically was when Nora went anywhere during the day. She also locked the doors and pocketed the key. She hated no longer feeling safe and secure with the doors unlocked.

With her umbrella protecting her against the wet, she headed down the road toward Larksbeck. Every few minutes, she glanced over her shoulder to see if Colin and Lyle were coming up behind her yet. They still hadn't appeared by the time she reached the bridge, leaving Nora to assume they'd driven instead of walked.

"Ready for our song today, Miss Lewis?" Mr. Bagley asked when she reached the church.

Nora stood on the doorstep and shook the water from her umbrella. "I think so, yes."

"I have no doubt your solo will be perfect."

"Thank you."

She slipped into her customary pew in front of Bess's family, making sure to leave enough room on the end for Colin and Lyle. The church soon filled, despite the steady rainfall outside, and the pastor stood to welcome the congregation. Nora twisted in her seat to look at the door. Where was Colin?

He'll be here, she reassured herself.

Colin had said as much, and she trusted him. He wouldn't have forgotten about their choir number or her solo today. Despite his grumblings about Nora roping him into regularly attending church, he hadn't missed a performance yet.

Still, she couldn't stop fidgeting. She shifted on the hard bench, glanced in the direction of the door, folded and unfolded her hands in her lap. The pastor began his sermon, but Nora couldn't concentrate. Perhaps Colin and Lyle had chosen to sit in the back instead of causing commotion by coming forward to her pew. Once she'd convinced herself that's where they must be, she was able to listen better.

When the pastor announced the choir's song, Nora stood with the rest of the singers, her heart beating fast with nervousness. She could do this. One look at Colin's reassuring grin and her confidence would return.

She filed into her place and looked toward Colin's customary spot, down and to her left. Another man stood there. Nora scanned the faces of the congregation. Colin wasn't seated in any of the pews either. Icy threads of panic made her stomach clench. As if from a distance, she heard the first notes of the organ. Mr. Bagley smiled at her from his place in front of the choir. Her solo was first.

Where are you, Colin?

Nora stared into the eyes of the villagers, but instead of friendly gazes, she imagined hard glares. One of them had tossed a rock through her window; one of them wanted her gone from this place. Or was it all of them? She'd felt accepted into the community this week, but now she wasn't sure who to trust.

Her mouth felt dry, her throat clogged. Could she even get the notes out?

The organist repeated the song's introduction. Nora had missed her cue. Mr. Bagley frowned, then nodded to her. She shut her eyes for a brief second, gathering her resolve. Whoever wanted her to leave was mistaken if he or she thought Nora would simply tuck tail and run. She wouldn't give up. This was her home now. She had a right to be here.

Opening her eyes, she tilted her chin upward and began to sing.

* * *

The whoosh of curtains being pushed aside nudged Colin awake. He sat up and rubbed at the kink in his neck as dim light flooded his room. Raindrops pattered against the window.

"Good morning, sir," Gibson said in his usual monotone. "Your breakfast is ready." He motioned to the tray on the nearby table. "Unless of course you want lunch."

Colin stood. "What time is it?"

"Half-past eleven."

After eleven? He hadn't slept this late in years. Colin sat at the table and drew his napkin over his lap. His stomach rumbled in anticipation of food.

"What will you be doing on this wet Sunday, sir?"

Sunday usually meant church with Nora.

Colin jumped up, his napkin dropping to the carpet. Nora was supposed to sing her solo today, during the choir number, and he'd slept through both. How could he have let her down, especially after last night at the dance? He hadn't been able to get the image of her dancing out of his head. The way her red hair had flowed down her back and her blue-green eyes shone with enjoyment.

"I'm going out, Gibson."

His valet arched his thick gray eyebrows. "Out, sir?"

"Yes," Colin grumbled with mounting impatience. "Is Mr. Lyle up yet?"

"I don't believe so." Gibson stepped forward to assist Colin into a day suit.

Once dressed, Colin grabbed some toast from off the breakfast tray. "Tell Mr. Lyle I'll be back in a few hours."

"Shall I call for the automobile?"

Colin shook his head. "I'm not going far."

"Very good, sir."

He turned toward the door, but not before he caught a flash of emotion in Gibson's weathered gaze. Did his valet suspect what Colin was only beginning to realize? He was falling for Nora. The idea sent a thrill shooting through him, but it disappeared as quickly as it had come. What would that mean for his father's plans?

Colin shoved the troublesome question to the back of his mind as he bounded down the stairs. Right now, he knew one thing for certain—he needed to see Nora and apologize.

Rain pummeled the ground outside, but Colin didn't want to waste any more time going back for an umbrella or a hat. Streams of water ran down the road, cutting paths through the mud. Colin stuck to walking on the narrow strip of grass on the road's side, though here and there a protruding hedge forced him into the mire for a few moments.

The road leading up to Nora's home wasn't much better. By now, his suit was completely soaked and he had to keep wiping water from his eyes. He sloshed his way up the hill to the cottage and knocked on the front door. Phoebe barked from inside.

A minute or two passed before he heard Nora call out, "Who is it?"

"It's me. Colin."

To his surprise, he heard the sound of the latch being released. When had Nora started locking the door, and during the day, too?

The door swung open and he hurried inside. Nora hadn't yet changed out of her church attire. She wore a dark blue dress that heightened the blue in her eyes, and her hair was arranged in such a way to show off the long lines of her neck.

After closing the door behind him, she stood in the

entryway, making no attempt to invite him to sit down. "You're dripping an ocean onto my floor." She fixed him with a stern glare.

Colin glanced at his shoes and the water he'd tracked in. "I'll clean it up."

Phoebe came forward from behind Nora to sniff the hem of his trouser legs. When she'd finished, the dog turned and trotted down the hall, as though she, too, wanted nothing to do with him.

Colin shoved his hands into his sodden pockets and cleared his throat. "I'm very sorry, Nora. For missing church today . . . and for missing your solo."

Her gaze wouldn't meet his as her shoulders lifted in a shrug. "I'll get a rag for you. To wipe up that puddle."

She started down the hall, but he caught her wrist in time to stop her. He gently pulled her around, grateful when she didn't jerk away from him.

"I wanted to be there—I had planned to be there, believe me." His thoughts derailed as he stared into her large eyes. They revealed the hurt she was trying so hard to mask with anger. Why hadn't he been at church with her, watching her face light up as she sang? Being with Nora brought him the greatest happiness.

"What happened?"

Her accusing tone broke the trance he'd been under. "It was Lyle. He had a nightmare last night. He was reliving the flight when he got shot. We stayed up quite late, talking about the war. I suppose I was more tired than I thought."

The rigidness in her shoulders and face melted at his words. Colin allowed himself an inward sigh of relief. Perhaps she would forgive him after all.

"Is Lyle all right today?"

"He was still asleep when I left." Colin couldn't help rubbing the soft skin of her wrist with his thumb as he continued. "I think he'll be fine, but the nightmares will likely last a long time. He's had a hard go of it since coming home."

"What about you? Do you have nightmares?"

Recollections assailed him at the simple question. He was no longer in the small cottage but sitting in his biplane flying toward a squadron of German planes—the air filled with explosive sounds, the mix of fear and adrenaline in his gut, the innate drive to shoot instead of be shot.

"Colin?" She covered his hand where it still gripped hers.

He shook himself back to the present. "I'm fine. On occasion there's a bad dream, but nothing as real as what Lyle experiences."

"But the memories are still there."

She voiced it as a statement, not a question, but he dipped his head in a simple nod anyway. Nora would understand. While she might not have fought over a battlefield as he had, she was battling the repercussions of the war, too. Would she be forever scarred by those outcomes? he found himself wondering. Would she someday have room in her heart for someone else besides her deceased fiancé?

Nora broke free first. "If it was Lyle who made you miss today, I forgive you."

Though he suspected she was teasing him, a rumble of jealousy rolled through him. "Just for Lyle?"

She gave a soft laugh, but the merriment ended as fast

as it appeared. Her whole demeanor appeared unusually somber this morning. "I'll get that rag."

He let her go this time. A shiver stole up his back, making him acutely aware of his wet clothes. Despite a fire glowing in the parlor hearth, the cottage still felt cold and abnormally drafty. The source of the slight breeze seemed to be emanating from the dining room. Colin looked inside and noticed several pieces of wood had been propped into the broken window, but air still leaked through.

"A rather unusual window covering you have there," he said, pointing at the wood as Nora came down the hall, a rag in hand.

"It's not on purpose." She nudged him aside so she could wipe the floor.

He knelt and gently pried the cloth from her hands. "Allow me." Colin dabbed at the puddle, then wiped at his shoes and the hem of his pant legs. "I thought you already fixed that window."

"I did." Nora climbed to her feet. "Someone threw a rock through it last night." Her voice, though calm, still held a hint of fear.

Colin stood slowly. "Was it a child's prank?" If so, he'd hunt down the culprit and have his backside tanned.

Nora shook her head. "I don't think so." She went into the dining room and held up a piece of paper. "I found this with the rock."

The single sentence was easily read, even from across the room—*Go back to where you came from.* Shock hit Colin in the gut at the threatening message. Someone wanted Nora gone. *Like you?* his mind argued. Guilt, hot and condemning, replaced his earlier cold. Though he would never stoop to tactics of fear or bullying, he, too, had been charged to get Nora to leave.

"Do you know who did this?" he asked, almost afraid of her answer.

"No." She folded her arms tight, the ugly note crushed in one fist. "I—I thought I was being accepted here. But I guess I was wrong."

The blatant hurt and vulnerability in her expression were too much for Colin. He gathered her to his chest and held her tight. She fit perfectly in his embrace, as if his arms were meant to hold her and no one else.

She sniffled once or twice, the only indication she'd shed a few tears, but there was no loud sobbing or hysterics. There couldn't be a braver, stronger woman anywhere else. Or one he would ever cherish holding half as much as he did Nora.

"What will you do?" he murmured after a few minutes.

She stepped back, despite his silent wish to keep her in his arms. "Fix the window again?" She brushed at her cheeks and lifted her chin. "I'm not going anywhere. This is my home now."

Colin wanted to kiss her soundly at hearing her resolve, while another part of him wanted to slink away in shame. He'd been right about one thing, though, when he'd told his father that Nora wasn't likely to give up easily.

Whoever had committed the act wanted her gone as much as his father. Could it be Sir Edward? Anger pulsed through Colin at the possibility, tensing the muscles of his neck and shoulders. He had a sudden desire to pound a fist into someone's jaw.

He'd promised his father he would help save

Elmthwaite, but he would do it on his own terms. His deadline wasn't until the end of the month—he wouldn't be pushed into securing an agreement with Nora any sooner.

"Since there'll be no walk today, I'll make you some tea," Nora offered. "You can dry out in the kitchen."

Colin trailed her down the hallway. With great effort, he swallowed his fury and guilt and took a seat at the table. No sense mulling over things he didn't know for certain yet. The minute he returned to the house, he would find out if his father was behind the act of violence against Nora.

Phoebe rose from her spot in the corner to lie against his shoe. He rubbed at the dog's ears as he tried to think of something he could do to make things up to Nora, to coax a smile back to her face.

"How would you like to go for a ride in my aeroplane?"

The sudden light in her eyes told him he'd hit upon the perfect solution for cheering her up. "Really?" she said, setting two cups and saucers on the table.

"If it isn't raining tomorrow, we'll go." It was high time he shared the thing he loved most with the woman he cared most about.

"I don't know anything about flying."

"Not to worry. Wear those trousers you did yesterday and I'll supply the hat and goggles. All you have to do is enjoy the flight."

"Sounds like a wonderful idea." She bestowed a full smile on him, the first one he'd seen since entering the cottage. The gesture warmed the room, and his heart right along with it.

* * *

Colin burst into the library where his father sat reading a book near a roaring fire. Another indication it was Sunday. Any other day of the week, Sir Edward would have been at his desk. Colin's earlier good mood, after talking with Nora for an hour or so, had quickly soured on the wet walk home as he contemplated her broken window and the malicious note.

"You look a bit drowned," Sir Edward said, glancing up as Colin stalked over to the couch.

He ignored his father's jab. "What do you know about a rock being thrown through Nor—through Miss Lewis's window last night?"

Sir Edward kept his gaze on the page in front of him. "I haven't a clue what you're talking about."

Angered by the man's indifference, Colin yanked the book from his father's grip. Sir Edward frowned but made no motion to retrieve his reading material. "Someone threw a rock through Miss Lewis's window, accompanied with a note that stated she was to go back to where she came from. I want to know if you arranged such an act."

"Of course not."

Colin might accuse his father of many things, but being a liar wasn't one of them. Now that his theory had proven false, the fury left him. He sank onto the opposite couch, his father's book still clutched in his hands. "You know nothing of this?"

Sir Edward shook his head. "I don't condone violence, Colin. Surely even you know me well enough to understand that." Something akin to hurt passed over his face before he lifted one foot and rested it on his knee in an unperturbed attitude. "I am curious to know if it worked, though. To persuade her to leave, I mean."

Colin strangled the book between his hands, his frustration mounting anew. "No, it did not. She's more determined than ever to stay."

"Ah, well, then we're back to your convincing her to leave, aren't we?" Sir Edward reached over, plucked the book from Colin's fingers, and settled back against the cushions.

"If it wasn't you, then who else wants her to leave?" Who would be spiteful enough, and for what reason, to do something like this to Nora? Once again, Colin had an overwhelming desire to slam a fist into the face of whoever had threatened her.

Sir Edward paused in leafing through his book. "Hopefully not someone who wants her land. If so, we might need you to secure things sooner."

"My deadline is the end of the month."

"And you will make that deadline?"

"Yes," Colin ground out, his gaze on the carpet.

"Good. With the shearing done and out of the way, the men I hired to work on the stables should be here Thursday." He hoisted his book again. "Everything's shaping up nicely, all according to plan."

According to plan? Colin fought a mirthless laugh. When it came to Nora and his feelings for her, nothing was going according to plan.

Chapter 11

To Nora's disappointment, the rain continued the next day, making a flight in Colin's aeroplane impossible. Instead he and Lyle came to the cottage. The three of them listened to the old gramophone and swapped stories.

The following day, while free of rain, saw the valley covered over in mist and low clouds. Colin still came with Perseus for their usual walk. But instead of circumventing the lake, he invited her to see the gardens at Elmthwaite Hall.

Nora hadn't been to the great house since her first day in Larksbeck, though she'd viewed the imposing structure from a distance plenty of times. The closer they drew to its stone walls, the more the turrets seemed to scrape the sky.

"How many rooms are there in Elmthwaite Hall?" she asked as she and Colin moved past the ornate front doors and up the drive.

"I believe there are fifty."

Nora laughed. "You believe?"

"At one point Christian and I counted them, but I can't recall the exact number." He threw her a rueful look. "It's really a small estate compared to most."

She sniffed in amusement. A dozen cottages, like hers, could easily fit inside the impressive hall, small or not.

Colin led her through a gate into a large walled garden. Neatly trimmed hedges, trees, bushes, and gravel paths stood in perfect symmetry across the expansive space. Here and there stone benches provided a place to sit and enjoy the beauty. Even in the misty afternoon, the greenery and splashes of color made Nora sigh with awe.

"It's gorgeous," she murmured.

A proud smile lit Colin's face. "I've always thought so. Of course, this is only one of three gardens."

"Are they all this enormous?" Nora crossed to a nearby flowering bush and bent to smell the blooms.

"No, this is the largest. If you don't count the grounds on the other side of the house, off the music room."

She wandered down one of the paths, her eyes drinking in the lush foliage. This was where she'd spend most of her time if she lived here. A flush filled her cheeks when she realized what she'd thought. Of course she'd never live here. Perhaps in fairy tales the sheep girl married the prince and came to live in the castle, but her life was far from being a fairy tale.

Colin allowed her to explore at her own pace, content it seemed to stroll behind her, answering as many of her questions about the different plants and flowers as he could. After some time, the clouds finally spilled their moisture. Within minutes the drizzle turned to drops.

"Come here," he called to her. "I want to show you something and it'll get us out of the rain."

Nora ran after him toward the opposite side of the garden. Colin stopped beside the wall. A room had been built into the stone. Three steps led up to the enclosure, with knee-high ledges on either side. The front stood open to the garden, while the other three walls were made entirely of rock. The roof appeared to be wood and thatch.

Colin helped her up the wet steps and into the room. It couldn't be wider than ten feet or deeper than five feet, but the place was surprisingly dry.

"What's this?" Nora looked around as she folded her arms over a sudden chill.

"It's a shelter from the elements," Colin said with a wave of his hand. "But as a boy, this used to be my sanctuary, my hiding place."

"Who were you hiding from?"

Instead of prompting a smile, Colin pocketed his hands at her question and shrugged. "From the world, mostly." He kicked at a loose piece of stone, sending it skipping across the floor. "If I lay down on my stomach, behind one of those ledges, no one could see me. I'd pick holes into the stones there. Of course, Christian would eventually find me. Or sometimes my mother."

"And your father?" she asked gently.

Colin's face hardened a bit as he shook his head. "No. Never my father."

This wasn't a story he'd shared with her and Lyle yesterday. Her heart squeezed at the thought of a young Colin lying on the cold floor, angry or hurting, as he chipped away at the stones in front of his nose. While he might have grown up with every privilege and comfort, his life hadn't been free of sorrow or pain.

Colin leaned his shoulder against the nearest wall, his face turned toward the watery garden beyond their shelter. "He wasn't always like he is now." Nora wondered if he meant the words more for himself than for her. "There were times, especially at the house in Scotland, when he would laugh or smile."

Nora couldn't keep the wonder from her voice when she asked, "You have a house in Scotland, too?" She went to stand beside him.

Colin chuckled. "Yes, but it's not nearly as large as Elmthwaite Hall. Only thirty rooms there."

"Is that all? How primeval."

His laughed deepened, as she'd hoped. "It's called Brideshall, named by William Ashby, who built it for his Scottish wife in the late seventeen hundreds. Every summer we'd ride the train there and stay for two or three months." He twisted to rest his back against the nearby wall. "The estate is on an island in the middle of the loch. The ideal spot for two boys to explore and play."

"Aren't you going there this summer?"

Some of the merriment left his dark eyes and he glanced away. "No . . . not this year."

Nora tried to interpret the tension behind his words. "Because of Christian?"

"Largely, yes." He gave no further explanation, and she chose not to ask for it.

"Does the house sit vacant the rest of the year?"

Colin nodded. "The staff would go ahead of us and prepare things, then a few of them would linger behind to close it all up again." A slight smile lifted his mouth.

"There were many times I tried to hide as we were ready-
ing to leave, hoping I'd get left behind for a little longer,
too."

Nora laughed softly. "I don't blame you. There's a certain peace that comes when you're living by a lake." She
gazed out at the rain, but she caught the appraising look
Colin threw her way.

"I hadn't thought of it that way, but you're right. Lyle
said something similar the other night."

"He's a good man."

"Yes." He straightened off the wall, bringing his arm
to rest against hers, his face forward. Even the light touch
set Nora's pulse skipping. "I think it's been very good for
him to be here. I just wish I knew what more I could do
to help him." Colin ran a hand over his face. "I'd like to
help others like him, too, but I don't know what I'd do."

Admiration for him warmed her heart, but a blast of
wet air set her shivering. Nora crossed her arms, wishing
she'd worn more than her thin sweater. Without a word,
Colin removed his jacket and set it around her shoulders.

"Thank you." She gripped the garment with both
hands, liking the way it smelled of him. "You'll figure
something out, I'm sure. Wanting to help other soldiers is
a worthy endeavor. God will help you."

A moment of quiet followed her words. "Do you ever
lose faith, Nora?"

She glanced up to find those dark eyes intently watching her. "It's all I have left," she half whispered, looking
back toward the garden.

"It's not all you have."

His low voice beside her ear resurrected her stuttering
heartbeat. He stood so close she could feel his warmth

through his jacket. His breath fanned her hair. Could he hear the pounding of her pulse? Every nerve was attuned to his nearness, every thought to the wonder of this man beside her. If she twisted slightly and lifted her chin, she knew she'd find his lips waiting for hers.

The desire to kiss him filled her from head to toe as they stood there, breathing in and out together. She turned her head and tipped it upward. In an instant his hands were cupping her face.

"Nora," he murmured.

"There you are." Lyle's voice broke over them like the clamoring of bells.

Nora jumped back, her face hot.

Lyle stopped at the bottom of the steps. "I've been looking all over for you two."

Recovering her composure, Nora glanced ruefully at Colin. "Apparently Lyle can be added to the list of those who can find you here."

"What is she talking about, Ashby?" Lyle's brow scrunched in confusion.

Colin laughed and shook his head. "Nothing, Lyle. We were only waiting out the rain."

"Well, it's stopped," his friend said, lifting a dry hand into the air as proof.

"Then we'll continue our exploration of the garden." He moved down the stairs and held his hand out to Nora. "Allow me, fair lady."

She eagerly pressed her fingers into his palm and descended the steps. Even when her feet touched the gravel, though, Colin didn't release her hand or ask for his jacket back. Instead he led her, fingers twined through his, down the path after Lyle.

* * *

Finally, midweek, Colin woke to a clear sky. He couldn't remember the last time he'd seen such a cloudless blue overhead.

He donned his flying clothes before sending word, by way of one of Mr. Green's young boys, that Nora should meet him at Elmthwaite Hall in an hour. Anticipation made him antsy. His foot kept up a steady tapping during breakfast and he couldn't concentrate on the conversation with Lyle.

"If I didn't know better," his friend said at the end of the meal, "you are anxious to have Nora to yourself this morning."

"You're right." Colin grinned as he tossed down his napkin and stood. "Now if you'll excuse me, Lyle."

He could hear Lyle chuckling as he exited the dining hall. After gathering his gloves and an extra hat, scarf, and goggles for Nora, Colin made his way outside. Davies, their chauffer, stood beside the biplane, waiting to help Colin start the engine.

Colin greeted the man, then ran his hand along the hardened cloth surface of the plane. The thought of being up in the air, far away from anyone or anything, never failed to lift his spirits. And today, he'd get to share that experience with Nora.

Once he made sure the front cockpit where Nora would sit was free of dirt and clutter, he stowed the helmets, scarves, and goggles on the seat. Then he climbed into the rear cockpit. A feeling of peace and excitement settled over him, as it did each time he prepared for flight. Like a worn-weary traveler who knew he'd find respite around the next bend, Colin found all the pressures and pretenses couldn't touch him when he was in his biplane. Here, he was home.

He flipped the switches to *off* and called to Davies, "Contact."

"Contact," the man echoed as he handed the propeller.

Colin switched everything to *on* and waited for the rumble of the engine. Except nothing happened—the plane sat silent.

"Give it another yank," he said to Davies.

The man obeyed, but again, the engine remained lifeless. Colin released an audible groan. Why today of all days did he have to run into trouble? He'd been looking forward to taking Nora flying and, as Lyle had unsubtly hinted at breakfast, spending more time alone with her.

Having ensured he had enough fuel last night for a long flight, Colin decided the problem must lie with the engine. He scrambled out of the cockpit, off the wing, and around to the front of the biplane. Davies came up behind him. Colin studied the engine, but for all his boasting to Nora about understanding machines, he couldn't isolate the problem.

"Any ideas?" Colin asked the chauffeur.

Davies shrugged and stepped back. "Sorry, Mr. Ashby. Automobiles are my expertise, not aeroplanes."

"Having trouble?"

Colin turned to find Lyle coming across the lawn. "She won't start, and I can't figure out why. I've never had that problem before."

Lyle shuffled forward. "Let me take a look."

Colin didn't suspect Lyle knew any more about planes than he did, but sheer desperation made him step aside. With another muttered apology, Davies returned to the house. Colin paced away from the biplane, his gaze on the road. Any minute now Nora would come walking up. He shoved his hands into his pockets and kicked at a clump of grass.

After more frantic pacing, and much watching of Lyle at the engine, Colin came to a stop, his eyes trained on the ground. Words rose unbidden into his mind, but they weren't entirely unfamiliar.

Please let this work out, Lord, according to Your will.

He might have scoffed at attending church or showing an outer belief in God through the years, but he'd repeated this same prayer in his mind every time he climbed into his biplane during the war—up until the day Christian had been killed. Only then did the daily petition to Heaven cease.

Colin lifted his gaze to see Nora starting across the grass toward him. He'd have to tell her their ride must be postponed—again. Then a roar filled his ears. He jerked around to see the propeller spinning and Lyle standing nearby, a wide grin on his face. Colin couldn't recall the last time he'd seen his friend that happy. Clearly Lyle had more talents than others gave him credit for.

He jogged over to Lyle. "How'd you get it to start?" Colin said loudly.

His friend shook his head. "I'll tell you later," Lyle shouted back. "You two climb in. I'll get the wheel chocks."

Lyle had saved their outing. There must be something Colin could do for him in return. His friend's quick fix of the engine gave him an idea. Colin would have to discuss it with his father first, but if Sir Edward agreed, Lyle might have a real chance at finding purpose again.

You owe the Lord, too, a gentle voice whispered inside him. A voice he hadn't heard in a long time. It both scared and pleased him. Colin offered a silent expression of gratitude for Lyle's help, then he waved Nora toward the biplane. It was time to fly.

* * *

Nora's stomach leapt into her throat as the plane rose off the ground. The acceleration pressed her to the back of her seat. Looking beyond the lower wing, she could just make out the lake sprawled below them. Mountains stood directly ahead, and she held her breath, her heart racing. Would they crash? As quickly as the rocky face loomed before them, though, it fell away as Colin expertly guided the plane over the top peaks.

She let out her breath and pulled her helmet more snuggly onto her head. The air felt cold against her cheeks but clear and exhilarating, too. She leaned over the side of the plane to see sheep scattering along the fell at their approach.

The plane leveled in the air, and Nora felt her insides return to their normal places. Any nervousness she might have felt before taking off had disappeared as quickly as the scenery they passed over. She trusted Colin and his skill as a pilot.

The world below reflected every shade of green, and the sky stretched sapphire blue above them. The plane flew over another lake and Nora craned to see their reflection in it. The scarf Colin had lent her streamed out behind her, a splash of white against the azure-colored water.

She twisted in her seat to look back at Colin. His

mouth was curved in a youthful grin. Even his leather hat and thick goggles did nothing to detract from his good looks. Nora faced forward again, her stomach twisting afresh with flurries of anticipation. This handsome, charming baronet-to-be desired *her* company.

His expression while flying matched the openness and joy she'd seen on his face last week when he'd sheared the sheep. Here was the real Colin Ashby, doing something he loved.

What do I love as much as Colin loves flying?

The lack of a ready answer punctured some of Nora's excitement. Did she love sheep farming? It was a question she'd asked herself numerous times since finding the rock through her window. She loved working hard and seeing the fruit of her labors, so raising sheep seemed as good a profession as any. Music was another source of great enjoyment—listening to it, singing to it. But was that enough to make a full life? Sheep farming and music? Her own silent reply came quick and piercing: "No."

Nora shut her eyes. *What more would you have me discover here, God?* Was she meant to find greater love? Of life, of another man?

Not so many years ago, she'd lived life with zest. It had been one of the qualities Tom loved about her. But where were those enthusiastic feelings now? After losing Tom, then her parents six months later, she had bottled up all that passion for life and locked it away. Feeling too much, even happiness, meant opening herself up to more pain and heartache. Better to rely on God and live alone than experience the sharp grief of loss all over again.

But is it relying on God to lock away my feelings, my dreams, my passions?

The question pummeled Nora's mind as hard as the wind slapping against her face. She'd been so certain she'd turned all her difficulties over to the Lord—being on her own, moving across the world, learning to be a sheep farmer. And yet she'd failed to give up her greatest burden, the lock on her heart.

"Forgive me." She whispered the words aloud, knowing Colin wouldn't hear her over the rushing air and the noise of the plane. "I want to live life fully, not cautiously anymore."

Her eyes still closed, she let the sounds around her fade into the background. In her mind, Nora pictured the faces of Tom and her parents. Next she reached inward and pulled out all her grief, her fears, her hurt over their deaths from the darkest places of her heart. She lifted her arms outward, the wind tugging hard on her hands and zipping wildly through her fingers. She imagined releasing her pain into the air, letting it fall away from her and the plane.

Several tears slid down past her goggles and froze against her cheeks, but they were more a product of relief than regret. With her arms still outstretched, she felt as if she were flying without the aid of the plane. Emotions she'd long since buried blossomed inside her once again—elation, freedom, hope, peace. No wonder Colin treasured his time flying. Nora had never felt so alive.

She felt the plane banking to the right. Opening her eyes, Nora peered down and caught glimpses of a large castle, crumbling stone walls rising high, and green fields falling away to a river. The pictorial view from high in the air stole her breath.

She wanted to fly forever, but Colin lowered the plane

and began circling around the castle. "I thought we'd walk through it," he shouted.

Nora nodded. There was still the flight back to Larksbeck, and the closer they drew to the castle, the more she became excited at the prospect of an exploration. When was the last time she'd gone exploring, not merely walking, for the pure delight of doing so? She couldn't remember.

As the plane dipped down and bumped onto the grass near the castle, Nora felt droplets of water smack her chin. Where had the clear blue sky gone?

By the time they'd glided to a full stop, the rain was falling faster. Colin climbed out of the plane first and helped her to the ground.

"So much for the good weather." He shook his head, though he didn't appear too upset.

Nora removed her cap and goggles and turned her face toward the sky. She'd never enjoyed an hour as much as she had this last one, and a little rain couldn't dampen her spirits.

She shot Colin a full smile and returned to letting the rain wash over her unbound hair. "It's absolutely perfect."

Chapter 12

Colin couldn't agree more—the day was turning out to be perfect. He took off his cap and goggles to get a better look at Nora. She completely entranced him with her raptured expression and the way her red hair fell loose below her shoulders. Did she know how pretty she was, especially with her face upturned to the rain like that?

She did look as if she was enjoying herself. He decided to follow suit and lifted his chin to the moisture. The rain ran over his jaw and into the collar of his flying jacket. But he felt too happy to care about getting wet today. He'd seen the way Nora had stretched out her arms to the wind. She appeared to love flying as much as he did. To share the sanctuary of the skies with her had been the right thing to do.

They stood side by side a few minutes longer, until the mild downpour became a torrent of water. "We can wait it out in the castle," Colin said, grasping Nora's hand. He led her at a run across the grass and beneath the covered archway of the castle's tunnel.

Water dripped off them both, creating puddles on the stones beneath their feet. Nora wiped some from her eyes and laughed. With her hand still captured in his, Colin reached out and brushed strands of dampened hair off her forehead. She gazed up at him, her large blue-green eyes full of sincerity and...longing? Her slightly parted lips seized his attention, and he tugged her closer. Could she hear the rapid thudding of his heart over the sound of the rain?

Yesterday they'd been interrupted before he could kiss her, but today, in this moment at least, they were alone. The castle was their own private world.

Colin leaned toward her. When her eyes fell shut, he needed no further prodding—he narrowed the hairsbreadth distance between them. He skimmed his lower lip against hers, the feel of it soft and smooth beneath his touch. The whispered kiss stoked fire within him and was all the proof he needed to know her lips were more delectable than he'd imagined. He wound his fingers through the damp hair at the nape of her neck and kissed her fully on the mouth.

It was as if he were soaring in his plane again. The euphoria and vibrancy of kissing Nora was the same as flying. Colin wanted it to last forever, to give in to the passion stirring between them, but he reminded himself he was still a gentleman.

Exerting great willpower, he stepped back. Nora opened her eyes and blinked as if startled from a dream. Colin bit back a smile—she'd enjoyed the kiss as much as he had.

"Come on," he said, pulling her gently after him. "I'll show you the castle."

He guided her to the other end of the tunnel and motioned to a nearby crumbling wall. "That wall outlined the courtyard and over there you can see there used to be another tower."

"Who did the castle belong to?"

Colin lifted her hand and satisfied himself with kissing her knuckles. "It actually belonged to a woman."

"Really?" Nora gave him a playful smile. "A sheep heiress like me?"

"Well...no." He laughed and she joined him. "A woman named Lady Anne Clifford eventually came into possession of this place, though it wasn't hers at first. She was meant to inherit all the Clifford properties upon her father's death, which was quite unheard of, even in the seventeenth century."

"What happened?"

Colin rested his back against the cool stones of the tunnel. "Apparently the properties went to an uncle instead, so Lady Anne Clifford spent a good portion of her life regaining them. She restored Brougham Castle here, and this is where she died. In the room where her father had been born."

Nora leaned into his chest, and he was only too happy to place his arms around her. "I like that story."

"I thought you might." He placed his chin on top of her hair, relishing the chance to hold her. Together they watched the rain from the dryness of the tunnel.

If only they could stay like this, Colin mused, without having to return to Larksbeck and all of the expectations and demands required of them both.

When the rain lessened, he straightened from the tunnel wall. "Do you want to see the view from the top?"

"Very much. Can we get up there?"

Nodding, he led her back the way they'd come to a winding staircase that would take them to the top of the ruins. The stairs were slick from the rain, so Colin kept a firm hold on Nora's hand and navigated them slowly to be sure she could easily follow.

When they reached the third floor, Colin guided her a few feet from the stairs before stopping. The view from here was one of his favorites, with the fields and trees spreading out like a carpet before him and the River Eamont lolling along a stone's throw away. Overlooking such beauty, his arms around Nora, Colin felt like a king himself, with his queen at his side.

"It's breathtaking," Nora murmured, her head turning from one side to the other to take in the scenery. "I thought Larksbeck was gorgeous, but this is almost…"

"Unreal," he supplied.

She nodded in agreement.

Much like you, he wanted to say.

How had he ever enjoyed life before Nora came along? How would he survive if he was successful in convincing her to leave? His father's pleas and Christian's entreaty to save Elmthwaite echoed in his head, but Colin fought them back. Why must he choose? His family's three-hundred-year-old estate for the woman he was beginning to love. Wasn't there a way to have them both?

Nora leaned her head back against his shoulder and released a sigh that resonated with pure contentment. "Thank you, Colin. Not just for taking me flying, but for bringing me here. I've not had such a wonderful day…"

Her voice broke. She cleared her throat to finish, "In a very long time."

The urge to kiss her once more filled him to distraction. He freed one arm and gently twisted her to face him. Tipping her chin upward, he pressed his lips to hers. The kiss lasted only a few moments, but it was long enough for Colin to decide he would fight to keep Nora here. Somehow, someway, he would figure out how to save the estate by the end of the month and still keep the affection of this woman he admired more than anyone in the world.

* * *

Humming to herself, Nora strolled down the road from Elmthwaite Hall to her cottage. She held the ends of the white scarf draped around her neck, which Colin had told her she could keep. She wanted to fly again, see the beautiful castle again.

Kiss Colin again.

Her cheeks flushed at the memory, but she couldn't help the broad smile that lifted the same lips he'd explored earlier. How many times had she contemplated kissing him? Yet even her imaginings had paled in comparison to the real thing, to how cherished she felt in his arms.

Her elation did come at a price, though. Almost at once, after that first kiss, she'd been assailed by dragons of doubt and guilt over kissing another man—and a wealthy, titled one at that. But Nora had refused to give in to the fear. Things would work out somehow.

If she ignored the incident last week with the rock, she could honestly say her life here in England was every bit as fulfilling and happy as the one she'd left behind in Iowa. Even more so, she had to admit, as she recalled standing on the castle tower, wrapped in Colin's strong embrace.

The past was the past, including the isolated threat against her. Perhaps it had simply been a mean joke. From someone jealous of her acceptance into the community or her success on the sheep farm.

She calculated the amount of money she'd received from the shearing and what she thought she could get when she sold her male lambs. While the total sum wouldn't put her anywhere near the Ashbys' social ranking, she figured she'd have enough to do some updating inside the cottage and put away a little in savings. Not bad for her first few months as a sheep farmer.

Nora switched from humming to singing as she walked up the lane to the cottage. She'd tied Phoebe out front today. The puppy began tugging on her rope the moment she caught sight of Nora.

"How was your morning, Phoebe?" She untied the dog and sat down to allow Phoebe to shower her with affectionate licks. "And my morning, you ask? It was absolutely wonderful. I flew in an aeroplane and..." she whispered into the puppy's ear, "kissed Colin. Twice."

The dog jumped from her lap and proceeded to wrestle with one of her shoes. Nora laughed and shook the puppy off. "Yes, we'll play in a bit. But first I need to see about those nasty weeds in the garden."

She climbed to her feet and headed to the back of the cottage, Phoebe running beside her. Thoughts of the garden brought back the memory of Colin covered in dirt from their fight. She chuckled softly. How she prized his friendship, his company, his attention. Could they make something more work between them, him as a baronet-to-be and her a lowly sheep farmer?

Eleanor hadn't been able to. Nora had read the night before how things had been forced to an end between Eleanor and E. When he'd returned after four months in London, E was different. While Eleanor still sensed he loved her, something in their relationship had changed. A few weeks later, he came to see her and confessed his father had learned of their secret two-year courtship. The man refused to condone a marriage between E and Eleanor.

Unwilling to go against his father's wishes, E bade Eleanor good-bye. Occasionally they saw each other at village functions, but they never acknowledged each other publicly or met alone on the fell again. A year later, Eleanor learned he'd married a wealthy young lady from Manchester.

Nora sighed as she came around the cottage and approached the garden. Poor Eleanor. Her heart had been broken. Nora certainly hoped to escape the same fate.

Now to the weeds. She went to the garden but stopped short of kneeling beside the plot. A horrified gasp escaped her throat at the sight before her. Nora covered her mouth with her hand. The garden had been completely destroyed, weeds and all. Not a single plant stuck proudly out of the soil anymore. Everything had been trampled or ripped up and tossed haphazardly aside.

Phoebe sniffed at the mess and barked. Nora sank to her knees in the grass. Had the rain and mud been the culprits? But she knew better. There in the dirt in front of her, still fresh, she saw the imprint of a boot sole. Someone had deliberately wreaked havoc here, just as he or she had done the week before with the window.

The rock and note hadn't been the end of it. If it was a mean prank, it wasn't over yet. Nora wrapped her arms around her middle as the breeze buffeted her. The day no longer felt inviting and cheerful, but cold and dark. Someone still wanted her gone.

* * *

The murmur of voices outside his window woke Colin the next morning. The clock on the mantel read ten minutes to seven o'clock. He climbed out of bed and went to pull aside the curtains. On the drive below, Sir Edward, already dressed for the day, was conversing with several farmers. Two of them held a ladder and a third had a tool box in either hand. As Colin watched, his father directed the men around the house and out of sight. Apparently the stable project began today.

Colin returned to his bed and shut his eyes, but sleep had already fled. Sitting up, he let his gaze wander over the lavish furnishings of his room. They reminded him of the old château in France where he, Christian, Lyle, and some of the other RFC pilots had lived. Unlike his life now, though, his days during the war had been filled with purpose and work.

Another glance at the clock confirmed it was still too early to go see Nora, as much as he wanted to after yesterday's shared flight to the castle. Colin propped his hands behind his head and grinned at the recollection of kissing her. What to do until he could go visit Nora? He thought of the sheep he'd sheared last week and the feeling of satisfaction the task had given him. They didn't own many sheep anymore, but what about the stables? He could help with the renovation project, especially if he slipped in after his father had finished giving the men their instructions.

Throwing off the blankets a second time, he went to the wardrobe, though he decided not to ring for Gibson. His valet would likely turn up his nose at the clothes Colin planned to wear today. He sifted through the wardrobe's contents until he found the well-used trousers and shirt he used to wear when he went hunting with Christian. Though the pant legs were an inch or two shorter now, Colin figured they'd do. He pulled on his flying boots and slipped downstairs. After snagging an apple from the dining room, he headed to the stables, eating as he walked.

The long, two-story building behind the house had been capable of handling up to fifty horses at once. Over time, though, the family's equestrian stock had dwindled to half a dozen and these were now housed in the barn. For years, the stables had sat empty.

Today all the doors had been thrown open. As Colin approached, he could see the farmers inside. He recognized Jack Tuttle, and a self-satisfied smile spread across his face. Maybe it was time to give Jack a taste of his own medicine. The young man might be the wrestling and shearing champion of Larksbeck, but Colin was no weakling when it came to hard work. He might not be as agile and strong as he'd been at the height of the war, but most mornings he still performed the same exercise regimen he'd done every day in France.

"Morning, gentlemen," he called out as he entered the

stables. He took a final bite of his apple and tossed it into a nearby rubbish barrel.

All three glanced in surprise at Colin, though Jack's expression soon became a scowl.

"Mr. Ashby," the oldest of the three, a Mr. Sodry, said with a tug on his cap. Colin remembered seeing him and the other fellow, Mr. Cripe, at the shearing at Nora's and at church.

"What are you tearing down first?" He eyed the rows of horse stalls. "I'm here to help, if you'll have me," he added as they continued to gawk at him.

"We don't need any help from the likes of—" Mr. Sodry held up a hand to stop Jack's protest.

The older man fixed Colin with a respectful gaze. "If you've a mind to help, we'd be glad for the extra hands. Though I can't say we're partial to splittin' our wages with you." He winked at Colin.

Colin chuckled. "My services are free for the day."

Jack muttered something inaudible, but Mr. Sodry grinned and rubbed his hands together. "Right-o, then. Since there'll be four of us, Mr. Ashby and I will take this side, and Cripe, you and Jack, can start at the other end."

"Shall we race then?" Mr. Cripe asked, his brows lifted in amused challenge.

"What say you, Mr. Ashby?" Mr. Sodry turned to look at him. "Up for a little competition?"

Making sure to keep his eyes trained on Jack, Colin nodded. "A pint of ale to the winners? My treat."

"Done." Mr. Sodry hoisted one of the tool boxes and motioned for Colin to follow him. "The one with the most stalls demolished by lunch is the winner," he threw over his shoulder.

Colin hurried after the man. He'd brought along his flight gloves, which he removed from his pocket and put on. Mr. Sodry slapped a hammer into his palm and directed him to tackle the part of the stall that butted against the back wall of the stables.

The building soon filled with the sound of metal striking wood. Most of the boards had weathered, which meant a few strikes with the hammer or a good firm jerk with the hand released them from the places they'd stood for at least a hundred years. Colin tossed the soft boards into a pile, noting Mr. Sodry was working as quickly as himself.

They worked in silence, which suited Colin. As he hacked and ripped at the old stalls, he recalled the many times he and Christian had played hide-and-seek in here as children. Those had been happy times. He'd idolized Christian, and in turn, his older brother had looked out for him. They'd both known from early on that Christian would be baronet and a good one at that—he had the seriousness and aptitude to run the estate.

"What about you, Colin? What would you do if you could be baronet?" Christian had asked him one day when they were children.

"I'd buy a pony for every child in the village!"

Christian laughed, reminding Colin too much of their father.

"Aren't you supposed to help others as baronet?" he argued hotly. "Father's always going on about your responsibility to other people."

His brother instantly sobered at the reminder. "You're right." He reached over and mussed Colin's hair—something he knew Colin hated. "I think you would make a good baronet, little brother."

Colin paused to stare at the hammer in his hand. He'd
forgotten about that conversation, until now. Did Christian still think he'd make a good baronet? As his eight-
year-old self had emphatically stated, being baronet was
more than running the estate; it was about helping others.
Was there more he could do in his position to better the
lives of those around him? Perhaps even those who lived
beyond Larksbeck, such as ex-soldiers like him and Lyle.
It was new train of thought, a way of looking at the in-
evitable passing of the title of baronet to him in a more
positive light.

"Hurry, lad." Mr. Sodry pushed his cap up. "I think
we're in the lead."

Colin glanced at Jack and Mr. Cripe. Sure enough,
they appeared to have only demolished two stalls to his
and Mr. Sodry's three. A feeling of gratification broke
over Colin.

Who's the champion now? he thought with a grin as he
wrestled the next set of boards.

One thing was certain. He wouldn't wile away his
time at a desk when he was baronet. He much preferred
being out among the villagers, like this, working alongside them.

When they'd finished taking out the present stall, he
and Mr. Sodry started in on the next. Sweat ran down
Colin's neck and forehead, soaking his collar and the
back of his shirt. Good thing he'd worn old clothes. Gibson would skin him alive if he'd attempted to work in one
of his regular suits.

He stopped only once, long enough to take a swig of
the water Mr. Sodry had brought in a stone jug. The liquid
tasted delicious. Colin wiped the moisture from his lips

and thought of Nora. Had he missed their typical time to go for a walk? Hopefully she'd understand. He sensed she liked and admired his willingness to try his hand at farm tasks.

Mr. Green arrived sometime later, and although clearly stunned to find Colin among the workers, he praised both teams for their efforts and volunteered to be the one to call the competition at noon. Tiring of his own thoughts, Colin asked Mr. Sodry about his farm and family. To his surprise, he learned the man had lost two sons to the war. Mr. Sodry had also been sheep farming for more than twenty-five years and claimed to have married the prettiest girl in all of the Lake District. He, in turn, asked Colin about his biplane, and even expressed a desire to ride in it.

Colin agreed to take him someday soon. It was high time he shared the heady experience of flight with others, though he was secretly glad Nora had been his first passenger.

Mr. Green removed a watch from his shirt pocket. "Fifteen minutes, gentlemen."

"Let's make it a strong win," Mr. Sodry said to Colin as they started in on the next stall.

He nodded and attacked the rotting boards with renewed energy. The stall was no match for him and Mr. Sodry. By the time Mr. Green counted down the seconds to twelve o'clock, Colin tossed the last of the boards into the giant pile on their side of the stables.

"Mr. Sodry and Mr. Ashby win," Mr. Green declared. He gave both men a congratulatory handshake.

Jack and Mr. Cripe wandered over, their faces looking every bit as red and dirty as Colin's felt. "Good work, young man." Mr. Cripe shook Colin's hand. Jack merely dipped his head in acknowledgment, without meeting Colin's gaze.

No matter. Despite being sticky with sweat, his clothes covered in dirt and loose bits of hay, Colin felt prouder of his work than he did besting Jack. "What do you say to pints for all of us?"

Someone stepped into the barn behind him. The men immediately removed their hats. "Miss Lewis," Mr. Sodry said with a nod.

Still euphoric from what he'd accomplished, Colin turned, lifted Nora off her feet, and swung her around. "I missed you," he murmured before setting her down. Her cheeks flushed with what he guessed must be embarrassment, but her eyes glowed with momentary pleasure. Conscious they were being watched, by his father's land agent no less, Colin led her from the stable and around the building.

"What were you doing in there?" she asked when he stopped.

Colin pressed his forehead to hers. "Sweating mostly, but we're tearing down the stalls to make room…" He paused, not sure how much of his father's plan to share. "My father wants to use the building for something else." He eased back and rubbed her cheek with his knuckles. "I lost track of time, but we can still go on our walk, once I take these fellows to the pub and—"

"Someone destroyed my garden yesterday, Colin." Nora lowered her gaze to the ground.

Concern rippled through him. "You sure it was deliberate?"

She nodded. "I found a boot print and a good portion

of the plants had been torn up, not washed away from the rain or mud."

Colin tightened his jaw, anger following quickly on the heels of his unease. Whoever wanted Nora gone wasn't finished with the threats.

"I don't know what to do." Nora lifted her eyes to his. "I've already taken to locking the doors, but I can't prevent things from happening outside the cottage."

"This has to stop." Colin pounded a fist against the stone wall of the stable. The shot of pain to his hand barely registered in his mind. "I promised these men a drink. But while I'm at the pub, I'll ask around. See if anyone has noticed or heard anything suspicious."

"All right." She folded her arms as if cold.

He drew her against him, certain she wouldn't mind his dirty clothes, and wrapped his arms around her. "We'll figure this out, Nora."

"They can't scare me away," she murmured. "I'm here in Larksbeck to stay."

Resting his chin on her hair, he hoped with all his heart her statement would prove true. Time was running out to find a solution that satisfied both his father and his own heart—but he was praying he'd find one.

Chapter 13

Can't sleep either, girl?"

Nora twisted onto her side and stroked Phoebe's fur. The puppy had been restless, starting the night on the bed, then moving to the floor, and finally returning to the bed.

Rolling onto her back, Nora stared up through the darkness at the ceiling. How could one day be so different from another? Yesterday, she'd felt alive, accepted, happy. Tonight she felt wary and tired. Colin's inquiries at the pub hadn't turned up any information. She wished he'd been able to talk to Jack, but he'd refused to go with the others. Nora would have to remember to ask him later if he'd heard anything suspicious.

She draped her arm across her forehead and shut her eyes, willing sleep to come. It wasn't that she felt unsafe. The doors were locked, and neither act of violence had been life-threatening in any way. But Nora couldn't rid herself of the unsettling feeling of being watched and disliked. Which made sleep nearly impossible.

With a sigh, she sat up. Phoebe lifted her head in question. "I'm going to read," Nora explained.

She lit the lamp beside her bed and picked up Eleanor's diary. Removing the ribbon that marked her place, Nora scooted back beneath the covers. She would never have suspected a journal to be so riveting, but she found herself caught up in the details of Eleanor's life.

After E married, the young woman had remained some time without a beau, though she did mention exchanging letters with Matthew Galbert, the farmer and fiddler. Apparently the young man had some sort of illness that often confined him to bed, so he greatly appreciated Eleanor's letters. When they did see each other at village functions, he often accompanied her singing on his fiddle. The people of Larksbeck loved the musical duo and would request their performance for holidays.

While Nora knew the two would eventually marry, since Eleanor's last name had changed from Lewis to Galbert, she still found the story of their courtship interesting. Especially knowing E had been Eleanor's first love.

After locating the last entry she'd read before bed, Nora began reading again. Eleanor wrote of a growing affection for Matthew—from friendship to something more. Nora could relate. She was beginning to feel the same way toward Colin.

She couldn't help smiling as she read about Matthew finally asking for Eleanor's hand in marriage and her acceptance. But Eleanor's next words made her pause.

*Some may wonder if I regret falling in love with an-
other before I met Matthew. But I would answer:
never. Loving E allowed me to recognize love when
it presented itself a second time and made me more
determined than ever to overcome the challenges. If
anything, my love for Matthew is stronger because
of all I've experienced.*

Nora read the words through twice, her finger skim-
ming the worn handwriting. She'd loved Tom with all her
heart and had yearned for a future together, before that
dream had been broken. Did that mean she could never
love another man as strongly? Eleanor certainly didn't
think so.

The next few entries were about Eleanor and
Matthew's wedding plans and the day itself. After a short
trip to Scotland, the pair moved in with Eleanor's father.
The dates at the top of the pages grew farther apart as
Eleanor settled into her new life. She mentioned moments
of great happiness as well as moments of great struggle
over Matthew's health. Two years into their marriage,
Eleanor became pregnant and several entries expressed
her delight at the prospect of being a mother.

Then Matthew lost his fight against the illness that had
plagued him most of his life. Tears dripped off Nora's
chin onto the page as she read Eleanor's entry of the
event, written a month after Matthew's death.

*I thought I knew love when I loved E, but I see now
that was more a girlish fancy. I thought I knew love
when I married Matthew, but I was wrong then, too.
Holding my beloved's hand as he crossed from this*

*life to the next, I experienced true love and its infi-
nite power.*

   *Matthew's last request was about our sweet
baby's name. If a boy, he asked that I name him
Matthew. And if a girl, he asked me to give her the
shortened version of my name—Nora.*

The book tumbled from Nora's hands to her lap. She
stared at it as if it might rear up and bite her. Her heart
thudded hard against her ribs. She'd heard Eleanor and
Matthew had a daughter who'd gone to live with relatives
as a baby after Eleanor died. But surely she would have
heard if she had a distant cousin with her exact same
name.

Goose pimples broke out along her arms and she shivered. If there was no other Nora in the family, could that
mean...? All the references she'd heard since coming to
Larksbeck about her likeness to Eleanor repeated through
her mind.

"No," she told herself firmly, shaking her head and
folding her arms tightly against her nightgown. The idea
was preposterous. Her parents had been Frank and Grace
Lewis.

She shoved the book onto the bedside table and blew
out the lamp. No more reading tonight. It was merely a
coincidence she and Eleanor's daughter shared the same
name. Perhaps the relatives had changed the girl's name
to something else—that would explain why there wasn't
another Nora in the family.

Things all around were bound to look better and more
sensible in the morning. Nora settled on her side next to
Phoebe and shut her eyes, but sleep was still long in coming.

* * *

On hands and knees the following morning, Nora wiped up the rainwater that had once again leaked through the broken window onto the floor of the dining room. It had been almost a week since she'd found the rock and note. If she didn't fix the window soon, she feared the floor beneath it would start warping.

"We're off to the village this morning, Phoebe," she announced as she went to fetch the puppy from where she'd tied her outside earlier. Phoebe jumped and barked in anticipation as if she understood the outing in store.

Nora untied the dog and allowed her gaze to sweep for a moment over her field. Something wasn't right. She studied the line of her stone walls until she located the problem. Something—or more likely, someone—had toppled several feet of the wall she and Jack had painstakingly fixed three weeks ago.

The garden two days ago and now this. Nora squeezed her eyes shut against a rising headache. At least she could fix this. The garden was another story. She wasn't sure how much she could expect to reap even if she replanted.

A feeling of despair threatened to overwhelm her. Who wanted her gone so badly? And why? Her only wish was to carve out a life for herself here. Was that so offensive to the other farmers?

She opened her eyes and blew out a long sigh. It was time to start repairing the damage that had been done. Time to show whoever wanted her gone that she wasn't leaving.

With Phoebe's leash in hand, she collected the basket Mr. Bagley had kindly given her and locked the doors. The puppy dashed as far down the lane as the rope would allow, coaxing a smile from Nora. How grateful she was for the energetic puppy. She felt less isolated with Phoebe around for company.

Of course, Colin had come to mean as much to her as Phoebe. *More so*, her heart argued. Watching him interact with the other farmers yesterday and basking in the comfort of his strong arms, she'd realized how much she'd come to rely on and cherish his presence in her life. The anticipation of seeing his playful smile, or teasing and talking with him, or feeling the touch of his hand on her face buoyed up her spirits. He had become the sun to her recently cloudy days.

Her thoughts returned to what she'd read in Eleanor's diary the night before—how Eleanor felt no regret at loving someone else before she loved Matthew. Did Nora have the courage to do the same? She'd locked her heart after Tom's death, but Colin had successfully breached the barricade. Wouldn't he be pleased to know that? A hint of a smile pulled at her lips.

The gesture soon faded to a frown, though, as other questions crowded her thoughts. If they were to marry, would Colin be willing to give up his grand house to come live on her sheep farm? Or would she be required to fit into his high-society life instead?

With no ready answers, Nora pushed the troubling queries to the back of her mind and sucked in a deep breath of clean, dew-drenched air. She would salvage the day, regardless of what had transpired with her stone wall.

She and Phoebe traversed the bridge, and Nora waved

to several of the women in the village who were busy working outdoors today. They cheerfully returned her greeting, prompting a mixture of happiness and confusion inside her. If most of the families enjoyed having her here, who didn't?

She reached Mr. Bagley's shop, but embarrassment kept her from heading straight inside. After all, she'd already ordered one windowpane from him. Would he think her careless when she announced she needed another?

There was no reason to feel ashamed, she reminded herself. She wasn't the one who'd broken the window either time. After tying Phoebe out front, she opened the door and marched into the shop.

Mr. Bagley looked up from his newspaper and smiled. "Good morning, Miss Lewis." He folded his paper and set it on the long counter. "Splendid job on your solo last Sunday." He leaned his elbows on the counter as he added, "Though I did wonder if nerves had gotten the better of you for a moment."

"For a moment," Nora admitted, "but then my courage returned."

"How about Mr. Ashby?" Mr. Bagley frowned. "Is he returning to our choir? Can't say I'd blame him if he didn't. Not after missing our performance this week."

"I promise you he had a very good excuse for not being there. His friend, Andrew Lyle, the one visiting him, was feeling poorly."

The grocer straightened, sympathy emanating from his gray-blue eyes. "Aye, then. I suppose that's a good enough reason to miss services. Now what can I do for you today?"

"I need just a few things." Nora collected some goods from around the shop and brought them to the counter. "I'd also like to order another windowpane."

Mr. Bagley arched his eyebrows. "Another? What are you doing to your windows, Miss Lewis?"

Nora forced herself to join in his good-natured laughter. "Nothing out of the ordinary, I assure you. I'm afraid an errant rock made its way through one of the panes last week."

"How did that happen?" he asked with a puzzled frown.

Not wishing to divulge more than she had to, Nora settled for sharing the simple truth. "I don't know. It might have been an innocent prank." Though the note, her ruined garden, and the toppled stone wall this morning all suggested otherwise.

Mr. Bagley's frown deepened to a scowl. "Prank or not, such a thing isn't right. I'd like to take a belt to whoever did it. And I'd be willing to bet the lad's parents would feel the same."

Nora doubted it was a child who wanted her gone. "Is there anyone who might be…" She paused for the right words. "Might be upset by my coming here and taking over Henry's place?"

"Certainly not." Mr. Bagley shook his head, a smile breaking through his grim expression. "We were right pleased to hear you might be coming. To have Eleanor's daughter home again—it was great news for all of us."

Nora's heart seemed to stop, then began beating again, twice as fast. The floor felt suddenly uneven beneath her feet. She gripped the counter to keep from swaying. Mr.

Bagley's words echoed the ones she'd tried to drown out last night as she lay awake, long after putting the diary aside.

She couldn't be Eleanor's daughter—she'd never even been to England before now. At her age, she certainly knew who her parents were and who they weren't.

Unbidden wisps of memory drifted into her mind, things Nora had wondered about over the years, questions to which her parents had only vague answers. Why they'd never had more children. Why she didn't look like either of them. Why her mother couldn't recall details of Nora's birth or those first few months of her life.

"Miss Lewis? Nora?" Mr. Bagley's voice sounded far away. "Are you all right? You look rather pale."

Nora shut her eyes a moment, to clear the confusion swirling through her head. When she opened her eyes again, she pasted on a smile. "I'm fine."

"I'll order your windowpane today," Mr. Bagley said after she'd paid for her purchases and put them into her basket. "And we'll see you Saturday at choir rehearsal."

She managed a nod before escaping the shop. Phoebe pawed at her boots as Nora untied the dog's leash. She couldn't go back to the cottage now. Not with Mr. Bagley's announcement about her being Eleanor's daughter still ringing in her ears. She had to know if it was true, and there was only one person who could confirm or refute it.

Bess.

Whatever the woman's reasons were for keeping silent, or mostly silent, about Eleanor the last two months, Nora determined she would wrestle the truth from Bess today. She would not leave the Tuttle cottage until she had the answers she needed.

Nora gently pulled Phoebe into step beside her and hurried up the road, away from Larksbeck. At her quickened pace, she reached the Tuttles' cottage in minutes. She proceeded to the back door, where she stopped to catch her breath, praying she'd catch Bess alone. After giving the door a good knock, she gathered Phoebe into her arms, along with her basket, and waited for Bess to answer.

The door opened a minute later, and Bess appeared in the doorway, a dish cloth in her hands. "Nora. Come in, come in."

Nora stepped into the warm kitchen. No one else appeared to be about. The smell of baking bread filled her nose. "Smells delicious."

"It'll be done in about ten minutes and you can have a slice." Bess moved to the sink, lifted a dish, and dried it. "Already been to the village, have you?" She nodded at the basket Nora set on one of the benches drawn up to the table.

"Yes." She took a seat and let Phoebe down onto the floor, though she kept hold of the puppy's leash.

Bess put the dish away, but she paused in her return to the sink to ask, "Are you all right, love? You look like you could use a nice cup of tea."

"Yes...I mean, no." Nora cleared her throat. Best to just come out with it. "I want to know who Eleanor is." That wasn't right either. "What I mean is I want to know who Eleanor is, to me."

Bess faced the sink, her back to Nora. Her silence stretched over several long seconds.

"Please, Bess," Nora pleaded. "You know the truth. I need to know it, too."

Heaving a sigh, Bess turned slowly. Her eyes glistened with unshed moisture, but they held Nora's. "I didn't think it my place to say, but then again, everyone else has passed on, you see." She gave a humorless chuckle.

Nora waited for Bess to continue, her heart drumming as fast as it had in Mr. Bagley's shop. Her fingernails dug deeper into the leather of Phoebe's leash.

"Eleanor Lewis Galbert was your mum, love."

Though Bess's words confirmed her suspicions, the simple declaration still pounded Nora like a rush of cold wind, tearing through the idyllic memories of her childhood. "My—my mother?"

Bess nodded. "Henry wasn't really your great-uncle. He was your grandfather." Several tears slipped down her round cheeks, but she was smiling. "I got to hold you a few hours after you were born, you know. Your hair was the same rich red as your mum's, even then."

Nora tried to imagine the scene—Bess holding her as a baby, while Eleanor and Henry looked on. But she couldn't quite visualize the faces of her real mother and grandfather.

Something damp nudged her hand. Looking down, Nora mustered half a smile for Phoebe as she rubbed the puppy's soft brown fur. "How did my..." The word *parents* didn't roll so easily off her tongue anymore. "How did Frank and Grace Lewis come to raise me? I know from Eleanor's diary she died shortly after...I was born."

"You found her diary?" Bess sat down on the bench. "I searched for it after she died, but never found it. Where was it?"

"Tucked inside a cracker tin in one of the stone walls."

Her eyes glowed with delight. "Eleanor was always clever like that."

"What about Frank and Grace?" Nora prompted.

Bess shook her head, as if casting off old memories. "Your poor grandfather was beside himself with grief over Eleanor's death. He'd lost his wife, his son-in-law, and his daughter. He loved you fiercely, he did, but he knew he couldn't care for a wee babe on his own.

"So he wrote to his brother James in America, asking what could be done. James wrote back about his son Frank and his lovely daughter-in-law who couldn't have children. Would Henry consider allowing them to rear you as their own."

Nora blew out her breath. She felt as if she were living a scene from a dream—to find out her life had begun so differently than she'd always believed. That she was different than she'd always believed.

"I remember the day your American mum and dad came here." Bess's voice sounded full of the past again. "I'd thought of taking you myself, since I'd been caring for you a great deal, but Henry said 'twas better this way. When I saw that beautiful blond woman hold you and smile, I knew he was right." She swiped at her cheeks. "Still, Henry looked mighty forlorn when they drove away with you in the wagon."

She climbed to her feet and motioned Nora up as well. "Come here, love. I've something to show you."

As though moving through a fog, Nora tied Phoebe's leash around a chair leg and followed Bess into her parlor. The woman removed a thick volume from the bookcase. She sat on the settee and patted the empty spot beside her. Nora dropped onto it. The book wasn't one for reading—it was a photo album.

"I borrowed this from Henry's cottage after he died." Bess flipped through several pages before she stopped on one. A single photo filled the page. In it a man in a suit and a woman in a white dress, holding a small bouquet of flowers, stood outside Henry's cottage. Nora peered closer. The woman's heart-shaped face and large eyes were identical to her own, though her nose more resembled the man's.

Nora ran a finger over the two faces. "I read about how they met and fell in love. How Matthew would play the fiddle and Eleanor would sing." She couldn't yet call them Father or Mother.

Bess patted her hand. "They were very much in love, those two. Your mother was devastated when your father died, but she was strong—for you. She kept his wish to call you Nora."

"And Frank and Grace agreed to do the same?"

"It was the one request your grandfather made of them."

"I wonder why they never told me."

Nora searched her memory for some hint, some chance word from her parents that might have implied her true origins, but she couldn't think of one. Not even on their death beds had her mother or father shared anything but their love for her. Of that, she had no doubt. Even if she hadn't been the natural daughter of Frank and Grace Lewis, she had not been loved any less than if she had been. The realization wrapped itself around her like a comforting blanket, soothing some of her earlier shock.

"Ah, who knows," Bess said with a lift of her plump

shoulders. "They had their reasons, I'm sure. The heart is a funny thing, love."

"And Henry? Didn't he ever wish to contact me directly?" The letters from England had always been addressed to her father, Frank Lewis, though he'd occasionally shared portions with Nora.

"Dozens of times, I imagine. But I think he felt it best to let you live your life there. He wanted you happy most of all."

Bess flipped to a different page. Nora recognized the photo of a little girl in a rocking chair. It had been on top of the piano at the farm in Iowa for as long as she could remember.

"That's me."

Bess dipped her chin. "They were kind to send it to your grandfather. They wrote every six months or so to tell him about you, though the letters stopped a few years ago."

"They died, from the influenza." Nora stared at herself in the photo and tried to imagine Henry doing the same.

"That leaves just you and us then."

You and us. A glimmer of expectancy rose inside Nora. "If Eleanor's your cousin, then Jack and the others are my..."

"Is it second cousins or third cousins once removed?" Bess laughed. "I never can remember. But no matter— you're family." She closed the album and gently pushed it onto Nora's lap. "This is yours now."

"Are you sure? I already have her diary."

Bess brushed a piece of dust from the album's cover. "Then it's only fitting you have the few photos that go with it."

On impulse, Nora leaned forward and gave the older woman a kiss on the cheek. Bess was the closest thing to an aunt Nora had ever had. "Thank you—for the photos, but even more, for telling me the truth."

A blush spread over Bess's face, but a grin graced her mouth. "You are more than welcome, love." She released a deep sigh and laughed. "It's a relief, actually, to have you knowing the truth. Don't know how many times I had to stop myself or one of the children from saying too much. They've always known about their distant cousin in America."

"Why did you wait to tell me?"

"Because I knew when the time was right, you'd come asking yourself." She stood and shooed Nora off the settee. "Time to pull that bread out of the oven, and feed you proper. You're as skinny as your mum was." With a hearty laugh, she led Nora back into the kitchen.

Once she'd eaten her fill of bread and jam, Nora bade Bess good-bye. As she and Phoebe walked past the fell and the gray-blue lake toward the cottage, she realized something looked different. The colors were sharper, and the beauty of the valley touched her soul deeper. Of course she knew the scenery hadn't really changed, but she had.

It was Nora Lewis from Iowa who'd walked down the road this morning, but it was Nora Lewis Galbert from England who walked back now. She hadn't come to live in a foreign place, after all; she'd come home. And here she wasn't alone—she had family nearby.

Home and family. The words swept through her like a gentle breeze, clearing away her earlier melancholy. If this was indeed her home, then no amount of persuasion—violent or otherwise—would induce her to leave.

I felt you wanted me here, God. Nora lifted her eyes to a patch of blue sky directly overhead. *Now I think I understand why.*

Chapter 14

Colin?" His mother's voice followed him down the corridor and halted his hurried steps. Lyle had agreed to go flying with him and Colin was looking forward to a good, long flight before supper. He needed an escape to the skies right now.

Releasing an impatient grunt, he turned back to the open doorway of his mother's sitting room. "Did you need something, Mother?"

She sat at her desk, a stack of papers near her elbow. "Come in a moment, will you?"

Colin pulled off his flying cap and stepped into the room. Had he been in here since coming home? He couldn't remember. The room hadn't changed much since his days as a youth. The blue-flowered wallpaper and light-colored furnishings were still the same—a sharp contrast to the darker hues of the rest of the house.

He felt a measure of satisfaction that the war hadn't altered everything.

He perched on the edge of one of the white chairs drawn up near the cold fireplace. "What are you working on there?"

"Invitations for the party to celebrate Elmthwaite's three-hundredth anniversary."

Colin recalled his father mentioning something about the party at breakfast that morning, but his mind had been on other things. He was still reeling from the news Nora had shared with him yesterday about her being Eleanor Galbert's daughter and about someone destroying a part of her stone walls.

His jaw tightened at the thought of further sabotage against Nora. He wished he could figure out who was behind it. A few choice words and a well-placed fist or two ought to settle the matter. The damage to her property wasn't the only reason, though, for the annoyance roiling through him. Colin didn't like the idea of Nora spending the entire day with Jack, repairing her wall, even if the young man was now her distant cousin.

"Colin? Did you hear me?"

He cleared his throat. "Yes, you were talking of the party."

His mother shook her head, her dark eyes sparkling with hidden amusement. "I asked if Lyle will still be here, to attend."

"I believe so."

"Wonderful. I've very much enjoyed his visit."

Colin leaned back in the chair and lifted one foot onto his knee. "I don't know that Father has."

"Don't worry about your father. His attention is elsewhere right now." Lady Ashby reached for what he assumed was another invitation. "How is the stable renovation going?"

"Quite well." A deep sense of fulfillment rose inside him at what he and the other men had accomplished in a few short days. Lyle had even volunteered to help. The work was hot and tiring, but Colin enjoyed every minute of it. His father, on the other hand, had objected to his son assisting the local hired help, but he hadn't forbidden Colin from continuing. Colin hoped in time to change Sir Edward's opinion about the benefits of laboring alongside the villagers.

"You like the work." She didn't phrase it as a question.

Colin fingered his leather cap. "I'd like to find something else to do when we're finished. Maybe I can fly Father's hotel guests around or something. I need to do more here than simply sit at a desk. I want to help people, feel useful." He lifted his gaze to his mother's. "What about you? Don't you miss what you did during the war?"

Lady Ashby shifted to face him, a sad sort of smile on her lovely face. "Very much. I met so many interesting people working in that canteen—soldiers like you and Christian, other wives and mothers. There were always people to talk to." She lowered her eyes toward the floor. "Those two or three days were the best part of my week."

"Then why not insist Father let you do something else?"

Her chin lifted. "My place is here, with the two of you, and I willingly accept that. Though I will be forever grateful for the experience of seeing the world beyond Elmthwaite and Larksbeck." Her probing glance made Colin suspect she wasn't talking solely of herself. Was it time he also accepted his place here, while being grateful for the things he'd learned and experienced away from the estate?

"Lady Sophia and her parents will be coming to stay a week in conjunction with the party." She bent over the stack of invitations again.

Colin didn't bother stifling a groan. "Father must be overjoyed."

"He wants you happy, Colin." Like Nora, his mother's perceptiveness was uncanny.

"I rather think being yoked to a silly, rich heiress is the antithesis of happiness."

A frown creased her brow, but she remained silent. Colin released a breath through his nose as shame replaced his irritation.

"Forgive me, Mother. I shall hope to find an heiress as genuine as you." Though he doubted it would happen. The only woman he'd met who possessed the same type of unpretentiousness as his mother was Nora, and his father certainly wouldn't classify inheriting a sheep farm as equal to being wealthy.

"He loves you," she said, her pen still, her gaze distant. "Losing Christian nearly killed him, but not for the reasons you may think. The death of a child changes you." She lifted her eyes to Colin's, the pain there evident. "He's determined to save this place because I think he believes it's the only thing of permanence in this world. Elmthwaite Hall is his lifeblood. I knew that when I married him."

"So duty must always come before love?" Colin countered in a gentle tone.

Her face paled at the implication of his words, but

she kept her head erect. "Before we married, I saw the way he prized this estate and knew he would extend that same care and respect to me. And he has, Colin. We've been happy together." She fixed him with a compassionate look. "I want the same for you, whomever you choose to marry."

Colin rose to his feet. How did she manage to make him feel both chastised and comforted at the same time? He crossed to her chair to kiss her cheek. "You are the real treasure, Mother. To both of us."

She smiled and rested her hand against his jaw. "As are you, my boy."

He started for the door but paused on the threshold. "May I invite someone to the party?"

"Certainly. Who?"

"Miss Nora Lewis. She's Henry Lewis's granddaughter."

"Ah, yes. The one you've been spending so much time with."

Colin lifted his eyebrows in silent challenge. Lady Ashby chuckled. "I don't occupy all my time indoors, Colin. I have noticed a couple who like to walk around the lake nearly every day."

A boyish grin tugged at his mouth. "Nora may come then? I can deliver her invitation myself."

Her merriment faded. "You're welcome to invite her, but do you think that's wise?"

"Of course. Why wouldn't it be?"

A flicker of something passed over her face, but Colin couldn't read the emotion. "No reason. I'm more than happy to have her join us. I've been hoping for a chance to meet her for some time now." She addressed an invitation and stood to hand it to him.

"Thank you, Mother," he said, pocketing the invite. "I'm looking forward to introducing the two of you."

He left her room and headed downstairs, a whistle on his lips. Lyle would be wondering what had taken him so long. But he wasn't sorry his mother had detained him. The idea of his father's party was no longer abhorrent— Nora would be there with him.

* * *

Nora slid the invitation across the table to Bess and took another sip from her teacup. She'd never cared much for tea back in Iowa, but living here, it had become as much a part of her day as it clearly was for the rest of the villagers. Perhaps it was her English background.

Bess lifted the invite and read it through. "You're to go to the party at Elmthwaite tonight, are you? My Mary has talked of nothing else all week. Don't know how the Ashbys' cook does it, what with the sugar ration still on, but Mary says the woman's got all manner of sweet dishes prepared."

"There's only one problem." Nora clinked her cup onto its saucer.

"You don't want to go?"

"No, that isn't it."

At least not entirely, although the idea of being in that grand house with all those wealthy, sophisticated people turned her stomach into a hive of nerves every time she thought about it.

She was very much looking forward to seeing Colin, though. They'd only been able to snatch small stretches of time together over the past two weeks, while Nora had been busy walling and selling off the male lambs with Jack's help. Jack had even repaired her window. Thankfully there'd been no more acts of vandalism to her property.

"The problem is I'm not sure what to wear," Nora admitted. "I don't own anything fancy."

"Did you have something in mind, love?"

"Let me get it." Nora stood and went upstairs to collect the dress she'd worn to Livy's wedding. She loved the soft lavender color and the silk material, but was it elegant enough for an estate's three-hundredth anniversary party?

She returned to the kitchen and held the dress up for Bess's inspection. The older woman studied the garment, her fingers testing the cloth.

"I hate to say it, but I don't think it'll do."

"It won't?" Nora sank into her chair. What was she going to do? None of her church dresses were extravagant enough. Perhaps she could procure a ride to the larger town of Keswick, but she might not find anything suitable there either.

"It's a pretty color and the silk is nice, but according to my Mary, it's the wrong style." Bess sipped her tea before continuing. "The society women coming to the party will likely be wearing the new drop-waist dresses."

"What do I do then, Bess?" Nora fiddled with one of the small pearl buttons on the bodice, desperation causing a lump in her throat. She didn't care what the other women thought of her, but if she planned to enter Colin's world tonight, she wanted to do so without embarrassing him or appearing the country bumpkin.

Bess gave her a thoughtful look over her teacup. "Are there any of your mum's things still up in the attic?"

"Yes, a whole trunk full. But those clothes will be more outdated than this one."

Climbing to her feet, Bess shooed Nora from her chair. "Never mind that, love. You go collect what's up there and we'll get to work."

Nora obeyed, though she wasn't sure what sort of plan Bess was concocting. At the moment, her dear cousin was her only hope. In the attic, she removed all the dresses and garments that had once been Eleanor's. She brought everything back downstairs to the parlor, where Bess waited with the lavender dress. Nora spread the clothes out on the settee and stepped back to let Bess peruse the pile.

"This might work, and this," Bess muttered to herself as she considered each item. Those she wanted she piled into Nora's arms, including a fur-lined cloak. "I think that's everything. So we're off then."

"Off to where?" Nora asked with a laugh.

Bess opened the front door and waved her through. Phoebe raced outside ahead of them. "Do you have a sewing machine?"

Nora shook her head.

"Then it's to my house, love."

After tying up Phoebe in the Tuttles' front yard, Nora followed Bess into the cottage, her arms still overlaid with clothes. The older woman directed Nora to use her room to change into the silk dress. All of Bess's girls, except for Mary, were home and they trooped into the parlor as Nora came out. Bess gave Nora a shrewd looking over, placing straight pins here and there as she did so.

"What are you doing?" Ellie asked from her seat on the settee. She held a doll in the crook of her arm.

"Getting ready for the Elmthwaite party tonight," Nora answered. "I think your mother is going to transform my dress."

Ellie's eyes widened. "Like Cinderella?"

Nora chuckled. "I hope so."

"Go change back, and we'll get started," Bess directed.

By the time Nora returned to the parlor, Bess had the twins hard at work, cutting and unstitching pieces of Eleanor's old garments. Nora handed over her lavender dress, and soon, Bess had the sewing machine humming.

"How are you going to do your hair?" Margaret—or Martha—asked her. Nora still couldn't tell them apart.

Nora sat beside Ellie on the settee, feeling a bit useless. She could wield a needle well enough, but not to create something as fancy as an evening gown. "I'm not sure."

Both twins studied her. "Why not wear it long with a headband in your hair?" one of them suggested.

The other nodded and looked around at the cluttered parlor. She scrambled to her feet to pick up a piece of lavender silk Bess had cut away from the dress. "We could turn this into a pretty headband." She approached Nora and carefully placed the material at the top of her forehead and tied it around her hair. "What do you think, Martha?"

"It's perfect," Martha said, clapping her hands. "I'll get a mirror so you can see, Cousin Nora."

The girl returned with a hand mirror, which she held in front of Nora. Nora eyed her reflection in the mirror. She did like how the band swept the hair back from her face but left most of it to hang long over her shoulders and back. "I think that works nicely."

Martha beamed. "We'll have Mum sew the edges."

With Bess hard at work, Nora volunteered to make lunch. Ellie helped her, keeping up a constant chatter. Jack and his brothers tromped in as Nora was setting the food on the table.

"Didn't expect you here," Jack said, removing his cap and shooting a surprised grin at Nora.

"Mum's making her dress for the royal ball. Isn't that right, Cousin Nora?"

Smiling, Nora ran a hand over Ellie's copper-colored hair. "Something like that."

"You mean the party at Elmthwaite?" Jack's expression turned sour. "You're going?"

"I've been invited, yes."

Jack plunked down into a chair and grabbed one of the plates of food. "Sounds like a waste of an evening to me."

Nora ignored his sullen remark as she called the twins and Bess to lunch. Though Bess declined, the rest of the family sat down at the table. Nora slipped onto the bench next to Ellie. After the blessing on the food, the twins struck up a conversation about what Mary had told them regarding the party and their speculations on what the other ladies might be wearing. Ellie listened, her eyes wide with fascination.

When they'd all finished, the boys spilled out the door, except for Jack. The twins went back into the parlor to help their mother, leaving Ellie to assist Nora with the dishes.

Jack paused at the back door. "You aren't going to fit in up there, Nora." His voice was as brittle as dead corn stalks.

Nora pressed her lips together. She hated the way his

words echoed the ones that had been running through her mind since Colin had given her the invitation.

"You're not like them—and you never will be. Just like the rest of us." He jammed his cap on his head. "You're fooling yourself if you think they're going to accept you as one of them."

She whirled away from the sink, an angry retort on her tongue, but he left before she got out a single word. In silence, she finished washing the dishes. Was Jack right? Was she simply fooling herself into thinking she would be accepted by Colin's family, simply because he accepted her? The nervousness in her stomach returned, making her wish she'd skipped lunch.

A tug on her arm pulled her attention back to Ellie. "Don't listen, Nora," she said with wisdom well beyond her five years. "He's only mad 'cause we've never got invited to the big house."

Nora crouched down and gave the young girl a hug. "Should we go see how the dress is coming along?"

Ellie threw her dish towel onto the table and grabbed Nora's hand. Bess glanced up as they entered the parlor. "Give me another hour, love, and I'll have her done."

The twins soon wandered outside, but Ellie chose to stay with Nora. She read the little girl a book to pass the time while they waited for Bess to finish. Before long, Ellie's eyes closed and her head found its way onto Nora's lap.

Nora watched the child sleep, her small chest rising and falling with gentle breaths. Having never experienced life with siblings, she'd always envied Tom's large family. She brushed an errant red curl off the girl's forehead, and a motherly longing she hadn't felt since holding Livy's baby daughter wrenched her heart.

She and Tom had talked about having lots of children after they married. Was it possible that she might still be a mother one day? She'd told herself for so long she was content to live the rest of her life alone, but now Nora recognized it as a lie.

Deep down, where she'd buried most of her dreams until recently, she still longed for love with a husband and children. Was it silly, as Jack had said, for her to hope she might find that with Colin? There were so many moments when it seemed possible—when they'd gone flying, or when he'd sheared the sheep and worked on the stables, or when they walked around the lake. But tonight she would see a part of his world, a part of him, she hadn't before.

"Ready to try it on, love?" Bess's question broke through Nora's troubled thoughts and woke Ellie. Sitting up, the girl yawned and stretched.

"Go on and use my room again to change," Bess instructed.

Nora stood and accepted the dress without examining it too closely. She wanted her first proper look to be alone, with the dress on. Her heart hammered with both dread and hope as she went into Bess's room and closed the door. She shed her work dress and slipped the lavender silk over her shoulders. Once she had the dress in place, she turned and faced the bureau mirror. Her breath caught in her throat at the vision before her.

Bess had completely transformed the dress. While she'd kept most of the lavender silk intact, she'd added a lace and bead overlay of ivory to the short sleeves and bodice, which now fell loosely to a lower waistline. A swath of fur ran from the back of the dress to right below Nora's knees in a V shape that revealed the lavender-colored underskirt. The whole ensemble made for a luxurious evening dress.

A soft knock sounded at the door. "Come in," Nora called.

Bess appeared in the doorway, a smile gracing her round face. "Well?"

"It's absolutely gorgeous, Bess." Nora did a little spin. "I can't believe it's the same dress."

Ellie squeezed past her mother. "You look like a princess, Cousin Nora."

"I feel like one."

Bess disappeared for a moment, then returned with the lavender headband the twins had suggested. The sides were evenly hemmed now. Nora positioned it onto her forehead and tied the band of material around her hair. "What do you think?"

Bess's eyes glimmered with tears. "You're the picture of your mum. She'd be right proud."

Fighting tears herself, Nora embraced Bess. "Thank you, Bess. You truly are a wonder."

The woman waved away the compliment, but her eyes glowed with pleasure. "We'll let you change back now, so you can carry it home." She guided Ellie from the room and shut the door behind them.

Nora studied herself in the mirror once more. She might not be a rich heiress, but dressed in her new gown, her confidence returned. Whatever happened tonight, she would keep her chin up and be proud of where she came from. She wasn't wealthy or from high society—she was the daughter of Eleanor and Matthew Galbert of England, and Frank and Grace Lewis of Iowa. And that was exactly who she wanted to be.

Chapter 15

Colin stretched his shoulders in a vain attempt to loosen his tailcoat. His eyes swept the music room, now crowded with guests for Elmthwaite's three-hundredth anniversary party. A band played music in one corner and the notes mingled with the hum of conversation.

"Colin, may I introduce the Lord and Lady..."

He shook hands with the white-haired man and his fierce-looking wife, their names instantly forgotten the moment his father said them. Where was Nora? She'd told him yesterday she was coming.

"Colin," a cool feminine voice murmured near his ear. Lady Sophia attached herself to his arm, a coy smile playing at her lips. She was dressed in a black dress with a low neckline. "As a friend of the family, I insist on having the first dance."

He stifled the urge to shrug her off. Lady Sophia and her parents were the most esteemed of the party attendees. Still, that didn't mean he enjoyed their company as much as his father did. Dinner followed by conversation in the drawing room with Lord and Lady Weatherly and their daughter the night before had been a long and tedious affair.

Forcing a smile, Colin artfully extracted Lady Sophia from his side, while still gripping her hand in a solicitous manner. "Of course."

"I look forward to it." She gave him an unabashed look before sauntering away.

Colin glanced at the music room's double doors. The line of guests continued to wind their way inside, but he couldn't see Nora among them. In the past, he'd never stayed in the receiving line for long. Instead he'd left the dreary job to Christian and his parents, while he wandered off to visit or dance.

He plucked at his white bow tie, certain Gibson had meant to strangle him by securing it so tightly. If only he could stand closer to the open doors that exited onto the terrace outside, then he might manage to feel a breeze in all this stuffy, warm air.

After what felt an eternity of standing and smiling, his parents left their positions near the inner doors to mingle with their guests. Colin headed straight outside. Leaning over the stone railing, he breathed in lungfuls of the cool, night air.

"I thought I might find you here."

Colin grinned at the sound of Nora's voice behind him. He straightened and turned around. The sarcastic retort on his tongue died at the sight of her. Back-lit by the lights of the party, her red hair glowed like fire beneath her headband, falling in cascades over one shoulder. Her light purple dress highlighted the pink of her cheeks and lips.

Her eyes sparkled with satisfaction and confidence, then with hidden laughter, as Colin stood there gaping. "Nothing to say?" Those delicious lips turned up in an impish smile, revealing her dimple. "I think that's a first, Mr. Ashby."

"You're late, Miss Lewis," he said, finding his voice at last. He crossed the terrace to take her hand in his.

The look she gave him was more amusement than contrition. "I apologize. But you'd be late, too, if you had to walk up the road in these heels and without getting them muddy." She lifted one of her white shoes. "I nearly wore my wellies instead."

She'd walked from her cottage to Elmthwaite Hall in an evening dress and heels? Colin battled the temptation to kiss her mouth right then and there. Instead he twisted her hand and pressed his lips to the skin of her wrist. He was glad she wasn't wearing gloves like the other women. "I'm glad you came. You look exquisite."

His compliment succeeded in infusing more color into her cheeks. "Thank you. You look very sophisticated yourself." She fingered the sleeve of his tailcoat. "I haven't seen you this dressed up since my first night in Larksbeck."

"Believe me, I prefer those old work clothes from last week to this," he muttered, leaning close. Her hair smelled of roses and Colin allowed himself a moment to breathe in the sweet scent before he straightened and motioned toward the music room. "Would you like to meet my parents?"

She nodded, though she didn't make a move to follow.

A look of trepidation had chased some of the spark from her eyes.

"They're going to like you," he reassured, "I promise."

At least his mother would. He wasn't sure about his father. It had taken some serious convincing for Sir Edward to agree to Colin's idea to invite Nora. He'd finally helped his father see the wisdom in the decision. If Sir Edward meant to buy her out, then having Nora at the party might show her and the villagers he meant no ill will with the business endeavor.

Niggling doubts still irritated Colin's conscience regarding his father's plans, but he'd nearly replaced them with thoughts of self-assurance. He would come up with some way to keep his father happy and Nora here. He had to. The idea of Nora leaving him was unthinkable.

"All right." Her shoulders rose with a sigh, but she followed after him.

He guided her into the crowded room and searched for his mother. She was talking with Lyle. Colin led Nora over to them. Clapping his free hand on Lyle's shoulder, Colin caught his mother's eye and smiled. "May I interrupt? Mother, I'd like you to meet Nora Lewis. Nora, this is my mother, Lady Ashby."

Nora stepped forward and extended her hand. His mother took it between both of hers. "Miss Lewis, thank you for coming. I'm so happy to make your acquaintance." She bent close as she added, "Even more happy to learn you've willingly put up with my son's antics."

The two women exchanged a smile. "I assure you, Lady Ashby, he is the perfect gentleman." Colin bit back a chuckle as Nora threw the last word over her shoulder at him.

"I'm pleased to hear it."

Nora and Lyle exchanged greetings as Colin scanned the room for his father. The band's lively music had changed to a waltz. He spied his father at last, in what appeared to be a heated debate with Lord Weatherly and another man.

"Come with me. I want you to meet my father." He captured Nora's hand again and wound his way around the perimeter of the room. Space had been cleared away in the middle to allow for dancing.

"Colin." Lady Sophia blocked their path. "I've been looking all over for you." She glanced past him to Nora, then down at their joined hands. One eyebrow rose. "Who's this?"

"Lady Sophia, Nora Lewis."

"It's nice to meet you," Nora said, her voice void of sarcasm despite the other woman's unfriendliness.

"An American, how charming. No wonder you're enthralled, Colin." Lady Sophia gave a simpering sniff. Colin sensed Nora stiffen behind him at the other lady's condescending tone. "What a quaint dress. I had one that looked nearly the same, last year."

How could he possibly entertain the idea of marrying someone so superficial and self-absorbed? "If you'll excuse us—"

"But, Colin, you promised me the first dance." Her eyes narrowed as she turned to Nora. "You don't mind, do you, Miss Lewis? He did give me his word."

Nora shook her head and slipped her hand from his. "Go ahead, Col—Mr. Ashby. I can meet your father later."

He threw her a pained look as Lady Sophia latched on to his arm. "Don't leave," he mouthed.

"I won't," she whispered back.

Lady Sophia dragged him toward the dance floor and he lost sight of Nora in the press of people. His mother's words from the other week echoed loudly in his mind: *You're welcome to invite her, but do you think that's wise?*

Had his mother known something Colin hadn't? Did she suspect, even then, the sort of reception Nora would receive from their so-called friends? He hoped to prove her wrong. But as he forced himself to take Lady Sophia in hand for the waltz, he feared the person who might be wrong was himself.

* * *

Nora intended to return to Lady Ashby and Lyle, who were still conversing, but a young man with a mustache asked her to waltz. She accepted. He led her onto the dance floor as Colin and Lady Sophia spun past. The two of them made a handsome couple, with his dark hair and her blond. The other young lady oozed wealth and society, but Nora had recognized in a matter of seconds the black heart beneath Lady Sophia's black dress. Colin's mother, on the other hand, had been surprisingly genuine and kind. Nora saw much of Colin in Lady Ashby's demeanor.

"You're American," her dance partner said with a smile as they began waltzing. "Are you here on holiday?"

Nora shook her head. "I live nearby."

"In Keswick?"

"No. My home is down the road."

The young man frowned. "I saw only farm cottages on the way to Elmthwaite Hall."

"Yes, and one of those cottages is mine." She lifted her chin a notch. "I inherited my grandfather's sheep farm a few months ago."

"You don't say? How interesting." The words sounded more sardonic than sincere.

Nora attempted conversation, but the young man kept his answers short and kept gazing about the room as if searching for someone else. When the dance ended, she felt great relief. Nora looked for Colin, but she couldn't find him. Once again she tried to make her way to Lyle, only to be asked to dance by another man.

The pattern repeated itself several more times. The young men would comment on her being American, which they seemed to find fascinating. However, the moment they learned she was simply a sheep farmer from down the road, their reception turned cool. At one point she even overheard one of her former dance partners mutter the words *social climber* to another young lady. Nora didn't have to guess who he meant.

Fighting a headache, she declined to dance a sixth time. She needed something to drink and a reprieve from the constant affronts to her humble life and her reasons for being at the party.

Nora made her way through the press of people to the refreshment room and requested some tea. Cup and saucer in hand, she turned to watch the people milling about the room. An older gentleman entered and approached the table, his hair a mixture of gray and white. Nora recognized enough of Colin in his height and jawline to know this was Sir Edward Ashby.

She lowered her teacup to introduce herself, but the words stuck in her throat. Would he also disapprove of her? When he noticed her standing there, his steps came to an abrupt halt. His eyes widened as he stared at her, and his face drained of color.

"Eleanor?" The name was hardly more than a whisper, but Nora heard him nonetheless.

"No. I'm Nora Lewis. I inherited Henry's farm. Eleanor is my moth—" The explanation died on her tongue. Realization crashed over her and Nora sucked in a sharp breath. "You're E, aren't you? You knew my mother."

Sir Edward flushed a deep red. "I—I don't know what you're talking about, young lady. If you'll excuse me." He spun on his heel and marched from the room.

Her hand trembling slightly, Nora set her nearly full teacup and saucer back onto the table. A keen sense of regret filled her as she returned to the ballroom and took in the glittering display before her. The young men sporting tail coats and slick smiles, the young women playing coy in their expensive gowns and jewelry. Her eyes followed Colin, dancing with Lady Sophia again. When he chuckled at something the other young woman said, Nora's stomach twisted in response.

She didn't belong here—nearly everyone she'd met, including Colin's father, had made that perfectly clear. Just as he had to her mother, Eleanor.

Tears swam in her eyes, but she willed them back. The soft night beckoned beyond the crowded room and Nora gave in, escaping to the terrace. Outside, the fresh air washed the flush from her face. She leaned against the rough stones of the railing, much like Colin had when she'd found him. Had it really been less than an hour ago that she'd felt so full of hope and promise? The way Colin had gawked at her, speechless, had left her feeling like the most beautiful woman in the world. But did he still think so now?

She considered going home, but she didn't want to leave without telling Colin good-bye. Running her fingers along the railing, she started down the three steps that led to the manicured grounds. A firm hand claimed hers and stopped her retreat. Nora turned to find Colin standing above her on the terrace, a questioning smile on his handsome face.

"Where are you off to?"

Nora glanced at the path ahead. "I thought I'd walk around a bit."

"Then I'll join you."

She moved over to allow him down the steps. He didn't release her hand, much to her gratitude, as they walked along the gravel path. Their shoes crunched softly in the moonlit night. Colin stopped her beside a beautiful, flowering bush. The music from inside still reached them.

"What do you think of the party?" He rubbed his thumb over the back of her hand. "I saw you dancing."

Nora swallowed, grateful the shadows hid her true expression. "Elmthwaite is as beautiful as ever."

She sensed his frown. "But?"

"I very much enjoyed meeting your mother," she hedged in a bright voice.

"Yes, Mother is extraordinary. I'm sorry I wasn't able to introduce you to my father earlier."

Nora plucked a flower from the bush and brought the bloom to her nose. "I met him," she said, inhaling the heady scent.

"You did? When?"

"While you were dancing." She let the flower tumble to the ground. "He called me Eleanor."

"Eleanor?" Colin repeated in surprise. "You mean he knew your mother, too?"

"Colin, he's E. From Eleanor's diary."

He didn't respond right away. "You're sure?"

"Yes. He looked at me as if he were seeing her again. Then when I asked him if he was E…"

Colin's free hand tilted her chin upward. "What did he say?"

"He excused himself and left without another word."

"Ah. Therein lies the proof."

The sting of Sir Edward's rebuff lanced through her again. In need of Colin's strength, she wrapped her arms around his waist and rested her head against the lapel of his tailcoat. He held her, one hand playing with the waves of her hair. Neither of them spoke until the present song ended and another began.

"What happened between E and Eleanor?" Colin inquired in a soft voice.

Nora squeezed her eyes shut, wishing he hadn't asked. The similarities between her and her mother and their love for these wealthy Ashby men were uncanny and a bit frightening. Would history repeat itself? She pushed out a sigh and opened her eyes. "His father wouldn't condone a marriage between them, so E eventually told her goodbye."

"So…my father and your mother might have married?"

She eased back to look at him. "We could have been brother and sister."

His eyes, though shadowed, gleamed with intensity.

"Then I must say I'm grateful things didn't work out between them."

The music spilling into the garden was another waltz. Colin glanced in the direction of the house, then back at Nora. "Would you do me the honor of this dance, Miss Lewis?"

She couldn't help a tiny smile—he'd been the only one she wanted to dance with. "Yes, Mr. Ashby."

He led her to a patch of grass beside the path and they began to dance. She followed his lead, even as he began improvising the familiar steps with fancy spins.

"Where did you learn to dance like this?" she asked with a laugh.

"Christian." It was the first time she'd heard him mention his brother without the undercurrent of regret. "I taught him how to converse with the young ladies and he taught me how to dance with them."

"What was he like?"

Colin slowed the pace of their steps. "He was serious, prone to thinking first and acting second. I'm sure you can guess I was quite the opposite." Nora smiled at the vision in her head of Colin as an exuberant, impulsive boy. "But he also had a way of coaxing me out of a bad mood when Father had said or done something irritating. One couldn't be unhappy for long when Christian was happy."

"He sounds like a good brother."

"He was." Colin spun her away from him. "He would have liked you, very much." He pulled her back and resumed dancing. "I want you to like my family, Nora. I want you to like it here...at Elmthwaite."

The snubs she'd experienced the last hour repeated in her mind. Could she imagine herself being happy in this sort of life? While Colin easily slipped from her world of necessity and toil to the ease and affluence of estate life, she found the contrast jarring and uncomfortable.

"I do like it here." She bit her lip to stop the rush of emotion in her throat as he dipped her back. "But my place is in the cottage down the road, not in an elaborate drawing room like you. I don't think I can—"

His lips met hers, stealing away her protest and setting Nora's pulse to galloping. He eased back, leaving her breathless, and lifted her gently to her feet before he kissed her again. Nora encircled her hands around his neck. His tender kiss, though brief, succeeded in chasing away her doubts.

Colin pressed his forehead to hers, their breath mingling in the cool night. "We'll make it work, Nora. Somehow. I promise." His mouth lifted in a smile that sent a ripple of feeling through her middle. "And a..." He paused, waiting for her to supply the answer.

"Gentleman," she finished in a whisper.

"Always keeps his word."

Chapter 16

With his hands tucked into his pockets, Colin crunched up the drive toward Elmthwaite Hall, after seeing Nora to her lane. She'd encouraged him to return to the party rather than walking her to her doorstep, and he'd agreed. The temptation to kiss her again—more soundly this time—might have proven too great if they'd lingered in the dark by her cottage. So he had contented himself with placing a kiss on her palm before bidding her good night.

Ahead of him he spied Lyle standing in the alcove of the front doors. Colin lifted his hand in greeting. "Escaped the party, did you?"

Lyle shrugged. "Lady Sophia is looking for you."

Colin frowned at the news. "No chance she'd buy a story of my drowning in the lake during a midnight swim?"

His friend chuckled. "Might be worth a try."

"You don't like her?" Colin came to stand next to him,

his eyes on the few stars he could see through the clouds.

"Wealthy, beautiful, and extremely smug. Most definitely not my type."

They stared at the sky in comfortable silence until Lyle asked, "Did Nora enjoy the party?"

"I believe so." Colin thought of their kiss. If her response was any indication of her feelings, he felt confident she was ready to put the past behind her and consider him a true contender for her heart.

"What now?" Lyle's question wiped the grin from Colin's face.

Colin turned to him. "What do you mean?"

"Are you going to marry her?"

He wanted to, and that desire increased every minute he spent with Nora, but would Sir Edward ever allow it? "My father has his hopes pinned on someone else. Someone like Lady Sophia and her father's pile of riches."

Lyle frowned and shook his head. "I've never seen you this happy before, Ashby. And that's Nora doing."

Colin ran a hand over his jaw as the old guilt and doubts assailed him. "It's complicated." How much should he share? The burden he'd been carrying since meeting Nora begged to be lightened. "My father wants her land—to build a hotel."

"What does Nora say about that?"

Shame coated Colin's throat so he could hardly voice his response. "She doesn't know." Lyle's eyebrows rose in challenge, bringing a frustrated sigh from Colin. "He charged me to get to know her and persuade her to leave. I tried, at least in the beginning, but... well, I failed, Lyle."

"Because you're in love with her."

"Yes," he murmured to the gravel. "But that doesn't change the fact that my father needs this hotel. It's the reason we converted the stables—to bring in more cars and provide guests with transportation from the railway to Elmthwaite."

Lyle leaned against the nearby stone wall, his cane clutched in both hands. "Is the estate really in need of the revenue?"

"Yes." Colin kicked at a pebble and sent it skipping over the drive. "If we do nothing and I choose not to marry someone wealthy like the earl's daughter, we'll have to sell Elmthwaite eventually. And that is something I promised Christian I would never do."

"What will you do then?"

Colin gave a bitter laugh. "I was hoping you might have some advice."

A sad smile settled on Lyle's face. "I don't think I'm qualified to give the best advice in terms of marriage or women. But…" He threw a pointed look at Colin. "Nora Lewis seems to be the kind of woman a man ought to fight for. She's worth a hundred of those stuffy heiresses here tonight."

The truth of Lyle's words pierced Colin deep, scattering his worries like bits of wool. How could he stand by and let someone like Nora walk away? While Elmthwaite Hall might mean the world to him now, his world meant nothing without Nora. "You're right. It's time I told her what she means to me."

"What about your father and his plans?"

A sense of loss moved through Colin at the reminder. He wouldn't live up to Sir Edward's expectations after all and he would let Christian down in the process. But Nora was worth far more to him. "He'll have to make other arrangements."

Lyle met his level gaze and seemed to understand the price of Colin's simple statement. "Good luck, ol' chap." He clapped a hand onto Colin's shoulder.

"We're both going to need it," Colin said with a chuckle.

"And why is that?"

He turned toward the door. "Because Lady Sophia will be staying on a few more days."

"Ah, but it is your illustrious company she desires." Lyle grinned as he shuffled past Colin.

"Don't remind me."

"Forget luck then, Colin. I'd say you're going to need something much stronger."

* * *

Nora let Phoebe out the back door. The morning air drew a shiver from her, but it couldn't erase the smile playing at her lips. She might have felt out of place at the party last night in the company of women like Lady Sophia, but not in Colin's presence. With him, she felt cherished, beautiful, important. And when he'd kissed her...it didn't matter if she was a sheep farmer and he was the son of a baronet. They were simply a man and a woman in love.

The faint sound of someone knocking at the front door reached her ears. Who would be coming around at this early hour? Could it be Colin? Her heart leaped in anticipation.

"You wait here," she told Phoebe.

She quickly tied the dog's rope to one of the gate posts

and hurried back into the house. Thankfully she'd already dressed and brushed her hair. Another knock drew her down the hall. At the front door, she smoothed her hair back.

"Good morn—" She choked on the words as she threw open the door and found Sir Edward standing there.

The older gentleman looked equally uncomfortable. "I apologize for coming here so early, Miss Lewis, but there's an important matter I wish to discuss with you."

Nora swallowed her surprise and stepped back. "Come in then."

Sir Edward crossed the threshold and stopped in the entryway. Nora managed to close the door behind him, but he remained where he stood.

"It's been more than thirty years since I was last inside this house," he murmured, his eyes taking in the parlor and the dining room.

Though she wasn't sure he'd give an answer, she couldn't help asking, "What was my mother like back then?"

The slightest smile crinkled the corners of his mouth. "She had a contagious passion for life and was very beautiful." He frowned at the cap in his hands. "I wanted to attend her funeral, but I wasn't sure your grandfather or the other villagers would appreciate my presence. I don't know that they ever forgave me for breaking her heart all those years ago."

"She did marry for love later on," Nora said, hoping to dispel the sadness and guilt hanging like a shroud around him.

"Yes, Matthew Galbert. A good man, though very ill. And you're their daughter?"

She nodded and maintained a steady gaze, despite the way he scrutinized her. Why was he willing to acknowledge her and her mother today when he hadn't last night?

"I'd heard Eleanor had a daughter, who went to live with relatives, but I had no idea you'd been sent all the way to America."

A strained silence clouded the space between them. "Would you like to sit down?" Nora waved in the direction of the parlor.

Straightening to his full height, Sir Edward marched into the parlor and took a seat in the armchair. Nora sat on the settee.

"I'll get straight to the point, Miss Lewis." Something in his curt tone told her he wasn't here to reminisce. "I want to buy your land."

"What?" She gave a startled laugh. "Whatever for?"

"I want to build a hotel on this property, to bring tourists to Larksbeck and Elmthwaite Hall."

He wasn't joking. Nora frowned at the realization. "I don't understand."

He glowered at her as if she were a simpleton. "You have the best view of the lake, apart from Elmthwaite Hall, of course. So naturally this would be an ideal setting for guests to experience the Lake District."

She drew herself up. "But this is my home."

"Yes, and Elmthwaite is mine," he shot back. "Or it will be as long as we move forward with this plan. We need the extra funds, I'm afraid."

"We?" Every piece of this conversation was proving to be a study in confusion.

Sir Edward lifted his boot onto his knee, a hard sort of smile twisting his face. "Yes, myself and Colin."

The air felt sucked from Nora's lungs. "Colin?" she repeated in a strangled voice.

"Of course. The boy's to inherit my title and the estate
someday. Naturally he wants to see it continue to flourish.
A hotel here would ensure that."

Why did it feel so difficult to breathe? Nora pressed a
hand to the base of her throat. Colin wanted her land for
a hotel?

"I asked him to charm you, to convince you to go
elsewhere, but I realized last night that you may have
charmed him instead. Therefore, I've taken it upon myself to deliver my request."

Nora's thoughts were a snarled mess. Colin had been
given the task to charm her? To convince her to leave?
She thought of their kisses, their time together. It had all
been an act? Heat crept into her cheeks. She'd been a fool
to think the son of a baronet would take sincere interest in
her.

Anger followed on the heels of her embarrassment
when she thought of the broken window, the destroyed
garden, the fallen stone wall. Colin had clearly grown
desperate these past few weeks to stoop to such means of
persuasion.

She dug her nails into the palm of her right hand, the
very palm Colin had the audacity to kiss last night. He'd
even promised to find out who was doing the vandalizing
when all along it had been him.

"What do you say, Miss Lewis? Are you willing to
sell?" Sir Edward lowered his foot to the floor. "I'll pay
you enough to give you a fresh start somewhere else."

A fresh start was the reason she'd come here in the
first place. Nora scanned the simply decorated room,

taking in the things her parents and grandparents had owned. Could she leave this place, now that she knew it was the place of her birth, a place where she still had family?

Her eyes fixed upon the gramophone. Memories of listening to it with Colin and Lyle traipsed through her mind. This cottage held more than forgotten times with her family—it held countless moments with Colin, too. Could she remain here with those recollections, knowing all the while it had been a ruse?

Tears blurred Sir Edward's image, but she blinked them back. She would not cry in front of this arrogant man. "I'd like a week to make my decision. I'll let you know then if I intend to sell."

"Very good." He jammed his cap back on and stood. Nora didn't bother to join him. He could let himself out. "A pleasure doing business with you, Miss Lewis. I'll be in touch in one week. Good day."

At the click of the door behind him, Nora dropped onto her side, her cheek pressed to the couch. The tears fell from her face onto the worn fabric, but they did little to ease the hurt lancing through her. She'd given her heart away, only to lose it all over again. But this time, there wasn't the knowledge she'd been loved in return. No, this gaping hole couldn't be partially filled with happy memories of the deceased.

"Oh, Mother," she whimpered, not sure if she meant Eleanor or Grace, or both. A wave of loneliness crashed over her, stealing her breath with its intensity. She hadn't felt this alone and abandoned in a long time. At least she still had Phoebe.

She sat up and dried her cheeks with the back of her

hand. Wherever she ended up, she still had the puppy. In that, she could be thankful for Colin.

Grabbing her sweater from the kitchen, Nora stepped out the back door. She needed a walk, a chance to clear her head and think carefully over her decision. "Ready for a walk, Phoebe?"

She shut the door and turned toward the gate. Phoebe wasn't there, straining at her rope as usual. Concern gripped Nora's heart as she walked to the post. The top of the dog's rope was still tied, but somehow the rest of the line had snapped in half.

"Phoebe?" she called. "Phoebe, come here."

The dog didn't appear. Nora pushed through the gate into the field, looking for the puppy. There was no sign of her. Her worry churned to desperation in her stomach and brought a resurgence of her earlier tears. She brushed them away and leaned over the stone wall, scanning the ground for paw prints. After a few moments, she caught sight of something long and thin lying in the grass.

Nora scrambled over the wall and reached down to pick up the rest of Phoebe's rope. It was still attached to the dog's collar. How had the puppy managed to wriggle out of it? There was no telling where she'd run off to now. Nora lifted her eyes to the fell, rising into the gray clouds in front of her. Would Phoebe venture that far from the cottage? There was only one way to find out.

She started up the face of the mountain, her shoulders pulled back in resolution. "Phoebe?" she yelled every few feet. Rainy mist soon dampened her sweater, but she didn't turn back. She had to find Phoebe—the dog was the only thing she had left.

* * *

A firm knock at Colin's door had him glancing at the mantle clock. It was early in the morning still, but Gibson was already helping him dress. He didn't want to wait any longer than he had to before going to tell Nora how he felt.

"Come in," Colin said, curious as to who else in the house had awakened early. Perhaps it was Lyle.

The door opened and there stood his father. A feeling of dread began to fill Colin's gut at the sight.

"Will you excuse us, Gibson?" Sir Edward directed as he entered the room.

"Yes, sir." Gibson finished buttoning the cuffs on Colin's sleeves before he exited the room and shut the door.

"What can I help you with, Father?" Colin worked at the buttons on his shirt, his jaw clenched in forced patience.

Instead of answering, Sir Edward dropped into one of the armchairs and leaned back. Colin caught the man's self-satisfied smile in the mirror. What was his father so happy about this morning?

"I believe congratulations are in order, my boy. I have done in one morning what it's taken you weeks to do."

Colin's fingers stilled as he slowly turned around. The trepidation inside him grew stronger, heavier. "What are you talking about?"

"Miss Lewis, of course. I simply walked over and made her my offer."

The words sliced through Colin like knives, each one leaving him more bloodied and battered than the last. He gripped the cushioned back of the other armchair. "That is not what we agreed to. You told me I had until the end of the month to talk to her."

"Yes, and we both know that wouldn't have happened." Sir Edward drew one foot onto his knee. "I'm not blind, boy. I saw the way you looked at her last night. You've gone soft over a pretty face." He tugged at the top of his shoe. "Just like I did with her mother, all those years ago."

"What did you say to her?" Colin challenged, his fury giving bite to each syllable.

"I told her I wanted to buy her land, for the hotel. She didn't refuse outright, which I'd fully expected. Instead she told me she'd let me know in a week."

Something inside Colin snapped at his father's casual tone. Nora wouldn't give up the cottage so easily. Which meant Sir Edward had clearly said more than he was letting on. He stalked to his father's chair and stood over him, his hands clenched into fists. "What *else* did you say to her? Did you mention me?"

Sir Edward frowned up at him. "Well, of course I did."

Colin ran his hands through his hair and paced back toward the mirror. The happiness and dreams he'd enjoyed last night had vanished like morning fog against the heat of the sun. What must Nora think of him now? He'd managed to win her heart, but now she must think it was only because he wanted to gain her land for the hotel.

He hurried to do up the last of his shirt buttons and jerked his jacket off the bed where Gibson had placed it. Forget his vest and tie. Shoving his arms into the jacket, he marched to the door.

"Where are you going?" his father demanded as he rose to his feet.

"To explain the truth . . . to Nora."

"Nora?"

"Miss Lewis." Colin threw open the door.

"I forbid you to leave. I've already settled things there and you'll only make matters worse."

Colin spun around. "You still don't understand, do you, Father? I love her." His finger shook with anger as he pointed it at his father. "And I will not sit back while you run her off. Just like you allowed your father to do with Nora's mother."

Sir Edward's face twisted into a hard glare. "You don't know the first thing about the past. I had to choose, as you must. I could not afford to throw my life away on the daughter of a penniless farmer, and neither can you. You must choose this estate over young love, as I did. I chose Elmthwaite. And so must you. Without more capital, we cannot build the sort of hotel I intend to or continue to run the estate until this business venture begins to pay for itself."

Colin fought the urge to take his father by the collar and shake him. He would not be ordered into a loveless marriage. "You are mistaken if you think I'll marry for money alone as you did."

"How dare you." Sir Edward's voice held no warmth, only stony reserve. "Your mother and I have been happy all these years. Even if love took time to grow, I have cared for and respected her from the very first. Unlike my own father, my eyes have never wandered to another woman. It has been your mother, and her alone, whom I have honored."

Shame doused some of the flames of Colin's anger. Whatever his faults, his father had always been faithful to his mother. "I'm sorry, Father. But do not force me to choose between the estate and my heart." He inhaled a deep breath and let it out slowly. "Because I will choose differently than you did."

Sir Edward turned his back to Colin. "Christian wouldn't," he threw over his shoulder.

The accusation punctured Colin's heart, leaving him breathless with the pain. "You're right. Christian wouldn't. But I am not Christian, and I never will be." He straightened to his full height, reining in the hurt, as he spoke the words he'd longed to since coming home. "I'm Colin, your other son. Remember? The one who's still living."

His father didn't turn around, but his body no longer stood erect and proud. He seemed to slump forward as if unable to bear the weight of the painful memories.

"You raised Christian to successfully take over for you, but none of us imagined he wouldn't be here to follow in your footsteps." Colin took a step back into the room, wanting to make him understand. "But I'm still here. To help, in my own way."

"You go after that woman," his father countered, "and you're throwing away all we've worked for. What the Ashbys for three centuries have fought for."

"What they worked for is the desire of their hearts, Father. That's something Christian understood, perhaps better than all of us. Elmthwaite was the object of his heart."

"But not yours?" Sir Edward asked, his tone low and despondent.

Colin shook his head. "It is important to me, yes. But it isn't first in my heart."

He waited for his father to speak, to reassure Colin that he did understand, but Sir Edward remained silent. After several moments, Colin strode out the door and down the hallway. He stopped when he saw his mother standing in the doorway of her sitting room. Her pale face told him she'd caught a good portion of the shouted conversation between him and his father. Was this the first she'd heard about Sir Edward and Eleanor? From the look on her face, Colin guessed not.

"I have to go to her, Mother."

She nodded, tears shining in her eyes. "I know." She gripped his hand as she walked past him. "And I must go to your father." Her unyielding devotion softened Colin's heart in ways Sir Edward's angry words and accusations never could.

Colin bounded down the stairs and out the front door. He would have to face his father again—and the consequences of his choice—when he returned from Nora's. But he put those thoughts from his mind. A sense of urgency propelled him down the lane toward the cottage at a fast walk. First things first, he had to set things right with Nora.

Chapter 17

Colin found the yard in front and behind the cottage devoid of life, including Phoebe. Nora didn't answer his loud knocking on the front or back door either. Colin jammed his hands into his pockets, as much for warmth as from habit. The morning had turned cool and the heavy clouds overhead promised rain before the afternoon.

Was Nora so angry she refused to open the door? He shook his head. If she were inside, he would have heard Phoebe barking in response to his knocks. So where had they gone? He set off down the lane to the main road, where he paused. From what he could see of this side of the lake, Nora wasn't close by. Perhaps he'd try the village, though the thought of facing her in public after what his father had told her nearly made him turn around.

With his jaw clenched in determination, Colin headed for Larksbeck. Nora was likely getting groceries, and the sooner he found her, the sooner he could explain everything. A few droplets of rain dripped onto his jacket as he crossed the bridge. He went to Mr. Bagley's shop first, but the man informed him Nora hadn't been by that morning. It was the same at the apothecary—neither Mrs. Smith nor her husband had seen Nora.

Undeterred, Colin left their shop and walked at a quick pace back up the road toward Elmthwaite. The rain still remained light enough he didn't need an umbrella. Perhaps Nora had gone to Bess's cottage. If she had, would she have told her cousin about Sir Edward's plans? Colin cringed at the thought of having Bess Tuttle angry with him, but he had to find Nora.

He knocked on the Tuttles' door. A small, redheaded girl answered and stood there mute, staring at him. "Has Nora been by here?" he asked.

The girl shook her head.

Relief mixed with disappointment. His involvement in his father's plans was still a secret to Nora's relatives, at least for now. "Thank you."

Not waiting for her response to his abrupt visit and departure, he retraced his steps in the direction of the cottage. Instead of returning up the lane, though, he decided to circumvent the lake. Nora might have sought solace on the opposite side.

Colin trudged along, through the misty rain, around the lake. Choppy waves faded against the rocky shore. What would he say to her when he found her? Would she listen long enough for him to share his true feelings?

He'd come to know her with the full intent of doing his father's bidding, but somewhere along the way he'd changed his mind. Had it been that first night when he'd walked her to her cottage? Or when he'd attended choir rehearsal with her for the first time? Perhaps it had been the day he'd given her Phoebe. Or maybe something greater than himself had been at work the entire time, helping him see the error in his father's plans and the absolute joy of having Nora in his life.

Each stretch of beach and jumble of rocks stood empty. Colin appeared to be the only one outside at the moment. When he reached the bridge to Larksbeck once again, he could no longer deny the uneasiness tensing the muscles in his shoulders and jaw. The valley wasn't large, which meant there weren't any other places for Nora to go.

Hopeful he'd missed her during his walk around the lake, he went back to the Lewis cottage. He pounded on the front door until his fist hurt. When he still received no answer, he circled to the rear of the house and tried the handle of the back door. It wasn't locked. Colin pushed through. "Nora? Are you here? It's Colin." The room echoed with silence.

He walked through the kitchen and down the hallway. "Nora? If you're here, please say something." The parlor and the dining room stood empty as well. He hated to intrude farther, but he needed to confirm she wasn't in the house. A quick inspection of the upstairs settled the matter—Nora was gone. Had she left Larksbeck altogether? Colin dismissed the thought. All of her belongings were still in place, minus the sweater she typically hung on one of the pegs in the kitchen.

Swallowing his dry throat, Colin let himself out the back. He walked to the field gate and leaned against it. Where else could she be? Something scratched his hand and drew his attention to the gate post. It was

Phoebe's rope or what was left of it. The fibers appeared to have been snapped or cut less than a foot from where it had been tied. Had something happened to the puppy? Had she escaped? If so, Nora would no doubt search everywhere, just as he was now searching for her.

Colin lifted his gaze to the mountains that circled the valley. Gray clouds hung like a scarf around them, obliterating the view of their tops. It was the one place he hadn't looked. The one place he hoped Phoebe, and therefore Nora, hadn't run off to.

On a good day, a person had to know the terrain in order not to get lost up there. Colin was sure Nora had only hiked the mountains a few times, and always with someone. Would she be able to return home on her own, especially on a wet day such as this one? He didn't know, but he wouldn't sit around waiting to find out.

The task of finding Nora had suddenly become larger than what he alone could do. It was time he recruited help. At a run, Colin tore down the lane back toward Bess's cottage. He pounded on the door again until it opened. The same little girl stood there.

"Cousin Nora isn't—"

"I need to talk to your mum."

Before the girl could move, Jack appeared in the doorway. His usual hate-filled gaze dropped into place when he saw Colin. "What do you want?"

Colin straightened. "Nora's missing. I think she went up on the fell. I need you to go to the village and round up others to help look for her."

Jack's face went white and his eyes widened.

"Did you hear me?" Colin snapped. Every minute

he stood there was a minute he could be looking for Nora. "Please go get some of the other farmers to help. Now!"

With a nod, Jack dashed past him. The little girl had begun to weep, probably from fear. Colin didn't wish to leave her upset. "It'll be all right..." He put a hand on her thin shoulder, knowing the words sounded as hollow to him as they likely did to her.

"What's all the fuss out here?" Bess bustled to the door.

"It's Nora," Colin said, lowering his arm to his side. "I believe she's up on the fell. I sent your son to get others to help search, but I'm starting up there now."

"Dear Lord, keep her safe." Bess pressed her hand to her ample bosom. "We're right behind you, Mr. Ashby. Come on, Ellie, help me get my coat."

Satisfied additional help was on its way, Colin spun around and headed back up the road. His legs and feet were beginning to feel the effects of all his brisk walking, but he wouldn't slow down. Not when Nora needed him.

* * *

"Phoebe?" Nora's hoarse cry wasn't likely to reach farther than a few feet. Her throat hurt from yelling for the puppy. "Here, Phoebe." How far had the dog come? How far had she herself been walking?

She stopped along the narrow trail carved into the side of the mountain and looked back over her shoulder. Gray fog obscured her view. She shivered and folded her arms, though she doubted it would bring her much warmth. Her sweater and socks were already damp from the light rain that continued to fall.

Brushing a wet strand of hair off her forehead, she shuffled forward, careful to keep her balance tipped toward the hill. No telling where she'd end up, or how hurt she'd be, if she slid down the soggy grass.

"Phoebe? Come on, girl. Where are you?"

The bleating of a sheep was her only answer, though Nora couldn't see the creature through the clouds. Hidden away up here, she felt her earlier loneliness return with a vengeance. She pressed her lips together tightly to keep from crying all over again. She'd shed enough tears over Colin and her broken heart.

"I never should have believed him," she muttered as the pain of his betrayal knifed through her again. She shook her head in disgust.

Ahead the clouds bunched higher up on the fell, revealing more of the rocky mountainside to her view. Nora picked up her pace. Perhaps the stormy weather was receding.

No sooner had the thought passed through her mind than the rain began to pour in great, angry drops. It blurred her vision again and ran cold down her collar. Her shivering grew more forceful, and she clenched her jaw to stop her chattering teeth. She'd be able to wring an entire bathtub worth of water from her clothes by the time she returned to the cottage.

A large rock came into focus. Nora paused when she reached it and leaned against its sturdy surface to rest. Her stomach rumbled with hunger, reminding her that she hadn't eaten breakfast before Sir Edward's awful visit. Should she turn back? She scanned the thin path ahead and behind her. If she was cold and miserable, Phoebe was surely the same. She couldn't give up yet, but she needn't search alone either.

"Please let me find her, God," Nora whispered.

She pushed off the rock and drudged through the growing mud at her feet. Surely she'd stumble onto Phoebe soon. The poor dog was probably huddled down somewhere, waiting out the storm. Nora stopped again to wipe her eyes and peer through the downpour. Several yards ahead she spied the edge of the fell, where it sloped downward before becoming another mountain on the opposite side. It would require careful traversing in this weather.

Squaring her shoulders, Nora offered another silent plea for help as she continued forward. She reached the edge of the trail and paused to ascertain the descent. From what she could see through the rain, a series of steps had been cut into the side of the mountain.

"Just like walking down stairs," she reassured herself, "albeit muddy ones."

She leaned back against the hill so she was nearly seated and stepped down the first step. So far, so good. Confident, Nora stood up straighter to traverse the second and third steps, though her knees were beginning to feel the effects of the steep, downward walk. She unfolded her arms to help keep her balance and climbed down again.

As her foot hit the next stair in the mountain, she heard a sound behind her. Like someone shouting her name. She spun toward the noise, but her shoe didn't stay put in the mud. Instead it flew out from under her, dropping her hard onto the slick ground beside the carved staircase.

Nora scrambled to grab on to something to stop herself

from sliding. But her clawing fingers wouldn't hold fast
to the wet grass. She screamed in terror as her body slid
faster down the mountain. "Oh, please..." she started to
pray. Then stabbing pain exploded inside her head and total darkness jerked her downward.

* * *

Colin paused to catch his breath. Though tempted to remove his jacket, he decided against it. The garment was
the only thing keeping his upper body from being completely soaked by the rain. The storm had increased in
fury since he'd started up the fell.

The oppressive clouds made visibility difficult, but he
recognized the spot where he'd stopped. He was almost
straight south of Nora's cottage and Elmthwaite Hall. He
wasn't even sure Nora had come in this direction. If she
hadn't, then hopefully the other searchers would find her
elsewhere on the mountains.

Straightening, Colin set off again. "Nora?" he called,
his hands cupped around his mouth to increase the sound.
"Nora?"

The narrow path became muddier the farther he hiked.
Colin wished he'd thought to change into boots, but that
couldn't be helped now. Urgency and concern drove him
onward.

Time seemed to expand up on the mountain. Colin
felt as though he'd been walking for months, though he
guessed he'd been at his search for only an hour or so.

"Nora? Can you hear me?"

His cries went unanswered as the mist pressed in
closer. Soon Colin struggled to see more than six feet in

front of him. With a loud groan, he stopped once more. He'd never find her in these conditions. What he needed was his plane. It was time to abandon one form of searching for a more effective one. Of course that meant waiting for the clouds to disperse, but he felt confident he could spot her from the air more easily than walking the face of the fell.

Colin set his jaw and turned around, retracing his steps back down the trail. Despite the scant visibility from the rain and clouds, he didn't slow his pace. He knew these walks as well as his own house.

Closer to the bottom of the mountain, the clouds receded, revealing to his view two dozen or more people. He spotted Jack and Bess, Mr. Bagley, and even old Ebenezer Snow among them. All of the villagers were calling Nora's name as they moved along the fell.

The sight brought a lump of emotion to Colin's throat. The people of Larksbeck cared about Nora, and not just because she was Eleanor's daughter. They cared because she was one of them. She'd come here with no prior experience with the land or the sheep, and yet, she'd been successful. Nora belonged here, among these relatives and villagers who would do anything to help her.

Colin hurried toward Bess. She was likely the one, other than himself, who would be most worried about Nora.

Bess caught sight of him and waved her arm. "Any sign of her?"

He shook his head. "The weather's turned nasty higher up. I'm going to get my plane and see if I can't spot her from the air."

"Good idea." She wrung her hands, her eyes red-rimmed. "We've got to find her. I can't lose her..." Her voice broke. "Now that she's come home to us."

"We'll find her, Bess. I won't stop until we do."

"Should we keep searching?"

"Yes," he said over his shoulder. "When I see where she is, I'll tip the wings of my plane to let you know."

She nodded. "God go with you, Mr. Ashby."

He hit level ground at a run and didn't slow his steps until he reached the gravel drive to the house. After throwing open the door, he plowed up the stairs, only to bump into Lyle at the top.

"Sorry, chap." Colin made certain Lyle was still standing before he hurried down the hall.

"Where are you off to in such a hurry? Going to confess to Nora?"

Colin turned around. The smile on Lyle's face faded at seeing Colin's frown. "Nora's missing on the fell. I'm going to take the biplane up to see if I can spot her."

"What can I do?"

"Help me start the plane." He opened his bedroom door. "And pray," he added in a low voice.

Colin exchanged his wet clothes for a dry set. The weather would make flying cold enough without his clothes being soaked through. He grabbed the rest of his flight gear and left his room. Lyle was waiting for him outside, beside the plane.

Colin climbed into the rear cockpit. He worked the magneto and throttle as Lyle spun the propeller. The engine coughed, then roared to life.

"Be careful," Lyle yelled over the noise. He removed the wheel chocks and the biplane began to roll.

"I will," Colin shouted back.

Less than a minute later, the plane was speeding across the grass toward the lake. Right before the beach, Colin pulled back on the stick and the nose of the biplane rose into the air. He guided the plane upward, then leveled her out. The bitterly cold, damp air pierced his flight jacket and the exposed parts of his face, but he ignored it. He circled the plane over the lake and the village, toward the mountains ringing the north end of the valley.

The rain had lightened considerably since he'd been on the fell, but the clouds still obscured his view until he cleared the mountains. Colin didn't fear crashing into anything, though. He'd flown over these valleys and mountains so many times he no longer had to think about when to use the stick or the rudder petals. His hands and feet responded without conscious thought.

He circled the next valley, searching the ground as he banked, then headed back toward Larksbeck. The cloud cover meant he couldn't fly low enough to get a good look at the mountains. Colin grit his teeth in frustration as the plane zoomed south of Elmthwaite. If the weather didn't improve, he'd be forced to keep circling aimlessly until he ran out of fuel.

"Come on," he hollered at the clouds. He hadn't felt this helpless since the day Christian had been killed. What if something happened to Nora before he could explain? Before he had a chance to tell her he loved her?

His stomach roiled with anxiety, and unshed tears stung his eyes. What more could he do? He was only one man against the power of nature.

Though like the wanderer, the sun gone down,
darkness be over me, my rest a stone;

Where had he heard those words recently? He searched his memory. They were from the hymn he'd sung that first day at choir rehearsal with Nora—the hymn Christian loved. Colin whispered the rest of the verse, "*Yet in my dreams I'd be nearer, my God, to Thee.*" If there was ever a time he needed to be near God, it was now.

"God." The address felt foreign in his mouth, but he plunged on. "I need Thy help. I need to find Nora, but I can't see her with the clouds. I know You care for her, even more than I do…" His voice cracked with emotion. "Please don't let me lose her now."

Clearing his throat, Colin turned the plane in another wide, slow circle and flew back toward Larksbeck. A patch of green off the right wing caught his attention— it was one of the fell peaks. Could the clouds be lifting? Had God heard his awkward but humble prayer? Colin steeled himself against full hope, but he sensed a tiny seed of it still taking root inside him, despite his doubts.

He guided the plane north of Larksbeck, circled the valley there, and headed back. This time he spotted several splotches of green on either side of him. By the time he circled south and flew toward Elmthwaite again, the only clouds remaining were those gracing the very top of one peak. The rest had receded high above him.

Colin stared in awe at the uncovered mountains. A feeling of optimism filled his heart until he hardly noticed the sharp cold anymore. God was not only near him, but he felt certain He was near Nora, too. Colin wasn't alone in his search for her.

"Thank you, Lord," he murmured as he lowered the

plane and leaned over the side to scrutinize the terrain below. Sheep ran helter-skelter at his approach. He spotted the villagers combing the mountainside. Nothing else looked out of place among the grass and rocks.

He flew away from the valley once more, searching the next. How far could Nora have gone? Colin guided the plane back toward Larksbeck, his gaze jumping from one side of the mountains to the other. In the basin between two of the peaks, a flash of color caught his eye. He circled back, his eyes pinned to that spot.

There it was again. A piece of blue near a large rock. He allowed himself a quick breath of relief at finding something and nosed the plane down as low as he dared to get a better look.

A figure lay prone against the rock. Colin recognized the blue dress as Nora's. Horrified, he nearly forgot to pull up to keep the plane from crashing into the mountain. Questions raced through his mind as he and the biplane shot back into the sky. What had happened? How badly was she hurt?

Fear sprung up like vines inside him, snaking their way outward to tighten his lungs and constrict his breath. He wasn't staring down at the grassy slopes of the fell anymore, but at Christian's shattered plane and broken body, though he hadn't seen them himself. Grief cut through him. He couldn't lose another person he cared about.

What of the miracle you witnessed moments before? his heart gently entreated.

Colin lowered his chin in shame. Why did he so easily doubt the help of Someone far greater than himself? He may have once believed God had abandoned him and his family when Christian took his last breath, but he could no longer cling stubbornly to that way of thinking. Not after what he'd seen and felt today.

For the first time, he viewed the last year of his life with different eyes. He had much to be grateful for, despite losing his brother. He still had family, health, and Nora's friendship. God had brought her here, of that Colin felt certain. Loving her had reminded him that what he cherished most about life—love, laughter, acceptance, purpose—hadn't been permanently ripped from him at Christian's death.

Colin set his jaw—he wouldn't give in to the panic. There had been nothing he could do to save Christian that fateful day, but he could do something to save Nora.

He flew in another circle and came in low over the other searchers. They lifted their heads as the biplane zoomed low overhead. When he neared the spot where he'd seen Nora, Colin moved the plane's stick left to right to rock the wings. Once the villagers began rushing in the direction he'd indicated, he headed toward Elmthwaite Hall. The sooner he landed, the sooner he could go to Nora.

His petitions to Heaven started up again as he circumvented the lake and lowered the plane onto the lawn in back of the house. *Please let her be all right. Please let us reach her in time.*

Once the plane had stopped, Colin threw off his cap and goggles, tossed them into the front cockpit to retrieve later, and clambered to the ground. He didn't bother with the wheel chocks. His long strides ate up the grass as he headed back up onto the fell. Every footstep, every heartbeat, echoed with uncertainty of what he might find on the fell, but the fear he'd felt earlier had lost its over-whelming grip. His faith, however fledging, had made him stronger.

Colin met the other rescuers halfway up the trail. Mr. Bagley held Nora in his arms, while the rest of the group followed single-file behind him. The somberness of the villagers hit Colin from several yards away. The closer he came, the more details came into focus—Nora's limp body, her mud-strewn clothes and face, her matted hair.

"Is she..." Colin couldn't finish. He took a deep breath, bracing himself for the worst.

"She's breathing," Mr. Bagley said. Relief nearly drove Colin to his knees in the wet grass. "It looks like she took a nasty hit to the head. I think she might have slipped. We've got to get her warm and out of this weather."

Colin removed his mostly dry jacket and draped it over Nora as Mr. Bagley passed by him. He wished he were the one holding Nora tight to his chest, but he appreciated the others' willingness to help. Bess gave his hand a squeeze of gratitude as she and Jack walked past. Jack still appeared to be in shock. Colin fell into step at the back of the group. They moved in a slow line back down the mountain.

When they reached Nora's cottage, Mr. Bagley carried her inside and upstairs. Bess began issuing orders for hot water to be boiled, for Dr. Chutney to be sent for, and for Jack to go tell the rest of her children that Nora had been found. Colin stood in the parlor, hands in his pockets, feeling in the way and useless. He could have been the one to go for the doctor, but he was glad someone else volunteered. He wanted to stay near Nora.

The doctor arrived soon after and hurried up the stairs. Colin paced between the parlor and the dining room, ignoring the small crowd that milled about and their conjectures on Nora's condition. He saw Bess come down once and fetch water from the kitchen, but she returned to the second floor without a word to anyone. Eventually the group dispersed as the villagers slipped away to their own homes.

When they'd all gone, Colin summoned his courage to venture upstairs. Would he be allowed to see Nora when no one else had? The door to her room stood ajar. The murmur of quiet conversation floated into the hallway.

Colin gave the door a soft tap. Bess appeared in the doorway. "Mr. Ashby?" she said with evident surprise. "I thought you might have left with the others."

"Not yet."

Her face relaxed into a smile. "Thank you again for your help today. We might never have found her if you hadn't gone up in your aeroplane."

"May I see her?"

She looked him up and down a moment, then nodded. Opening the door wider, she gave Colin a view of the room. Nora lay in her bed with blankets up to her neck. She'd been cleaned up, all traces of mud erased from her face and hair. Her eyes were still shut, but her chest rose and fell with the even breaths of sleep. Dr. Chutney was putting his tools into his black bag.

"You located her just in time, Mr. Ashby," the doctor said, straightening. "Any longer in this weather and her hypothermia might have been much worse."

"Will she be all right?" Colin looked the man square in

the eye—he wanted the truth, however painful it might be to hear.

Dr. Chutney glanced at Nora and back to Colin. "With plenty of rest and warmth, I believe she'll be fine. She likely suffered a concussion when she hit her head, so she will need to be watched carefully for any signs of complication. But I don't think she'll suffer any lasting consequences from the ordeal."

Once again relief flooded Colin, bringing hope in its wake. Nora would be all right. As he studied her peaceful expression, a longing to touch those lips and reddened cheeks nearly drove him across the room to kneel at her bedside. If only he could be the one to stay with her, sit near her, tell her everything the moment she awakened, but he doubted Bess would allow it.

"May I come by tomorrow?" he asked instead. "To see how she's doing?"

"I can't say she'll be up to having visitors," the doctor said in a kind tone, "but you're welcome to stop by. If that's all right with you, Auntie Bess."

"Course." Bess settled into the hardback chair pulled up near the bed. "Will you let my Mary know what's happened, Mr. Ashby? And that I'll be staying here for the time being? She can swing by on her way home."

Colin nodded. "I'll let her know."

With nothing more to say or do, Colin bade the two of them good-bye and let himself out the front door. The rain had stopped, and a shaft of sunlight shone down onto the lake. The sight bolstered the feeling of optimism stirring inside him. He'd been led to find Nora—of that he had no doubt.

What would she say when he told her how he'd prayed

and how the clouds had parted for him? The thought brought a trace of a smile to Colin's face, the first he'd felt all day.

Tomorrow he'd tell her about the miracle in finding her and how much he loved her. Tomorrow everything could return to the way it had been.

Chapter 18

Something warm and wet lapped at Nora's chin. Curious, despite the ache in her head, she cracked her eyelids open. A wriggly ball of brown fur stood with its hind paws on her chest.

"Phoebe," she croaked out. "You're back."

The dog continued to lick her face as Nora lifted her hand and scratched Phoebe's ears.

"Jack found her last night and brought her home straightaway." Bess was seated next to the bed, a bit of mending in her hands. "Good to see you awake, love."

"How long have I been asleep?"

"Since yesterday midmorning. It's going on eight o'clock now. Looks as though it'll be a sunny day."

Nora settled Phoebe at her side and glanced at the window. Beams of sunlight streamed through the curtains into the room. The sight warmed her nearly as effectively as the extra blankets.

"How did I get home?"

"We found you on the fell. It looked as though you slid down the trail, then hit your head on a rock." Bess cut a thread with her teeth. "Though that rock stopped you from ending up all the way at the bottom."

Nora gingerly touched her head. She remembered searching for Phoebe on the fell and being very wet and cold. There was also a vague recollection of traversing some stairs before she felt herself sliding. After that, all she could remember was the feeling of being lifted into the air and the rise and fall of voices around her. She'd been too tired, her head too full of pain, to pay much attention or respond.

"Dr. Chutney will be along soon. He believes you should be up and around in a few days, mind you stay in bed and rest." Bess motioned to the tray on the bedside table. "Care for something to eat?"

The poached egg, toast, and steaming tea made Nora's mouth water. She couldn't even remember the last thing she'd eaten. "Yes, please."

Bess helped her sit up, with the pillow propped behind her. A wave of dizziness engulfed Nora, but she shut her eyes against it and the feeling soon dissipated. After Bess settled the tray on her lap, Nora sipped at the tea. The hot liquid felt heavenly sliding down her dry throat and warming up her insides. She still felt chilled.

"Where did Jack find Phoebe?" Nora asked, her hand brushing the dog's fur. Phoebe lifted her head at hearing her name, then lay back down. Nora smiled at her—she'd been so worried she'd never see the puppy again.

"Somewhere on the fell, I suppose. He was very upset

at seeing you hurt." Bess cleared her throat. "We all were. Half the village turned out to look for you."

Gratitude mingled with remorse inside Nora at Bess's words. "I'm sorry to have worried everyone. I probably shouldn't have gone up the fell alone, but I had to try to find to Phoebe." A memory nibbled at the back of her mind—some event that had transpired before she'd gone looking for her dog—but Nora sensed it was unpleasant and she drove it from her thoughts.

Bess's serious expression perked up into a smile. "How's your head feeling?"

"Sore. But other than feeling cold, I'm all right."

With a scrape of the chair, Bess stood and gathered another blanket from the foot of the bed. She draped it around Nora's shoulders. Nora snuggled into the warmth. "Better?"

Nora nodded. "You don't have to stay here. Your family needs you more than me."

Bess shook her head as she sat back down. "You are family. And my young'uns will be fine until you're fully better."

The feeling of appreciation expanded in Nora's heart. She and Phoebe weren't alone. She needed to remember she had family here. "As soon as I'm well, I'll have to thank everyone who helped."

"You can start with Mr. Ashby. He said he'd be along today to see how you're faring."

Nora set her cup onto the tray with a loud *clink*, drawing an odd look from Bess. Memories fired through her mind like gunshots—Sir Edward's visit, his request to buy her land and farm for a hotel, Nora's discovery that Colin had known about the plan from the beginning. "Wh-why does he want to stop by?"

"He was the one who discovered you were missing in the first place, love. Found you on the fell, he did, using that aeroplane of his. Without him, I don't know that we would've found you until it was too late."

Colin had saved her life? The realization was as unsettling as the thought of seeing him. He didn't want her; he only wanted her land. If she'd died out on the fell, it would've made things much easier for the Ashbys.

Nora frowned at her own dark thought. Colin might have broken her trust and her heart, but he wasn't a fiend. That didn't mean she had anything she wished to say to him, though. In a few more days she'd have to give Sir Edward her answer about the farm, and she would make that decision without succumbing to the charms of Colin Ashby ever again.

"Please tell him I'm fine, but that I don't wish to see him."

Bess gave an absent nod. "That's all right if you're not up to him visiting today."

"Today or any other day." Nora kept her chin up, even while her heart and dreams split further at saying the words out loud.

"I see." Bess shot her a veiled look before she resumed her sewing. "Something happen between you two?" Her tone sounded causal enough, though the question certainly wasn't. "My Mary's talked about seeing you and Mr. Ashby together quite often."

Nora slid her tray back on the bedside table, her appetite gone. She slipped down onto her pillow. How much should she reveal? She considered telling Bess about the acts of vandalism to her property, but she decided against it. She didn't have actual proof that Colin had stooped to such tricks, though she had no reason to doubt his involvement now. It was humiliating enough to have to admit she'd fallen for the man's lies.

"We did spend a lot of time together." She feigned intense interest in the hem of one of the blankets. "But I learned yesterday his interest was an act."

"How do you mean?" Bess didn't sound convinced.

Nora cringed as she recalled her conversation with Colin's father. "Sir Edward wants to buy my land, to build a hotel and bring in more income for Elmthwaite Hall. Apparently Colin—Mr. Ashby—knew this from the start and was charged to persuade me to sell."

Bess's mouth fell open. "Buy your land? But you've only just come home. What did you tell the man?"

"I told him I'd think about it and give him an answer in a week."

"What for, love? How come you didn't send the baronet packing with a 'no'?" She studied Nora's face with such intensity Nora lowered her gaze. "Ah. You still care for Mr. Ashby."

"Yes." Tears swam in Nora's eyes. "I mean, no. How can I? I was wrong about him."

She waited for Bess to speak, to get as angry as she felt over the whole mess. Instead the older woman gave a sad shake of her head. "You have every right to be upset with him. But…"

"But?" Nora repeated, her frustration making her tone sharp.

"If you'd seen him yesterday." Bess stared down at the sewing in her lap. "The look on his face when he told me you were missing, and then again, when he found us carrying you back."

Despite her best efforts, a flicker of hope attempted to ignite inside Nora. She pressed her lips against it. She wouldn't be fooled again. "He was probably worried if something happened to me, my land would go to you and your children and he'd never get it."

Bess met her eye. "I think your land was the farthest thing from his mind."

Nora pulled the blanket tighter around her shoulders. Bess didn't understand. Nora had allowed herself to love again, only to learn it wasn't real.

Her head began to hurt. She twisted onto her side to face Phoebe and drew the other covers up to her neck. Only with her back to Bess did she allow the tears to come. "I'd like to sleep now. Please tell him that I don't wish to see him."

* * *

After knocking on Nora's front door, Colin stepped back and waited for Bess to answer. He eased his grip on the bundle of flowers in his hand. Hopefully Nora would like them. He'd picked them from one of the Elmthwaite gardens this morning.

He knocked again, knowing the sound needed to carry all the way upstairs. After another minute or so, Bess opened the door. Colin noticed her usual animated demeanor had been replaced by a somber one. Had Nora's condition worsened in the night?

"Good morning, Bess."

She dipped her head in acknowledgment.

"Is Nora worse today?"

"No, thank the Lord. She woke up about an hour ago

and drank a little something. She's tired and says her head still hurts, but she seems to be improving."

Relieved, Colin smiled and hoisted his flowers. "May I see her? I won't stay long, I promise."

Bess shifted her gaze to the floor. "I'm afraid that's not possible, Mr. Ashby."

"Is she sleeping? I can come by later."

The older woman shook her head. "Isn't that." She lifted her chin. "She won't agree to see you—today or any day. I'm sorry."

Nora refused to see him? Colin fell back a step and lowered the flowers to his side. He'd expected anger, even distrust. But he hadn't counted on Nora not even giving him a chance to explain—to tell her he wasn't the man his father had portrayed him to be.

"It's about her land, isn't it?" he asked, though he knew the answer.

"Yes."

"Can't I have five minutes, to tell her the truth? Please, Bess."

"I can't be going against her wishes. I'm sorry," she repeated, her voice nearly as sorrowful as his own. Why hadn't she condemned him, too? After all, it was his father who wanted to throw out her relative.

As if she'd heard his unspoken question, Bess threw a glance over her shoulder and leaned forward. "I want to thank you again for saving her life, even if she won't. Whether for her or her land, that was a brave thing you done. I only wish it could've made things right between you. Good-bye, Mr. Ashby."

The finality of her farewell wasn't lost on Colin as Bess quietly shut the door. She might not convict him completely, as Nora had, but she wouldn't choose him over a relation either. Colin stared at the flowers in his hand; he'd forgotten to give them to Bess. Their cheery heads mocked the pain squeezing his lungs.

He tossed them at the stone wall of the cottage and watched them fall to the ground, crushed and battered. Just like his hopes for the future—ones that had included Nora, until yesterday.

With his hands jammed into his pockets, he walked down the lane. Regret and anger warred inside him. If only she'd given him a chance…But he didn't blame her for not wanting to either. He'd broken her trust, from the moment he'd agreed to his father's plan. Someone like Nora, who'd already lost so much, wasn't likely to trust again where she'd found deceit. And yet his feelings for her had been—still were—genuine. In that he'd never lied.

Could he avoid seeing her, once she was well? As his father and Eleanor had clearly avoided each other. Perhaps. But even without seeing her, Colin knew it would be a long time—the rest of his life maybe—before he would be able to forget Nora.

The walk home succeeded in driving away most of his hurt and frustration, leaving only numbness. Colin entered the house and stopped in the entryway. What should he do now? He'd spent nearly every day for the past three months in Nora's company.

"Colin!"

He looked up to see Lady Sophia sweeping her way down the stairs.

"I've been looking for you."

"Have you?" He suddenly felt too exhausted to play her games.

"Will you take me for a ride in your aeroplane?" She came to stand beside him, her hand moving possessively to his sleeve. "Father's given his approval and it's a gorgeous day."

Was it? Colin hadn't even noticed the lack of cloud cover or rain. He glanced out the door, which he'd mistakenly left open. Sure enough, sunshine shone down on the gravel drive outside.

"You look as though you need cheering up, and I know how much you love to fly."

Colin studied her hazel eyes, which appeared to be largely free of pretense today. He didn't particularly like Lady Sophia—he'd witnessed more than his fair share of her shallow, petty opinions during her two visits. But flying was exactly what he needed today. With her aboard the plane, he might actually be able to forget Nora and her refusal to see him, at least for a few minutes.

"You've convinced me," he said, forcing an exaggerated smile. It felt unfamiliar to his mouth. For weeks now, he'd been himself—the real Colin Ashby—because of Nora. And though she might not want him anymore, he didn't have to go back to living behind his pretentious façade again. That, at least, was something he could keep from his time with her.

He let the fake smile fall away. "You are correct, Lady Sophia. I'm very much in need of a good, long flight. And you are welcome to join me."

* * *

Bess opened Nora's door and stepped inside. "You've a visitor."

Had Colin tried to come by again, as he had yesterday? Nora's heart beat faster at the thought. "Who is it?" she asked.

"Mr. Lyle."

Nora blew out her breath in relief and sat up straighter against the pillows. She hadn't seen Lyle since the party at Elmthwaite Hall. "I'd love to see him."

Bess nodded before disappearing out the door. A few moments later, Nora heard the methodical thud of Lyle's cane and footsteps against the stairs. When he reached her doorway, he paused and rapped a knuckle against the wood. "May I come in?"

"Yes, please." She motioned to the chair drawn up near the bed.

He crossed the room and sat down, resting his cane across his lap. "You're looking quite well."

Nora laughed as she fingered her loose braid. Except for the occasional dizzy spell, she was feeling much better, though the doctor still insisted she rest as much as possible. "That's what visitors are supposed to say."

"Yes, but it's especially true in your case, Nora."

She blushed at his compliment. If only she hadn't given her heart foolishly to Colin, perhaps she and Lyle might have been more than friends. As it was, she was finished with romantic attachments. "Thank you. What have you been occupying your time with?"

"Automobiles," he said with a grin. "Sir Edward had four sent up from London. Fascinating machinery."

"What does he need four cars for?"

Lyle kept a steady gaze. "To bring guests from the rail station to the hotel."

Nora fiddled with the cuff of her dressing gown. "You

mean the hotel he and Colin plan to build here, on my land?"

"Do you plan to sell then?"

"I don't know." She'd gone back and forth in her decision. Half the time she was convinced she ought to stay, to be near the only family she had left in the world. The other half of the time she wanted very much to be gone, away from Colin. "I have to give Sir Edward my answer in five days."

"And I shall be off in five days."

She lifted her head to look at him. A feeling of sadness washed over her. First she'd lost Colin and now Lyle would be leaving her, too. "You're going back to London?"

"I'm sure I've worn out my welcome. I've been here more than a month now."

"Are you sad to go?"

He rubbed the top of his cane. "Very much so. You and Colin and Lady Ashby... and the others... have made me feel accepted. It's different here than in the city."

"These others you mention wouldn't happen to include a certain brown-haired maid," she teased, "who works at Elmthwaite?" She'd noticed the way Mary and Lyle had been conversing at the dance after the shearing and guessed they'd managed to have other conversations since.

Lyle's face grew red, making Nora chuckle. "It might." He cleared his throat and his color returned to normal. "Speaking of people at Elmthwaite, why did you refuse to see Colin?"

It was Nora's turn to blush. "I just... couldn't. I'm sorry—I know he's your friend."

"Last I remember, he was your friend, too."

"He lied to me, Lyle." She didn't bother to hide the undercurrent of anger from her voice. "He was sent by his father to win me over so they could buy my land."

"At first."

Nora blinked in confusion. "What do you mean, at first?"

Lyle bent forward and rested his arms on the edge of the bed. "He didn't plan to start caring for you, Nora, but that's what happened."

The traitorous seed of hope attempted to sprout inside her again, but Nora mentally tore it up. She wouldn't be fooled into trusting where she shouldn't. "Maybe so, but he has a very odd way of showing it. Like throwing a rock through my window with a note telling me to leave. Or destroying my garden or pushing over a section of my rock walls."

Lyle's brow furrowed. "Whatever are you talking about?"

"Someone did all those things to get me to leave. And as far as I know, Colin and his father are the only ones who want me gone." The admission stung her throat.

"I don't know who did those things, but I'm confident it wasn't Colin."

Nora shook her head. The room was beginning to feel stiflingly hot. "How can you be so sure?"

"Because I know Colin," Lyle said, sitting up straight. "Even if he was charged to persuade you to leave, condoning violence isn't in keeping with his character." Nora gave a snort of disbelief. Lyle waited to continue until she met his gaze again. "The other reason is that the night of the party, Colin told me everything—about his father's plans and about his willingness to go along with them. Until something happened."

"What?" The word was out before Nora could stop it. She didn't want to hear this, did she? It would only make not seeing Colin that much harder.

"He wasn't getting to know you for his father anymore; he was doing it because...he loves you."

Nora rested her head against the bed frame. She felt too tired to sit up any longer. Could Lyle be right? Did Colin love her? A part of her thrilled at the possibility, while her more practical side balked. Love or not, he'd still been nice to her under false pretenses. "Is Elmthwaite Hall that important?"

"Is this place?" Lyle waved his hand to encompass the humble room.

"Yes," Nora whispered.

She of all people knew what it was like to give up her childhood home. Is that why Colin had agreed, in the beginning, to Sir Edward's plans? Not only had Elmthwaite Hall been in his family for centuries, but the house held memories of his brother, too. Was it so wrong then that Colin would want to hold fast to it?

"Thank you, Lyle, for telling me. I understand a little better now," she admitted. "Though I still think Colin should have told me right away what he was playing at."

"Would you have bothered to get to know him if he had?"

Nora wanted to say "yes," but she wasn't sure. What if she hadn't befriended Colin? Despite his betrayal, she'd learned so much from her association with him, especially things about herself. "I don't know..." She pressed her lips over the emotion rising up her throat. "But I also don't know if I can trust him again."

"Fair enough. I ought to let you rest now." Lyle set down his cane and climbed to his feet. "You should know, though, Lady Sophia has wasted no time in filling Colin's vacant hours with outings together. She's already been flying with him twice."

Flying with Colin? Jealousy swept through Nora at the thought of someone else in his aeroplane, experiencing the thrill of flying with him, seeing his eyes shine with pure joy. She tamped the feeling down, though. Why she should care if Colin favored the smug heiress now? "Will I see you again before you leave?"

Lyle nodded. "Good day, Nora."

"Thank you again for stopping by."

"My pleasure."

After he left, Nora whistled for Phoebe. She didn't want to be alone. The scraping of claws on the stairs preceded the puppy's entrance. Phoebe hopped onto the bed and settled against Nora's side. She stroked the dog's soft fur as she tried to make sense of the cyclone in her mind.

She could almost excuse Colin's actions, except for the acts of vandalism. But if he hadn't done those, as Lyle firmly believed, then who had? And why? Not knowing made her decision to stay in Larksbeck or sell the farm all the more difficult.

A wave of dizziness crashed over her, making the room tilt and spin. Nora laid her head onto her pillow, her eyes shut tight, and prayed sleep would come. Only then would she be free of the confusion and frustration that had become her constant companions.

Chapter 19

From the air, Nora's cottage looked so small. Tomorrow would mark one week since Colin had seen her last—one week since the night of his father's party. How drastically life could change in a matter of days or moments.

Colin guided the biplane in a wide circle over Elmthwaite Hall. Over the stately towers, the gardens, the lawn. Over the blue lake reflecting the green, cloud-shrouded mountains. The beauty of it hit him today as it hadn't in a long time. No wonder his father wanted to bring tourists here. People of all backgrounds, even troubled ex-soldiers like Lyle, could find peace in this lakeside valley.

The place was not only the lifeblood of his ancestors for three centuries, but Colin's, too. Could he stand by and watch the place parceled off piece by piece until nothing remained? This place where he'd been born and lived, like his father and his grandfather and so on, back to the first Ashby who'd fashioned the beginnings of the house out of rock from the fells.

No. He couldn't give up Elmthwaite, but he wouldn't take Nora's home to keep it either. Whatever her feelings were for him now, she deserved to keep her home as much as he did his. So where else could his father build a hotel?

Colin flew in toward the lawn and guided the plane downward. Lady Sophia twisted in her seat to smile back at him. He smiled in return. While the heiress might still be a bit self-absorbed, he hadn't loathed her company the last few days.

The biplane's wheels touched the grass and Colin cut the engine. The plane rolled forward across the expansive back lawn. Its length had always made the perfect spot for taking off and landing, with plenty of room to turn the craft around in preparation for his next flight.

As the plane came to a complete stop, Colin gazed at the house in the near distance. Ideas began to coalesce in his mind and filled him with sudden anticipation. One meant sacrifice on his part, but it was worth it if Nora could keep her farm. The other meant a way he could help some of the returned soldiers.

Colin climbed out of his seat and helped Lady Sophia to the ground. "Did you enjoy that flight as much as your first one?" he asked as he set the wheel chocks into place.

"Very much." They both removed their helmets and goggles. "I wish we might have stopped at that castle we saw. Those were beautiful ruins."

He settled for a nod. He'd flown over Brougham Castle so she might see it, but he hadn't wanted to stop. That place would forever remain his and Nora's, regardless of the way things had turned out between them.

"I believe I'll go change," Lady Sophia said, falling into step beside him as they walked toward the house. "Then perhaps we might go for a walk?" The eagerness behind the question was unmistakable.

"I need to speak with my father first. But I shall see you at dinner."

"Very well." She walked beside him in silence for a minute before she stopped. "Colin?" He came to a stop as well and waited for her to continue. "We leave tomorrow for home, as you know, but I was wondering if perhaps..." Her cheeks turned an attractive shade of pink. "Well, I thought perhaps you might want to join us. You could stay with us for a few weeks, or longer, if you decide. We could run up to London while you were there. You could fly your aeroplane."

Colin studied the helmet and goggles he carried. Did he want to go with Lady Sophia and her family? Perhaps a change of scenery would do him good. "Thank you for the invitation. I'd be honored to consider it."

She smiled. "I hope that means you'll say 'yes.'" She linked her arm through his as they returned to the house.

Inside Lady Sophia excused herself to go upstairs, while Colin halted in front of the closed doors of the library. He and his father hadn't spoken directly to each other since their confrontation about Sir Edward's visit to Nora.

Colin expelled a long breath and pushed open one of the doors. Sir Edward sat with his back to his desk, his face toward the window. Colin stepped unnoticed into the room.

Dressed as he was in his pilot clothes, prepared to speak to his father, time felt as though it had wound backward, to the morning nearly three months before when he'd agreed to help with the plans for the hotel. How much things had changed since then—how much he'd changed.

He cleared his throat to announce his presence. "Father?"

Sir Edward glanced over his shoulder. "Colin. I didn't hear you come in."

"May I speak with you?" Colin crossed the room and sat on the short couch, facing the desk.

"Yes, of course." Sir Edward turned his chair around. He sat stiff and straight, as though steeling himself for something unpleasant.

Their interactions hadn't always been this way, had they? Colin tried to remember happier times between him and his father. A long-forgotten memory nudged its way forward in his mind—a summer day in Scotland when Christian had been in bed with a cold, and Colin and Sir Edward had gone fishing in the loch, just the two of them. Colin recalled the warmth of his father's hand on his shoulder as he'd cast his line and the easy laughter they shared when he caught a twig instead of a fish.

"What do you wish to discuss?" his father asked, his tone bordering on impatience.

"I have a proposal—for the hotel."

"Let's not be hasty. Miss Lewis is to give me her answer tomorrow and I believe she'll agree to sell."

Colin set his goggles and helmet on the couch beside him and bent forward, his elbows on his knees. "She may, but I've come up with another idea so we don't have to rely on her agreement or the money from someone like the earl."

"Go on." Sir Edward laced his fingers together and rested them on the desk.

For a brief moment Colin allowed himself to grieve what he was about to lose, then he recalled Nora's face the night she'd first seen her cottage. He was doing the right thing. "I think you ought to build the hotel on the far edge of the back lawn."

His father studied him. "That's where you land your aeroplane."

"I know, and it would mean building a much smaller hotel." Before his father could protest, he hurried to explain. "I recognize it's not ideal, but it would give guests access to the gardens and house them closer to the automobiles as well."

"Interesting thought." Sir Edward leaned back in his chair. "You realize we have no other property for your plane, though. You're prepared to give that up?"

Colin gave a resolute nod. "I am."

"Why?"

He lowered his gaze to his empty hands, unwilling to give voice to the reason.

"You want to do this," Sir Edward interjected into the ensuing silence, "even though Miss Lewis no longer shares your affections?"

Colin lifted his head. "How do you—"

"Come, my boy. You wouldn't be spending time with"—he lowered his voice—"the earl's daughter if Miss Lewis were still around." He chuckled when Colin gaped at him. "I don't always need your mother to tell me what's going on under my nose."

"So you agree then?" Colin pressed. "Would a smaller hotel still save the estate?"

Sir Edward tapped his fingers against his chin. "Building on our own land would allow us to cut out outside investors and keep more revenue for ourselves. But I don't think it would allow us to live as we've been."

Colin hung his head, tasting bitter disappointment, until his father continued. "However, if you are willing to sacrifice your enjoyment of flying, then I believe your mother and I could forgo some of the niceties we've come to expect."

"It will work then?" The question came out a plea.

"We can easily extend the drive to the back lawn and the gardens would be a nice draw for visitors." After a long moment, Sir Edward gave a decisive nod. "Yes, I think it may work. Well done."

His father's praise seeped into Colin's soul, eradicating any remaining sorrow at giving up his flying days. In the end he'd done his duty as future baronet to save Elmthwaite Hall.

"There's something else." Colin picked up his stuff and stood. "I'd like you to give Lyle a job."

One of Sir Edward's graying eyebrows rose in challenge. "Doing what?"

"He's actually quite handy with machines. He fixed my aeroplane the other week when I couldn't get her started. I think he'd do an excellent job maintaining the cars." Colin changed his tone from confident to entreating. "Things haven't gone well for him in London since the war. I think he'd welcome a permanent change."

"All right then. I'll consider it. Anything else?"

"Yes." Colin gave a decisive nod. Nora had told him

the idea to help other soldiers would come eventually, and it had. He only wished he'd thought of it sooner. "I wish to use Brideshall."

"Whatever for?" Sir Edward asked, his expression baffled.

"I want to turn it into a home, a hospital of sorts, for soldiers. Ones worse off than Lyle even. Those who haven't been able to adjust to life at home yet." He took a step forward, earnestness fueling his motions. "Brideshall is the ideal setting. It's away from the village and has the loch surrounding it."

"How would you pay to care for these men?"

Colin swallowed hard. "I don't know for certain. I envision the men will help around the home, to earn their keep so to speak. But we'd likely need to organize some sort of charity to fund their care."

When he'd finished, Colin waited in the growing silence for his father's response. This, more than flying even, was what he was meant to do, at least for the next few years. Colin felt it in every cell of his body.

Sir Edward studied him for a long moment, then glanced away, an unmistakable sheen to his eyes. "I rather like the idea of helping others who served in the war, as you and Christian did."

Elation soared through Colin. "Does that mean we can do it?"

"It will take much planning. Nearly as much as the hotel. But yes." A rare show of excitement lit his blue gaze. "I believe we can do it."

Colin couldn't help grinning. "Thank you, sir." He started for the door, but his father called him back.

"I am…" Sir Edward coughed and shifted in his seat.

"What I mean to say is I may have misjudged...certain things." Colin kept silent. "These new ideas of yours show real ingenuity and selflessness. I didn't know quite what to do with you when you came home. I know you didn't want to be baronet, but we had no choice."

He lowered his hands to the armrests of the chair and rubbed the worn fabric. An air of exhaustion seeped from him, reaching Colin across the room. "I know you're not Christian." Colin felt his gut tighten at the words, but his father's next admission erased the tension. "And that is good. I think these times call for someone like you, Colin, to run things here. Christian would have done it the way I have, the way my father did, the way my grandfather did. But the world is changing, and for good or ill, we must change with it. I believe you're the man for the job."

Regret for their contention in the past and happiness at his father's approval made it impossible for Colin to speak. He'd waited his entire life for this moment, and yet, it might have come earlier if he'd been content to be himself sooner.

"I'll see you at dinner," Sir Edward said, bending over the papers on his desk.

Colin recognized the dismissal as a way for both of them to remain stoic, at least outwardly. With a nod, he exited the library and drew the door softly shut behind him. Neither of them may have said all they wanted to, but Colin sensed something significant had changed between them. He no longer saw his father as unyielding and incapable of understanding, and his father no longer saw him as a poor substitute for Christian. If nothing else, Colin had Nora and the hotel project to thank for that.

Chapter 20

A knock at the back door of the cottage set Phoebe to barking. "Come in," Nora called from where she sat at the table. Her response to Livy's latest letter, announcing the arrival of their son, Tommy, was almost finished.

Somehow Nora had managed to fill several pages, despite leaving off any mention of Colin or the vandalism to her property. If Livy got wind of what had happened, Nora felt certain her dear friend would hop ship to England, new baby in tow, and storm Elmthwaite Hall intent on righteous retribution.

Jack opened the door, a towel-covered dish in his hands, and stepped into the kitchen. Phoebe growled in protest.

"You silly dog. It's only Jack." Nora nudged the puppy with the toe of her shoe. "I thought Mary might come over again." Bess's oldest daughter had brought dinner to Nora the night before—and stayed a good hour, talking all about Lyle. It pleased and pained Nora to hear Mary prattle on about how much she liked the young man.

"I asked to come. Where should I put this?"

Nora motioned to the counter. Phoebe finally stopped making noise at their guest, but she didn't return to her spot under the table. Instead she sat beside Nora's feet, ears alert. Nora shook her head at the dog's strange antics. "Please tell your mother she doesn't need to make dinner for me anymore." She'd been on her own for two days now, though she did appreciate the meals Bess had provided.

"I'll tell her, but I doubt she'll listen."

Nora laughed. "True." She stood slowly to avoid the dizziness she still felt if she moved too quickly or remained on her feet too long. "Want to join me?"

Jack hesitated. "Is there enough?"

"If there's as much as there was last night, we'll both have plenty."

"All right." He took a seat and set his cap on the table. Phoebe let out another low growl.

"I wonder what's gotten into her," Nora said, removing two plates from the cupboard. She dished her and Jack some of the sausage and set the plates on the table. After offering grace, she began to eat.

"What happens with the sheep in September?" she asked after swallowing a bite.

Jack pushed his sausage around with his fork. "It's hefting." He clearly caught the blank look she gave him over her dinner. "That's when the ewes return to their particular spot on the fell with their lambs. If they don't *heft*, then the lambs will wander all over the mountain."

"Kind of like me," Nora quipped, but Jack didn't laugh. Instead he took a bite and set his fork down.

"There's something I need to tell you, Nora." His expression was uncharacteristically serious, even for Jack.

"Okay." She stopped eating to listen.

"There's no easy way to say it." He stared at his plate. Nora could hear his boot tapping a steady beat under the table. A flush had begun creeping up his neck. "I need to tell you...I mean I want to tell you..."

"Tell me what, Jack?" she prompted, hoping to ease his nervousness.

He lifted his head to look at her. "It was me who threw the rock through your window."

Nora's mouth fell open, her mind reeling, unable to make sense of what he'd just said. "Wh-what are you talking about?"

"The note, the garden, the stone wall—it was all my doing." He hung his head.

Prickles of ice ran up Nora's spine and she shivered. Jack had been the culprit?

"That isn't all, though. I...um...took your dog...and hid her." His face turned as red as his neck now. "I only meant to worry you, honest, not send you up the fell by yourself."

The revelations were coming too fast. Nora folded her arms against the chill racing through her and shook her head, trying desperately to think clearly. She only managed to get out one word, "Why?"

Jack ran a hand under his nose and gazed in the direction of the door. "Mary told me about Colin's plans to persuade you to leave so he could buy your land. She overheard him and his father talking at breakfast one day." He twisted his head in her direction again, his eyes full of sorrow. "I thought if I could make you believe Colin was behind those pranks, that you'd…"

"Choose you over him." The answer was so startlingly clear Nora couldn't believe she hadn't suspected Jack before. Each act had come on the heels of her spending time with Colin—the shearing day at her farm, flying in his plane, seeing him after he'd worked in the stables with Jack, and finally, the party at Elmthwaite Hall. Jack had been jealous.

"I'm sorry, Nora. You may not believe me, but I am. I didn't mean for it to go so far that you got hurt." He fingered his cap beside his plate.

"I might have died, Jack. If Colin hadn't found me…" She couldn't finish her sentence. A lump clogged her throat. She wanted to lash out in anger at him, but at the same time, shame at herself made her hold her tongue. She'd condemned Colin for something he hadn't done.

Jack scraped back his chair, causing Phoebe to bark again. Nora was no longer surprised the puppy wasn't friendly toward him. Phoebe had witnessed his treachery firsthand. "I think I'll go." He stood up and plopped his cap back on his head.

"Yes, I think you should."

He paused at the door. "I don't blame you for being angry, Nora. I just hope you won't hate me forever."

"I need some time, Jack, but I don't hate you. You, your mother, and brothers and sisters are the only family I have left." Especially now that Colin was out of her life. She pressed her lips together, knowing she was seconds away from crying.

"Good night, Nora."

She nodded in response. The door clicked shut behind him as the first few tears escaped her eyes. Jack's confession changed everything. She rested her elbow on the table and pressed her hand to her forehead. Her head had begun to hurt.

Her shoulders shook with her quiet sobs. Phoebe stretched her hind legs onto Nora's knee and licked her free hand, but Nora couldn't muster the strength to soothe her.

She'd thought herself a fool for trusting Colin, but she felt more foolish at having convicted him without proof. He hadn't tried to make her leave after all, as his father had requested. Instead he'd been kind and solicitous.

"What am I going to do?" Her question sounded loud in the quiet kitchen, though she'd hardly spoken above a whisper.

No longer hungry, she set her and Jack's plates on the floor for Phoebe to finish. She needed to do something, anything to get out of this silent house. She couldn't weed the garden—she hadn't replanted it—but there might be something out front to pull up. The need to rip up something drove her down the hallway and out the front door.

The flowers and plants below the window had grown a bit wild with neglect. Nora knelt down and began pulling out the weeds. When she finished one area, she moved across the doorway to the other. Among the grass, she spotted some shriveled flowers. She picked up the small bundle. They weren't like any of the other flowers growing around the cottage.

Nora studied the withered heads and tried to remember where she'd seen this type of flower before. The memory of dancing outside Elmthwaite Hall with Colin entered her mind. She'd plucked a flower similar to these from a bush while they'd been talking. These flowers came from Colin's house. Had he brought them to her? If so, he must have tossed them aside after she'd refused to see him.

The dead petals crumpled under the weight of her fingers and resurrected her tears. While Colin hadn't been completely honest about his motives, at least not in the beginning, he had genuinely cared for her—according to Bess and Lyle. Did he still? Or had her hurt and stubbornness cost her what her heart most desired?

She might have hurt him in return, but perhaps she hadn't lost him—not completely anyway. Nora climbed to her feet and brushed the bits of flower from her hands. There was a way she could set things right, a way to prove to Colin that she was no longer angry. That deep down she still loved him more than anything else.

First thing tomorrow morning, she would go to Elmthwaite, as promised, to give Sir Edward her answer about the farm. Then she'd ask, beg, demand, whatever it took, to see Colin. She no longer cared if she made a fool of herself in front of his family or their guests. It was time to silence her practical side and let the passionate one have sway for once.

* * *

The morning sunlight warmed Colin's back through his jacket as he gripped Lyle's hand in a firm handshake. It was shaping up to be a perfect day for flying, with hardly a cloud in the sky. "Take care of yourself—and those cars—while I'm gone, all right?"

Lyle nodded. "I still can't believe your father gave me a job. He won't say how the idea came to him, though." He threw Colin a suspicious look. "Only that I'm the right man for it."

"You are, so never mind how he came up with it."

"How long do you think you'll be gone?"

Colin glanced in the direction of Nora's cottage, though he couldn't see it from here. "A month, I think, maybe longer. Depending on Lady Sophia," he added with a rueful smile. The earl and his family had already departed for the train station. Colin would fly his aeroplane and meet them at their home outside London.

Lyle chuckled. "I'll admit she has improved upon further acquaintance." His expression sobered. "But I don't think she'll ever quite measure up to..."

"Nora." The name tasted as sweet as it did bitter on Colin's tongue.

"You're certain you don't want to try to talk to her again?"

Colin shifted his weight, his hands finding their way to his jacket pockets. "It wouldn't do any good. She would only see it as me attempting to persuade her again." He shook his head. "I've given her enough reason to mistrust me—if she wants to change things, I have to let her do it."

"You think some time away from her will make a difference?"

He lifted his eyes to Lyle's. "I need to go, Lyle. It's difficult...being so close and yet unable to see her."

His friend clapped a hand on his shoulder. "I promise not to sweep her off her feet in your absence."

Colin laughed, easing the tension that roiled through him whenever he talked or thought about Nora now. "That's because you'll be too busy sweeping some other girl off her feet. Rather convenient now that you both work at the same place."

Lyle's face flushed, but his smile didn't diminish. He'd told Colin the night before about his attraction to Mary Tuttle. Colin hoped the two of them would be happy. Perhaps someday he'd find that same happiness, or at least a portion of it, with someone else.

"I noticed a picture as I was walking by your room this morning," Lyle said, artfully changing the subject. "I don't think I noticed it before. It's the one of you and Christian from the *Daily Mail* article, isn't it?"

"Yes."

Colin had returned it to the spot on his wall the night before. Afterward, he'd stood for some time staring at the grainy image. His and Christian's grins were almost identical, their arms draped around each other's shoulders in mutual comradery. Instead of grief and regret, a feeling of peace had filled him as he studied his brother's face. This was exactly how he wanted to remember Christian.

"I'd better go." Colin shook Lyle's hand once more and climbed into the aeroplane. At his signal, Lyle jerked the propeller. When the engine roared to life, Colin lifted a hand in farewell. Within seconds, the plane was speeding down the lawn for the final time. His father would start digging the hotel foundation in a few days.

Colin pulled back on the stick, and the biplane climbed toward the sky. Of their own accord, his eyes sought out Nora's cottage as he flew over the lake.

"Take care, Nora," he murmured before setting his face forward. He had a long flight ahead of him.

* * *

A noise, like the incessant buzz of a fly, filled Nora's head. She waved her hand in front of her face, without opening her eyes, in hopes of driving the insect away. Just a few more minutes of sleep, then she'd get up.

Ever since her accident on the fell, she'd had a much harder time rising at her usual early hour. But she couldn't remain in bed all day—there was something important to do, though she couldn't quite place what it was at the moment.

She twisted onto her side and burrowed farther beneath the blankets. Sleep had been long in coming last night. She'd been thinking about Jack's confession... and about Colin...and about the flowers he'd thrown away.

At the memory of the flowers, her eyes flew open. She'd planned to see Sir Edward and Colin, first thing this morning, so they could put the last week behind them for good. Nora darted a glance at the clock and gasped. It was nearly nine. She'd slept in.

She threw off the covers, upsetting Phoebe in the process. The dog hopped up from the foot of the bed and barked in protest.

"Never mind that, Phoebe. I'm late."

Nora changed into her green Sunday dress, the one she'd worn to the dance at the pub. After running a brush through her hair, she settled for tying it back with a ribbon instead of taking the time to arrange it up. She placed her matching green hat on her head and scooped Phoebe up into her arms on the way out the door.

She didn't want to waste any more time preparing breakfast, so she grabbed a couple of biscuits from the tin in the cupboard and went outside. Sunshine filled the morning with light and warmth. Nora tied Phoebe up to the gate post. Now that she knew Jack was the one behind the puppy's disappearance, she no longer feared leaving her alone outside.

After a quick pat on Phoebe's head, Nora set off down the lane. Each rapid footfall matched the swift beating of her heart. Would Colin see her? Would he be pleased with what she planned to say to his father?

She reached the main road and turned left, toward Elmthwaite Hall, eating her meager meal as she went. As she drew closer to the grand house, she slowed her steps. It wouldn't do to arrive sweaty and out of breath. When she reached the front doors, she stopped to straighten her hat and brush any crumbs from her dress.

"Here goes." She knocked loudly, surprised she could hear the noise over the pounding of her heartbeat.

Nearly a minute surely passed before one of the doors was opened by the Ashbys' butler. He stared down his angular nose at her, blocking her way with his tall frame. Though it was morning, unlike the first time she'd come knocking here, the moment felt ironically similar to her first night in Larksbeck. Only she wasn't the same this time.

She'd come to England, lost and grieving, with the hope of slipping into this new life largely unnoticed. What she'd discovered instead was that she didn't want to live isolated and wholly independent anymore. She needed others, just as they hopefully had need of her. Not only had she found a new family in this small valley, a family which included the villagers and a man she loved with all her heart, but she'd found herself, too.

"Good morning, Mr. Martin." She gave him her most beguiling smile, in the event he'd been told not to allow her admittance. "I need to speak with Sir Edward."

"Is he expecting you?"

"I believe he'll want to hear what I have to say."

The butler eyed her hat and dress, then to her surprise, he stepped back. "Come in, Miss Lewis. Sir Edward is in the library."

She stepped inside and waited for him to shut the door. Here in this entryway she'd first seen Colin, looking so dashing in his dinner suit. Her gaze wandered to the grand staircase. Was he awake yet?

"This way," the butler said.

Nora followed him farther into the house to a set of closed double doors. The butler knocked softly and entered. The murmur of conversation reached Nora's ears.

"He will see you," the butler announced as he exited the room. He motioned Nora forward.

She straightened her shoulders and walked through the doorway. Nearly every wall, except the ones with large windows, held bookcases filled to capacity. Across the room Sir Edward sat at a long desk. When the door clicked shut behind her, he stood.

"Miss Lewis. Have a seat." He motioned to a small couch opposite his desk.

Nora walked over and sat down. "Thank you."

He resumed his seat and folded his hands on top of the desk.

"I'm here about your business offer, Sir Edward." When he didn't respond, Nora shifted her weight on the couch. "After a considerable amount of thought, I've decided..." She wet her dry lips, reminding herself she was doing this for Colin. "I've decided to sell my property to you."

"I see." His expression remained indifferent.

Nora plucked at an errant thread on her dress. The conversation wasn't going at all as she'd imagined. Why wasn't the man more excited at finally having her land? "I'll need to find another place to live first, but then we can make the needed arrangements—"

"I'm afraid that won't be necessary, Miss Lewis." He brandished a pen and tapped it against the desk. "You see, I no longer have need of your property."

"I'm sorry?" She shook her head, unsure she'd heard him right. "I don't understand. Are you still planning on building your hotel?"

Sir Edward nodded. "I am."

"But you don't need my land anymore?"

"Quite right."

Had she missed something? "Are you using your home in Scotland then?"

"No. My son has decided to put that to use as a temporary home for soldiers recovering from the war."

"Oh...how wonderful." So Colin had found his way to help at last. Which meant he would be gone soon, to Scotland. Perhaps she could assist in some way from here, if he no longer cared for her. She very much liked the idea of helping soldiers who, unlike Tom and Christian, had survived the war but were still suffering.

"May I ask where you plan to build your hotel then?" she asked, still confused.

"Colin has graciously given up the back lawn, so we can build it there."

Nora sank back against the couch, her thoughts awhirl. Colin wouldn't give up the place where he landed his plane, unless... Her gaze jerked from the carpet to Sir Edward's face. The tiniest bit of a smile lifted the corners of his mouth.

"My son found a way to honor his duty—and his heart. Unlike his father, all those years ago." Sir Edward rested his elbows on the chair arms, his smile deepening. "Then again, perhaps my decision back then wasn't so injudicious as it seemed to some. Since it has led to the happiness of more than one couple. Wouldn't you agree, Miss Lewis?"

Colin still loved her, enough to give up flying so she could keep her home. The realization drove her to her feet. "May I see him, please? I need to thank him. And there are other things that need to be said..." She let her voice trail off at the sudden return of Sir Edward's somber countenance.

"He's not here."

The finality with which he said it snuffed Nora's elation as quickly as a candle in a breeze. "Has he gone flying?"

"He has, but he won't be back for some time. He's gone to stay with Lady Sophia's family near London." Nora's knees gave way and she dropped back onto the couch. "I imagine he'll be there for a few weeks, perhaps longer. It all depends."

She knew exactly what it depended on—how well

Colin came to like Lady Sophia. While Nora didn't think he favored the heiress, she was beginning to see how quickly things could alter in a week's time.

"I'm sorry," Sir Edward said, his tone surprisingly genuine.

"You disapprove of him going?" Nora couldn't stop the question from slipping out. She'd been so certain Colin's father wouldn't approve of them, and yet he seemed nearly as sad as she at the news of Colin spending time with the earl's daughter.

He fiddled with the pen in his hand. "I would have gladly welcomed such a thing before this week. But now..." He lifted his eyes to hers. Nora saw only sincerity in their blue depths. "I want him happy, Miss Lewis. Will he find that with Lady Sophia? Perhaps. Although I thought, before he left this morning, that he may have found such happiness closer to home."

Nora recognized the meaning behind his carefully crafted words. If Colin had chosen her, Sir Edward would not have put up a fight. But both their revelations had come too late. Colin was already gone, and with him, her chance to make things right.

She climbed to her feet once again and held out her hand to Sir Edward. "Thank you, sir."

"For what?" He stood and clasped her hand.

"For allowing me the chance to know your son." Her voice broke and she hurried to clear her throat so she could continue. "Whatever the reason, at first, his friendship made being here much easier. He's an exceptional person, and I hope you'll be proud of him."

"I am." He lowered his hand. "And I owe you some appreciation as well."

"I don't know what for."

"Because Colin was . . . well, a bit lost before you came here, Miss Lewis. Befriending you appears to be the best thing he could have done, in finding himself and his place here."

Nora tipped her head in acknowledgment. Tears stung her eyes. If she didn't leave soon, she'd fall into a weeping mess before the baronet. "Good day, Sir Edward."

"Good day, Miss Lewis. Shall I have Martin escort you to the door?"

"No. I'll see myself out."

She made it down the hall to the front doors before the moisture in her eyes could no longer be checked. Tears leaked down her face as she fled outside and down the gravel drive. The sunny day mocked the pain splitting her heart in two. Why couldn't it be gray and rainy? That sort of weather wouldn't be such an affront to the regret inside her. If only she hadn't been so stubborn in refusing to talk to Colin.

She neared her lane, but the thought of returning to the quiet cottage, even with Phoebe around, was unbearable. Alone, there would be no escape from the despair of her loss. But she also loathed the idea of going into the village, or to Bess's, and making small talk when her world had been turned upside down—again.

Where to go? Nora twisted in a circle, taking in the lake and the mountains. The valley felt suddenly too small and confining. She needed to go somewhere with open space and few people. The memory of such a place slipped into her mind—Brougham Castle. She could explore the ruins in the sunshine, in a place where she and Colin had been happy.

Nora hurried up the lane to the cottage to collect her purse and some money for the train fare. It would be a long trek to the castle, but she didn't care if it took all day. However silly or irrational her plan, at least she had something to do and she wouldn't be swayed from doing it.

Chapter 21

After setting out bowls of food and water for Phoebe, Nora set off for the long walk to the train station. She had to go through Larksbeck first, though she feared someone would see her and want to talk. Thankfully luck was on her side, and she managed to get beyond the village without incident. The sun seeped through her dress, making her warm. Thankfully she had her hat.

By the time she reached the station, she felt hot and dizzy. Nora purchased a ticket and dropped onto a bench outside to wait for the train. If only she'd eaten more than a few biscuits this morning. She fanned her flushed face with her hat and watched the people around her.

Wealthy guests to Elmthwaite Hall would arrive here, much like the elegantly dressed family standing near her bench. The couple were exclaiming over the town and the mountains, while their two boys chased themselves around their mound of luggage. Nora could understand their awe at the beauty of the Lake District. Surely there would be plenty of people who would want to take advantage of the Ashbys' hotel.

Could she remain living near the estate and Colin, if he brought Lady Sophia back as his wife? The idea cut deep enough that she brought a hand to her throat. Maybe they'd move to Scotland to oversee the home for soldiers and she would be free to continue her life here, alone.

"Are you all right, miss?"

Nora looked up. The mother of the two boys joined Nora on the bench. "Oh, yes, I'm fine."

"You look as warm as I feel." The lady had friendly brown eyes. "Charles?" she called to her husband. "Would you and the boys be so kind as to procure some refreshment for us and this American young lady here?"

"You don't have to—"

"It will mean a moment's peace," she said with an impish smile. "My boys need to stretch their legs after being on the train all the way from London and I need a little quiet." Her husband, with the boys in tow, moved away from the station.

"Do you live here?" she asked Nora.

"No, I'm from…" Nora nearly finished with saying she came from Iowa, but that didn't feel right anymore. "I actually live in a village south of here. It's called Larksbeck."

"Have you lived there long?"

"Only a few months," Nora said with a laugh. "But it's home." The words were out before she could analyze them, but they rang true to her heart. Larksbeck was home. No matter what happened with Colin and his future bride, she couldn't leave the village.

They fell into companionable silence until the

woman's husband returned with some pastries and peppermint sticks. Nora accepted a pastry, though she declined the candy. The little bit of food in her stomach did much to revive her stamina. She thanked the couple several times for their kindness and wished them a pleasant holiday.

Her train arrived shortly after and Nora stood to board. A thought had her hurrying over to the family who were manning their luggage again. "If you decide to return to the Lake District next year, I know the perfect place to stay. There's a hotel being built beside Elmthwaite Hall near Larksbeck, and it will be brand-new next year."

They thanked her for the information and Nora climbed onto the train, feeling pleased with herself for possibly securing some of the hotel's first guests. She did want the place to succeed, if only for Colin. She settled into her cushioned seat. Once the train began moving and her ticket had been collected, she shut her eyes and allowed herself to doze.

The announcement for her stop penetrated Nora's sleepy mind. She sat up as the train pulled to a stop at the station and she disembarked. With some food and sleep, she felt ready for the last part of her journey—the long walk to the castle. She headed out of the city limits, trading shops and side-by-side housing for farms and fields. Perhaps when she returned in a few hours, she might wander through some of the stores. She kept close to the river as she walked since she knew it ran directly alongside Brougham Castle.

Just when her feet were beginning to feel sore, she spotted the topmost tower of the castle above the trees. She was close.

Nora crossed the bridge to the east side of the castle and climbed the small hill toward the ruins. A few sheep grazed nearby. They lifted their heads at her approach, but they soon returned to their eating. She could see no other visitors about the place.

The half-crumbled walls were as intriguing and beautiful as they'd been the other week when she and Colin had flown here. Nora entered the tunnel where they'd sought protection from the rain. She stopped to run her fingers over the rough stone, remembering Colin's kiss in this very spot. It was that day she'd realized how much she was falling in love with him.

She walked down the tunnel, the click of her shoes echoing off the ancient walls. At the other end, Colin had told her the history of the castle while she'd basked in his strong embrace. She peered out at the courtyard, a slow ache beginning in her heart. Perhaps this had been a terrible idea. She'd come seeking peace and closure, not torture from sweet memories she'd never experience again.

No longer excited at the prospect of lingering, Nora decided to take in the view from the third floor before she walked back to the city and the train. She left the tunnel the way she'd come and circled the ruins to reenter near the winding staircase. As she reached the stairs, the thud of descending footsteps filled the air. Nora paused. She wasn't alone after all—someone else had come to admire the castle.

She retreated to the other side of the walled room, away from the stairs, to allow the other person to come down before she headed up. Her moment at the top needed to be hers alone.

Nora stared at the moss-covered walls rising three

floors above her. She tried to visualize what they might have looked like in Lady Anne Clifford's day, with ceilings and rooms and furniture.

The footsteps sounded closer, no longer near the top of the staircase. Nora moved toward a wall where a fireplace appeared to have been. She ran her hand over some of the charred stones. What sort of events, joyful and sorrowful, had this hearth witnessed? She could no longer hear the other person's footfalls. Had he or she slipped away unnoticed, anxious for some privacy, too?

Ready to climb to the top, she turned toward the stairs and froze. A figure stood in the shadows, but it wasn't his presence that caused her heart to skip several beats. It was the cap and goggles dangling from one hand.

"Colin?" she whispered, the name barely making it out of her suddenly dry throat.

She squeezed her eyes shut, certain she was imagining things. How foolish she'd feel when she opened them again to find a complete stranger standing there.

"Nora."

The familiar voice washed over her like gentle rain. Her eyes flew open as he emerged from the staircase. He was dressed in his flying jacket and trousers and looked every bit as handsome as he had the night of the party. Had it really been a whole week since she'd seen him last? It felt more like a lifetime.

With measured steps he walked toward her, but he came to a stop several feet away. His eyes watched her intently, his lips in a tight line. Nora realized she was holding her breath. She let it out in a quiet whoosh, which somehow loosened her tongue enough to speak. "I thought you were on your way to London."

"I was—I am. The plane is sitting not far from here."

He was still leaving.

"How did you get here?" he asked.

"I walked and rode the train." She couldn't seem to collect enough air to breathe properly. Her earlier dizziness threatened to engulf her. She put a hand to the stones next to her to keep from swaying. At once, Colin was beside her, gripping her elbow. His nearness, and warm touch, after such a long absence made the shaky feeling worse.

"You need to sit down." He led her to a line of stones that must have formed a wall at one point. Nora sat. To her disappointment, Colin released her arm at once. He set down his flying gear but remained standing. "You're clearly not well. Why did you come all the way out here?"

A twinge of anger rose inside her at his reprimand. He was the one who'd left without saying good-bye. *Of course, he probably thought you'd turn him away*, her mind scolded. "I met with your father this morning, to tell him he could have my property. But apparently, he received a better offer."

Colin rested one boot on the stone in front of him, his hands in their customary spot inside his pockets. "I didn't see the need for your land, when there was a perfectly fine spot near the house that we could use."

How could she break through the cautiousness he wore around him like a shield? She tasted bitter regret in her mouth at the realization of how much she'd hurt him. "I didn't get..." She tried again. "I didn't take the chance to thank you the other day, for saving my life."

His shoulders lifted in a shrug, his gaze taking in

everything but her. "It was God who helped me see you through the clouds that day. The credit ought to go to Him."

Nora stared at him, disbelief rippling through her. Colin's tone no longer sounded doubtful or angry at the mention of God. "What happened?"

He remained silent, long enough that she thought he wouldn't answer, but he finally spoke again. "I couldn't see anything on the ground because of the clouds, so I prayed." Beneath his indifferent tone, Nora sensed the wonder and faith the experience had inspired in him. "It wasn't a minute later that the clouds started to disappear. Then I spotted you."

Shame burned her cheeks. "I'm sorry, Colin. I was angry and hurt, and I thought you'd committed those acts of vandalism. But I had no right to be horrid."

"You thought I did those things?" His eyes swung to meet hers. The surprise and pain in them twisted Nora's heart all the more.

"I know I had no proof, but I couldn't think of who else wanted me gone. And then Jack"—she blew out another sigh at the memory of her cousin's confession—"admitted it was him."

"Jack?" Colin straightened.

"He hid Phoebe, too. That's why I couldn't find her on the fell."

His jaw visibly tightened. "I ought to fly back there and teach him a lesson."

"No." Nora set down her purse and hat and slowly got to her feet. "It was me who needed the lesson. I realized the moment Jack told me what he'd done that I wasn't angry with you anymore—for going along with your father's plan." She took a wary step toward him. "I never should have refused to see you."

Colin didn't speak, just watched her. Nora clasped and unclasped her hands. The air between them still felt heavy with unsaid hurt and remorse. Was there any way to make things right before he left?

"Your father told me of your plan to turn Brideshall into a sort of home for soldiers who need extra help." She wet her lips and plunged on despite his continued silence. "I think it's a wonderful idea, Colin. Hopefully a good many of them can begin to heal in a place I imagine must be just as beautiful as this one. I would love to help if I can."

"That may be a possibility." A quizzical light entered his eyes, but he made no further comment.

"I...um...heard you're going to visit Lady Sophia and her family."

"Yes. They expected me this evening."

Nora gave a friendly nod, though hearing the news from Colin's own lips made it ten times harder to bear. Maybe it would've been better if she hadn't come to the castle at all, but now that Colin was here, she couldn't leave without saying everything she needed to. Including telling him the idea she'd been pondering most of the day.

"I was wrong, Colin, about a great many things. I know that now. Whatever your reasons for being my friend, I'm grateful." She pressed her lips together to keep from crying. She had to finish. "Which is why I want you to take my land and use it for a runway, for your plane. Please don't give up flying. Not on my account."

He studied her openly. "What would you do?"

It was her turn to shrug. She hadn't sorted out every

detail yet. "I could combine my sheep with the Tuttles'. That way I could still live in the cottage, but farm with them."

"Is that what you want?"

The tears were getting harder to hold back. "If it means you get to keep flying." She lifted her chin, though it trembled. "I want you to be happy, Colin. You are and always will be my friend." She swallowed hard and forced out her next words. "That is, if Lady Sophia approves."

His expression had softened during her impassioned speech. He stepped toward her as she finished, closing the distance between them. "Why should we care what Lady Sophia thinks?" He brought his thumb to her chin and stroked the skin there. Nora's pulse thrummed as fast as the train's wheels earlier, especially when his finger brushed her lips. "You still didn't answer my earlier question. Why did you come here, Nora?"

"Because..." A tear slid down her cheek. Colin gently skimmed it away with his finger, his dark eyes intent on her face. The tenderness in his look made her want to cry all the harder. How could she let him go? "I came because I love you. And while I want you happy, Colin, even if that means you choose Lady Sophia..." Another tear escaped her stinging eyes. "I suppose I foolishly held out hope you might still choose to be happy... with me."

Without a word, Colin bent to kiss away the lingering tear from her cheek. Nora shut her eyes and leaned into his touch. How she'd missed him this last week. Then his lips were moving softly down her skin until they found her mouth.

A lightning bolt of feeling catapulted through Nora's stomach at his kiss. Her heart beat wildly in her throat.

His other hand clasped her waist firmly but affectionately, drawing her closer. Nora cupped his face between her hands and fervently kissed him back. How wonderful and familiar his clean-shaven jaw felt beneath her fingers. When he eased back several heartbeats later, Nora felt faint again, but this time it was a wonderful, dizzy kind of feeling.

"You haven't asked why I'm here," he said, his voice low.

"Why are you here?"

"I didn't plan on flying this way, but somehow I ended up in this direction." He captured a lock of her hair between his fingers and began to play with it. "The closer I came to the castle, the more I knew I couldn't visit Lady Sophia. It would give her the wrong idea. So I landed and sent her a telegram informing her I wouldn't be coming after all. Then I flew here."

Nora drew back. "But you said you were still going to London."

Colin gave her a slow smile that made her stomach spiral again with pleasure. "I am, but not to see the earl's family."

"Why then?"

"Because a proper bride needs a proper ring."

Nora feigned a suspicious scowl, even as happiness coursed through her at his words. "Who is this proper bride, and how do you know she plans to accept your ring?"

He chuckled. "I planned to sleep out in front of her lane until she agreed to see me. I would have waited there for years, if need be. You see, I recently discovered the power of hope." His expression turned serious. "That being said, I should have told you in the beginning about the hotel plans. But I thought if I did, it might end any chance I had of getting to know you better. Can you forgive me, Nora?"

She went up on tiptoe to kiss him, relishing the feel of his lips against hers once more. "I already have."

"Will you be my wife then?"

"Yes," she said emphatically, "if you're sure. The poor sheep heiress from next door and the baronet-to-be. Whatever will people say?"

The love and desire shining in his deep, dark eyes set Nora's pulse to racing once more. Inexplicable joy washed over and through her.

"You are the heiress of my heart," Colin said softly. He held her open palm against his chest, allowing her to feel the steady drum of his heartbeat. Nora couldn't think of a more comforting rhythm. "And that, my dearest Nora, is the only inheritance and title that will ever matter to me."

Epilogue

Iowa, December 1921

It's so wide... and empty here."

Nora chuckled at Colin's insistent tone. She lifted her head from where she'd been resting it against his shoulder and followed his gaze out the train window. Snow-covered fields and bare trees whizzed past them. "Much different than Larksbeck or Scotland."

"Indeed." He lifted their joined hands and kissed her knuckles. "How are you feeling?"

"A little tired." Her free hand went to the slight bump protruding from her drop-waist dress. "I'll be fine."

"I'm glad we didn't come sooner, when you were sick."

The thought of crossing the ocean during the earlier months of her pregnancy made her stomach turn. Thankfully they'd postponed their trip and Nora hadn't been ill at all. "Coming for Christmas was a much better idea."

"What are the Campbells going to think of your British husband, my dear?"

Nora pulled him toward her so she could press her lips firmly to his. "They are going to love you, just as I do." She released him and feigned a worried expression. "However…"

"However what?" Colin actually looked concerned. Nora bit back a laugh. She could understand his nervousness. Her own stomach had felt full of butterflies this morning at the thought of seeing Livy and her entire family again after eighteen months away.

"If you think Brideshall is full of noise and people with our fifteen soldiers there, wait until you meet the Campbells." She smiled at the exaggerated look of horror on Colin's face. "Joel and Livy will both have their spouses and children there. And I think Livy's husband, Friedrick, may have brought his two siblings down with them as well. The farm is going to be quite full."

"Good thing we're staying in town then." He bent close and brushed his lips against the skin of her neck. Pleasant shivers rose up Nora's back and down her arms.

She leaned against his shoulder again, savoring his solid nearness and warmth. "How do you think everyone back home will spend the holiday?"

Colin draped his arm around her. "Mother will probably host the hotel guests for a grand dinner. I still can't believe the number who wanted to spend Christmas in Larksbeck." He squeezed her shoulder. "All thanks to you, my dear, and your good friends the Ingrams."

The couple Nora had met the day she'd found Colin at Brougham Castle had heeded her suggestion to return to the Lake District and stay at the Ashby Hotel. They'd been among the hotel's first guests in the spring. Having enjoyed their time in the little valley, they made reservations for themselves and a number of their friends to stay through Christmas. They'd also contributed a sizable donation to the soldiers' home at Brideshall after learning of Nora and Colin's work there the last year.

"Do you think Lyle and Mary will be all right managing everything in our absence?"

Colin's friend had married Bess's daughter, and like Nora and Colin, the couple divided their time and employment between Elmthwaite in England and Brideshall in Scotland.

"Yes. The men know them well enough now, and Dr. McFadden is in the village should they have need of him." Colin playfully tapped her nose. "No more worries, dearest. If anything you should be concerned about Father. He's quite upset that you won't be around to challenge him in chess this Christmas."

Nora chuckled. How nervous she'd been to live under Sir Edward's roof, while the house in Scotland was being prepared, despite his obvious approval of his son's choice in a wife. Her fears had been unfounded, though, especially when the two of them had discovered a mutual enjoyment of chess.

A man in a railway uniform walked past their door and announced the next stop. "This is it," Nora said, sitting up. She watched the train pull into the familiar station. The depot platform stood largely empty. Most of the patrons were inside, out of the cold.

Colin collected their bags, then helped Nora to her feet. They made their way out of the car and off the train. The winter air stung Nora's cheeks. She drew her thick coat tighter around her as she and Colin crossed the depot to the station. He shifted the bags to open the door for her. Stepping inside, Nora searched the faces of those waiting.

A cry of excitement erupted from one corner. Nora saw Livy jump up and hurry toward her. "Nora!"

Nora embraced her friend, tears of joy leaking onto her frozen cheeks. "You cut your hair."

Livy touched her short blond locks. "Do you like it?"

"It suits you perfectly." Nora threaded her arm through Colin's. "Livy, this is my husband, Colin Ashby. Colin, may I introduce my dearest friend in the world, Livy Campell Wagner?"

Livy dropped a quick curtsy. She blushed when Nora laughed. "I don't know what to do when one meets a baronet-to-be."

"It's nice to finally meet you, Livy." Colin extended his hand, which Livy shook enthusiastically.

"I'm so glad you came." She waved the two of them toward the corner bench where Friedrick stood, a little boy in his arms and a girl holding his pant leg. "Come meet my family."

Friedrick gave Nora a hug. "It's good to see you again." He and Colin were introduced and exchanged a handshake.

"This is Tommy," Friedrick announced, hoisting the brown-haired cherub. Nora felt a twinge of emotion in her throat. She'd known Livy had named her son after her brother Tom, but meeting the little boy in person brought things to a happy full circle.

Friedrick gave the girl at his side a gentle push. "You know Kate. Kate, can you say hello to Nora and Colin?"

Nora squatted down in front of the blond-haired girl. She could hardly believe how much Kate had grown in her absence. "Do you remember me, Kate?"

The girl scrunched her nose and shook her head.

"That's all right. How old are you now?"

She held up two small fingers.

"Two already?"

"Do you wive in a castle?" she asked, her voice tinged with awe.

Nora and the others chuckled. "Sort of," she said with a smile at Colin as she stood.

"The car's out front." Friedrick led them out of the building.

After stowing their luggage, Colin helped Nora and Livy into the backseat of the car. Livy held Tommy and Nora held Kate. The girls began chattering away as the two men slipped into the seat up front.

As the car pulled away from the station, Nora kept her eyes peeled to the landscape out the window. Nearly every store in town held some memory from her childhood. Livy pointed out the few new ones that had sprung up. Soon they left the town behind for the farms, and before long, they pulled to a stop in front of the Campbells' home.

Memories washed over Nora as she and Kate exited the car and she faced the two-story farmhouse. Most of the recollections were happy, some sad. Colin took her hand in his, a gesture that imbued her with renewed confidence. Together they followed Livy and Friedrick up the porch steps and through the front door. A cacophony of friendly conversation and laughter greeted them as she and Colin stepped inside.

"Nora!" someone cried. In a moment she and Colin were surrounded by Livy's parents and siblings. Nora exchanged a hug with Livy's mother, introduced the group to Colin, and exclaimed over how much Livy's younger sister and brothers had all grown. When the crowd parted, she looked down to see her dog Oscar sitting there. She crouched down to pet the dog's head.

"It's so good to see you, boy," she murmured, ruffling his ears. "I wish you could've met your rambunctious cousin, Phoebe, but we had to leave her behind."

Livy's oldest brother, Joel, came up and gave her a hug. How many times had she, Tom, Livy, and Joel gone places together before the boys had left to fight? She was pleased to see that, like Livy, he was happily married and held no ill will toward her or Colin.

Joel introduced her and Colin to his wife, Evelyn. The pretty, dark-haired woman smiled warmly and had their adopted son Louis say hello. Several other young men from their boys' home in Michigan were also introduced. After meeting Joel's family, Nora presented Colin to Friedrick's brother and sister, Harlan and Greta, whom she'd often seen during her visits to Livy.

Once all the introductions and reunions had been completed, Livy's mother invited everyone into the dining room to eat the feast she'd prepared. Nora sat beside Colin, her left hand tucked in his beneath the table. She listened with amusement to the different conversations bouncing around the room until someone asked her about life in England. A sudden quiet descended over the group as she and Colin did their best to describe Larksbeck, Elmthwaite Hall, and Scotland.

From their earnest expressions, Nora knew the others

wanted to see it the way she and Colin did, but they couldn't quite grasp how tall the fells were, or how green the valley was most of the year, or the changing of the seasons beside the loch. "I suppose you'll just have to come for a visit," she announced. Everyone laughed and agreed a trip across the ocean was in order.

After the meal, Nora pulled Colin aside. "Care to go for a walk?"

"Is there a lake around here?" he teased. They still took their daily walks, rain or sun.

"No," she said, laughing. "Although there is a pond."

"Where to then?"

"I want to show you the old farm."

Nora told Livy they'd be gone for a bit. She and Colin slipped out of the house and headed up the road. A weak sun had come out, warming the temperature and turning the snow into sparkling diamonds.

At the crossroad, Nora led Colin to the right. "It's not much farther from here." Her heart sped up at the thought of seeing the old place again. Was the same couple who'd bought it from her before she left for England still living there?

The house came into view along with the barn and the oak tree across the road. Nora was grateful the yard stood empty so she could observe the place without someone watching. Everything looked exactly as she'd left it, minus the new paint on the barn. She stopped Colin beside the tree, now stripped of leaves, and stared at the house. She'd been happy living here.

"So this is what a non–sheep farm looks like."

Nora elbowed him in the ribs. "Yes."

"It's very nice." He nodded his approval. "I still can't

believe you ran this place by yourself. It looks rather large
for one person."

"It seems a simple enough challenge now," she said
with mock exaggeration. "At least in comparison with
running a sheep farm in England and winning over the
baronet-to-be next door."

Colin chuckled. "Glad to hear I didn't make it quite so
easy." He pressed a kiss to her forehead. "Did you want
to see inside?"

Nora hesitated. How envious she'd been of the couple's happiness when they'd come to look at the place.
She'd felt certain she would never have another chance
at her own dreams of marrying and having children. Now
she'd returned with the man she loved, and their first child
would be born in another four months.

"That's all right. I only wanted to see the place once
more." She gave the farm a final glance-over and turned
to head back to the Campbells', her hand still snug inside
Colin's.

"Now that you've had the luxury of trying out several
houses," Colin said, kissing her knuckles, "which do you
prefer, my dear? The Iowa farmhouse, the lakeside cottage, or the ancient hall?"

Nora stopped walking, her heart suddenly filled to
overflowing with gratitude. Before going to England,
she'd thought a home was something made of wood or
stone, a building that housed one's family. Now she knew
the truth—the people one loved made up a home.

She gazed up at her husband, into the face she cherished most of all. "I'd be content to live in a cave the
rest of my life, so long as you are there beside me, Colin
Ashby."

"I couldn't agree more, Mrs. Ashby." His mouth parted in a slow grin as he pulled her close. Nora knew exactly what he wanted. With a laugh, she wrapped her arms around his neck and kissed him fully on the mouth, in the middle of the snowy, country road.

From the Iowa heartland to
battle-torn France, take a journey
back to the Great War in Stacy
Henrie's sweeping romance!

An excerpt from
Hope Rising
follows.

Prologue

France, May 1918

Evelyn Gray breathed in the briny smell of the sea as she fingered the five shells in her gloved palm. One for each year without her father. From beneath her velour hat, she peered up at the gray sky overhead. The cool temperature and the possibility of rain made her grateful for the warmth of her Army Nurse Corps outdoor uniform, with its dark blue jacket, shirtwaist, and skirt.

"Nurse Gray, come on." One of the other three nurses down the beach waved for her to join them in their walk along the shoreline toward the white cliffs in the distance.

Sighing, Evelyn turned in their direction. She wasn't in any hurry to rejoin their conversation. The other girls on leave with her were full of talk about home and families and sweethearts, while she had only her aging grandparents waiting for her back in Michigan. As for a beau? Her lips turned up into a bitter smile. She'd been too busy with nurse's training to worry about any of that.

She lifted the first shell—a smooth, white one—and tossed it into the sea. "I still miss you, Papa," she said as the seashell slipped beneath the surface of the water.

Five years today, since you left us. She could easily picture how he'd trudged up the porch steps that afternoon after tending to a patient—he'd never established a doctor's office in town, preferring instead to make house calls or take visits in their home. He hadn't looked well, but Evelyn's medical knowledge at seventeen wasn't what it was today at twenty-two. She still wasn't sure if he himself recognized the signs of the coming heart attack.

Tossing the second shell into the water, she swallowed hard against the flood of memories. She'd gone upstairs to make sure he was lying down and found him on the floor next to the bed, already gone.

She rid her hand of the third, fourth, and fifth shells in quick succession, then brushed the granules of sand from her gloves. The wind and the ache in her heart brought salty moisture to her eyes, but she straightened her shoulders against both. No one else needed to know what day it was or how much the loneliness tore at her.

"Afternoon."

Evelyn whirled around to find an American soldier watching her from a few feet away. He wasn't overly tall, less than six feet, but his handsome face, broad shoulders, and dark eyes were an impressive combination and made Evelyn's pulse skip from more than being startled.

"I didn't mean to disturb you." He smiled, looking anything but apologetic. "Beautiful view."

The way he said it, she knew he wasn't talking about

the ocean. Evelyn didn't blush, though. She was used to lingering looks and flirtations from the wounded soldiers at the hospital where she worked. Some, like this young man, were quite handsome; others were sweet; and a few pressed her to keep in touch once they left the hospital. But Evelyn put a firm stop to any such nonsense. She wouldn't break the rule forbidding fraternization between nurses and enlisted soldiers.

Being a nurse was demanding enough; doing so while pregnant or with a venereal disease would make it twice as difficult. Not to mention she would be discharged if it were discovered she was with child. No, nursing was too important to her, and to her grandparents, to throw her job away for some soldier. Nowhere else but in a busy hospital ward, performing her duties, did she still feel close to her father.

Time to catch up with the other nurses.

Evelyn turned in the direction of the cliffs and started after the girls. They'd managed to cover quite a bit of distance while she lingered behind. To her dismay, the soldier fell into step beside her.

"I'm Private First Class Ralph Kelley." He held out his hand for her to shake. "And you are?"

"Not supposed to talk to you," Evelyn said in her firmest nurse's tone. "You know the rules, soldier." She tried to maintain a brisk pace across the beach, but the stones and sand underfoot made it difficult.

He chuckled as he lowered his hand to his side. "You on leave?" he asked, doggedly ignoring her rejection. "With those other nurses?"

She refused to answer, but his next question caught her off guard.

"Do you collect pebbles? I saw you picking some up earlier."

How long had he been watching her? Heat rose into her cheeks at his intrusion upon her private mourning. "I need to go." She attempted to outdistance him again, but his feet kept tempo with hers.

"Have lunch with me."

The request, spoken in an almost pleading tone, halted Evelyn's retreat in a way his earlier attempts at charm hadn't. She circled to face him. Perhaps a gentle rebuff would serve her better than her usual abrupt one.

Before she could say anything, he spoke again. "I can't say I don't make it a habit of talking with nurses." He gave her a sheepish smile as he removed his cap and fingered the olive drab wool. "But you looked like you could use a friend back there. Like there was something weighing on your mind."

The perceptive observation took her by surprise, and she fell back a step. Could there be more to this soldier than his ladies' man demeanor? Her earlier feeling of isolation welled up inside her, nearly choking her with its hold. "It's the anniversary of my father's death—five years today." The admission tumbled out, despite the voice of reason screaming in her mind to keep walking away. "I've been thinking a lot about him lately."

"Do your friends know?" He nodded in the direction the other girls had gone.

Evelyn folded her arms against the battering breeze and shook her head. "I didn't want to spoil their time away from the hospital."

"That's rather generous." He cocked his head to study her. "Will you at least tell me your name?"

She could feel her defenses crumbling beneath the sincerity in his black eyes. "It's...um...Evelyn. Evelyn Gray."

"Evelyn."

Hearing his deep voice intone her name brought butterflies to her stomach, and the smile he offered afterward made her heartbeat thrum faster. When was the last time she'd felt this way? Probably not since she and Dale had kissed after high school graduation. Dale Emerson had been her first beau, until he moved to Sioux City, Iowa, and Evelyn had put all her time and energy into becoming a nurse. Last she'd heard, Dale had graduated from medical school and was serving as a surgeon at the front lines.

"I discovered a place yesterday that serves excellent fish," he said, his tone coaxing. "If you like fish..."

Despite her best efforts to stop it, a smile lifted the corners of her lips. "I think I'd like anything that wasn't cooked at the hospital. Our food there isn't much better than Army fare, I'm afraid."

Private Kelley laughed; it was a pleasant sound. "I owe it to you then, to at least provide you a decent meal while you're on leave." His expression sobered as he added, "Especially today."

Evelyn glanced over her shoulder at the three nurses far down the beach. She ought to refuse. But logic was growing less and less persuasive inside her mind. For the first time in months, she felt valued and important. This soldier's genuine notice and concern soothed the loneliness she wore as constant as her nurse's uniform.

She pushed at the sand beneath her shoes, her lips pursed in indecision. Could any real harm come from simply sharing a meal in a public place? At least she'd be spared having to listen to the other girls prattle on about their big families and parents who were still alive. She would only be trading one conversation for another.

Inhaling a deep breath, she let her words slide out on the exhale. "Let me tell them I'll meet up with them later."

He grinned and replaced his hat on his head. "I'll wait right here for you."

Evelyn moved with new purpose toward the retreating group. She called to the girls from a distance to avoid any questions. The three of them turned as one. "Go on ahead without me. I'll meet up with you before supper."

They glanced at one another, then one of them shrugged and waved her hand in acknowledgment. A sense of freedom rolled through her as Evelyn retraced her steps to where Private First Class Ralph Kelley stood waiting.

"All set?" He extended his hand to her.

Evelyn stared at it for a long moment, then placed her fingers in his palm. With a smile, he tucked her hand over his arm and led her away from the beach.

Fall in Love with Forever Romance

A HOPE REMEMBERED
by Stacy Henrie

The final book in Stacy Henrie's sweeping Of Love and War trilogy brings to life the drama of WWI England with emotion and romance. As the Great War comes to a close, American Nora Lewis finds herself starting over on an English estate. But it's the battle-scarred British pilot Colin Ashby she meets there who might just be able to convince her to believe in love again.

SCANDALOUSLY YOURS
by Cara Elliott

Secret passions are wont to lead a lady into trouble... Meet the rebellious Sloane sisters in the first book of the Hellions of High Street series from bestselling author Cara Elliott.

Fall in Love with Forever Romance

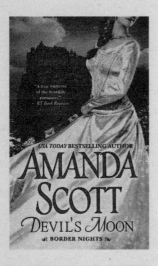

DEVIL'S MOON
by Amanda Scott

In a flawless blend of history and romance, *USA Today* bestselling author Amanda Scott transports readers again to the Scottish Borders with the second book in her Border Nights series.

THE SCANDALOUS SECRET OF ABIGAIL MacGREGOR
by Paula Quinn

Abigail MacGregor has a secret: her mother is the true heir to the English crown. But if the wrong people find out, it will mean war for her beloved Scotland. There's only one way to keep the peace—journey to London, escorted by her enemy, the wickedly handsome Captain Daniel Marlow. Fans of Karen Hawkins and Monica McCarty will love this book!

Fall in Love with Forever Romance

A KISS TO BUILD
A DREAM ON
by Kim Amos

Spoiled and headstrong, Willa Masterson left her hometown—and her first love, Burk Olmstead—in the rearview twelve years ago. But the woman who returns is determined to re-build: first her family house, then her relationships with everyone in town...starting with a certain tall, dark, and sexy contractor. Fans of Kristan Higgins, Jill Shalvis, and Lori Wilde will flip for Kim Amos's Forever debut!

IT'S ALWAYS BEEN YOU
by Jessica Scott

Captain Ben Teague is mad as hell when his trusted mentor is brought up on charges that can't possibly be true. And the lawyer leading the charge, Major Olivia Hale, drives him crazy. But something is simmering beneath her icy reserve—and Ben can't resist turning up the heat! Fans of Robyn Carr and JoAnn Ross will love this poignant and emotional military romance.

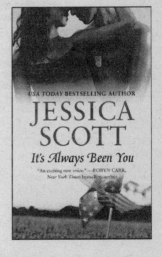

Fall in Love with Forever Romance

TOTAL SURRENDER
by Rebecca Zanetti

Piper Oliver knows she can't trust tall, dark, and sexy black-ops soldier Jory
Dean. All she has to do, though, is save his life and he'll be gone for good.
But something isn't adding up...and she won't rest until she uncovers the
truth—even if it's buried in his dangerous kiss. Fans of Maya Banks and
Lora Leigh will love this last book in Rebecca Zanetti's Sin Brothers series!